"NO ONE CAPTURES THE MAGIC AND ROMANCE OF THE BRITISH ISLES LIKE MAY McGOLDRICK."
—Miranda Jarrett

Praise for *The Promise*

"Filled with warmth and emotion . . . *The Promise* is a wonderful book for any lover of historical fiction. . . . Cuddle up in a chair and simply enjoy . . . don't miss it."
—*New York Times* bestselling author Heather Graham

"This vibrant Georgian historical is perfect for readers who like a nice mix of history and passion." —*Booklist*

"*The Promise* is a tender, emotional love story. . . . History springs to life in this latest from an immensely talented storyteller." —*Romantic Times*

"If you like passionate stories about people you can care deeply about, that take you on an emotional ride, that tell of battles between good and evil, I promise you will love *The Promise*." —Romance Reviews Today

"Readers will strike gold with this fabulous historical romance." —BookBrowser

continued . . .

Previous books by May McGoldrick

THE REBEL
THE PROMISE

Highland Treasure Trilogy
THE FIREBRAND
THE ENCHANTRESS
THE DREAMER

FLAME
THE INTENDED
THE BEAUTY OF THE MIST
HEART OF GOLD
ANGEL OF SKYE
THE THISTLE AND THE ROSE

Borrowed Dreams

May McGoldrick

A SIGNET BOOK

SIGNET
Published by New American Library, a division of
Penguin Group (USA) Inc., 375 Hudson Street,
New York, New York 10014, U.S.A.
Penguin Books Ltd, 80 Strand,
London WC2R 0RL, England
Penguin Books Australia Ltd, 250 Camberwell Road,
Camberwell, Victoria 3124, Australia
Penguin Books Canada Ltd, 10 Alcorn Avenue,
Toronto, Ontario, Canada M4V 3B2
Penguin Books (N.Z.) Ltd, Cnr Rosedale and Airborne Roads,
Albany, Auckland 1310, New Zealand

Penguin Books Ltd, Registered Offices:
Harmondsworth, Middlesex, England

First published by Signet, an imprint of New American Library,
a division of Penguin Group (USA) Inc.

First Printing, June 2003
10 9 8 7 6 5 4 3 2

 REGISTERED TRADEMARK—MARCA REGISTRADA

Printed in the United States of America

PUBLISHER'S NOTE
This is a work of fiction. Names, characters, places, and incidents either are
the product of the author's imagination or are used fictitiously, and any resemblance to actual persons, living or dead, business establishments, events, or
locales is entirely coincidental.

For Judy Spagnola.
Thank you for all you do.

Chapter 1

London
January 1772

"We are going in the wrong direction!"

Instead of turning west at the ancient Temple Bar, the carriage had turned east on Fleet Street, and the driver was now whipping his team through the busy traffic going into the City. The lawyer raised the head of his cane to the roof of the carriage to get the attention of the driver, but the touch of Millicent's gloved hand on his sleeve made him stop.

"He is going where he was directed, Sir Oliver. There is an urgent matter I need to see to at the wharves."

"At the wharves? But . . . but we are already somewhat pressed for time for your appointment, m'lady."

"This shall not take very long."

He sank back against the seat, somewhat relieved. "Since we have a little time then, perhaps I could ask you a few questions about the secretive nature of this meeting we have been summoned to attend this morning."

"Please, Sir Oliver," Millicent pleaded quietly. "Can your questions wait until after my business at the wharves? I am afraid my mind is rather distracted right now."

All his questions withered on the man's tongue as Lady Wentworth turned her face toward the window and the passing street scene. A short time later the carriage passed by St. Paul's Cathedral and began wending its way down through a rough and odorous area in the direction of the Thames. By the time they crossed Fish Street, with its derelict sheds and warehouses, the lawyer could restrain himself no longer.

"Would you at least tell me the nature of this business at the wharves, m'lady?"

"We are going to an auction."

Oliver Birch looked out the window at the milling crowds of workmen and pickpockets and whores. "M'lady, I hope you intend to stay in the carriage and that you will allow me to instruct one of the grooms to obtain what you are looking for."

"I am sorry, sir, but it is essential that I see to this myself."

The lawyer grasped the side of the rocking carriage as the driver turned into the courtyard of a tumbledown wreck of a building on Brooke's Wharf. Outside the window, an odd mix of well-dressed gentlemen and shabby merchants and seamen stood in attendance on an auction that, from the looks of things, was already well under way.

"At least give me the details of what you intend to do here, Lady Wentworth." Birch climbed out of the carriage first. Despite the biting wind off the Thames, the smells of the place—combined with the stink of the river's edge—were appalling.

"I read about the auction in the *Gazette* this morning. They are selling off the estate of a deceased physician by the name of Dombey. The ruined man moved back from Jamaica last month." She pulled the hood up on her woolen cloak and accepted his hand as she stepped out. "Before he could be put in debtor's prison, he succumbed to ill health some ten days ago."

Birch had to hurry to keep up with Millicent as she pushed her way through the crowd to the front row. "And what, may I ask, in Dr. Dombey's estate is of interest to you?"

She didn't answer, and the lawyer found his client's gray eyes searching anxiously past the personal articles that were laid out on a makeshift platform. "I hope I am not too late."

The lawyer did not ask any more questions as Millicent's attention turned sharply toward the set of wide doors that led into the building. The bailiff was dragging out a frail-looking African woman wrapped in a tattered blanket and wearing only a dirty shift under it. A crate was placed on the platform, and the old woman—her neck and hands and feet in shackles—was pushed roughly onto it.

Birch closed his eyes for a moment to control his disgust at this evidence of the barbaric and dishonorable trade that continued to curse the nation.

"Lookee, gennelmen. This here slave was Dr. Dombey's personal maid," the auctioneer shouted. "She's the only servant the medical bloke carried back with him from Jamaica. Aye, sure, she's a rum thing with her wrinkled face. And she's of an age to rival Methuselah. But gennelmen, she's said to be a weritable African queen, she is, and bright as crystal, they tell me. So e'en though she's worth a good thirty pounds, what say we start the bidding off at . . . at a pound."

There was loud jeering and laughter from the group.

"Look, now, gennelmen. 'Ow about ten shillings then?" the auctioneer announced over the roar of the crowd. "She's good teeth, she has." He pulled open the woman's mouth roughly. There were crusts of blood on the chapped lips. "Ten shillings? Who'll start the bidding at ten shillings?"

"What bloody good is she?" somebody shouted.

"Five, gennelmen. Who'll start us at five?"

"The woman is nothing more than a refuse slave," another responded. "If we were in Port Royal, she'd be left to die on the wharf."

Birch glanced worriedly at Millicent and found a look of pain etched on her face. Tears were glimmering on the edges of her eyelids.

"This is no place for you to be, m'lady," he whispered quietly. "It is not right for you to be witnessing this. Whatever you came for must be already gone."

"The advertisement said she was a fine African lass." A middle-aged clerk, sneering from his place at the edge of the platform, threw a crumpled *Gazette* at the old woman. "Why, she's too old to even be good for—"

"Five pounds," Millicent called out.

Every eye in the place turned to her, and silence gripped the throng. Even the auctioneer seemed lost for words for a moment. Birch saw the woman's wrinkled eyelids open a fraction and stare at Millicent.

"Aye, yer ladyship. Yer bid is in fer—"

"Six pounds." A second bid from someone deep in the crowd silenced the auctioneer again. All heads in unison turned to the back of the auction yard.

"Seven," Millicent responded.

"Eight."

On the platform the man's face broke out into a grin as the crowds parted, showing a nattily dressed clerk holding up a rolled newspaper. "Why, I see Mr. Hyde's clerk is in attendance. Thank ye fer yer bid, Harry."

"Ten pounds," Millicent said with great vehemence.

Birch scanned the number of carriages in the yard, wondering from which one of them Jasper Hyde was issuing his commands. A large plantation owner in the West Indies and supposedly a good friend to the late Squire Wentworth, the Englishman had wasted no time in taking over all of the squire's properties in the Caribbean after his death in payment for debts Wentworth had owed him. And if that were not enough, since arriving in England, Mr. Hyde had positioned himself as Lady Wentworth's chief nemesis, buying up the rest of the bills of exchange and promissory notes the squire had left behind.

"Twenty."

There was a loud gasp of disbelief and the crowd began to shift uncomfortably.

"Thirty."

The lawyer turned to Millicent. "He is playing with

you, m'lady," he said quietly. "I do not believe it would be wise—"

"Fifty pounds," the clerk called without a trace of emotion.

A group of sailors near the edge of the platform turned and scoffed loudly at the clerk for pushing up the price.

"I cannot let him do this. Dr. Dombey and this woman spent a great deal of time on Wentworth's plantations in Jamaica. From the stories I've heard from Jonah and some of the others at Melbury Hall, she became a person of some importance to them." She nodded to the auctioneer. "Sixty pounds."

Birch watched Jasper Hyde's clerk appear to squirm a little. The man turned and looked toward the line of carriages. The rolled newspaper rose in the air before the caller could repeat the last bid. "Seventy."

The rumbling in the crowd became more pronounced. There were sharp comments to the effect that he should let the woman have the slave. A couple of the sailors edged threateningly toward the clerk, muttering derisive obscenities.

"This is all a sick game to Mr. Hyde," Millicent whispered, turning away from the platform. "There are many stories of his brutality on the plantations. The stories about what he did after taking possession of my husband's land and slaves are even worse. He is answerable to no one and has no regard for what few laws are observed there. This woman has witnessed it all, though. He will hurt her. Kill her, perhaps." Her hands fisted. "Sir Oliver, I owe this to my people after all the suffering Wentworth caused. I cannot in good conscience turn my back when I can save this one. Not when I have failed all those others that Hyde took."

"That it, yer ladyship?" the auctioneer asked. "Ye're giving in?"

"Eighty," she replied, her voice quavering.

"You cannot afford this, m'lady," Birch put in firmly but quietly. "Think of the promissory notes Hyde still holds from your husband. You've extended the date of repayment once. But they will all come due next month, and you are personally liable, to the extent of every last thing you own. And this includes Melbury Hall. You just cannot add more fuel to his fire."

"One hundred pounds." The clerk's shout was instantly swallowed up by a loud response from the crowd. Birch watched the man take a few nervous steps toward the carriages as the same angry sailors moved closer to him.

"One ten, milady?" the auctioneer, grinning excitedly, called out from the platform.

"You cannot save every one, Millicent," Birch whispered sharply. When first asked by the Earl and the Countess of Stanmore to represent Lady Wentworth in her legal affairs a year ago, he'd also been informed of the woman's great compassion for the Africans whom her late husband had held as slaves. But his expectations had not come close to the fervor he'd witnessed since then.

"I know that, Sir Oliver."

"For all we know, he might already own this woman. In the same way that he has been acquiring all of the late squire's notes, he may have done the same with Dombey. This may just be Jasper Hyde's way of draining the last of your available funds."

As his words sank in, Millicent's shoulders sagged. Wiping a tear from her face, she turned and started pushing her way toward the carriage. Halfway out of the yard, though, she swung around and raised a hand.

"One hundred ten."

A round of exclamations erupted from the crowd. Gradually, people parted until she was facing the pale-faced clerk across the mud and dirt of the yard. Having already retreated to back edge of the crowd, the man shook his head at the auctioneer and looked back at Millicent.

"Lady Wentworth can have her Negro at the price of a hundred ten pounds."

The mocking tones of the man, accompanied by his sneer, caused the sailors to lose the last of their restraint, and two took off after him. The clerk turned and bolted from the yard. Watching him run, Birch felt the urge to go after the clerk himself. There was no doubt in the lawyer's mind that this ordeal had been arranged. In a moment, the sailors returned empty-handed.

She laid her hand gently on his arm. "Regardless of Mr. Hyde's actions, I had to save this woman's life, Sir Oliver."

Millicent Gregory Wentworth could not be considered a great beauty, nor could her sense of style be called *au courant* by the standards of London's *ton*. But what she lacked in those areas—and in the false pride so fashionable of late—she made up in dignity and humanity. And all of this despite a lifetime of oppression and bad luck.

Birch nodded respectfully to his client. "Why not wait in the carriage, m'lady. I would be happy to take care of the details here."

A small writing desk was being handed up and placed exactly where the slave woman had stood a moment earlier. Millicent watched several members of the crowd edge forward for a better look at the piece of furniture. They were far more interested in this item than in the human being who was auctioned off before it. Only the competition of the bidding had attracted their attention. She turned to watch the woman being led across the yard, with Sir Oliver trailing behind.

Appalled by the entire proceeding, Millicent pushed her way through the crowd to the carriage.

"She will be brought to my office this afternoon," Birch said as soon as he had climbed in some time later. "And, since you do not wish to have her delivered to your sister's home, I will arrange for a place for her to stay until you are ready to leave for Melbury Hall."

"Thank you. We shall be leaving tomorrow morning," Millicent replied.

"Rest assured, m'lady, everything shall be handled with the utmost discretion."

"I know it will," she said quietly, looking out the small window of the carriage at the door of the shed where the old woman had been taken. Millicent couldn't help but worry about how much more pain these horrible people would inflict on her before she was delivered to the lawyer's office that afternoon.

As they rode along in silence through the city, she thought of the money she'd just spent. A hundred ten pounds was equivalent to seven month's worth of salaries of all twenty servants she employed at Melbury Hall, not counting the field hands. It was true that the purchase of the black woman would cut deeply into her rapidly diminishing funds. And she wasn't even considering the money that she needed to pay Jasper Hyde next month. Millicent rubbed her fingers over a dull ache in her temple and tried to think only of how much good it would do, bringing this woman back to Hertfordshire.

"Lady Wentworth," the lawyer said finally, breaking the silence as they drew near their destination, "we cannot put off discussing your appointment with the Dowager Countess Aytoun any longer. I am still completely in the dark concerning why we are going there."

"That makes two of us, Sir Oliver," she replied tiredly. "Her note summoning—or rather, inviting me—to meet with her arrived three days ago at Melbury Hall, and her groom stayed until I sent her an answer. I was to arrive at the Earl of Aytoun's town house in Hanover Square today at eleven this morning with my attorney. Nothing more was said."

"This sounds very abrupt. Do you know the countess?"

Millicent shook her head. "I do not. But then again, a year ago I didn't know Mr. Jasper Hyde, either. Nor the other half-dozen creditors who have endeavored to come after me from every quarter since Wentworth's death." She pulled the cloak tighter around herself. "One thing I've learned this past year and a half is that there is no hiding from those to whom my husband owed money. I have to face them—one by one—and try to make some reasonable arrangement to pay them back."

"You know that I admire you greatly in your efforts, but we both know you are encumbered almost beyond the point of recovery already." He paused. "You have some very generous friends, Lady Wentworth. If you would allow me to reveal to them just a hint of your hardship—"

"No, sir," she said sharply. "I find no shame in being poor. But I find great dishonor in begging. Please, I do not care to hear any more."

"As you wish, m'lady."

Millicent nodded gratefully at her lawyer. Sir Oliver had already served her well, and she trusted that he would honor her request.

"To set your mind a little at ease, though," he continued, "you should know that the Dowager Countess Aytoun is socially situated far differently than Mr. Hyde, or your late husband. She is a woman of great wealth, but she is rumored to be exceedingly . . . well, careful with her money. Some say she is so tightfisted that her own servants must struggle to receive their wages. In short, I cannot see her lending any money to Squire Wentworth."

"I am relieved to hear that. I should have known that with your attention to detail we would not be walking into this meeting totally unprepared. What else have you learned about her, Sir Oliver?"

"She is Lady Archibald Pennington, Countess of Aytoun. Her given name is Beatrice. She's been a widow for over five years. She is Scottish by birth, with the blood of Highlanders in her veins. She comes from an ancient family, and she married well besides."

"She has children?"

"Three sons. All men now. Lyon Pennington is the fourth Earl of Aytoun. The second son, Pierce Pennington, has apparently been making a fortune in the American colonies despite the embargo. And David Pennington, the youngest, is an officer in His Majesty's army. The countess herself led a very quiet life until the scandal that tore her family apart occurred this past summer."

"Scandal?"

Sir Oliver nodded. "Indeed, m'lady. It involved a young lady named Emma Douglas. I understand all three brothers were fond of her. She ended up marrying

the oldest brother and became the Countess of Aytoun
two years ago."

That hardly sounded scandalous, but Millicent had no
chance to ask any more questions as their carriage rolled
to a stop in front of an elegant mansion facing Hanover
Square. A footman in gold-trimmed livery greeted them
as he opened the door of the carriage. Another servant
escorted them up the wide marble steps to the front
door.

Inside the mansion's entrance hall, yet another servant
greeted them. As Millicent shed her cloak, her gaze took
in the semicircular alcove at the far end of the hall and
the ornate gilded scrolls and rosettes that decorated the
high, patterned ceiling. In a receiving area beyond an
open set of doors, she could see upholstered furniture
of deep walnut by Sheraton and Chippendale tastefully
arranged about the room, while handsome carpets covered the brightly polished floors.

A tall, elderly steward approached and informed them
that the dowager was waiting.

"What was the nature of the scandal?" she managed
to whisper as they followed the steward and another
servant up the sweeping circular stairs to a drawing
room.

"Just rumors, m'lady," Birch whispered, "to the effect
that the earl murdered his wife."

"But that is—"

She stopped as the door to the drawing room was
opened. Trying to contain her shock and curiosity, Millicent entered as they were announced.

There were four people in the cozy, well-appointed
room: the dowager countess, a pale gentleman standing
by a desk that had a ledger book open on it, and two
lady's maids.

Lady Aytoun was an older woman, obviously in ill
health. She was sitting on a sofa with pillows propped
behind her and a blanket on her lap. Blue eyes studied
the visitors from behind a pair of spectacles.

Millicent gave a small curtsy. "Our apologies, my lady,
for being delayed."

"Did you win the auction?" The dowager's abruptness caused Millicent to look over in surprise at Sir Oliver. He appeared as baffled as she was. "The African woman. Did you win the auction?"

"I . . . I did," she managed to get out. "But how did you know about it?"

"How much?"

Millicent bristled at the inquiry, but at the same time she felt no shame for what she'd done. "One hundred ten pounds. Though I must tell you I don't know what business it is of—"

"Add it to the tally, Sir Richard." The dowager waved a hand at the gentleman still standing by the desk. "A worthy cause."

Sir Oliver stepped forward. "May I say, m'lady—"

"Pray, save the idle prattle, young man. Come and sit. Both of you."

Millicent's lawyer, who probably hadn't been addressed as "young man" in decades, stared open-mouthed for a moment. Then, as he and Millicent did as they were instructed, the countess dismissed the servants with a wave of her hand.

"Very well. I know both of you, and you know me. That pasty-faced bag of bones over there is my lawyer, Sir Richard Maitland." The old woman arched an eyebrow in the direction of her attorney, who bowed stiffly and sat. "And now, the reason why I invited you here."

Millicent could not even hazard a guess as to what was coming next.

"People acting on my behalf have been reporting to me about you for some time now, Lady Wentworth. You have surpassed my expectations." Lady Aytoun removed her spectacles. "No reason for dallying. You are here because I have a business proposition."

"A business proposition?" Millicent murmured.

"Indeed. I want you to marry my son, the Earl of Aytoun. By a special license. Today."

Chapter 2

Faced with the threat of another life in hell, Millicent shot to her feet. In an instant, propriety and decorum were cast to the winds.

"You've made a grave mistake, Lady Aytoun."

"I do not think so."

"Your servant must have delivered the message to a wrong address."

"Sit down, Lady Wentworth."

"I am afraid I cannot." She glanced in the direction of her lawyer and found him standing as well.

"If you please, Lady Wentworth. There is no reason for panic." The dowager's tone was gentler. "I am well aware of your fears. I have been advised fully of the suffering you endured during your marriage. But what I am proposing to you now has no similarity to the situation you were forced to endure under the brutal tyranny of your first husband."

Millicent stared at the old woman, trying to understand how she could know any of that. The dowager was speaking of her life as if it were public knowledge, and a queasy feeling gripped her stomach. The urge to run for the door was strong. She wanted nothing more than to go out of the house and return to Melbury Hall.

To Millicent, marriage meant being owned by a man. She had felt the chains of that "blissful" state for five endless years. There was no protection for a married woman. Marriage was a state of mental and physical abuse. Period. The vows of matrimony were nothing more than a curse contrived by men to control women. And after Wentworth's death, she had sworn never to allow herself to be subjugated to that life again.

Millicent took a step toward the door.

"At least allow me to explain my purpose for this confusion." The dowager raised a hand to her. "I know at first I spoke in haste. I believe if you would be so kind as to allow me to explain the unpleasant situation in which I find my family, then you shall better understand the reason for the offer."

"Any explanation of your family's situation, m'lady, is completely unnecessary. If you know anything of my history, then you should also know that my revulsion to the very notion of marriage is unrelated to anything you might tell me of your own family. The topic is repugnant to me, Lady Aytoun, and under no circumstances am I willing to—"

"My son is a cripple, Lady Wentworth," the dowager interrupted. "After a horrible accident last summer, he has been left with no use of his legs. He has no strength in one arm. He has plunged into a state of melancholia from which he cannot lift himself. I thank God for the loyalty and persistence of his personal manservant and a half-dozen others who see to all of his needs, for without them I would have been lost. Indeed, without them I would have had no choice but to place him in a hospital for the insane. I do not mind telling you that such a situation would surely have killed me."

The distraught tone of the old woman's words tugged at Millicent's heartstrings. "You have my deepest sympathy, m'lady, but I fail to see what I could do."

The dowager's hands trembled as they absently straightened the blanket on her lap. "Despite all of my bravado, Lady Wentworth, I am quite ill. To be blunt, I am dying. And my physicians, the devil take them, are very happy to give me daily reminders that I might not see the next sunrise."

"Really, m'lady, I—"

"Don't take me wrong. I don't give a pin about myself. I've had a full life. Right now my greatest worry is what shall happen to Lyon when I am gone. That is why I have asked you here today."

"But . . . but surely there are other options. Family. Friends. Other acquaintances who are not complete strangers to you. Lord Aytoun is a peer of the realm. You have so many venues available to you, so many treatments."

"Please, Lady Wentworth. Please sit down. I shall explain."

Millicent turned and found Birch standing attentively a couple of steps away, awaiting her decision whether to go or stay. She looked back at the aging countess. The façade of strength she had encountered in the dowager when first entering was completely gone. What Millicent saw now was simply another woman. A dying woman. A mother who was just trying to secure the future well-being of her son.

She hesitantly sat down. The expression of relief on the dowager's face was immediate.

"Thank you. You asked about family. Well, those remaining believe that if something were to happen to me, then Lyon should be put in a madhouse." Temper flashed in the old woman's blue eyes. "The Earl of Aytoun is not mad. He doesn't belong in Bedlam. I won't have him tied and tortured, bled and purged, dosed with opium and put on display for the rest of London's *ton*."

"But there must be other treatments for his condition. Every day there seems to be a new cure for yet another ailment."

"I have tried every method and paid a great deal of money, and seen no improvement in him. Just this past week, there was an advertisement in the *Gazette* by a Mr. Payne at the Angel and Crown in St. Paul's Churchyard. It claimed that sufferers from 'loss of memory or forgetfulness' for two shillings, six pence could buy a pot of 'a grateful electuary' that would enable them to 'remember the minutest circumstances of their affairs to a wonder.' I had Lyon try it, hoping to spur *some* response in him. Nothing." She gave a dismissive wave. "I am tired of the charlatans and the Merry-Andrews who eagerly endorse the claims of these quacks. I am tired of giving my son highly colored pills that have no good in them at all. You see, his legs and arm were broken, but now they are healed, and yet he has no ability to move them. He cannot walk. He cannot even lift his right arm. So the so-called doctors say he must have a secret disease. Those from the university have but one answer: Bleed him and bleed him again. But it has no effect."

"I am sorry, m'lady—"

"So am I," the dowager said, looking at her directly. "But I'll have no more of that. And I'll have no mad-house for my son. And I'll definitely have no more of these quacks with their dung tea, stewed owls, and crushed worms. I am done with them all."

"I know there are many, many charlatans out there. But there must be some reputable doctors, as well."

"Aye, there are. But the *reputable* ones, as you call them, are also at their wit's end. Aside from bleeding and purging, their only other suggestion is to keep him sedated."

"Why? Is he violent?"

"Of course not," the dowager assured her. "But he has been terribly unhappy at Baronsford, the Aytoun family seat southeast of Edinburgh. That's where the accident happened. In fact, this past fall he went so far as to insist on transferring control of all his inherited properties to his brother Pierce, my second son. Not that his hasty decision did any good for anyone. Pierce is not in England at present, and he has no interest whatsoever in the family fortune. Besides, Lyon is the earl. He is the one whom our dependents look up to and—" She abruptly stopped and waved a dismissive hand. "But Baronsford is the least of my problems right now. The reason I brought it up is so you would know why I needed to get him away from it. I need to find my son a place where he shan't be reminded of his past and what he has lost."

Millicent's nerves had once again settled. She was calm enough to realize that no one could force her into

anything. The choices were hers; so were the consequences. "I still cannot see how your proposal could
improve the earl's life. I am no physician, and I am
hardly capable of—"

"He needs to be out of Scotland. He needs a home
with people who will care for him. Since your husband's
death, 'tis no secret that you have provided a safe haven
for the people Squire Wentworth enslaved." The dowager paused for a moment before continuing. "But you
should know that I intend to make this arrangement as
advantageous to you as 'tis for my son."

Without waiting for the younger woman's response,
she motioned to her lawyer to hand her a large sheet of
paper lined in the ledger style of banking clerks.

"My dear, this is a summary of all the loans and promissory notes that Squire Wentworth left you. We went
to a great deal of difficulty in gathering them together.
It may be that there are some that we have missed. Your
lawyer here can scan them at his leisure and let us know.
And as you know, there are a number of individuals
who take great enjoyment in revealing the painful layers
of your indebtedness just to watch you unravel."

Millicent reached for the proffered paper and glanced
down the list of debts. The totals at the bottom were
huge, but she would not allow her distress to show. She'd
known for some time that she was drowning. The depth
of the water made very little difference. The end result
was the same. She handed the paper to Sir Oliver.

"What is it exactly that you propose, Lady Aytoun?"
she asked dully.

"A marriage in name only. A business arrangement,
pure and simple. If you were to agree to the terms, the
Earl of Aytoun shall come to reside with you at Melbury
Hall. But he will arrive with his own manservant and
servants. We have a new doctor who can travel up from
London on a regular basis. All you need to do is arrange
for space for these people. In return, my lawyer Maitland here, will have all the debts listed on that paper—
and any others that are unfamiliar to us—paid in full. In
addition, these two gentlemen shall settle on a generous

amount that will be paid to you on a monthly basis to support the upkeep of Melbury Hall. It shall be more than enough for you to continue to pursue your causes."

Millicent's head reeled with all that the dowager had just proposed. She had spent endless nights awake, tossing and turning as she worried about her expenses. The last six months had been especially difficult. Lady Aytoun was offering her an opportunity to free herself of the shackles of her husband's debts once and for all. But the thought of the price she would have to pay kept pushing itself forward in her mind with terrifying clarity. Marriage again.

"What shall happen to our arrangement, m'lady, if the Earl of Aytoun recovers from this affliction?"

"I am afraid there is no hope. No doctor who has seen him recently believes . . ." The countess paused to quiet a quaver in her voice. "None of them believes there is any chance of him recovering."

"But he might."

"I envy your optimism."

"I want a provision in the agreement that, in the event of his recovery, a divorce will be uncontested."

The dowager glanced at her lawyer.

Sir Richard nodded curtly, rising from his chair. "Considering the nature of the marriage and the earl's present health, an annulment or a divorce could certainly be arranged."

Sir Oliver agreed. "His present state of mind makes it an arguable case for annulment."

Millicent couldn't believe how far she had been persuaded. In her mind, she was actually weighing the benefits versus the loss, and the scale was definitely tipping.

"Anything else? Any concerns that you have been left with?"

The dowager's question lifted Millicent's chin. "Aye, m'lady. Why me? I am a stranger to you. Why did you decide on me?"

"We did not settle on you without serious consideration. Faced with my requirements, my lawyer here had a great challenge laid at his door. His search has been painstaking. But I must tell you that your history and your reputation for goodness, combined with all that Sir Richard was able to gather about your present financial situation, made you the perfect candidate." The older woman nodded approvingly. "I hope you are not offended by the amount of poking and prodding that my people have been doing into your past and present affairs. When they concluded, there was very little about you that I did not know."

Millicent raised a curious brow. For all her life, she had maintained a very private lifestyle. She doubted there was much out there for anyone to dig into.

"This surprises me, m'lady, and I should like to hear a sample of what your people might have discovered about me."

"If you wish. You are Millicent Gregory Wentworth, twenty-nine years of age. You have been widowed for a year and a half. You were entered into an arranged marriage by your family."

"These are facts easily obtainable. They don't say anything about the person."

"That is true. But my meeting with you today has settled my mind about that. With the exception of an overnight stay at their residence now and then, as in the case of this trip to London, you are practically estranged from your kin. Not that I blame you. Your family consists of two older sisters and an uncle whom you do not trust, since he gave you to Wentworth without any inquiries into the man's character." The old woman's hand smoothed the blanket tightly over her lap. "There is little correspondence between any of your family. During your five years of marriage, you never once confided to any of them about the abuse you were receiving at the hands of your husband. You have very few close friends, but your pride does not allow you to ask for help, even when you are desperate. What else? Yes, you are involved in freeing your slaves—"

"My late husband's slaves."

"Indeed. Partly because of your efforts to correct that situation, however, you are on the verge of being crushed under the resulting financial burdens." The dowager's gaze swept over Millicent's face. "On a much more trivial level, you appear contented with your unadorned looks and your obvious disinterest in style. Actually, you have never been an active member of London's fashionable set and, since becoming a widow, have taken shelter within the walls of your country residence, Melbury Hall, at Hertfordshire."

"I have missed nothing important by staying in the country, m'lady."

"Quite true. And this attitude is one of the things that I find most advantageous. You shall not miss the parties in town during the Season nor hold a grudge against your husband for not escorting you to London, or Bath, or wherever the *ton* is running wild at the moment. In addition, you are a bright woman who is endowed with great compassion. You have finally discovered the value of independence, and you are now striving to wield the power that goes along with it. But to succeed, you could very well use the protection of a husband's name to keep the wolves from the door."

The battle inside Millicent raged. She did indeed need the protection of a husband's name in order to pursue her goals. Already she had found it nearly impossible to hire and keep a capable steward to manage Melbury Hall. Even in going to an auction by the Thames, she found that society demanded the presence of a male overseer, since obviously a man had such a higher level of intelligence than any woman.

Millicent did her best to control her temper and instead thought of her best friend's story of the ten years that she had spent in Philadelphia. Going under the assumed name of Mrs. Ford, Rebecca had used the ruse of having a husband to establish herself and a newborn in that city.

"What do you think of the offer, Lady Wentworth?"

Millicent shook off her struggle and met the dowager's direct gaze. "Why today? What is the significance of this marriage taking place today?"

"You don't stay away from Melbury Hall more than

a day or two at the most. My guess is that you are traveling back there tomorrow morning."

"I am."

"When I add that to my physicians' predictions about the scarcity of sunsets and sunrises in my future, I could not bring myself to tempt fate by waiting. There is too much at stake."

"How does his lordship feel about this great scheme you have been devising?"

The dowager drew a deep breath and released it before answering. "I did not know if I would be able to convince you, but I explained to my son that it would be out of your need for financial support and not out of charity that the marriage might be arranged. Once he heard that, he was resigned to it. He'll not be pitied. Whatever else might be stripped from Lyon, he will always have his pride."

Lyon Pennington, fourth Earl of Aytoun, remained motionless in the seat before the window. The muscles of the peer's gaunt face were drawn tight beneath the dark, untrimmed beard. His eyes were fixed on an invisible point somewhere out beyond the glass, out amid the dreary scenery of Hanover Square.

The earl's two valets had laid out a brocade coat, a silk waistcoat, a black cravat, breeches, stockings, and silver-buckled shoes for the wedding. Neither man dared to approach him, though, and they stood by the door, exchanging nervous looks.

"She's here," a young woman whispered, coming in with a tray of tea.

She hurried to put the tray down on a table near the earl. With a curtsy, she backed away and returned to where the men were standing.

"The dowager thinks," she whispered to one of them, "that the visitor'll be looking to meet with his lordship before the ceremony."

Another serving girl walked in carrying a tray of pastries. Following her, the earl's man, Gibbs, entered the chamber.

"What're ye waiting for?" he growled at the valets. "His lordship should be dressed by now."

As Gibbs took a step toward them, the two men moved to do his bidding. The earl's man was as tall and as broad as the great oaks in the deer park at Baronsford, and they both had felt the weight of his displeasure in the past. One of the valets reached for his master's buckskin breeches. He looked uneasily at his lanky fellow servant, who was picking up Lord Aytoun's shirt. They were both still hesitant to approach the master.

The one called John whispered warily to Gibbs, " 'Slordship was none too keen about dressin' this mornin'."

The two serving maids hurriedly escaped the chamber.

"Aye, Mr. Gibbs," the other valet put in quietly. "By 'slife, sir, Lord Aytoun near killed us both while we was tryin' to dress 'im. Not till we gave him the tonic the new doctor left for 'im did he settle down at all."

"His lordship had that already this morning!" Gibbs exploded, quickly lowering his voice to a fierce whisper. " 'Tis not to be given any bloody time ye fancy giving it to him."

"Aye, sir. But what he had weren't enough."

"If I had the time right now to wring your necks and kick ye from here to . . ." Gibbs tried to compose himself. "But the lack of time is going to save yer bloody arses. The company is already downstairs, and he's still not dressed."

" 'Tis only a minute or two that he's calmed 'imself."

Scowling at them, he motioned for the two men to follow him as he moved to the earl's chair. "M'lord?"

Lyon's gaze never wavered from the window. He was neither asleep nor awake. Gibbs closed the shutters and stepped in front of the sitting man again.

"We need to get you ready for company, m'lord."

The earl's face was blank as he looked up at the three men now standing before him.

"Lady Wentworth and her lawyer have arrived, sir," the earl's manservant said calmly, pulling the blanket off the man's unmoving legs. "The bishop has been waiting in the library an hour. Ye're expected, m'lord."

One of the valets reached down to undo the buttons of the double-breasted dressing gown. Perceiving the scowl being directed at him by his ailing master, he stopped and shrank back a step.

"Put me in the bed," Lyon growled in slurred tones.

"I cannot, m'lord. Her ladyship insisted that we should have ye ready."

With no thought for the legs that did not move—that had not supported him in months—the Earl of Aytoun pushed himself up from the chair. Before the hands of his panicked servants could reach him, he fell heavily to the floor.

"Bloody hell . . . !"

". . . landed on 'is right arm!"

"Help me roll him off it." Gibbs was down on his knees beside the earl in an instant.

"I 'eard the doctor say he'd have a surgeon amputate if that arm breaks again."

Gibbs flashed John a killing look for his comment and gently turned the earl over.

Lyon Pennington was as large a man as Gibbs. His months of confinement had detracted somewhat from his prior robustness, but moving him still required several men. Even more when he was not in the best of temperaments.

"M'lord, if I may remind ye . . ." Gibbs gingerly bent and straightened the earl's right arm. The bone didn't appear to be broken again. "Your lordship promised the dowager that ye would go through with this plan of hers."

"Put me back in bed." Anger was woven tightly into the words that escaped his lips. His good hand formed a fist and pounded once on the floor. "Now!"

"Your mother had another sick spell last night, m'lord. We had to send for the doctor." Gibbs crouched nearby, knowing better than to maneuver the earl when his anger was on the edge of exploding. The man's blue eyes were boring holes in the manservant's head. "The only thing pushing her from her sickbed this morning was your promise to abide by her wish. If she hears that ye have decided to throw it all down the well, then that could be the last straw. If ye please, m'lord, her ladyship has gone to a great deal of trouble to arrange this for ye. I'm thinking ye might give her a wee bit of peace for the few days she might have left in this world."

Whether it was the sedating medicine the valets had administered earlier or the realization on the earl's part that he had few choices left, Gibbs couldn't tell. Whatever it was, the servant was relieved when Lyon Pennington did not fight them when they lifted him again into the chair.

"And what of this woman, Gibbs?" he muttered. "Do you think this new bride of mine will ever have so much as a moment's peace?"

Chapter 3

Jasper Hyde pulled his pocket watch from his waistcoat and looked at it. It was nearly three in the afternoon, though there was no sign of his blasted clerk or Platt, either.

White's Club was crowded, as it was every day, and Hyde glanced around at the other gentlemen. He was beginning to recognize some of the faces of the players and the others who simply milled about drinking and being entertained by the sight of those intent on losing their fortunes. It didn't seem to matter what time of day it was here; the card and dice tables were nearly always full. Hyde knew, though, that the crowd would soon start to thin as some went off to the dinners and parties and the many other vices that London offered in abundance.

Hyde stared at the dice cup in the Earl of Winchelsea's hand. He himself had already lost more than he cared to, but he knew it was well worth it to be rubbing shoulders with such members of the *ton*. And it didn't hurt to lose money to them, either.

"All bets down," the periwigged croupier called in a bored voice.

Behind the man, by the large open hearth, a harpist and horn player were playing, and the director was upbraiding a servant for being slow with his delivery of a bottle of wine to a hazard table in the corner.

Lord Winchelsea rattled the dice once more for luck and rolled them out onto the table.

"Seven." The men crowded around the table responded with groans and shouts of victory, depending on their wagers, and Hyde watched Winchelsea smile arrogantly as the dice were passed back to him.

"Now *this* is what I call a celebration," Winchelsea said to the Earl of Carlisle, standing to his left. The other nobleman snorted in response, and Winchelsea smiled at Jasper Hyde. "Still betting with my erstwhile friend here, Hyde?"

The plantation owner glanced down at the quickly dwindling sum before him. Hyde knew the young earl had easily lost three thousand pounds this week. Winchelsea's luck, however, had definitely turned today.

"If you don't mind, m'lord, I believe I shall wager with you."

"Smart move, Hyde. By the way, I have reserved a private room at Clifton's Chophouse down by the Temple Bar before we go on to Drury Lane. Care to join us there for dinner?"

"I would be delighted." Extremely pleased at being included, Hyde doubled his initial wager on the table.

"Considering your good news today, you should invite everyone here for dinner," Lord Carlisle challenged.

"Damn me, but you're right about that, Carlisle. You can all come." Winchelsea started rattling the dice cup amid of the loud laughter and calls of approval by those gathered around the table.

"If I may be so bold as to ask, m'lord, what is the nature of your good news?"

Carlisle answered Hyde's question. "Rumor has it that our friend's chief nemesis is escaping to the country first thing in the morning."

"Aytoun is leaving London?" someone said from across the room.

"Carried away, to be more accurate," Lord Carlisle answered.

"Finally sending him to Bedlam, are they?" the same person asked.

"Despite my heartfelt recommendation, no." Winchelsea shook the cup more savagely. "But he is being sentenced to a lifetime of imprisonment all the same. We hear that he is getting married again this afternoon."

"All bets down," the croupier intoned.

"What simpleton would give their daughter to him?" another person asked. "Didn't he kill his first wife?"

"That was only an unsubstantiated rumor," Carlisle said in defense of the absent nobleman. "No truth to it whatsoever."

"I disagree with that," Winchelsea argued, putting the cup of dice on the table. "Having faced the man's brutal temperament, I find him perfectly capable of murdering his wife."

"You faced Aytoun's *brutal* temperament because you were dallying with his wife," Carlisle scoffed. "And you just say that now because he was the only man to best you in a duel. You've only just lately stopped complaining of the shoulder wound you sustained against him. If you'd beaten him, I say you would not be slandering him with such accusations."

"Are you accusing *me*?" Winchelsea challenged hotly.

"No . . . and you shan't convince me to face you in the park in the crack of dawn, either, my friend." Carlisle handed the cup of dice back to the earl. "I say we continue with our celebration and let Aytoun and his new wife just go to hell."

Voices rose in agreement around the table at that. Still scowling at his friend, Winchelsea grudgingly took the cup and rolled out the dice.

"Six," the croupier declared, handing back the dice.

Carlisle smiled smugly. "Hope this doesn't mean your luck has changed."

"Wishful thinking on your part."

"Next we'll be hearing that your tailor's at the door waiting to be paid."

"You are the devil himself, Carlisle, to wish such horrible things upon me."

Paying no regard to the give and take of the two men, Hyde closely followed the roll of the dice across the table again. *Seven.* Winchelsea's violent curse was mild compared to how Hyde felt at that moment. Losing five hundred guineas at a single throw might be insignificant among this group of gentry, but for Hyde it was another link in a lengthening chain of bad luck.

The plantation owner held his breath as a stabbing pain suddenly wracked his chest and shoulders. Hyde waited until the spasms subsided. He knew they would pass, and he did not want to draw any attention to them. Occurring with no warning and more and more frequently of late, the sharp pains came and went, but not before draining him of his vigor. He leaned on the table.

The dice cup passed on to Lord Carlisle, and once again wagers were being laid on the table. Turning his head, Hyde was relieved to see his lawyer finally appear at the doorway. He made his excuses at the table and made his way across the room to where Platt stood waiting. Without saying a word, the lawyer led him down the stairs to where the clerk, Harry, stood squirming just inside the front door.

A servant handed Hyde his cane and hat and gloves and helped him on with his overcoat. All the while, Hyde kept his gaze fixed on his servant. The pain in his chest had started to ease a little, but the air in his chest was scarce.

Hyde motioned to the two new arrivals to follow him into a small chamber beside the entryway. It was obvious that all had not gone as planned.

"Where is she?"

Platt closed the door of the chamber before breaking the news. "Harry was not able to buy the slave woman."

Rage, like a strong gust of wind, rushed through him in a single sweep. The clerk shrank back against the wall as the end of Hyde's cane jabbed him hard in the chest. "You had your instructions. All you had to do was to continue to bid on her until you won her."

"I did, sir. But the price kept climbing."

"Lady Wentworth showed up at the auction unexpectedly," Platt offered from a safe distance.

"I couldn't win the woman, sir, but I made her ladyship pay a fortune for her. She was a worthless refuse slave."

Jasper Hyde's fury boiled over, and he struck the man hard on the side of the head with the cane. "*You* are the worthless refuse. I should turn you out now. Did you hear nothing of what I told you before? Your specific instructions were to bid up and win that slave. What worry is it of yours about the price?"

"But she went for a hundred ten pounds, master," Harry blurted out, rubbing his head with one hand and ready to deflect the next blow with the other. "And the crowds were against me. They thought I was pushing the price up on Lady Wentworth and took her side, sir. I looked for yer carriage, but ye and Mr. Platt here were nowheres to be seen. I never thought ye'd be meaning to go anywhere above fifty pound. But I braced myself and went double, and—"

The cane flashed again, striking the clerk on his upraised wrist and causing him to howl in pain.

"This will solve nothing," Platt said nervously. "There are other ways of getting the slave back."

Jasper Hyde labored to breathe as he sank onto a nearby chair. He gripped his cane with both hands and tried to fight the pain that was once again raging through him.

"It is fortunate that Lady Wentworth was the one winning the slave," Platt offered reasonably. "She owes you a fortune in promissory notes. And she has no credit available to her at all. She bid five times the value of the slave woman and might not even have enough funds available to pay for the purchase. Either through Dombey's creditors or Lady Wentworth's lawyer, I could have the slave woman in your possession by the end of the week."

Hyde considered that for a moment, waiting for the pain to pass. When he stood up, the clerk, Harry, cowered against the wall. The plantation owner turned to Platt.

"You make certain of that," Jasper Hyde instructed his lawyer. "Time is running short."

The articles lay before her on the brick hearth of the small fireplace. They were no more than a few things

Ohenewaa had been able to hide in the sleeves of her ragged shift. A few stones, the crumbled broken bark of a tree, some dried leaves, a small satchel with a few strands of hair. The old woman poured a few drops of water onto the hearth and placed a small piece of bread as an offering next to the charms. She had much for which to give thanks, and she knew the spirits were listening as she knelt by the makeshift altar.

Reaching into the hearth, Ohenewaa took a fistful of warm ashes and spread them on her face and hands and arms. The ancient chant started low in her chest. Rocking back and forth where she sat, she thanked the Supreme Being, Onyame, for her deliverance from Jasper Hyde. She chanted her gratitude for having the shackles once again removed from her hands and feet and neck.

What was to become of her was still a mystery. She had been delivered to the office of the lawyer, Sir Oliver Birch, in the early afternoon. The tall Englishman had the name of a tree, she thought. Perhaps he had a soul, as well.

The lawyer had looked in on her a little later and had explained that the lady at the wharf had already signed the papers freeing her. A free woman, he had said. The words were difficult to comprehend fully. A free woman.

But the lawyer had also said that this same woman, Lady Wentworth, would be pleased if Ohenewaa would accompany her to her country estate in Hertfordshire. The lawyer had explained that there were many freed slaves who lived and worked at Melbury Hall, and Lady Wentworth thought that Ohenewaa might know some of them from her years in Jamaica.

Ohenewaa remembered the name Wentworth very well. She remembered clearly the people's celebration when news of Squire Wentworth's death reached the sugar plantations in Jamaica. But that was before Jasper Hyde's iron fist had closed around their throats.

At the sound of a knock on the door, she ceased her chanting. The door slowly opened, and a young woman's face appeared, peering in with uncertainty. "May I come in?"

The blue eyes were large and curious, taking in the articles on the hearth. They turned soft and the lips thinned when she looked at the ragged shift and the blanket covering Ohenewaa. Neither bit of cloth did much to hide the ugly bruises around her collar or her wrists.

"I'm Violet," the young woman said softly, opening the door a little. Ohenewaa could see the woman was holding a tray in her arms, but she did not enter immediately. "I'm Lady Wentworth's personal maid. She sent me here to see to your needs until we are ready to leave for Melbury Hall tomorrow morning. May I come in?"

Ohenewaa studied the young woman's pretty dress, no doubt a hand-me-down from her lady's wardrobe. The old woman nodded slowly, but did not rise.

"They told me there was some water and bread left here, but I brought you some hot food. My lady said that—good as he is—we shouldn't put too much faith in an old bachelor like Sir Oliver." She placed the tray she was carrying on the table beside the narrow bed and glanced around. A pitcher of water and a washbasin were on a small chest by the foot of the bed.

"I am sorry not to have thought of bringing you a dress to change into. But I'll leave you my cloak, and we'll be at Melbury Hall by tomorrow afternoon. Once we get there, Lady Wentworth—and Mrs. Page and Amina, of course—will see to it that you have everything you need."

The girl rubbed her hands up and down her arms. "Would you mind if I added some more wood to the fire? 'Tis really quite cold in here."

Ohenewaa was surprised that the servant asked. The girl was waiting for permission from an old slave.

"Do as you please."

Rubbing the chafed skin on her wrists, Ohenewaa pushed herself to her feet and went to sit on the edge of the bed. The young woman walked cautiously—perhaps even respectfully, she thought—around the items on the hearth before kneeling down and stacking more wood in the fireplace.

"You were praying," Violet said. Soft golden curls framed the woman's pale face when she glanced over her shoulder at Ohenewaa. "I admire that."

"As a Christian, that does not bother you?"

"No! I admire it. This is an altar, is it not? I know you see the altar as the threshold of heaven, as the 'face of God' . . . more or less."

"How is it that you know as much?"

"I have many African friends at Melbury Hall, and I have the opportunity of spending many hours with them, especially with the women. For some of them, their beliefs are much stronger than mine, even if they aren't . . . well, strictly Christian."

"Is that so?"

"I realized, for one thing, that they believe they are never alone, despite being taken away from their kin, as they were. They believe the spirits of their ancestors are always with them."

"You do not like to be alone."

"No. To be honest, I do not." Violet shook her head and stood up. "And I'm glad you're coming back with us. I'll be back in a moment. I need to find a tinderbox."

Ohenewaa watched the servant leave the room, and she stared at the open door. For the first time in her sixty years of living, she was free.

That knowledge alone, though, brought little joy. She knew how hard a place the world was. She knew what misery it could inflict. She might be free, as the lawyer said, but she had no place to go. No money to buy her bread. No job to earn money. She continued to be a slave in their society.

The one thing they had not asked her about was if she was willing to go with these people to the country. They assumed she would be grateful for the chance. Perhaps she should be. Ohenewaa went to the basin and washed her face and hands. She was finally a free woman, but the world remained the same.

As Violet came in again and bent to the task of lighting the fire, Ohenewaa considered Lady Wentworth's
gesture. The woman had sent her own servant to see to
the needs of a slave.

Perhaps going to Melbury Hall would be a new beginning. Or perhaps not. For a slave, nothing but death was
a certainty.

Chapter 4

"I know this news is quite sudden, so please apologize to our people for the additional burden I am putting on them with all that must be done. But Lord Aytoun could be arriving at any time, and I truly need everyone's assistance in readying ourselves."

Millicent stood by the fire in the library, warming herself as she addressed the steward and the housekeeper. The journey up from London had been damp and cold. With her maidservant, Violet, and the old black woman riding in the carriage, Millicent and a groom had ridden behind, and a bitter winter wind had cut into her the entire way. But the physical discomfort of the trip had been nothing compared to the upheaval in her mind. Making a simple country house like Melbury Hall presentable enough to receive an earl was a challenge that Millicent had no confidence in facing. During her brief time in the dowager's company, she had heard a great deal about Baronsford, the Aytoun castle. She'd even seen a painting of it on one of the walls. And, having seen the magnificence of his town house in London, she could only imagine how grand her new husband's home was in the Borders of Scotland. Millicent's mind now reeled from her feelings of inadequacy.

"But really, m'lady!" The steward's protest cut through her thoughts. "Doing all of this today? What you ask is absolutely impossible. 'Tis already midafternoon. There is certainly not enough time to—"

"Mr. Draper," Millicent interrupted, already well acquainted with the man's querulous nature and finding herself short of patience. "We shall certainly have *less* time if we dally here and argue over what can or cannot be done. Now, kindly relay my instructions to the grooms in the stables regarding the necessary space for his lordship's carriage . . . or carriages . . . and horses. Then relay the news to Jonah with my instructions for the rest of the servants regarding the urgency of the situation. Mrs. Page and I need to see to the immediate need for living accommodations."

The tip of the steward's thin nose rose a few inches in the air before he turned toward the door. Millicent hoped the man was smart enough to realize that there was also an immediate need for a change in his attitude before he was introduced to Lord Aytoun. She saw Draper pause by the door.

"What about the African woman? She refuses to speak. Even her own people have not been able to convince her to take more than a step into the kitchens. Why, the woman won't let go of that horrid rag she has wrapped about her, either. Do you wish to have her left where she has situated herself, blocking one of the kitchen doors?"

Millicent silently reproached herself for not seeing that the woman was immediately situated. Violet had mentioned that she had refused the food last night and even declined the offer of wearing a cloak over her rags.

"She is to be treated as a guest in this house, Mr. Draper, but I will go and see to her needs myself as soon as I am finished here with Mrs. Page."

"Before you uproot and offend everyone in the household, m'lady," the steward commented sharply, "you should know that there is no space remaining whatsoever on the third floor. With so many of the field hands who were formerly housed in the Grove now cluttering up the household staff's quarters, there isn't a spare place for her. Therefore, I recommend once again that you reconsider your decision not to use the Grove shacks. Any of those places would be a castle compared to where she has been."

Along a bend in the river just beyond the glen lay the cluster of decrepit huts where Wentworth used to house many of the Africans he'd held as slaves at Melbury Hall. It was called the Grove. After his death, one of Millicent's first projects had been to move the people from that dark and dismal area of the manor land.

"I told you I will look after her myself, Mr. Draper. You may leave now."

Neither woman spoke until the steward had left the drawing room.

"You can always house her in one of Mr. Draper's rooms, m'lady. He is forever complaining that the two rooms he now occupies are unsatisfactory compared with what he was accustomed to with his previous employer."

"Do you think he would willingly surrender his sitting room to our new guest?"

There was mischief dancing in the housekeeper's eyes. "I think he'd quit at a mere suggestion of such a thing, m'lady."

Millicent shook her head. "I'm afraid I cannot allow that to happen right now, Mrs. Page. Though Mr. Draper maintains the record for anyone holding the steward's position since my husband's . . . my previous husband's death, this would not be a very good time to lose him. Finding and keeping a steward who believes in what we are attempting to do here is a daunting task, it seems."

"The problem is not with you, m'lady, but with these ignorant men who think that because you have no husband ordering you about, they should be taking over the job."

"Perhaps, Mary. But the real truth is that you are the one whom I really cannot do without." She touched the woman appreciatively on the arm. Millicent's previous worries edged again into her thoughts. "As to the rooms, how difficult would it be to prepare Squire Wentworth's old chambers for the earl?"

"The rooms have been kept clean. I had the bedding aired while you were in London, and with some fresh sheets and bedclothes, they'll be ready. I can go up and start right now."

"I should have arranged for some new furnishings in there before now."

"You haven't been in there for some time, m'lady. But they are just fine as they are."

"You should have a fire prepared to be lit if his lordship should arrive today," she said resignedly. "We also need to have the small guest room across the way ready for the earl's doctor. I am not really certain if he will be traveling with his lordship or how long he will be staying, but I want to be ready. Also, the other room by the servants' stairs. Hopefully, that would be suitable for the earl's manservant."

"It should, m'lady. He'll be able to hear his master call from there, I should think. As for the rest of them, I know that some of the field hands have put the loft in the dairy to rights for their own quarters. They could move out there anytime, now. Then, if need be, I can move two of the girls in with Vi and that will make space for . . ."

The housekeeper continued her planning, but Millicent's mind was caught up with the problem she'd been facing for some time now. After moving everyone out of the Grove, she had housed as many as she could in the few empty cottages in the outlying farms, and the rest in the servants' quarters in the house. But all of that had been temporary and very difficult during the hectic harvest days. With her limited funds, she had not even been able to think about any new buildings or renovations. But now, with her marriage, so many exciting possibilities presented themselves. Perhaps clearing more land along the river and building decent cottages for the field workers. Perhaps draining the marshy lowland and erecting a stone wall to contain the river during the spring. She paused, wondering if the Earl of Aytoun would consider staying at this crowded country manor long enough for her to start any of these projects.

"How many servants will be accompanying his lordship, m'lady?"

"Half a dozen, I should think. Perhaps more."

"And what should I instruct the kitchen staff as far as the earl's likes and dislikes?"

"I am not really certain. He is a Scot. What do Scots eat?"

"I'm sure I don't know, m'lady. Where would you think he'll be taking his meals?"

Millicent shook her head. "He is confined to a chair or a bed. We shall simply have to wait until he is here before we can make those decisions."

"And what about the furnishings in this room? Do you believe the earl will be spending his mornings here?"

Millicent glanced about at the old but comfortable chairs of the library and realized she wasn't sure how her new husband would be spending his days. There was a great deal she didn't know about him. She had never really thought of Melbury Hall as being small until now. Millicent's own bedchamber would be on the same floor as his. She would be within hearing if he should call, too. There would be no ignoring his presence.

Doubts about what she had done began to nag at her. "I am afraid he might find this place completely inadequate."

"You're worrying about too much right now, I think, m'lady. This is a fine home, and you're a perfect hostess. There is no use in upsetting yourself by guessing what he might think or do. The good Lord is sure to get everything working properly."

Mary's consoling words made Millicent nod in resignation. The two of them started for the door.

Beneath the vaulted ceiling of the entry foyer, four servants stood by the open front door, obviously agitated. At the sight of Millicent, the doorman ran toward her. "In the courtyard, m'lady. A carriage, two wagons, and a half-dozen serving men riding behind. He's here. His manservant said I should tell ye the Earl of Aytoun has arrived."

"Run, Mrs. Page! Get a couple of your people to ready the rooms. Also, find Mr. Draper. I need the two of you and everyone else in the yard to greet his lordship.''

Receiving a quick nod from her before the house-keeper scurried off, Millicent rushed past the wide stair-case toward the front door. Before she reached it, though, a panicked voice from behind brought her to a sudden stop. Millicent whirled toward the young maid-servant hurrying toward her.

"What is it, Violet?"

"She's dead, m'lady! Ohenewaa! She just went down where she was standing in the kitchen. I don't think she's breathing.''

Without hesitation, Millicent turned her steps toward the kitchen. She waved a hand at the doorman. "Tell his lordship's people I shall greet him in a mo—"

"M'lady!" a groom shouted as he ran in a doorway leading to the gardens. "They're killin' each other, for sure.''

"Who is killing whom?"

"Mr. Draper and Jonah, ma'am. Something the stew-ard said. I saw old Moses headin' that way. Now, you know there's no stoppin' him if he thinks someone is hurtin' Jonah.''

"Oh, no!" Millicent lifted the hem of her skirts and ran toward the door. "Go to the courtyard and help with the Earl of Aytoun's entourage.''

As she went out, she prayed under her breath that the old woman was still alive and that the earl would not be offended by her tardiness in greeting him. Most of all, though, she prayed that Moses would not do anything that might cause irreparable harm to himself or to any-one else. Not again.

The dawn mists hung between the shadowy trees, the dew dripping from dark green leaves. The pistol, silver and pearl, looked to be but an extension of Lyon's hand. He glanced briefly in the direction of the two men in the distance, their images blurred by the mist enshroud-ing them.

A somber voice called out, the sound echoing and

then dying away. Lyon listened to the far-off burbling of the river, to the waking cry of a startled bird. He inhaled the damp, earthy smell of the park as if this were the last he might have the privilege to breathe.

As his foe raised his pistol, pointing the muzzle at the steel-gray sky, Lyon did the same. *How many men must die,* he thought. He watched the fop by the tree extend his hand. A kerchief dangled from his lily-colored fingers . . . and then fluttered to the ground.

Before Lyon could pull the trigger, the mist cleared around the ghostlike face of his opponent.

Pierce stood facing him. David, their youngest brother, stood as his second. And then the shot rang out.

Lyon awoke with a start, sweat drenching his face.

Only another dream, he told himself. *Just another nightmare.* He struggled to shake himself free. He had been sleeping for what felt like an eternity. They had given him one of those damned drinks again before they had set out on the road this morning.

The carriage was not moving, he realized. He looked about the confined space and found that his manservant, Gibbs, was not there, either.

The curtain on the far window of the carriage had been tied back. He stared out and all he could see were walls of brick and a high iron gate. He could not rise above the confusion clouding his mind. He could not think clearly. Then, though he fought to contain it, panic began to gnaw at him.

Bedlam. They had told him they were taking him to the woman's house in the country, but they had lied. He was at Bedlam.

Anger swept away his panic as quickly as a Highland storm sweeps away the sun. *One more bloody betrayal.* He tore the blanket off his lap with his good hand. He would not be a prisoner in an institution. He was not insane.

Lyon shoved himself away from the seat, away from the images of high iron gates. But even as he tried to escape, his body collapsed under him in a heap of twisted bones and flesh. Jammed painfully between the carriage seats, he stared out through a small opening between the curtains covering the opposite window. All he could see were the tall chimneys of a house.

At that moment, where they had taken him made no difference to Lyon. He was a lonely cripple, less than half a man. His real life was over, and he wanted release. If they would but give him a pistol, he would put a quick end to this accursed existence.

"You are dismissed, Mr. Draper."

Millicent's voice echoed against the garden walls that bordered the path leading down the hill toward the Grove. She'd heard the steward's shrill voice as soon as she left the house, proclaiming both her incompetence and her corrupted nature in bringing the infamous Scottish "Lord of Scandal" under her roof as husband. Jonah had stepped forward to defend her, and now violence was clearly imminent.

"You are fired. Dismissed." She stood short steps from the two men. The steward's contemptuous gaze never moved from Jonah's angry face. He didn't appear to be listening. "Now! You are to get your things and leave Melbury Hall immediately."

"This business has nothing to do with you, m'lady," he said, still glaring at Jonah. "This is between me and this insolent slave."

"There are no slaves at Melbury Hall, Mr. Draper. You are the insolent one here. I heard what you said just now. Jonah, as my servant, has every right to defend me against the disrespectful things you said about me."

Millicent glanced at old Moses and thanked the Lord that he had remained a bystander thus far. Beneath his hair of mottled gray, the man's face showed the scars of innumerable beatings by slavers and by owners like Wentworth. Millicent knew, though, that despite his size and the fierce look born of his mutilated features, Moses was one of the gentlest souls alive . . . so long as no one tried to hurt Jonah. She turned back to Draper.

"Now I tell you again, return to the house and pack your belongings this instant."

"Not until I am finished with him." The steward took a step toward Jonah.

Millicent quickly put herself in the path of Moses as the large black man moved toward the steward. She placed a hand on his arm and shook her head at him.

She shot a look toward the house, hoping that some of the servants would be coming. She feared that Jonah would not defend himself. After so many years of being beaten and abused as a slave, he could not be expected to assert his rights as a free man. Bright and competent as he was, Jonah was still struggling with his new job as bailiff. The freedman was extremely capable, but lacked confidence.

Someone was indeed coming down the path, though it took Millicent a moment to realize it was Gibbs, the earl's personal servant, whom she had met for the briefest of moments yesterday after the marriage service in London.

"The mistress told you to pack your bag, Mr. Draper," Jonah ordered.

"I'll teach you to open your ugly mouth to your betters."

Millicent turned in time to see Jonah being pushed backward off the path.

"Stop. This instant," she screamed at the steward as her hands clung desperately to Moses's arm to keep him from advancing. If Draper struck Jonah, Moses would kill the man. Of that Millicent was certain. She didn't know if she could hold him much longer. "I ordered you to leave these premises."

As the steward lifted his fist, Millicent was shocked to see Gibbs stride past her, grab the back of the attacker's coat, and throw him to the ground with no more effort than one might expend plucking a bad apple off a tree.

"Ye have a wee bit of trouble following the mistress's directions, sir?" He put his silver-buckled shoe on the back of Draper's neck and shoved the man's face hard against the frozen ground.

The earl's manservant was a tall, barrel-chested Scotsman with thick black hair tied at the collar. In addition to his menacing dark eyes and bushy eyebrows, it was impossible not to notice the size of Gibbs's huge fists. This was not a man to be trifled with, she realized. Obviously Draper thought so too. It was stunning to see the fight knocked out of the steward so quickly.

"I heard her ladyship tell ye to leave, ye bloated cur."

"I was about to. I am, sir. As soon as you release me."

Still not lessening the pressure of his boot, Gibbs nodded politely to Millicent. "If your ladyship would like to go in out of this cold, these men here can help me dispose of this ill-mannered dog on the road to St. Albans."

"I believe Jonah and Moses would be happy to assist you, Mr. Gibbs." She turned her attention to the man on the ground. "Your things will be sent to the Black Swan Inn at Knebworth Village."

The look on Draper's face, beneath the shoe of the Scotsman, was not that of a happy man.

Millicent glanced up toward the house. "Has his lordship been brought in, Mr. Gibbs?"

"Nay, m'lady. Lord Aytoun was sleeping, so I left him in the carriage. I thought ye might prefer to greet him yourself before we moved him."

"Of course," she whispered, knowing the importance of such protocol. But Vi's earlier news about the collapse of Ohenewaa in the kitchen preyed on her mind. Gibbs must have noticed her gaze in the direction of the house.

"If ye please, m'lady. As I came through the servants' hall, your wee housekeeper asked me to relay a word to ye about the African woman in the kitchen. The woman is fine and has come about."

"Thank you." Millicent was indeed grateful for Gibbs's intervention, and Jonah appeared much more at ease as well. She saw him grab Draper by the scruff of his neck and yank him roughly to his feet when the Scotsman removed his boot. "I think I shall go around the house to the courtyard and greet his lordship."

Not until she rounded the corner of the manor house did she feel the cold wind penetrating her dress. She started to shiver. For the first time since charging out, Millicent realized that she had on no cloak or shawl.

At a respectful distance from the carriage, a number of her servants had lined up in greeting. As she went past them, she saw Mrs. Page rush out of the front door and—with a curtsy to Millicent—take her place beside the assembled staff.

The earl's servants as well stood waiting by their horses and wagons in the courtyard. Intensely aware of the dozens of eyes on both sides watching her every move, Millicent tried her best to hide her nervousness and approached the carriage with confident steps.

From the outside, she could not see in clearly through the curtains, but there appeared to be no one sitting in the carriage. At her nod, the footman opened the door.

The earl was twisted, helpless, wedged between the seats in the most awkward position. She saw her new husband's eyes open as the light from behind her poured inside the carriage. Millicent hurriedly stepped over his sprawled boots and climbed in, pulling the door closed behind her. He didn't have to say anything. She knew this was not the way he would wish to be introduced to his new household.

"I am so very sorry, m'lord. You have fallen down from the seat." Trying clumsily to find solid footing in the cramped space, she tried to bend his knees and straighten his boots. "The roads traveling up from London are not in the best condition, and nothing is worse than enduring a long trip like that to a strange place and . . ."

Millicent knew she was jabbering, but her embarrassment at not greeting him immediately was compounded by the sharpness of the earl's glare. She crouched down in the cramped space between the seats and searched for his right arm. It was twisted behind him.

"If you would be kind enough to place your other arm around my neck, perhaps I could lift you a little, and we could free this arm."

The earl did not respond, and she glanced up at his bearded face. His expression was intimidating, but she decided the tenseness she saw in his blue eyes had to be caused in some part by pain. This made her all the more determined.

"Please, m'lord. If you could just—"

"Gibbs. Get him."

Millicent was relieved to get some response. "He is coming, but—"

"Get Gibbs," he said louder.

"I have no intention of moving you inside by myself. I just thought it would be more comfortable for you to be sitting on the seat, instead of where you are."

She stopped, feeling like a liar for not speaking the whole truth. For a moment, she vividly recalled a time when she herself had sat inside the carriage, battered by Wentworth, desperate to hide her face from the prying eyes outside the door. Hiding the truth had always been Millicent's way of avoiding the embarrassment of her husband's horrible treatment. But the Earl of Aytoun's condition was nothing like hers.

"I am sorry, m'lord. I was acting without thinking."

She drew back and sat on the edge of the seat. "Your steward was kind enough to get involved with a problem I had with one of my workers. He should be back momentarily."

"*Gibbs!*"

The man's shout in the confined space of the carriage was startling. A vision of Squire Wentworth with the veins bulging in his neck, with his clutching hands reaching for her face, flashed before Millicent's mind. She quickly buried the terrifying image in the recesses of her mind. With her heart pounding in her chest, Millicent quelled her impulse to fling open the door and leap out. Through the small window, she could see the curious glances of the servants in the courtyard.

"I told you that he would be coming back shortly, m'lord," she said, keeping her tone reasonable.

"*Gibbs!*"

The impotent fury that laced his shout drew Millicent off the edge of the seat. She crouched beside him again.

"Tell me how I can help you. It is your arm, is it not?" This time she didn't bother to ask for his cooperation. Instead, looping an arm around his waist, she desperately tried to shift him enough to free the arm. She just could not muster the strength to move him. And the earl was doing nothing to help her. Nonetheless, she continued to try.

When Gibbs yanked open the carriage door a minute later, Millicent's hair had already escaped the tight bun on top of her head, her dress was crumpled and twisted, and her body was tangled on the floor with the Earl of Aytoun's. Out of breath, her face flushed, she looked up at the manservant, who stopped to stare with one eyebrow raised.

"Pardon me, m'lady, I didna know ye planned to start your honeymoon quite so soon."

Chapter 5

"There is no physician traveling with them," Millicent advised the housekeeper a few minutes later as they were heading toward the kitchen. "But Mr. Gibbs informed me that a Dr. Parker will be coming once a fortnight from London and will remain with us overnight. So for the moment, I should like to put Ohenewaa in the chamber you've prepared for the doctor."

To Mary's credit, she never even batted an eye at the suggestion of putting the woman in one of the guest bedchambers.

"She needs a bath, m'lady, and some clothes. Violet tells me that on the ride up from London, the woman scarcely spoke a word. One of the girls was able to spoon some broth into her when she was just coming around, but as soon as she knew which end was up, the poor dear went back to her place by the kitchen door. Curious thing, though, as quick as word went round that she was here, I've had more field hands poking their heads into that kitchen to see her. But still she continues to stare at the wall. If you don't mind my asking, m'lady, who is she?"

"I believe she is seen as someone very special. I don't know her entire history, but I do know she belonged to a physician named Dombey, who traveled on many slave ships and lived in Jamaica between his travels. Before I even went to London, I had heard numerous stories of this woman's courage. Even as Dr. Dombey's slave, she was well known for the many ways she helped people on the sugar plantations there, my late husband's included."

In the kitchen, Mrs. Page went off to organize her staff of workers. Millicent was relieved to see Amina already there and speaking quietly with the old woman. Married to Jonah last summer, the younger woman was quickly becoming Mary's right hand in running the house at Melbury Hall.

"All of us are grateful to you, m'lady, for bringing her here," Amina said quietly, joining her mistress in the middle of the kitchen.

"She looks hungry and weary." Millicent watched the tall, thin frame of Ohenewaa sway near the door. "Why is she refusing to come inside?"

"Her pride. Not knowing what is expected of her here."

Giving an understanding nod, Millicent walked toward the old woman. Ohenewaa's dark eyes remained fixed on the wall in front of her. Hers was a face lined by age and disappointment.

"We're happy you're here, Ohenewaa," Millicent said softly. "There is no need for you to stand by the door. Would you please come in?"

"I was told I am a free woman."

"You are."

"Then I do not wish to step inside a slaveholder's home." The old woman's gaze shifted to Millicent's face and then back to the wall again.

"I do not hold any slaves, Ohenewaa. I do not believe in owning or abusing innocent people. All the workers you see at Melbury Hall today, regardless of the color of their skin, or where they were born or came from, are here of their own will."

"I have seen how Wentworth treated his workers in Jamaica."

Millicent could hear the diamond edge of the woman's voice draw steadily across glass.

"That was my husband. Not I," Millicent replied passionately. "And I am trying, Ohenewaa. Since the death of the squire, I am doing my best to mend some of the injustices done to the people. I lost those plantations in Jamaica before anything could be done. But I am trying here."

The black woman's gaze once again moved away from the wall and rested on Millicent's face. "What do you wish from me? What do I have to do to earn my keep?"

Millicent paused to answer. The dark, penetrating gaze continued to look into her soul.

"It would be a lie if I said you have to do nothing. We need help of all kinds. The truth is that I don't know yet what you can do here." This time she was the one who fixed her gaze on the cracks running in every direction on the wall. "I came to the auction yesterday because I recognized Dr. Dombey's name in the notice in the newspaper. I came because I had failed to act effectively when Jasper Hyde took over Wentworth's plantations. There were so many lives that I did not save. Thoughts about if I were a stronger person, if I had acted quickly enough, continue to plague me. I wonder if, had I traveled there myself, I could have kept the plantations."

She turned to face the older woman. "In freeing you, I suppose I hope to lessen my guilt. And in bringing you here, I hoped to remind my people—and myself—that strength and courage like yours are to be aspired to."

"I am a healer. Nothing more."

"In Jamaica, you were the one person whom they knew they could trust. That was everything to them." Millicent noticed more than a few of the kitchen helpers and servants had paused in their work. Many eyes were on them, curious as to the outcome. She gentled her voice. "At least for now, until you have the opportunity for employment, will you please stay at Melbury Hall as my guest?"

"If I step across this threshold, it will not be to ease your conscience, but to ease my hunger."

Millicent smiled. "I respect that. We both have a reason. They do not conflict. And that is as good a place as any to start."

Ohenewaa looked about the room at the cluster of

hopeful faces before stepping through the door and into the house.

The air was frigid, the ground frozen. The night was dark, and the woods were threatening. Violet, however, scarcely gave the possible dangers a second thought. She had been passing through this deer park at least twice a week for over a month on her way to him. Lifting the hem of the quilted petticoats she'd been given by her mistress last month, she stepped over a fallen branch. Violet herself had embroidered the long apron she was wearing over the petticoats. And the pleated taffeta around her neck was a gift she'd bought herself when she and her mistress had been in London. She wanted to look pretty for Ned.

Ned Cranch—tall and broad with muscles as hard as rock—was a stonemason who had come in the fall to Knebworth Village to build the new grange. They had met outside church one Sunday morning. And after that, every time Vi had gone to the village, the handsome green-eyed giant had been there, tipping his hat or making some sweet remark about how good she looked or smelled.

Mrs. Page had witnessed Ned's sweet-talking a couple of times and had given Vi an earful about being careful, of course. But Violet was already eighteen, and she knew exactly what she was doing.

She was getting herself a husband.

Vi emerged from the woods and ran to the edge of the meadow above the village. He wasn't there, and Vi looked with concern at the lights in the windows of the cottages below. But before she could worry for long, powerful arms encircled her from behind, and she stifled a gasp as she was turned around in Ned's embrace.

He kissed her lips before she could whisper a greeting. His attentions were already becoming an obsession to her, and Vi dug her fingers into his thick, wavy blond hair and opened up to him so he could deepen the kiss the way he'd taught her. At last he tore his mouth away, but his hands continued to press her to him.

"I've missed you so much, Ned," she whispered while kissing the muscular column of his throat.

"Aye, lass, I know the feeling." He tossed his chin in the direction that she had come. "And with all the big doings at Melbury Hall, I didn't know if ye'd be getting away."

She looked at him in surprise. "You heard about it already?"

"Some. Ye know how village folk talk." His mouth dipped to her neck, and she shivered as his teeth nibbled and his lips brushed over her skin. "I've been looking forward to this since I saw ye last."

"You are the devil, Ned Cranch." She sighed.

"Who told ye?" he said with a laugh. "But tell me, Vi, is it true that yer lady has fetched herself a new husband?"

"As sure as I'm standing here," Violet managed to say, almost purring with pleasure as he kneaded her breast through the dress. Ned's caresses had become more and more intimate with each meeting. At the beginning, it had been only kisses. Over the past couple of weeks, though, Ned had begun touching her in places that made Violet shudder with excitement. But touching had been the extent of it. Vi knew that—in spite of Mrs. Page's words of warning buzzing in her head—not much could happen if they kept their pleasures at this.

"And they're saying she brought herself back a new slave as well." Ned's hand moved down over her stomach.

"An old woman." Vi closed her eyes and leaned into him as his hand reached the junction of her thighs. "Her name is Ohenewaa, and she is already freed."

"Ye can tell me all about it later." His lips took hers in a dizzying kiss. Suddenly he pulled away and wrapped his hand around her wrist. "Come with me."

"Where are we going?"

His eyes danced with mischief when he looked at her. "Back to my room at the Black Swan. We'll go in through the back door, lass. Nobody will see ye."

Violet hesitated. What he surely had in mind was the

one thing that she was hoping to avoid, at least until he asked her to marry him.

"What's wrong with staying here?"

Ned put his arms around her and placed his hands on her buttocks as he kissed her. She could feel the size of him as he rubbed himself hard against her. "What I want to do to ye, my sweet, means taking every stitch of your pretty clothes off and then kissing every inch of your skin. Now, we can do that here, if ye like, but 'twould be a mite cold, I should think."

Her body was on fire, but her brain was still working.

"Ned, I don't think we should." Vi was sorry the moment she voiced her objection, for a look of hurt came into his eyes. "You know I've never . . . well, never done this before. 'Tis just that I am nervous. Afraid, to be honest."

"Nothing to be afraid of. But I'm in no hurry, lass. We'll stay right here, if ye like." He smiled and led her to a fallen tree at the edge of the woods.

"You don't mind, Ned?" she said as he pulled her onto his lap. "Really?"

"Nay, my dream. And I know just how to get your mind off your worries." He caressed her thighs, sliding his hand slowly upward until she drew in a breath sharply. "Aye, ye just think of Melbury Hall and tell me whatever ye want about it. And I'll kiss your neck—this pretty little spot here below your ear—and ye can keep talking. How's that?"

"Are you sure—" She gasped as he rubbed harder. "Are you sure you're not put off?"

"Put off? Nay, lass." He lifted his head. "In fact, I wasn't going to say this now, but perhaps 'tis for the best."

"What is it?"

"I love ye, Vi."

"You do?"

"Aye," he said, turning his attentions back to her neck. "But tell me what's doing at the Hall."

Chapter 6

It seemed quite awkward to Millicent, retiring for the night without having seen or spoken with the Earl of Aytoun again. His man, Gibbs, and two of the valets had taken their master to his chambers after the ordeal in the courtyard. At his request, she'd had dinner sent upstairs. The earl's servants appeared quite proficient in seeing to all of his needs.

No complaints. No requests. Everything had been deathly quiet since dinner. But as she left Mary in the servants' hall, Millicent couldn't shake off the nagging feeling that merely giving Lord Aytoun a suite of rooms was not at all what the dowager countess had wanted when she asked Millicent to marry her son. She had clearly stated that she wanted someone with compassion.

To bring herself to the point of getting closer to her new husband, though, Millicent had to crush the seeds of anxiety inside of her. In the few short hours that she had spent in London after marrying him, she had heard a number of grim reports about Lyon Pennington. The man had a notorious temper. He had definitely fought at least four duels during the spring before his accident. There were rumors of others, too. And there was a general belief that he had killed his wife.

Wentworth had killed his first wife. And on more than a few occasions, he had nearly taken Millicent's life, too. She cringed, remembering the first time. In her mind's eye, she could still see him taking his riding crop and approaching her. She had stood disbelieving at what was happening. They had been married less than a month. It was a miracle that she had survived him, survived their marriage.

Still shivering, Millicent recalled the first time she had met the earl, a silent man with dark hair and an un-trimmed beard covering a pale face. His blue gaze had been restless, but not hostile. Even today, when she had been trying to help him in the carriage and he had be-come angry, fear of him had never entered her mind. Sympathy and worry perhaps, but not fear.

Different situation, she told herself. *A very different man.*

Climbing the wide stairwell from the entry foyer, Mil-licent moved down the hallway past her own bedcham-ber. She paused at the door to Ohenewaa's room. The old woman had confined herself to her room tonight. Millicent felt better about that situation, at least, know-ing that Amina had gone in a couple of times, directing servants who had brought in a tub and water for wash-ing, and later food and several changes of clothing for the woman.

There were so many things pulling at Millicent's mind. Things such as how to make the old woman feel safe at Melbury Hall. And how she was going to advertise for the position of steward to replace Mr. Draper. And where she should spend her new income. She told her-self that she needed to sit down and decide what should be done first.

Too tired to put her thoughts in any manageable order, she turned toward the earl's chambers and lifted her hand to knock.

She paused, recalling the misery she had endured when Wentworth was in possession of these rooms. At times she would break into a cold sweat just coming this near the door. Once again, she pushed the fears back and knocked softly.

Gibbs opened the door, and one brow arched in sur-prise. "Lady Aytoun."

Millicent stared at him for a moment. No one had called her that before, and she was not accustomed to the name yet. Lady Aytoun. She managed, at least, not to look behind her in search of the mystery woman.

"Is the earl sleeping, Mr. Gibbs?"

"Aye, m'lady." He stepped back, opening the door wider.

Millicent could see part of the bed and the man sleeping on it. She didn't come into the room. "Did he have any dinner?"

"I am afraid his lordship had no appetite after so many hours on the road today. But he tried some of the soup, thank ye."

"Does someone stay with him all the time?"

"We try to, m'lady, at least when he's awake."

She gave a nod of approval, remembering how helpless he had seemed today, wedged between the carriage seats.

"What is the earl fond of doing, Mr. Gibbs?" It was an unexpected question, she realized, as the servant seemed perplexed as to how to answer. "What I meant to say was, how does he prefer to spend his days now?"

"Well, he spends most of it in bed or in his chair."

"No, what I want to know is whether he likes to read, or does someone read to him? Does he have a favorite newspaper that I should have delivered? Is he fond of playing at cards?"

"Nay, m'lady, none of that. His lordship likes to stare outside, and that is the extent of it, I'm sorry to say."

A twinge of sympathy pinched at Millicent. What kind of life was that for anyone? she thought. She made a silent vow to establish a better routine for her husband. She gave a final glance toward the sleeping man on the bed. He looked subdued, certainly not the hellion that he was reputed to be. "Are your own sleeping arrangements satisfactory, Mr. Gibbs?"

"Aye, they are far better than I expected, m'lady. I thank ye kindly."

"Very well. Good night, then." She turned toward her own rooms.

"Lady Aytoun." Gibbs stepped into the hallway after

her. "Since I'm to be here, if you think of anything around Melbury Hall that I might be helping ye with, speak out, for I'm willing. I do not think his lordship would mind."

Millicent knew from the dowager countess that the Scotsman had been with Lord Aytoun for years.

"You saw me fire Mr. Draper today. Perhaps you can help me as I try to find a replacement for him."

"Aye, m'lady. Whatever I can do to help, I am here to oblige."

Millicent nodded gratefully and turned away. As she walked back toward her own bedchamber, though, she found herself thinking not of the relief of having extra help, but of the man she'd found wedged helplessly between the seats of a carriage, and seeing in her mind the defeated look in his eyes.

"Why in the devil's name would you accept payment from her?" Jasper Hyde hissed at the other man. "You know damn well once she got the slave, everything changed."

"My apologies, sir, but—"

"You and your deuced apologies can go to hell." He pounded a fist on the table. "Blasted lawyers."

Mr. Platt, a small man, folded his hands on his desk. "It was clear, Mr. Hyde, that our plans had been frustrated. I could find no way to refuse the cash payment. The amount covered all of Lady Wentworth's outstanding debts to you. Her lawyer did not even try to wheedle out of paying the interest for this month. The entire amount she owed you, correct to the last farthing, was included in the settlement sum."

The sharp pain slicing through his chest made Jasper Hyde refrain from hammering on the desk again. His hand clutched a spot just below his heart, where he felt a dagger burn and twist its way in. There were never any bruises. No symptoms that anyone could see. The few doctors he had spoken to about his ailment had told him, in so many words, that there was nothing wrong

with him. The heart appeared strong, they said. He knew
better. As always the pain came on sharply, then gradually eased.

"Are you unwell, Mr. Hyde?"

"Did you offer to take . . . ?" He was gradually recovering his breath. "To take the black woman as part of
the settlement?"

"I did. But Sir Oliver would not consider it."

"Then you did not have to take the money."

"It was all done legally, you understand. I could not
reject the payment."

"And since when do you stick to legalities, Platt?"
Hyde planted both hands on the desk and glowered
menacingly at the lawyer. "You seem to be having a
hard time understanding me. You told me that she has
no credit at all available. That she would not be able to
pay for the woman."

"Mr. Hyde, there was no way of knowing that she
would marry the Earl of Aytoun that very day."

Hyde cursed his damnable luck. Yesterday, hearing all
the rumors about the fallen earl, he'd not once imagined
the crippled bastard would be ruining his plans.

"We are *not* going to let anyone stop us. Do you understand me?"

Hyde's fist landed hard on the desk again, scattering
a pile of papers and making the lawyer jump as the
candle wobbled in its holder. Platt tried to straighten the
documents before him.

"What is done we cannot und—"

With a sweep of his hand, Hyde cleared the lawyer's
desk of all the papers, scattering them across the chamber. "I want the old slave, Platt. *Now.*"

Sweat beaded on the lawyer's brow and ran down his
temple. Hyde knew Platt did not want to face his fury.
Many words were left unsaid between them, but the inti-
mation was clear. Hyde was certain the black witch had
cursed him. The pains in his chest. The change in his
luck. He did not need more proof than this.

"In a fortnight or so, sir, we may still be successful in
making another offer for the slave."

"You said yourself that she doesn't need the blasted money. Besides, she'll never sell the woman to me."

"Perhaps you might present yourself in a different light. Perhaps you can tell her you have seen the error in your ways. That you wish to employ the woman to help with the health of the slaves in Jamaica. She did have the benefit of assisting Dr. Dombey, I understand."

"You are a fool!" Jasper exploded. "There is not a chance in the world that she'd fall for such a ruse. She'd see through it in a moment."

"I am simply suggesting, sir, that money is not the only method we have to persuade her. She is just a woman, and therefore weak. In addition, she now has a crippled husband added to her burden."

"And no debts with which to crush her."

"True, and her money might not run out in the near future, so we shall need a new weapon to use against her."

"What?"

Platt's bony fingers formed a steeple. "We need to continue keeping a close eye on her."

"We need to find a way to pry her fingers off the old woman." Hyde straightened up, remembering the last meeting he'd had with Dr. Dombey. With what was practically his last breath, the old fool had spoken of honor, of how he would not sell Ohenewaa to someone like him for any price. Fearing Dombey might do something as stupid as actually freeing the woman before he died, Hyde had then simply helped the good doctor toward his eternal reward.

But his damnable luck had been against him that day too, as the slave was not there. A bailiff, representing a number of Dombey's creditors, stood outside, though, as well as several others who were attending to the dying man. Hyde knew there was no way that he would get his hands on her. He even had a good idea that she was somewhere nearby, waiting for him to leave.

"Perhaps we can somehow reason with the lady through the earl's lawyer."

Hyde dismissed Platt's comment with a wave of his

hand as a brilliant idea presented itself to him. "The
doctor. Find out for me the name of the doctor who is
attending to Aytoun while he is at Melbury Hall. I want
you to arrange a meeting with him."

Violet wasn't aware that her boots were wet. She paid
no mind to the quilted petticoats and the white apron,
all mud-stained and soaked through as well. She didn't
even realize that she was shivering violently. As she fled
along the path through the woods by the Grove, though,
tears continued to roll down her cheeks. It was still dark
when she emerged from the woods, and she quickly
moved up the knoll toward the back of the house.

Vi had no complaints about Ned. He had not forced
her to go back to the inn. When the cold rain had begun,
she'd gone willingly, giggling like a little fool the whole
way. Once there, he had not rushed her, either. He had
taken his time, teasing and kissing her and saying such
sweet things to her. And like a wanton hussy, she had
cried out in ecstasy as he had been doing all those
wicked things to her.

Once she'd left him and come out into the night,
though, shame had washed through her like icy rain. She
became more and more horrified as she ran home, thinking how she had simply spread her legs. What made it
worst of all, though, was that he'd had his way with her
without any definite commitment.

As she neared the gardens, she thought back over the
things he'd said. He'd said he was her man. He'd said
she was his true love. He'd said . . .

She stopped and leaned against the garden wall, covering her face with her hands. He'd never said he would
marry her.

"Oh God," she said in a moan. What if she was with
child now?

Her mother, long a widow, was no whore. She had
always been poor, but they'd always lived decently in St.
Albans. And her grandmother had always been so proud
of her. Years ago, her grandmum had spoken almost

boldly to Lady Wentworth about how Vi must be treated before allowing her to serve as maid to the mistress.

Vi stabbed away at her tears, remembering how her grandmum always referred to her as her own innocent thing. Where had that innocence gone? Before the squire had died, Violet had been ready to kill herself rather than let him touch her. She recalled how she had hidden in one of the slave huts in the Grove so he wouldn't find her. She had been terrified, but she had survived. She had kept her maidenhead. And now she had given it up like some slut.

She had to talk to Ned. She had to make sure he understood what kind of a girl she was. But perhaps 'twas too late? A sob caught in her throat.

The house loomed in the dreary predawn light. Pushing away from the wall, Violet ran toward it. As she reached the open garden gate, though, a tall, dark figure suddenly appeared in front of her, and she barreled straight into the man, who grabbed her arms to keep her from falling.

She gasped and looked up at the scarred face. "Moses!"

The man's hands dropped back to his sides.

"What are you doing out here at this hour of the morning?" she asked gently. She knew that Moses served as a watchman at night, but she had never returned this late and had not expected to run into him.

"Vi hurt?"

The gruff tone could not mask his concern, making her feel doubly guilty. She shook her head at him. "No, Moses. I'm not hurt."

"Why is Vi crying?"

" 'Tis nothing, Moses. I was just a little sad. But I'm better now. Truly." She touched his arm before going around him and heading quickly up the hill. When she reached the door to the house, she turned and looked back at Moses. Though she couldn't see his face, he was still standing where she'd left him, watching over her until she'd gone safely in.

Chapter 7

With the Chiltern Hills rising behind it, Solgrave sat on a ridge overlooking a long, narrow lake that stretched along a handsome valley. With its fine deer park and well-tended farms, the country house of the Earl and Countess of Stanmore was truly a beautiful place, one far superior to any of its neighboring country manor houses. But the mansion's grandeur did not diminish the value of its neighbors. Solgrave conferred on them greater status merely by having the good fortune of being located in the same vicinity. This added value had been reason enough for Squire Wentworth to purchase Melbury Hall.

Of course, Millicent thought, that was before Wentworth had married her to enhance his social status. How ironic that within a few years, Rebecca Neville would come back from the American colonies, marry Lord Stanmore, and provide Millicent with an ally who would help her fight for her liberty.

Despite the different roads that they had taken, fate had certainly brought the two school friends together again after nearly a decade apart. And Millicent would be forever grateful to Rebecca and Stanmore for helping her climb back onto her feet and manage to keep Melbury Hall after the squire's death.

Mrs. Trent, the housekeeper at Solgrave, was as friendly as ever when she led Millicent to the library. Inside, the young woman had only just managed to remove her hat and gloves before her friend rushed in to meet her.

"I was going to come to Melbury Hall to see you myself this afternoon."

Millicent returned Rebecca's embrace. "I couldn't risk not seeing you during the short time you were here. I heard you are only staying overnight."

"We are on our way to visit my mother-in-law in Scotland. Depending on the traveling conditions, we should only be gone for a month, but we had to stop here." Rebecca stepped back, holding Millicent at arm's length and studying her friend carefully. "Stanmore and I couldn't believe your news. You are *married* again."

"It is true."

"To the Earl of Aytoun."

Millicent nodded.

"But you didn't know him before, did you?"

"No, I didn't."

Seeing how puzzled her friend looked, Millicent sat down on the settee with her and told her about the dowager's letter. Short of getting into the exact details of their financial arrangement, she explained everything else.

Rebecca listened quietly and then chose her words carefully. "Did you know anything about the man? About his reputation?"

"Yes. Sir Oliver forewarned me, and I have heard a great deal since. But I consider much of it simply rumor and gossip."

"Then you know that some have openly accused him of pushing his wife off the cliffs at Baronsford."

"I believe she slipped and fell—as he did, trying to go down and help her. She died, but his fate has been almost as bad. He appears to be crippled, most likely for life." Millicent shook her head. "I spoke to the dowager at length about that accident, and about the other accusations. Lord Aytoun is a much different man now than he may have been a year ago. He is quite subdued in every sense."

Rebecca's hands clutched Millicent's tightly. "You know I am not one to meddle in anyone's life, but you have been married to him only a week, and already I see the strain in your face. You look tired."

She tried to smile. "I am the one to blame for that. Not him."

"And why is that?"

Millicent rose from the settee and walked to the large window overlooking the lake. This was the same question she had been asking of herself. "When I agreed to marry him, I convinced myself that I was simply offering his family a place where Lord Aytoun would be cared for." She turned to face her friend. "You know me, Rebecca. I have no illusions about love. They were crushed out long ago. But at the same time I know the importance of having a husband. This marriage to the Earl of Aytoun presented me with the most ideal situation I could ever have hoped for. By this union, I would have gained a husband without the fear that comes with having one. I am married without having to be a wife."

"Things are not going as you planned."

"No. I . . . I find that I feel sorry for him. He has no use of his legs, his arm. He spends most of the day in a silent stupor. He is as wretched as any beggar on the side of a London street. Yet I can see the pain in his eyes. He does not want this kind of existence."

"Is there no way you can help him? Perhaps different doctors. Or by finding ways of challenging his mind, at least. There are many ways you might be able to improve the quality of his life."

Rebecca would know about this. For ten years, she had lived on her own in the colonies and raised the earl's son, James. The boy had a misshapen hand and was partly deaf.

"But . . . but I fear I have married too far above my position," Millicent blurted out. "I am certain he sees how deficient I am, and what Melbury Hall lacks."

"Even without knowing him, I doubt that is true. I know you never give yourself the credit that is due." Rebecca's voice resonated with the passion of her belief. "You said yourself he spends his days in a stupor. So there is no way for you to know what he thinks or feels. Now, as far as improving on the condition of his life, I think you should be yourself. Do what your heart tells you to do and help him as far as he lets you. And there is no reason to worry about what happens beyond that. The future is as mysterious as the man you have married. But that is true for all of us. None of us can tell what awaits us down the road."

So true, Millicent admitted. She was worrying about forever, when tomorrow was the challenge that she had to face.

Through the mist and the gloom, he could catch only glimpses of Emma. She was holding up her skirts with one hand and running like a doe, weaving in and out between the stunted pines.

The wind-driven rain was on his face, in his eyes. Lyon wiped the wetness away, trying to see her. His legs were heavy, as if he were running in deep sand. The trees and brambles tore at his face and clothes, but he could not let her go. He glanced back at Baronsford, the walls rising gloomily in the gray of the gathering storm.

Turning, Lyon saw her again, her golden hair flying behind her as she disappeared in the mist by the cliffs. The rain was stinging his face, and he slipped and stumbled on the path.

Pierce's startling revelation was still clouding his mind. The hostile accusations of his brother continued to stab at his sense of honor. But how could he defend himself against something that he was ignorant of? Emma had the answers. She had to make Lyon understand. She had to come back with him and face the truth.

Lyon's chest was burning as he regained his balance and pushed himself to run harder.

The echo of Emma's scream filled the hills.

The break in the trees came quickly, and the path was slick where it turned at the cliff. Lyon could not see the far side of the river. All was bleak and gray. The path along the bluff was empty, except for the billowy mists.

And then he saw her—there at the bottom. Her

golden hair spread around her on the rocks. Her eyes
stared up at him, unseeing.

Lyon awoke with a start and stared at the unfathom-
able darkness that surrounded him. He was dead. He
had slipped and fallen down those same cliffs.

A shadow moved over him. Cold hands pressed
against the fevered skin of his new face. He stared into
the concerned face of his new wife. If he was dead, it
was clear that he had not won heaven.

At best, this was only purgatory.

Millicent stared out the window of the Morning Room
at the shining new chaise the physician had driven up
from London. A groom and his manservant stood at
the head of the handsome pair of geldings, talking and
stamping their feet in the cold.

Though they had been out there an hour, when Millicent had sent out hot drinks and asked them to come in
for something to eat, they had declined. Dr. Parker had
told them to wait with the carriage, as they would be
staying for only a few moments before going on to Lord
Eglinton's estate near Chiswell Green today.

She continued to pace the room. Dr. Parker had been
abrupt and dismissive when she'd greeted him upon his
arrival, and the doctor and his assistant had gone directly
upstairs to Lord Aytoun's chambers. Aside from asking
that some food be sent up, the physician had declined
with a wave of his hand her offer of spending the night
at Melbury Hall. His other patients, who were "too lofty
in London's social circles to name," needed him. And
he must return to the city immediately.

The physician's comment did not sit well with Millicent, as she again found herself being reminded of her
own social position. She would never have been in Lord
Aytoun's company if it were not for his accident. But
despite the slight, Millicent was quite happy that he'd
made the trip out, for she had dozens of questions about
the earl's condition, and they were becoming more pressing with each passing day.

Dr. Parker didn't keep her waiting much longer. While

the man's assistant went directly to the carriage, Gibbs showed the doctor to the Morning Room. Millicent gestured for him to sit down, but the man ignored her invitation and glanced at a watch he kept on a gleaming gold chain in his waistcoat pocket.

"All is well, m'lady," the physician said in a slightly hurried voice. "There will be no need for any new medicine, but I have directed Lord Aytoun's manservant to increase the frequency of the dosage that we began in London. So now, if you will forgive me, Lady Aytoun, I shall be on my way." He turned to the door. "I do not know when I shall return to Melbury Hall, but perhaps now that the earl is under such capable care, I could send out my very able assistant every fortnight or so, and I shall keep you advised as to his lordship's condition."

"I do have a few questions, Dr. Parker, which I was hoping you might answer for me." She took a step toward him, her voice shaking slightly with emotion. "They concern the earl's general health."

The physician paused and turned back to her. His bushy brows drew into a tight frown.

"I don't believe you need to be troubling yourself, m'lady. Lord Aytoun is in my care now, and I shall see to it that his lordship gets whatever care he needs."

"I am not doubting your abilities in the slightest, sir. I am certain that the dowager would have enlisted your services only if she had the greatest confidence in you."

"As I may have mentioned earlier," he began, puffing up with a pompous air, "my clients consist only of the most elite members of London's *ton*."

"I am certain that is true, and to have a physician of your stature journey all the way out to Hertfordshire is greatly appreciated."

Millicent watched as his attitude settled into one of benign condescension.

"Of course," he said slowly, smiling as if he had just learned something profound about her. "Your concern for your new husband is understandable, if not admirable. And I shall be certain to convey your concern to her ladyship, the dowager countess."

"That is hardly necessary, I assure you. But with regard to the earl's treatment—"

He raised a plump hand to stop her. "You do understand, m'lady, that I have never been involved with his lordship's external injuries."

"I understand that. But—"

"I have been informed that a Scotch surgeon from Edinburgh, named Wilkins or Wallace or something similar, set the bones after his lordship's . . . er, unfortunate fall from the cliff. Now, if that man's negligence has caused Lord Aytoun to continue having difficulty using his legs and his right arm, I cannot say one way or another. But after such a fall, I would tend to place the blame on the blow he received."

"My question has to do with my husband's treatment *now*."

The physician looked at her as if she were a child intent on trying his patience.

"As I said, Dr. Parker, I appreciate your coming to Melbury Hall. I simply want to know your view of my husband's condition and what your plans are for treatment. What, for example, did you do today?"

"Very well, Lady Aytoun," the doctor said shortly. "If you insist on knowing every detail, I checked his lordship's pulse and had a sample of urine taken. Lord Aytoun's condition is unchanged from ten days ago, when I saw him last."

"Indeed, you've hit on it exactly, sir," she replied. "Since the second night of his stay at Melbury Hall, I have been sitting with him for several hours each night."

"Have you, m'lady?" he said, his eyebrows going up in surprise.

"I have. And what I found was that at night his lordship is unsettled. He does not sleep soundly, so far as I can tell, and when he is awake he is not completely aware of his surroundings." Millicent's fingers twisted together. "Initially, I thought that perhaps my perception was skewed because of the hour of my visit, so I questioned his man, Gibbs, as to the best time to come.

But I was told that during the daytime Lord Aytoun is particularly unfit for company."

"I do not know what you mean by these comments, Lady Aytoun," Parker said defensively. He looked at his watch again.

"Gibbs has confirmed that his lordship's sleep is fretful. Moreover, when he is awake, Lord Aytoun is far more agitated than he has been in the past. Added to that, I have been informed that he does not wish to eat. He does not drink. Any nourishment he takes at all is forced upon him. I simply cannot help but think that something serious might be wrong, and that his condition is getting worse."

Dr. Parker fixed her with a disapproving glare. "Lord Aytoun is being administered some very powerful medicine, m'lady. To be exact, he is presently being given a tincture of opium, the preferred treatment for someone in his condition. That is, the preferred treatment for someone in his mental state and whom the family insists on caring for at home. The opium functions to calm him, to control the melancholia and avoid the need for securing him or locking him away."

"Why should he be locked away?"

"To keep his lordship from injuring himself during the blackest moments."

"But he appears to be getting less—"

"Now, with regard to that medicine, I can assure you this has been tried and proven to be highly effective. Before he left London, I increased his dosage several drops per day, and I believe he is responding well to my treatment."

"With all deference to your knowledge and experience, Dr. Parker, I see no—"

"M'lady," the physician said, holding his hand up again. "You must trust in that medical knowledge and experience. His lordship's life is far more pleasant than the lives of many who are similarly afflicted with the same melancholia. And I am ministering to his affliction with the most effective treatment known to medicine."

"I'm certain you have Lord Aytoun's best interests at heart, sir, but—"

"Now, you can do your part by concerning yourself with his diet. You must have your people take great care to keep the stomach of the patient settled, furnishing him with light meals, and . . . well, I have directed his manservant as to the importance of regular digestive function. And in the meantime, I shall continue to advise you as to the state of his mind. Now, I must say good day to you, Lady Aytoun. I have tarried here far too long. Far too long."

Lyon clamped his mouth shut and turned his face away as John, his valet, tried to feed him a spoonful of soup.

" 'Od's truth, m'lord, ye might help me here. Yer losing too much weight, and Dr. Parker says we have to force ye to eat more."

The man continued to talk, but Lyon ignored him. He was growing so accustomed to the cramping in his stomach that it was becoming almost tolerable. The intense nausea, however, which he'd been feeling since early this morning, before the pompous physician arrived, was something new. Or was it yesterday morning? The days were beginning to blur in his mind. Lyon tried to focus on which day it was but soon gave up. What did it matter?

The bloody doctor. He was just another lily-handed, potbellied charlatan who practically jingled with coin when he walked.

Lyon glared at John and turned his face again at the proffered food.

While Parker examined him, Lyon had said nothing to the man. He had mentioned nothing of the spasms of strength that every now and then ran through the muscles of his right arm, causing his fingers to curl and straighten. He had made no mention of the pain in his joints and had not asked the question of why it was that sometimes he was capable of actually bending his knee and not other times. He'd had no desire to prolong the bugger's stay. He hated the doctors and their prodding and poking. He abhorred their all-knowing attitude.

More to the point, though, he admitted inwardly, he was tired of wondering which one of them would finally persuade his family to have him sent to Bedlam. Not that very much persuasion would be needed once the dowager passed away. Lyon tasted bile in his throat and felt cold sweat breaking out on his brow.

The spoon touched his lips again. He jerked his head away irritably and tried to focus on the chaise that he could see through the window. As he watched, the fat doctor appeared and stepped into the carriage.

"We're only asking for a wee bit of help, m'lord."

Lyon recognized Gibbs's voice. The man was back . . . finally.

"Bed." He closed his eyes, wishing for the oblivion that so often surrounded him these days.

"Aye, but not before we'll be getting some food into ye."

The spoon was again at his lips, and Lyon slapped the annoying object away with his left hand. "Put me back in bed. Now."

The room was too hot. He felt his chair being turned around. He tried to focus on the face of John, still shoving a spoon at him. Beyond the valet, Gibbs was approaching with a crystal glass. The medicine. There was someone else behind him. Long Will, no doubt.

"Give him this only after his lordship has some food in him," Gibbs ordered, placing the cup on a table near him. "I'll be coming back shortly, now, so ye two mind what I say."

Lyon watched Gibbs move across the chamber and go out the door. He wanted to scream after the man to take this pair of imbeciles with him. But the bitter taste was still in his mouth, and he could feel himself shaking uncontrollably.

"We'll make it quick, if ye please, yer lordship. Eat jist a wee bit o' this, m'lord, an' we'll have ye back in yer bed in no time."

This time Lyon successfully dashed the bowl out of the man's hand, sending it crashing to the floor.

"Bloody hell," Will said from behind him, realizing his error as soon as the words had left his mouth. "Beggin' yer lordship's pardon, sir."

"The medicine," he managed to say. Oblivion. This was the only thing left to him. Opium and brandy. Laudanum. He started pushing himself out of the chair with his one good arm. "The medicine."

He didn't know which of the valets brought the glass to his lips, but the taste of it managed to push down the bitter bile. His stomach, though, cramped fiercely as soon as the liquid reached it. Lyon felt himself fighting back the involuntary desire to retch. As he tried to breathe, though, one of the two morons was trying to push bread into his mouth while the other held his shoulders pressed against the back of the chair. He reached out desperately to push the food away.

"Do *not* force him," a woman said sharply.

Through a haze of illness and frustration, Lyon watched her cross the chamber from the open doorway.

" 'Slordship ain't eaten not a bite all day, m'lady," John explained, the bread in his hand.

"We give 'im the medicine already, Lady Aytoun," the other one explained. "But Dr. Parker himself told us to mix it with 'slordship's food."

He tried to focus on her face, but it was all a blur. Her fingers were icy cold when they touched his face and brow.

"Take the food away," she ordered. "And bring that washbasin quickly. Give it to me."

His gut twisted painfully again and bile rose into his mouth. Lyon felt her arm wrap around his shoulder and lean him forward at the very moment that everything inside of him spewed out.

It was sympathy and not revulsion that washed through Millicent as the harsh smell of his sickness surrounded them. She wrapped her arm tighter around him and tried to give him some of her own strength. His left hand desperately clutched the basin on his lap. Streams of sweat dripped down his brow and blended into his dark, matted beard. She saw him close his eyes, and she wished she could soothe his suffering somehow.

"Get a towel and a clean bowl of water," she ordered the short valet.

Aytoun's wide shoulders shook as he continued to retch spasmodically.

"You! Give me another basin," she said to the one called Will.

As she was replacing the basin on Lyon's lap with a clean one, Gibbs swept into the chamber.

"Och! By the . . ." The manservant was at her side in an instant. "Forgive me, m'lady. A minute ago when I left, his lordship wasn't in such straits."

"Just support his shoulders like this, Mr. Gibbs," Millicent directed. She took the towel and clean water from John. She knelt again beside the earl's hunched, shuddering body, and started wiping his face and the corners of his mouth with the towel. He continued to heave, though nothing but bile was left in his stomach.

"This is not really the place for ye, Lady Aytoun," Gibbs said. "We can be doing all this if ye wish to—"

"I'm staying." She did not look up but dipped the towel into the water again and wiped her husband's face. "Does this happen often, Mr. Gibbs?"

"Nay, m'lady. The laird has been sick to his stomach twice or thrice over the past few months, but never like this, mum."

"What has he eaten today?" Millicent saw Gibbs look up at John and followed his gaze. The man answered with a shake of his head. "And last night?"

"A wee morsel. If that, m'lady."

"What about the medicine?"

"His lordship had a healthy dose of it last night," Gibbs told her. "But none yet today."

Will cleared his throat uncomfortably, and John reluctantly spoke up.

"Beggin' yer pardon. We give him more this mornin', but only because 'slordship forced us," he admitted in a small voice. "And some more jist now. Only but a wee taste, though, an' not a minute before 'er ladyship come in."

Millicent fought back the urge to scold the men for their carelessness. The poor man could have been poisoned. She knew, though, that the fault lay not with them, but with her. She had freely married this man. She had signed papers, stood beside his chair before a bishop. She had accepted his family's generosity in paying her debts, and she had vowed to care for him. But other than providing him with a set of rooms, she had done nothing of what she had promised.

Aytoun appeared to be improving slightly. The heaving was subsiding. She gently unclasped his fingers from the basin and wiped his mouth and face with the towel as Gibbs leaned him back in the chair. His eyes remained closed. His face was pale.

"Would you be kind enough, Mr. Gibbs, to put his lordship into the bed?"

She stood back while the three men skillfully followed her direction. She waited until he was settled before turning to them.

"I am very grateful for the care that you have been giving his lordship. From now on, however, I should like to be kept abreast of everything that is given to him, and you will tell me *before* it is done." She met the men's gazes directly. "If his lordship does not feel well, I will be told. If he has no appetite and misses a meal, you will tell me. I shall make a change in my own routine from this point forward. I am planning to spend much more time here than I have previously. Nonetheless, if Lord Aytoun is ailing and I am not here, I want you to find me. It is my express wish that you interrupt whatever it is I am doing. Is that clear, gentlemen?"

The two valets exchanged a glance and then nodded.

"Thank you. Would you be kind enough to clear these things away?"

With a bow, they quickly gathered up the dirty dishes and basins and left the room.

"Ye do not know what ye are asking, m'lady." Gibbs's quiet comment drew Millicent's attention. " 'Tis not without reason that his lordship has gone through so many surgeons and doctors since the accident. The pain is unceasing, mum, and the requirements of his care constant."

Millicent recalled the Scotsman's firm hold on Aytoun's shoulders, the concern that he showed for his master. She looked at the earl. His eyes were closed. He appeared to be asleep. She stepped away from the bed while the steward went about closing the curtains.

"I am not being critical of you in any way, Mr. Gibbs. I understand what you have done. I understand the pressures you must have faced watching over him all these months. He trusts only you. When he needs something, he asks only for you. This would put a great deal of strain on anyone, no matter how dedicated they are."

"Ye shall not be hearing any complaints from me, m'lady."

"I am certain of that." The last thing Millicent wanted to do was to hurt this man's feelings and lessen the care that Aytoun was already getting. "I only wish to be of assistance. Perhaps I can ease your burden a little, and do some good, too. This is what I think the dowager had in mind for me. Perhaps it is what she would do if she were in my position and in good health."

He gave a noncommittal shrug. "Good health or not, m'lady, I think the dowager would have sent Dr. Parker running, with his tail between his legs, if she had seen him here today. Ye will have to excuse my way of talking, for I was reared in the Highlands, where we speak plainly."

"Thank you, Mr. Gibbs. I appreciate your candor." Aytoun stirred, mumbling in his sleep, and she looked across the chamber at him. "Why do you say that her ladyship would have been displeased?"

"The good doctor had more interest in his meal than in his patient. Why, he barely looked at the master, and when he did, the rogue even had the nerve to complain about his lordship being but half awake." He snatched the glass off the table, saying angrily, "And then he orders us to give him more of this poison."

"The solution to this is quite simple. I shall send a letter to London, telling him that we no longer require his services. It was clear to me that he had no interest in coming out here anyway."

Gibbs cocked a bushy eyebrow at her. "Would ye do that, to be sure?"

"Indeed I shall. But we must find another right away. Someone better."

"None of them are any good, m'lady." He sent a thoughtful glance in the direction of the sleeping earl. "Most of them will press ye to have him bled till he comes to his senses or dies. The others will tell ye to purge him till he has no strength to fight. And those are the good ones, m'lady. The rest of them are charlatans and only after the money."

"I suppose you would include Dr. Parker among the last sort."

Gibbs shook his head. "I've no mind to be deciding any such thing. But I can tell ye that ye would have no trouble at all forming a line of his type from here to Bath. All he wants is to be doing one thing: keep his lordship sedated from now till doomsday and send his bill on to the family bankers once a month."

"You've been with his lordship since before the accident. Do you think he would have been content to live this way?"

"Not for a minute," the steward said passionately. "I know if he could do it, he would have ended his life long before now. I think his refusing to eat is part of it. 'Tis the only thing he can control. If we let him, his lordship would starve himself to death as sure as we're standing here."

"We cannot let that happen."

Millicent's gaze drifted toward the door. The valets had left it open when they'd gone out. In the hallway, she saw Ohenewaa, standing silently, staring at the sleeping form of the earl. The old woman had kept her distance for the entire week, and Millicent had not pressed her. She had simply let her know that she was welcome.

Ohenewaa's gaze drifted from the bed and came to

rest on Millicent's face. A moment later, like an apparition, she disappeared from the doorway.

"And we shan't let him spend his life in a stupor, either," Millicent whispered to the manservant. "There must be other ways of dealing with this condition. We just need to find the right kind of medicine and the right kind of doctor."

Instead of going downstairs, Ohenewaa walked to her own bedchamber and closed the door. The sight of a person's suffering was nothing new to Ohenewaa. For more years than she cared to count, pain and death had been all that surrounded her. On board slave ships, on the sun-scorched fields of the sugar islands, inside the walls of the rat-infested shacks she had seen the unspeakable; she had experienced the unimaginable.

Ohenewaa knew it was fate that she had been sold to Dombey, a doctor of mediocre skill and the deepest self-loathing. She had spent more than forty years with him, until his death. In that time she had always been at his side, assisting him in the islands and on the slave ships as well. She had learned the Englishman's medicine, what there was of it. But on those long, horrible trips from Africa, she had seen the rituals of *okomfo* and *dunseni* and the *Bonsam komfo* and had carried deep within her the ways of the Ashanti priests, and the medicine man, and the witch doctor.

Ohenewaa had gathered this knowledge and kept it safe, like the most precious gold, and with it she had tried again and again to help her people.

Her people. The whites didn't trust her ways, and she let them be. When Dombey himself had been sick—even though he knew she had gifts—he had sent for his own kind. Ohenewaa didn't know if she could have helped him. Cures lay in the hands of the goddess. But he did not want her, so she had let him be. Why bend her ways? Why touch the ice?

But with this woman, Millicent, she could feel the ice inside her melting. Since her arrival, Ohenewaa had spent many nights visiting with the black families at Melbury Hall. The stories they told of Squire Wentworth were horrifying. His brutal handling of the people here was much the same as what she had witnessed on the plantations in Jamaica. His bailiffs had obviously been the same brutes he brought back from there. While telling her all of this, however, every person's account had been filled with praise for the mistress. Though they had suffered terribly under Wentworth's cruelty, so had she—and often for her open support of them.

Ohenewaa had seen many white women of Millicent's station during her time on the islands. Whether they were a plantation owner's wife or a pampered mistress, the women there saw the slaves only when they were issuing a command or gathering for the entertainment of seeing a black man whipped, often by other blacks who had sold their souls to serve as overseers. In Jamaica, at a place called Worthy Plantation, she had seen a slave stripped and flogged while a group of white women stood with their children and stared openly at the man's genitals as he screamed in pain. And it was not the only time. In the islands, she had seen more than she ever wanted to see.

Ohenewaa walked to the table on which she had already collected bowls and bottles of seeds and herbs and liquids. Jonah had brought some of the ingredients back for her from his last trip to St. Albans. The black women of Melbury Hall who had brought seeds with them from Jamaica, or gathered them during past spring and summer months, gave other herbs to her. And even though it was winter, Ohenewaa had found other useful things as well in the kitchen and in the woods and fields around Melbury Hall.

Her collection was growing.

Tonight, instead of working with her herbs, Ohenewaa moved to the hearth and crouched before it. She spread some leaves from a nearby basket on the coals and picked up four stones.

There was a soft knock on her door.

Ohenewaa threw the stones on the floor before her and called to Lady Aytoun to enter.

*   *   *

Startled by the sight of the room, Millicent forgot to ask how it was that Ohenewaa had known it was she at the door. The simple guest room at Melbury Hall had been altered greatly. It was now a place somehow ancient and mysterious. Everything was changed. Jars of varying sizes sat on tables and on the floor. Dried herbs hung above the hearth. The closed draperies dimmed the chamber, which was lit only by the fire. Fascinating and exotic scents infused the air. But Millicent saw nothing menacing or frightening. In fact, the chamber had a calming, serene atmosphere.

Shaking off her surprise at the change, Millicent focused on her reason for coming. There would be time in the future for satisfying her curiosity about the woman and her ways.

"I am at the point of defying traditional English methods of medical treatment. I was wondering if there is any insight you might give me."

Ohenewaa continued to stare at the stones spread before her. Millicent quietly approached the hearth.

"Dr. Parker believes the only thing that can be done for Lord Aytoun is to keep him sedated with opium. My concern is that the drug is doing nothing for him. In fact, I wonder if it is doing him more harm than good." She sat down on the edge of a chair. "You worked with Dr. Dombey for a long time. If I were to cut back on the medicine, if I were to eliminate it completely, would I seriously hurt him? Could he die because of my meddling?"

Ohenewaa picked up a half-burned leaf from the hearth and waved it over the small stones. "He is drowning in a sea of mists. You have not seen him as he is." The dark eyes looked up and met Millicent's. "Are *you* prepared to see him and deal with him as a whole person? Do you have the courage to free his mind?"

Millicent remembered the rumors, the accusations, and the scandals. She had told her friend Rebecca that the Earl of Aytoun was not the man he had once been. Of course, the Aytoun she had seen had been a man

continually sedated by drugs. Was she ready to face a
changed man? She thought of the broken creature doubled over the washbasin.

"Yes."

Ohenewaa studied the stones for a long time and then
seemed to smile to herself. "You can take away the laudanum," she said, gathering up the stones. "And no,
'twill not kill him. Your instincts are correct. Heal the
mind first."

"But what of the pain? Is there anything else that I
should give to him instead? I do not want him to suffer
unnecessarily."

"We must wait and see."

Millicent looked about the room again, taking in the
aroma, the bottles, the dance of the shadows over the
smoke in the hearth. There was a presence in the room,
a power that she could not explain. She turned her attention back to the old woman. "Your knowledge is not
bound by the limits of English medicine, I believe. Is
there anything you would recommend that I do to help
improve his lordship's other ailments?"

"Wait until you have taken the first step. This will be
a monumental one. We will talk again after that."

Reluctantly, Millicent rose to her feet. There were so
many other questions that she had, but she understood
Ohenewaa's concern. Nothing could be done for the earl
until he had gained the full capacity of his mind.
"Thank you."

Ohenewaa nodded slightly; her gaze was fixed on her
fire again. Giving a last glance around the room, Millicent started for the door. Just outside in the hall, she
was surprised to find two of the African women waiting.

Millicent stood aside and watched them enter. One
was carrying a bowl and pitcher of water, another holding a folded linen cloth. The former slaves at Melbury
Hall respected Ohenewaa. They treated her like a queen
or priestess. And Millicent could see why. She had felt
the power of the old woman, too.

Chapter 8

Not having a steward to run the affairs of Melbury Hall was taking its toll on Millicent's time. Jonah was a wonderful help, but with the planting season approaching, many decisions that would affect them all needed to be made. Millicent knew she needed to speed up the process of finding a suitably experienced steward. Sir Oliver Birch was already contacting potential applicants, but London was simply too far away from the farmlands of Hertfordshire.

Sitting in the small study that she used for estate business, Millicent glanced at the guttering candle as she finished writing her letter to Reverend Trimble at Knebworth Village. He knew much of what went on in the surrounding countryside, and she hoped he might offer some help or some advice.

Millicent glanced up when she saw Violet enter.

"Can I help you get ready for bed, m'lady?"

"I am too restless to go up yet." She sealed the letter in her hand. "But why don't you go up yourself? You look tired, Violet. You probably are not getting much sleep since we moved those two girls into your room. I am sorry."

"No, m'lady. We're settled in nicely. I enjoy having them with me."

It was so much like the young woman not to complain. Over Violet's shoulder, Millicent's gaze was drawn to the door as she saw one of her husband's valets appear, holding a lit taper.

"What's wrong, John?"

"Beggin' yer pardon, m'lady," he said. "I know ye left 'slordship not an hour ago, but he's awake now and cross as a one-legged rooster, he is. Now, 'fore we give him anything, ye said ye wanted to be told, and we're doin' as ye said, mum. So I come runnin'."

"Thank you." Millicent immediately rose from the desk. "Why don't you go on to bed, Violet."

The young servant curtsied and moved off. Millicent followed the man toward the stairs. "Where are Mr. Gibbs and Will?"

"Will went down to the kitchen for some soup, jist in case 'slordship would allow a wee mouthful, and Mr. Gibbs is up in the room with 'slordship."

This afternoon, after leaving Ohenewaa, Millicent had returned to Aytoun's room and had watched him sleep. While there, she had pondered the physical ailments that were plaguing him. He had broken his arm and both his legs over six months ago, and she had no idea why he still could not use them. Gibbs said that one of the doctors had blamed it on the fall, referring to it as a form of "palsy." The dowager had commented about the earl's melancholia, but had not related it to his injuries, only to the accident. Considering that Aytoun had lost his wife and his independence of movement in the same horrible fall, Millicent could well understand the thinking of her mother-in-law.

As she approached her husband's bedchamber, Millicent thought about melancholia. It was an ailment that she herself had struggled with during one of the lowest points in her marriage to Wentworth. She had lost a child in the first part of her pregnancy because of the squire's violent rage. Physically beaten and feeling utterly defeated, Millicent had been more than ready to take refuge in the oblivion of the illness for the rest of her life. But at that stage of their lives, Wentworth had not been ready to commit her to Bedlam. He had still needed her for his social climbing. It was only when her friend Rebecca had come to the neighboring estate with Lord Stanmore that she had started fighting the disorder.

At the earl's door, she could hear raised voices, and she lifted a hand to knock. Neither man paused or looked at her when Millicent and the valet entered.

"You will do as I order, you cankered piece of dung, or you can just carry your wretched carcass out of my sight. Do you hear, you miserable, disloyal, dog-faced . . ."

Millicent paused just inside the door with John right behind her. She stared as the vehemence poured out of her husband. The number of words he uttered surpassed the total he had spoken in nearly a fortnight.

"Curse me as ye wish, m'lord, but ye'll not be getting a drop of this poison until yer wife gives her blessing." Gibbs stood between the bed and the table that contained the medicine.

"You filthy, spineless cur," the earl spat out. "You take orders from me, not from that foul bitch. Do you hear me?"

Gibbs turned in that instant and saw her. He shook his head in disgust as his master continued cursing one and all with equal vigor. Walking away from the bed, he joined Millicent by the door. "Do not take anything of what he says to heart, m'lady. Believe me, this is not his lordship talking. I think 'tis best if ye left him to us for tonight. He looks to be no company for man or beast."

She stayed where she was, refusing to be intimidated again in her own house. "Why is he so angry, Mr. Gibbs?"

"He wants the medicine. Stubborn as a goat he is, mum. He says he'll take no food, but only the laudanum."

"Is he in any physical pain?"

"I do not think so, m'lady," Gibbs answered in a low voice. "Those bones of his are long healed. Not that he ever complained of pain whilst they were mending."

Millicent sent a sharp look at the bed as the raging maniac referred to her as a lump of stale, mouse-eaten cheese.

"His lordship wants the medicine," the servant repeated, "because he knows 'tis sure to calm his mind. It makes him sleep, if ye wish to call it that—fretful as 'tis—but at least he rests."

The earl grew quiet, and Millicent realized that he was trying to catch his breath. For a moment, genuine worry overshadowed her desire to teach her new husband a lesson in manners. "Is this the worst you have seen him?"

"Physically? Nay, m'lady. But as far as that viper's tongue of his, he's lashing out sharp enough to kill a company of Dutch mercenaries."

And as if to prove Gibbs correct, Aytoun unleashed another string of obscenities.

"What do *you* think would happen if we refrained from giving him any more opium?"

Gibbs was astonished. "I'm sure I wouldn't know, m'lady. I'm no doctor. But I can tell ye that his lordship wasn't sleeping after the fall. Before he started taking the laudanum, he was miserable as a starving hound, though, and always made certain that every poor creature around him was sure to be miserable, too."

Millicent made a quick study of the chamber. Her husband was propped up in bed. The curtains of the windows were tightly drawn, holding out the chill of the winter evening. The brandy and the bottle of opium sat on a table. As she looked back at Aytoun, Will came in behind her, mumbling an apology and leading a servant girl who was carrying a bowl of soup and some bread on a tray.

Millicent told herself that she could handle this.

"None of you need to suffer his lordship's wrath tonight." She motioned for the servant to put the tray down on a table. "I want you all to go and catch up on your sleep. I should like to keep my husband's company for the night."

After a year and a half, Mary Page still considered herself new to the place and the job. Widowed as a young woman when her husband had died in a carriage accident in London, she had worked for almost ten years as a housemaid, putting in long, backbreaking hours of work, and getting treated with minimum respect. Then she had seen Lady Wentworth's advertisement for a housekeeper.

Mary had been impressed with Sir Oliver, and even more so with the mistress since meeting her. And she was forever grateful for the position and the opportunity she was given in coming down to Hertfordshire. And being new at the job no longer bothered the housekeeper, for the help was very good. The freed slaves worked as well as or better than the native English workers, and Amina, Jonah's wife, had become a good friend to her as well as a trusted helpmate.

Indeed, Mary Page loved her position, and she found she quickly came to love Melbury Hall as well. The addition of the Earl of Aytoun and his people was no hardship, either. In fact, she thought the mistress and the household had all adjusted to it quite readily.

Sitting in a settle by the fire in the servants' hall, her needlework on her lap, she raised an eyebrow as two of Lord Aytoun's personal servants trudged in from the master's bedchamber. When the tall Highlander appeared a few minutes later with a troubled expression in his eyes, Mary fought down the fluttering feeling she felt in her stomach whenever she saw him. She sensed, though, that something was amiss.

"Good evening, Mr. Gibbs. You and your lads are taking a holiday this evening?"

"Aye. Though 'tis not to our liking, I must say, Mrs. Page. Your mistress insists on staying alone with his lordship for the night. The lass does not know what she's getting herself into."

"Is that so?"

"Aye, mum." With a frown etched on his face, the Highlander sat on the settle beside her.

Mary spoke to him in a low voice. "Don't think I mean any disrespect, sir, for I have great affection for the mistress, but this is the second time she's been married. I'd say she knows her way about."

The dark brows of the Scotsman lifted in surprise. "She knows her way about *what*, Mrs. Page, if I might be asking ye?"

Mary felt a blush rise up in her cheeks. "I was simply jesting to ease your mind, Mr. Gibbs."

"Och, well. I'm delighted to know that ye care enough to be doing any such thing, Mrs. Page. I believe that in the course of this past sennight ye haven't seen fit even to return a lonely Highlander's morning greeting."

"I'm quite sure I have treated you with all due civility, sir."

"Ah, civility." He sighed dramatically. " 'Tis come to that, now?"

Mary felt herself growing warm. Despite his size and his fierce attitude to many around him, she found Mr. Gibbs to be quite attractive. Mary smiled as she remembered Vi's comment to a group of giggling serving maids when they were discussing the looks of the newcomers. *Handsome enough,* she'd said, *if you consider hairy monkeys attractive.*

"But now ye smile." His dark gaze lingered on her face. "Now, to what should I contribute this glimpse of heaven?"

"Surely, I don't know. It must have been something I ate for dinner," she answered flippantly. "But about your master. In spite of anything you have heard about her ladyship's circumstances during her first marriage, Lady Aytoun has worked hard to become a very capable individual. His lordship will do perfectly well in her care."

"To be honest, I was more worried about her. I doubt the lass has ever faced anyone with a temper as foul as he possesses this night."

"From everything I've heard, sir, she has survived a husband who was the devil incarnate. I think you can put your mind at ease." Mary patted his hand confidently. "She can handle him, Mr. Gibbs. She can handle him."

* * *

The heat of his fury was scorching the inside of his skull. He could feel it swelling in uncontrolled waves, burning the skin of his face, of his neck. His chest was a knot of anger, and if he could get his one good hand around her throat, he'd go whistling to the gallows.

Not much chance of having luck that good, though, Lyon thought as he continued to stare at the closed door. The stubborn woman was moving about far beyond his reach—sliding a chair here, straightening a table there, ambling about the room as if nothing were amiss. Why, the bloody woman was simply carrying on and pretending that she was not responsible in the slightest for turning those dogs he once thought of as loyal servants against their master. Like cattle at feeding time, the feebleminded cowards had dutifully lined up and marched from the room at her command.

He finally exploded. "Get Gibbs."

"You were looking for something?" she asked in a disgustingly cherubic voice.

He wanted to throw up again. "Aye. I said, get *Gibbs!*"

"I'm very sorry, m'lord, but Mr. Gibbs just left. And he won't be coming back for quite some time." She moved to the foot of his bed, a smile plastered on her face, behaving as if she were not bothered at all by his barking at her. "But I am here if there is something that you need."

He had been aware of her presence from the moment she'd arrived. Strange, he thought, that even in the midst of the haze and the anger, he was becoming aware of her. And how curious that even the horrible names that he called her seemed to have no effect on the woman. In becoming his wife, she had promised to take care of him, but Lyon knew that many a woman in her position might be thinking right now about how to rid herself of baggage as foul as he must seem to her. He prayed that she was thinking those exact thoughts. Poison would finish it all.

"Give me a drink."

She walked away from the table of medicines. He was

annoyed to see her pouring a glass of what he assumed was water. Lyon waited until she came back, glass in hand.

"Can you manage this yourself, m'lord, or do you need help drinking it?"

This close she didn't look quite so confident. When Lyon reached out with his hand, he saw the tremor in hers. He could make a grab for her throat now.

Almost against his wishes, he found his fingers closing around the glass. As soon as she released it, though, he let it fall.

The glass dropped onto the bed, spilling the clear liquid before tumbling off onto the floor. It didn't break, and he watched it roll away.

"I am sorry. I thought you had it," she said, immediately reaching for a towel and starting to soak the wetness from the blankets.

"Get me my drink. I'll have no more of whatever that was."

Her eyes snapped up to his. They narrowed as the realization flashed upon her that it wasn't an accident. She backed away quickly and picked the glass up from the floor.

Lyon waited, only vaguely pleased with the small victory. The weakness was back and the nausea as well. But he could only remain quiet for so long. He fully expected her to do as he commanded.

His mood soured even more than before when she sat down in a chair across the room. "You vile, inhuman wretch. Do you defy the doctor's o-orders to give me the med . . . medicine?" The struggle to form words smoothly increased Lyon's anxiety. He needed the medicine now. "If your p-plan is to kill me, then do it, by the devil. But don't t-torture me. Listen, damn you. I need it *now!*"

His plea must have penetrated her thick skull, for he saw her rise to her feet again.

"I shall give you that only if you eat something first."

"I have no desire for food," he snapped.

"You need to try, all the same." She started sitting down again.

"You are a hateful, withered hag," he said in a raspy voice. "I know now for certain that I d-died at the bottom of that fall, for this is hell. *You* are my eternal punishment."

"Say whatever you wish to me, but know that you shall receive the medicine only after we get some food into you."

"No. I'll have it before." Lyon wished he had throttled her when he had the chance. "You will give it to me now."

"Not before you eat," she responded without any further consideration. "That mistake was made today at noon. And last night. And God knows how many times before that. No one can remember when was the last time you had a meal."

"You are no woman. You have no warmth in you." He turned his face away. "Damn you. You can see that I cannot move. I have no appetite. Medicine, however, I need."

She went to stand by the tray of food, and he watched her. "Think of this as medicine, too."

Lyon cursed ferociously at the world, including in his verbal barrage Gibbs and Millicent and his damnable luck at being stuck with such a bloodless, unfeeling villain. When he leaned back to catch his breath, she approached with the tray of food. He considered upending it, grabbing the tray, scaling it across the chamber, and sending her scampering on her merry way. But already exhaustion was setting in. His body had begun to tremble badly, and his stomach was knotted with cramps and nausea. He just wanted the opium-laced brandy. He just wanted to forget.

"I should like you to feed yourself."

He turned his murderous glare on her. She was sitting on the edge of the bed, her fingers still clutching the tray tightly.

"You have one good hand. You feed yourself, and I

shall ready your medicine." She positioned the tray on his lap. "But I warn you. If you intentionally spill this food, then I shall need to go to the kitchen for some more. So keep in mind how much this will delay you from receiving your precious medicine . . . if that is what it is."

He continued to glare at her, making certain she saw the extent of his hostility. The damn woman, though, simply carried on as if nothing were wrong. She removed the cover from a bowl of broth. She put a spoon near his left hand and spread a napkin on his chest. Then she stood back, looking triumphant and watching him expectantly. He moved his hand over the spoon, and she turned to the table holding the tray with the bottles of brandy and opium.

If she wanted this to be a battle of wills, Lyon thought, then he could easily be the victor. She started counting the tincture of opium, drop by drop, into a small glass. He watched her add the brandy.

"I have done my part." She raised the glass to him. "Now let me see you do your part."

He waited for a long moment, but the desire for the laudanum overwhelmed his pride. Picking up the bowl of broth crudely, he brought it to his lips and—almost against his will—took a sip.

It was the smile of approval that crept across her face that killed him. Without a word, he flung the bowl away from him, soaking himself and the blankets with the broth. The bowl broke into a dozen pieces on the floor.

She didn't raise her voice or complain. She didn't even look startled, though the smile was gone from those lips.

Instead, calmly, she placed the glass on the tray and deliberately tipped it over.

"Oh, how clumsy of me. I have spilled your medication." Picking it up, she looked at the glass closely. "And only a couple of droplets are all that are left, it appears. I do hope this will suffice for the night."

He should have killed her. Next time he had the chance, he vowed, he would.

*   *   *

"So, ye vixen. Tell me what's new at Melbury Hall."

"Lady Aytoun spends a lot of time looking after her new husband. But other than that, nothing to speak of." Violet stretched leisurely on top of Ned's naked body. Her fingers played in the thick mat of blond hair on his chest. "She's sending me to St. Albans this Saturday to buy some woolens and other things. While I'm there, I might get a chance to stop and see my mother and my grandmum. Will you come with me?"

"Nay, lass. I'm far too busy a man to be traipsing around the country after ye."

"Then perhaps I can slip away some Sunday when you're free. I'm anxious to have you meet my family."

"What for?" Ned asked shortly. "Are ye so anxious to tell them ye've got yourself a good lover?"

"No. I just thought that since we've become so close," she said, blushing. "I just thought, now that you're my man—"

"What's this?" Ned rolled over on top of her. He smiled that devilish smile that made her quiver inside. She could feel his huge member was hard again. "Your man? And here ye've only come to my bed but twice."

"Aye, that's true, but now that you've said you love me—"

"To be sure, lass. But 'tis not a good thing, my wee Violet, making me wait more than a week before coming to see me."

He spread her legs with his knee and pushed his shaft deep into her. She was still sore from his rough handling of her when she'd first come to him tonight, but she bit her lip and didn't complain. Instead, she wrapped her arms around him tightly and hoped this time he would go slower.

"A man needs good reason 'fore meeting family, vixen."

"More reason than this?" she asked in a small voice.

"Aye. Much, much more," he said, beginning to slide within her. "But ye're a smart one. Ye're learnin' all the time."

An hour later, Violet felt somewhat queasy as she ran

back to Melbury Hall. He had done it to her again, and she'd let him. That was not the truth. She had gone to his bed willingly, only to walk away unhappy with the way he treated her. What was worse—and she hardly wanted to admit it, even to herself—she was already starting to doubt his words. He had said he loved her, but he was not interested in meeting her family. He told her how pretty she looked, but in the next breath he was asking the news of Melbury Hall. Why did he care about the place anyway? It was not like he worked there or even knew anyone there but her.

Violet was relieved that she had not said much about the place to him. Not that there was much to say these days that was any secret. But there were some things that no one could ever know. Secrets about the day that Squire Wentworth had died.

Violet saw Moses carrying a lantern at the end of a pole with his dog beside him when she broke out of the woods onto the curved drive. The watchman raised a hand and waved to her as the dog turned and wagged her tail. Two of a kind, Violet thought. As gentle as lambs. She turned her steps toward him.

"Your clothes are not dirty. You are not sad."

"No, I'm not sad." She smiled, leaning down and patting the dog on the head.

"No moon now, Violet. The nights are dark. You want someone to walk with at night?"

She shook her head and smiled up at the man. "I am fine, Moses. Thank you, but you have an important job here. You and your dog need to keep Melbury Hall safe."

He nodded slowly, then looked toward the stables. "I made a basket for you."

"Did you?"

He looked back at her. "I can go get it, if you wait. I soaked rushes I had from last summer and used a leather strap for a handle. Maybe you can wrap some of your pretty ribbons around it and use it when you go to the village, Violet. Wait until I get it?"

She nodded at him, feeling better. "I'll wait right here. I'll even hold the lantern until you get back."

Watching the old man go off to the stables, his dog on his heels, Violet took a deep breath of the night air. She would never reveal the secrets of Melbury Hall. Most of all, she thought, no one must ever know that Moses had been the one who really killed Squire Wentworth.

Chapter 9

She felt more like a soldier leaving a battlefield than a woman leaving her ailing husband's bedroom. When Gibbs arrived not long after dawn, Millicent gestured for him to follow her out into the corridor.

"Please help his lordship bathe and change once he is awake," she said in a weary voice. "Offer him breakfast, but give him no medicine until you fetch me. I shall have some sweet cider and some water sent up if he wants something to drink. Give him no spirits." She looked in past the partially closed door. "Oh. The bedding needs to be changed. And also a few spills on the rug need to be cleaned. I shall speak to Mrs. Page about that. And there might be a few pieces of broken dishes under and around the bed."

"Sounds like ye had quite a night, m'lady."

"Aye, Mr. Gibbs. Quite a night. Have you eaten anything this morning?"

"Aye, mum. Thank ye for asking."

"Very well," she said, turning to go.

"I hope ye are not already discouraged, mum."

The tall man's softly spoken words made Millicent pause. She turned to him. "No, Mr. Gibbs. I was asking a great deal of him for one night. I deserved what I received."

"No one deserves that trouble." He glanced over his shoulder. "But I want ye to know that his lordship was not *always* like this."

"I shouldn't think so." She spoke honestly, though

there had been moments last night when she might have seriously doubted it. "You have been with him a long time."

"I have, m'lady. And that's why I've not given up hope like the rest of them. His lordship has had his share of bad luck these past few years. But the way I see it, with him being here at Melbury Hall and with you looking after him, his luck might just be turning again . . . and for the better."

Millicent nodded, appreciating the man's confidence. "Please call me if you need me, Mr. Gibbs."

"Aye, m'lady."

As she moved off, her legs wobbled slightly, but Millicent paid no attention. She considered her own luck. Perhaps hers would change now as well, with Lord Aytoun as her husband. But first she had to learn to handle his temperament.

After what felt like a mile of walking, she made it to her own room. Inside, she eyed the bed, which looked like some heavenly cloud. Without removing her clothes, she simply stretched out on it.

Last night had truly been a test of her strength. Whatever assistance the dowager had offered her for marrying her son, there had been moments when Millicent had wished she had asked for double or triple the amount. Lyon Pennington was absolutely the most arrogant, difficult, and stubborn person she had ever crossed paths with in her life. And not having the use of his legs or his arm didn't hinder his virulent behavior in the slightest. On more than a few occasions during the night, she had wished he'd lost the use of his venomous tongue along the way as well. But then she remembered what Gibbs had said in the corridor. He had not always been like this. Perhaps there was hope.

Millicent pulled the covers on top of her and closed her eyes, hoping for a few hours of rest. Lyon had fallen asleep for the first time only moments before she had left the room. She was certain that he had to be even more exhausted than she.

When the knock on the door came, it took Millicent

a few moments to realize where she was and to rouse herself. Glancing at the clock on the fireplace mantel, she realized she had been sleeping for only half an hour. Will's voice was hesitant, but his message was clear: Mr. Gibbs wanted her ladyship to know that his lordship was fully awake and in as foul a mood as could be.

And he wanted his medicine now.

Ohenewaa sat quietly on a bench in the corner of the kitchen, listening to the worried conversation between the two servants. One was Violet, Millicent's personal maid, the other a young black servant named Bess. The two were about the same age, barely more than girls. They sat side by side on the settle close to the fire. She did not move—her eyes mere slits and her hands resting on the skirts of blue muslin Amina had given her. If anyone were to look at her, she knew, they would think she was an old woman sleeping contentedly.

"They say he's like a madman, cursing and shouting when he's awake, and fretting and feverish when he's asleep." The black woman's voice dropped low. "But she's still holding her ground about not giving him any of the medicine. Stubborn as can be."

" 'Tis not stubbornness but common sense, if you ask me," Violet answered. "I saw him same as you the first day that they brought him into the house. He didn't know who he was or where he was. This morning when I took a tray of food upstairs, his lordship was as mean as a starving dog, but he had no trouble recognizing anybody."

"I've been lucky not to be called up there myself, but I heard Mrs. Page say the mistress don't look too good."

"That's true," Violet agreed. "The mistress is starting to look more poorly than Lord Aytoun himself. And who'd blame her? She's spent nearly two nights and days now at his bedside with not a moment away."

The two women continued to talk, but Ohenewaa rose to her feet and moved away. The household was already accustomed to her quiet presence, to her silent comings and goings, and these two barely gave her a second glance as she got up to go. In the servants' hall she found Amina. .

"Come to my room at the noon hour. I will have a tea ready for the angry man upstairs."

"He is not drinking tea, Ohenewaa. He is not taking any food. If 'twas not for the mistress forcing him to drink water drawn straight from the spring, I don't know how he could have survived this long."

"Very well. Then we will mix it with his drinking water. It has very little taste."

" 'Tis good that you have decided to help her." Amina nodded gratefully. "How much should I tell the mistress to give him?"

"You will take what he needs the first day. After that we will watch to see how he does and then give him less and less each day. In a week or two, he'll be needing no more of it."

Doubt clouded Amina's features. "What happens if someone else or the mistress by mistake drinks some of it herself?"

The old woman nearly smiled. "She'll have a couple of hours of peaceful rest."

"Her ladyship is very distrustful of medicine, even English medicine."

Ohenewaa nodded reassuringly. "I understand her distrust. She will accept this from me. She might even be expecting it."

The edge of the feather bed sank beneath her weight. Millicent used a small towel to wipe the beads of sweat from Lyon's forehead. He had fallen asleep about one o'clock, but here it was not even an hour later, and he was caught in some type of nightmare.

She pulled the towel away as he jerked his head from side to side on the pillow. The words he mumbled in his sleep were gibberish. More glistening beads of sweat ran down his face and disappeared into his dark beard. He called something aloud that resembled a shout of warning.

Millicent pressed a hand to the side of his neck, check-

ing for fever. As she started to draw back, he reached up
with his left hand and trapped her arm against his chest.

She sat motionless on the edge of the bed, considering
the battles this man constantly waged, even in his sleep.
Her fingers were splayed on his chest, and the feel of
his heart pounding within overwhelmed her.

"No!" His hand clutched tight, squeezing her arm
painfully. "*No!* You cannot!"

"It is only a dream, m'lord." She leaned over him,
caressing his face with her free hand, pushing the strands
of wet hair off his brow, and talking to him reassuringly.

"Do not ever—"

"Wake up, Lyon. You're having a dream."

"Emma . . . do not . . . no!"

Millicent drew her hand away as if burned. *Emma.*
On his face, tears were mixed with sweat. She pushed
away from the bed and found Will standing in the
doorway.

"Stay with his lordship," she whispered to the valet.
"Please come and get me when he awakens."

Leaving the bedroom and heading downstairs, Millicent tried to push Emma's name out of her mind. The
woman had been Aytoun's wife—perhaps the most
important person in his life. She could not allow the
name to become a nightmare to her.

Instead, Millicent thought of Ohenewaa's medicine.
The drink had worked. In less than an hour after giving
it to him, her husband was sleeping, albeit restlessly. She
had to watch this closely, make certain how his mood
was when he was awake.

Downstairs, a servant hurried to her, carrying a letter.
A messenger had just brought it from Jasper Hyde. Millicent felt every nerve in her body go taut as she tore
into the letter. Again it concerned Ohenewaa.

"Please ask Ohenewaa to come to me in the library,"
she told the servant.

Sitting by a window in the library, Millicent read the
contents of it again. It angered her that Hyde was not
giving up. There were no more liens, no promissory

notes, nothing to give him any control over her, but he continued to persist. She could not understand the man's obsession about getting hold of the old woman.

When Ohenewaa walked in few minutes later, Millicent decided to not let her own feelings affect the healer's decision.

"Mr. Jasper Hyde has written to me, requesting a meeting with you. He states that he writes with no dishonorable intentions. He would prefer a London location, but if that is not satisfactory, he would even consider coming down to Hertfordshire."

As Millicent put the letter down on her desk, Ohenewaa stared at it with contempt.

"This is a most unusual request," Millicent continued. "My first reaction was to answer it with an abrupt no. But then I realized that it is not completely my decision, since the correspondence concerns you."

The young woman's tired face and gray eyes were disturbed when they looked up. "Before you give me your reply, though, I also want you to know that Mr. Hyde's lawyer has been in contact with Sir Oliver Birch half a dozen times in the past fortnight. Each time his offers and discussions have had something to do with you."

Though Millicent didn't voice it, the unspoken question hung in the room: *Why does he want you?*

Ohenewaa walked to the window and stared out at the dreary day and the gray, hunchbacked Chiltern Hills. She had been on one of the slave ships with Dombey when the rebellion erupted on Jamaica in 1760. It had been bloody, though; that she knew. The slaves of several plantations, fed up with the brutality of the masters and fooled by some old men into believing certain spells could make them invulnerable, had risen up and killed anyone who got in their way.

The revolt had been put down quickly and brutally, and she had seen the bloody aftermath. The years of cruelty that followed, fueled by fear of further uprisings, had become even more repressive. Wentworth and Jasper Hyde and his father and others like them had a free rein then, and in their hands the whip was wielded more viciously than ever. For over ten years the lash continued to fall without mercy.

"Jasper Hyde wants me because I have seen the fruits of his labors. I saw his ways when he took over Wentworth's plantations. I saw his calm disdain for the suffering of human beings. I saw the scars grow like the branches of trees on the backs of innocent men and women from the lash and the cane. I saw the rape of those who could not fight back."

Droplets of rain began to beat hard against the window, spreading over the cold glass and blearing the view of the hills.

"I, too, am branded. I, too, have felt the whip's sting. And now I am like the old mother of days gone by, suspected of witchcraft. Jasper Hyde would burn me alive if he could. He wants me because he believes I cursed him for what he has done. He believes in punishing the body to break the spirit. And he believes I am punishing his body to achieve the same end."

Ohenewaa turned back to the room. Millicent's face showed the pain that she was feeling for the suffering of all those enslaved workers.

"Hyde says his intentions are not dishonorable. That is true, because he feels there is nothing dishonorable in burning a witch with dry wood while her own people look on. He believes there is no dishonor in vengeance. But before he sees me die, he wants me to undo the curse that plagues him and release him from his sins. But that I cannot do."

Jasper Hyde knew that the doctor could do nothing to help him. But that was not why he had asked Parker to come and look at him anyway. He knew the only cure for his condition lay in what they could accomplish together.

"You have an unusually loud palpitation of the heart, Mr. Hyde, though I can see nothing physically wrong with you." The physician motioned to his assistant to pack up the instruments and leave the room. "Nonetheless, it is critical that you should start taking a few necessary precautions. There is always the possibility that a certain disease might be in its early stages, and we shall try to be ready for it when it surfaces. So before my next visit, I would like you to avoid all sources of unnecessary excitement. The meals should be taken at regular intervals, and should be very light. No violent exercise, and we should begin a series of regular bleedings."

Hyde watched until the physician's servant had left the room before interrupting Parker. "I am grateful that you were able to see me on such short notice. When I heard you are the chosen physician of the Earl of Aytoun, I knew you were the man for me."

"I see. Are you a friend of his lordship?"

"Not exactly. Just one who was greatly disappointed to see him thrown into the clutches of such an opportunistic woman."

The man's bushy eyebrows went up. "Then you are acquainted with the new countess?"

" 'Tis somewhat indelicate to speak of it, but I was her creditor until the lady's marriage to his lordship."

Parker's interest showed. "She was deeply in debt to you, sir . . . if you don't mind my asking?"

"Her first husband owed me a great deal, and she owed me more. I would have been forced to take possession of Melbury Hall in a couple of months' time, if she hadn't married. Like all women, she is a victim of her own poor judgment and is quite frivolous in her spending. I feel truly sorry for Lord Aytoun, finding himself in such an unpleasant situation."

The physician removed the spectacles from his nose and folded them. "Well, perhaps you don't know, but the wretched man had little choice."

"So when, Dr. Parker, are you going back to visit his lordship again?"

"I . . . well . . ." He cleared his throat. "I may not be going back. I find that Melbury Hall is too far from London, and I have many clients who demand my time here."

"She did not dismiss you, did she?" Hyde asked,

feigning great surprise and concern. At least his infor-
mants in Hertfordshire had provided one useful piece
of information.

"Lady Aytoun sent a letter indicating that it might be
easier for everyone involved if she searched out a more
local doctor for his lordship."

Jasper Hyde pushed himself to his feet. "You cannot
believe that, sir. This is all part of her scheme. First she
buys that black witch who killed Dr. Dombey, and takes
her to Melbury Hall. Next, she marries into that fortune
and takes Lord Aytoun back to the country, away from
everyone he knows. Now I find that she has dismissed
you."

"Well, I shouldn't call it 'dismissed' exactly, Mr.
Hyde."

"How convenient! What an easy way to kill another
husband."

"Kill her husband?" Parker said, suddenly alarmed as
the words began to sink in. "What witch? Who is this
Dombey? You must clarify this business, sir."

"Indeed, Dr. Parker. I believe you are correct. Won't
you please sit down, and I shall tell you my fears. I
believe, sir, that you may be the only man who can stop
this whole affair."

"I . . . ?"

"First sit down, and I shall tell you what I know about
Lady Aytoun's lack of character. Then you must promise
me that you will refuse her request to resign the commission Lord Aytoun's family bestowed upon you. You
must save his lordship from this black widow's deadly
venom. I'm certain, sir, that his family will be entirely
grateful."

"Yes, yes!" The man was quick to take a seat. "But
what was it you said about a witch?"

Chapter 10

The curtains had been left open, and a soft blue light imbued the room with a pervading sense of serenity. A light blanket of snow covered the countryside outside, and the moon shone brightly through the scudding patches of clouds.

Lyon's mind was clear for the first time in days. There was no nausea, no headache, no confusion. He tore his gaze from the rustic view and stared at the sleeping figure of the woman who was responsible for this recent improvement in his state of mind. Millicent was curled up in the uncomfortable chair near the foot of the bed. This was her eighth night here, and the first time he had seen her actually drop off to sleep. Exhaustion had finally set in, but not before she had succeeded in forcing him to clear his mind of the laudanum.

But sobriety, too, was a curse.

Lyon stared at his limp right arm on top of the blankets and felt the empty ache inside of him. He would never walk, never ride. He'd never sit in a chair unless someone propped him up. He would never lie with a woman. In his mind's eye he saw Emma with her wild blond hair spread across his pillow, her blue eyes smiling up at him, her arms pulling his weight down onto her willing body. She had been so young when he had first married her. But he had been a fool to think he was at the center of her world.

Pierce had been right about everything from the start. He had warned Lyon about Emma's true interests. Bar-

onsford was what she coveted, his brother had told him,
not the man who owned it. Out of arrogance, though,
Lyon had not believed him.

Of course, Lyon had always known that Emma had
been closest to his youngest brother, David. From the time
they were children, the two of them had played along the
cliffs at Baronsford, and the vision of them together was
etched in his—and everyone's—mind. David and Emma
had been inseparable through the years. And yet, when
Lyon had taken over Baronsford, Emma had come to him.

Selfish, vain, blind—he could think of a hundred
names for his actions. But at the bottom of it all, Lyon
had acted the fool, and his family had been torn apart
because of it. There was no one to blame but himself.

Lyon threw his good arm over his face and wished he
could free himself of the vision that was permanently
imbedded in his mind. The wet rocks. Emma's broken
body at the base of the cliff, staring up at him. She had
paid the price for her mistakes, as he was paying now.

Anger surged in his veins again, and he wished for
oblivion once more. Forcing his eyes open, Lyon stared
at Millicent's simple dress, her pale face and tightly
pulled-back hair. She was everything that he'd always
imagined plainness to be. She murmured something in
her sleep and then woke herself with a start. She stared
at him, sleepy-eyed.

"You want something?"

"I want the medicine tonight."

"No," she whispered quietly. She tried to return his
stare, but after a few moments started to nod off again.

Lyon wished he had enough use of his foot just to be
able to tip her chair backward. He considered shouting
an obscenity at her and making sure that she stayed
awake. But she drew up her legs tighter on the chair
and tried to get comfortable.

And Lyon found himself content just to stare at her.
His wife.

Sir Richard Maitland sat down on an armchair across
the way from his client, the Dowager Countess Aytoun.

" 'Twas a wise decision not to meet with Dr. Parker yourself, m'lady."

The old woman closed the book on her lap and stared at him over the tops of her spectacles. "That bad, was it?"

The lawyer nodded. "Dr. Parker accuses your new daughter-in-law of being a heretic. He believes she is deliberately endangering the earl's health and well-being by not following a single direction he gave to her a fortnight ago. He insists that Lord Aytoun is in dire peril and that you should remove your son immediately from Melbury Hall. And though 'twill be very difficult for him to manage, Dr. Parker assures me that he is willing to spend whatever time is necessary to restore the earl to where his lordship was before in his treatment."

"How generous of him! Did he mention a fee for this service?"

"Of course." Maitland glanced down at his notes. "The usual exorbitant amount was quoted."

The dowager picked up Millicent's letter from the table beside her. She read it once again. "And did Dr. Parker say a word about receiving a letter from my daughter-in-law, terminating his services at Melbury Hall?"

"It must have slipped his mind, m'lady, for he did not offer the information. Once I mentioned it, he made some excuses about being away from London and not receiving her notice until the day he was scheduled to go back to Hertfordshire. He felt the situation necessitated his return to Melbury Hall."

"He went anyway?"

"Aye. And the gentleman was quite eloquent about what he found. He felt compelled to report that the earl's condition is so severely worsened that if you do nothing about it immediately, his lordship's life is surely in jeopardy."

"And how is that?" she asked wryly. "Is Lyon any thinner? Does he suffer from excruciating pain? Has he broken any more bones?"

"Fortunately, you have in your hand, I am quite certain,

a more accurate report on Lord Aytoun's health than anything Dr. Parker might have related. Indeed, the messenger who carried Lady Aytoun's letter told me himself that his lordship is apparently improving every day."

"Then what the devil is this charlatan talking about?"

"His concern now is with his lordship's temperament." Maitland gave a small cough to hide his chuckle. "Upon being taken to Lord Aytoun's chamber at Melbury Hall, the physician was delivered a plateful of pastries, straight to the face."

"By Lyon?"

Sir Richard nodded politely.

"Were they intended for Dr. Parker?"

"Difficult to say, m'lady, though the result is a fine bruise to his well-padded cheekbone."

"How dreadful! But why is it difficult to say?"

"Well, apparently your son and your new daughter-in-law are given to daily battles that have all the elements of the siege of Edinburgh. And I am happy to report that she is far . . . well, hardier than we imagined her to be."

The dowager sank back against the sofa and actually smiled. "This is *most* encouraging news, Maitland. And did you throw Dr. Parker out of the house?"

"I certainly did, m'lady."

"Excellent. Most decidedly excellent."

With Gibbs trailing behind her with an armload of rejected books, Millicent entered the library and waved at a table.

"Pray, leave them there, Mr. Gibbs," she said, scanning the shelves and pulling out several volumes.

"Ye know his lordship is playing a game with ye, m'lady," the manservant said respectfully. "Ye might as well bring up a hundred more volumes. He'll be sure to find something wrong with all of them. With his mind clear Lord Aytoun is too capable of playing the devil with ye."

"Indeed, he is doing an excellent job at it, but I am not about to give up."

"Aye, m'lady."

Tucking the new selections under both arms, Millicent left the library. This was her third trip. Each time, the villain had found fault with her choices. She was determined to find a book this morning that would interest him, but still be something to her liking as well. There had to be *something* that they could agree on.

In the hallway and on the stairs, servants cleared out of her path. She had a suspicion, though, that no one was moving too far out of earshot. It was not hard to see that her disagreements with Lyon were quickly becoming a source of entertainment for the household.

The valets had moved the earl onto his chair by the window by the time Millicent returned to her husband's apartments.

"Here I am," she announced with an air of triumph, dropping the books on the table beside her own chair. "You cannot possibly find anything wrong with these."

Her challenge was answered with a defiant flash of the man's blue eyes. Millicent ignored the strange flutter of excitement inside of her and sat down on her chair, reaching for the first volume. "Dr. Johnson's *Rasselas*."

"You might as well burn that blasted book, for I refuse to listen to anyone reading it."

"Why?" Millicent managed to keep her calm.

"The man insulted the entire Scottish people in his dictionary, equating us all with horses."

"With horses?"

"Indeed. Look at his definition of 'oats' sometime."

She glanced down at the book in her hand, not truly sure of the truth behind the assertion. Finally, she put the volume aside and reached for the next one.

"Well, here is one written by a Scot. *Ossian's Fingal,* an ancient epic poem. Very exciting, I'm told."

"Written by James Macpherson. He is a Scot, but the man is a fraud. He made the entire book up of old Gaelic poems. There is not a shred of truth to it being by any Ossian. What else do you have there?"

Scowling at Aytoun, Millicent put this volume aside as well. She picked up the next. "Laurence Sterne's *Tristram Shandy*."

"Never. Open that book. I defy you to find a page that is not blotted with rows of stars and dashes and hand-drawn diagrams and every other bit of nonsense the author could contrive. Totally unintelligible! You call that a story? A wandering plot—if you can find it—and most of the tale is in the character's block-shaped head. Give me laudanum or read that book. The effect is the same."

"Very well," she replied shortly, putting this book aside too. "But I am telling you right now, m'lord, that there is nothing you could possibly find wrong with this next book. *Nothing.*"

He raised a brow, waiting.

"Mr. Pope's *Imitations of Horace.*"

"You must be joking."

"What do you mean?"

"The man was a virulent, malicious dwarf."

"Pardon me?"

"I refuse to listen to anything written by a man of his disposition."

"And is it the man's stature or his temperament that . . ." She glared across the room and then rose to her feet. "Oh, never mind! I don't even want to know. Just tell me, are we trying to read to broaden our minds? Or must we demean ourselves with trifling concerns about the authors that have nothing whatsoever to do with what it is written between the covers?"

"I cannot understand why you are getting so upset over something as trivial as finding a readable book," he said calmly. "All you have to do is ask me what it is that I would like to read this morning."

"How could I have forgotten? Oh, pray tell, what would you like to read, m'lord?"

"I do not know a thing about your collection."

"Other than the dozens of books I have already carried up here."

"Other than those. What else do you have?"

She sank back down on the chair. This was exactly where they were two hours ago. She would name the books, and he would find some fault with each of them.

Millicent knew she had to find a way to occupy this man's mind before he drove her so insane that *she* would be the one in need of laudanum. She picked up *Rasselas* and started to read. If Aytoun was representative of the Scottish people, then she was beginning to see some merit in Dr. Johnson's definition. But she wondered if the man hadn't meant to say "mules" in his dictionary.

Chapter 11

As always, the morning routine dragged on interminably. Lyon muttered his customary curses at his two valets as they helped him wash and dress. John, the turtle-shaped, flap-jawed rapscallion, and his scarecrow of a partner, Will, had both been somewhat tongue-tied when he harangued them for appearing in his chambers in "country" clothing rather than their customary livery. The poor devils had barely been able to utter an explanation about decisions the mistress had made about dressing the combined households. And Lyon made certain that he grumbled incessantly at Gibbs over the breakfast of which he refused to eat more than a bite.

But he was saving the worst of his temper for Millicent, knowing full well that she would be walking into his room about ten o'clock. Already weary from rising early to attend to the pressing affairs of the estate, she would no doubt be quite irritable after a nearly sleepless night. He knew that she would also be ready to deliver as hard a verbal punch at him as he was ready to afflict her with.

As the serving women finally cleared away the dishes in front of him, Lyon considered his wife. He couldn't fully understand it, but those moments when she was here arguing with him and berating him for his continual transgressions were the only moments of the day that he felt truly alive.

Of course, those were also the most frustrating times as well, for she never did what he told her or even asked her to do. She insisted on reading aloud despite his objections to her selection of books, ignoring him and only reading louder. She had even suggested that he leave these rooms occasionally. He'd argued bitterly against it, of course, flatly refusing and telling her that as the resident cripple, he had no wish to be paraded about for a houseful of gawking rustics.

Then, three days ago, with no regard to his wishes, she had bribed his own weak-livered servants into carrying him down to her drawing room. Naturally, he had made enough noise and caused enough damage that she had ordered him to be brought back less than half an hour later. Lyon had won the battle that day, but he was convinced she would launch another assault any day now. Vigilance was called for, without a doubt.

Ten o'clock came and went, but today there was no sign of her. Lyon felt his irritation rise. Half an hour later, when Millicent still didn't appear, he began venting his wrath in other directions. A young serving girl coming in to tend the fireplace fled teary-eyed after he hurled only the mildest of insults at her. Both John and Will tried to tiptoe about the chambers as they saw to his clothing, but when he upended a tray next to him and then flung a bound edition of the *North Briton* at them, the turtle John ran off, only to appear a couple of minutes later with Gibbs in tow.

"Can I fetch anything from the armory for your lordship?" the Highlander asked dryly.

"Indeed. Bring me my dueling pistols. I'd like to use these two dolts for target practice."

"Begging your pardon, m'lord, but perhaps 'twould be easier if ye'd just ask me where she is."

Lyon snorted and stared at him as if he were the village idiot.

"Very well, sir," Gibbs continued when Lyon said nothing. "Since ye insist on my telling ye, Lady Aytoun has gone to Knebworth to visit with the Reverend and Mrs. Trimble. Mr. Trimble is the rector at the church there. Quite the friends of your wife, they are. Her ladyship has been delaying this visit for two weeks now, on account of seeing to your needs. But today, it being bonny and warm for a late winter's day, she decided to take a horse out and ride over."

Lyon glanced at the beautiful sunny day outside the window. Of course she would be tired of being trapped in here with him day in and day out.

"When she gets back, I'll tell Lady Aytoun ye were pining after her," Gibbs offered with an innocent expression.

Lyon glared at his man. "And I will have your head on a platter for dinner."

"Ye shall have to be up and about before doing anything like that, m'lord."

"I should have let those dog-faced Edinburgh drunks at that oyster house in St. James Close hang you, Gibbs."

"Aye, m'lord, but that still doesn't put my head on any platter."

"The truth is, though, that all I have to do is tell my wife that I'd be sure to find my appetite if she'd only hang your ugly skull on a pole over my fireplace." The dark beard hid the trace of a smile. "Tell her that, and I have no doubt that she would make any necessary arrangements."

Mrs. Trimble's limp from an old carriage accident appeared more pronounced this winter. But to Millicent's delight the older woman's lively wit and high spirits were unaffected by the old injury. The two women sat together in the parlor, sipping tea and waiting for the rector to return from the village. Millicent was told when she arrived that he was expected momentarily.

"Things are happening in the village, m'lady," the kindly woman said. "Reverend Trimble took a walk to speak with the stonemasons who are building the grange. He was hoping to employ one of them in their off-hours to work on two of the rectory chimneys that are cracked and drawing poorly. But I am so glad you were able to come by this morning. Despite my bad knee, we were ready to drop by for a visit at Melbury Hall earlier this week. After talking to Mrs. Page last Sunday, however, we decided you might not be ready for any company just yet. She mentioned that Lord Aytoun's health is still a concern for you. Has his lordship shown any improvement yet?"

"Indeed, he has. Thank you." Millicent told herself she was not exactly misrepresenting the situation. Lyon's health had certainly improved in recent days.

"We were not envious of your position, my dear, in being faced with what must have been a very difficult decision to make. Not envious at all." Mrs. Trimble took Millicent's hand in hers and lowered her voice confidentially. "Lord bless you to take on such a responsibility. Caring for anyone crippled so badly is a true test, I'm sure. Both legs and an arm, I hear."

Millicent nodded.

"And a severe case of melancholia, too?"

This time she shook her head emphatically. Now that she had spent two weeks constantly in his company, Millicent was certain that Lyon's present temperament was not severe enough to be considered melancholia.

"Whatever my husband was suffering from when he first arrived at Melbury Hall, I believe his condition was being aggravated by the medicines he was being given."

"So you changed his treatment?"

"I did, and I believe he is feeling much more himself at present." Loud. Obnoxious. Occasionally bizarre. Awake practically around the clock. And Millicent liked him much better this way.

"You do look quite tired, my dear. If I might be also so bold to ask, how are *you* faring with this new arrangement?"

"I am doing quite well," Millicent answered honestly. "The changes have required some adjustment on the part of everyone, mostly due to the increase in the size of the household. But a shortage of living space has been my greatest problem right along."

Mrs. Trimble poured Millicent some more tea. "And I was so sorry to hear that in the midst of all this, you had to let go of your steward."

"That was inevitable. Mr. Draper and I did not get along from the start, and with each passing day things just seemed to get worse."

"But finding a replacement has been difficult."

Millicent nodded and took a sip of her tea before putting the cup back on the table. "I have interviewed three people thus far, but none of them seems to be the right person for Melbury Hall."

"And spring shall be upon us quite soon." She shook her head. "So much of the day-to-day responsibilities of the steward, then, are squarely upon your shoulders."

"Indeed, there is a great deal to do."

"And you were planning to improve the cottages on the estate, as well as building more. How can you possibly be holding up, my dear?"

"Fortunately, nothing has fallen to pieces yet." Millicent smiled. "Lord Aytoun's personal manservant, a very capable Scotsman who has been with his lordship for years, has been seeing to those responsibilities vacated by Mr. Draper for the past few weeks. Selfishly, I suppose, I'm hoping that he might consider taking over the job of steward permanently. Of course, I still have to convince Lord Aytoun of that."

Millicent thought that just asking the question should be good for at least a half-dozen overturned dishes. Lyon was quite fond of doing that.

"Your description of everything is so much more pleasant than the rumors that were initially floating around the village." Mrs. Trimble squeezed Millicent's hand affectionately. "I am so happy for you. I do hope we get a chance to meet his lordship soon."

"Well, perhaps once the weather improves, I'll persuade him to come into the village with me." She would have to do this persuading on the same day that she asked his opinion of Gibbs becoming the new steward. And perhaps the same day that she asked him to stop destroying the household furnishings. And the same day she asked him to talk rather than shout. Perhaps that would be the day to ask him to shave off that hideous beard as well.

Millicent glanced at the handsome clock above the hearth. It was approaching the noon hour, and she began to worry. She sincerely hoped Lyon had eaten some breakfast. She wondered what his reaction had been this morning when she had not come to his room, or if he had even noticed her absence. If he had eaten nothing for breakfast, she wanted to be there to encourage him to have something now. Well, either encourage or bully him.

"I cannot imagine what is detaining Reverend Trimble." The rector's wife, following the direction of her visitor's gaze, pushed herself stiffly to her feet and went to the window. She was a tall woman, and Millicent could see her looking out past the garden at the village.

"Would you consider me terribly rude if I were to curtail our visit today?" Millicent asked. "I know it sounds silly, but suddenly I find myself concerned for my husband. I have not left him alone for so many hours, and he is still recovering."

"I understand perfectly," Mrs. Trimble answered, turning back to her with a smile. "I am very sorry that Reverend Trimble missed you. The builders at the grange must be interesting fellows."

Millicent stood up. "I'm certain they are. In fact, I was hoping to ask his assistance in hiring one of these same men for the renovations at Melbury Hall. Aside from the new cottages, I was also hoping to build a stone wall to stop the river from flooding into the Grove every spring. I have quite a bit of work that needs to be done at the Hall."

"I know he'd be delighted to help out with that, my dear. Perhaps I could have him stop out at Melbury Hall sometime this week. Perhaps while he is there, he could meet his lordship."

"That would be very nice," Millicent said in a small voice, already wondering what kind of bribe she could use with Lyon to make him behave for the few minutes Reverend Trimble would be in his company.

The door to the earl's bedchamber was open. A few minutes earlier, Ohenewaa had seen one of the servants cursing and grumbling as he passed her with a tray. She took a step toward the door and looked inside.

The man was alone, propped up in a chair near the window. She was surprised to see he had a newspaper on his lap. His attention appeared to be divided between the paper and the view outside the window.

"Instead of hiding in the shadows, why not come in?"

He never turned his head, and he caught her off guard. Ohenewaa considered ignoring the remark and moving down the hall. Instead, though, she entered the chamber. There was a marked difference between what she saw in the room now and what she recalled seeing her first night here. There were no vials of medication. No smell of sickness. No sense of gloom. She inspected the painting and rugs and tables, and then looked over the man, studying him like any of the other furnishings.

"Why do you roam around the halls like a ghost? You can walk. You can talk. Why not make more noise?" His questions were abrupt, and this time his eyes focused on her from across the room.

"You make enough noise for both of us. Since we have started asking questions, though . . ." She motioned to the open paper on his lap. "Why don't you admit this to her? You appear perfectly capable of entertaining yourself."

"Perhaps I enjoy her company."

"Perhaps you need someone to torment."

"I do not ask her to come. She agreed to the arrangement. What she does, she does of her own free will."

"You haven't told her that you've improved. You might tell her that there is no need for her to fret over you every minute of the day."

"You care about her," he said, staring incredulously.

"You do not." Ohenewaa matched his expression for a long moment before turning and starting toward the door.

"Come back again. I enjoyed our lengthy visit."

Instead of going downstairs, Ohenewaa walked to her own bedchamber and stood looking at her herbs and bottles.

She had helped the earl and his wife once already. But her excuse to herself then had been that she was tired of listening to the two of them shouting and breaking things at all hours of the day and night. Her involvement, she told herself, had been as much for her own sake as for theirs. But what she planned next was far more complicated.

In fact, before today she wasn't certain that it might be a wise thing to go through the entire process of decocting to extract the oils for a particular mixture that she wanted. The salve she had in mind would serve several purposes. Thinking about him now, Ohenewaa told herself that she was a healer. Besides, from the first day on, she had been looking for a way to thank Millicent for what she had done for her.

The question of whether *he* was deserving of the effort Ohenewaa would expend had been answered today. She had seen today that he had a spirit within him, and—whether he knew it or not—he was helping his young wife to heal.

And that was a good enough reason, Ohenewaa thought. She would help him.

The ride and the bracing winter air had a noticeable effect on her. She looked far more relaxed—almost cheerful—and completely undisturbed by the complaints that he started with the moment she walked into the room.

"A swarm of dung flies would not sit on this bread. And this soup must surely be the result of some mangy cur lifting his leg and pissing in the pot. Are you and your bloody cooks trying to poison me?"

"With images like that running unbridled through your mind, m'lord, I don't blame you for not wanting to eat it. Indeed, you must surely detest the food simply for being weary of it. I must have a talk with the cook. You are beyond the need for these watery broths and dry bread. There is no reason that you should not be served what the rest of us are eating."

As she took the untouched tray off his lap, the profanities that he was preparing to deliver withered on his tongue. For the mere seconds that Millicent had leaned close to him, he had smelled the scent of fresh air in her hair. He found himself admiring the touch of sun on her cheeks. He watched her deposit the tray on a table beside the door. *Bloody hell,* he thought, recovering his composure.

"I don't want to eat anything you bring up here," he barked shortly.

"I perfectly agree."

"By the devil, I think this is a first."

"I assure you, it is only the first of many agreements we shall have."

He scowled at her bright face suspiciously. "What is this all about?"

"You should not be served your meals here in this room at all. The surroundings are too restricted. The air is too stale. I also believe that an ill-tempered disposition tends to linger in a place. And I must say that with your temperament, this chamber already reeks of it."

"Well don't leave your own temperament out, as long as you're going on about it."

"Very well, m'lord. *Our* temperaments."

"And don't call me 'm'lord,' " he grumbled. "I won't have my wife calling me that. You'll call me Lyon when we're alone, and Aytoun when we're not."

"As you wish." Millicent held her hands folded before her and gave him a bright smile. "But starting tonight, you and I will have our meals in the dining room."

Lyon would have told her she was daft if he weren't momentarily arrested by her smile. She was damned bewitching with those soft dimples in her cheeks and the mischief dancing in her gray eyes.

"That settles it." She clapped her hands once and reached for the servant's bell.

"The devil it does!" he finally managed to get out. "I am no wooden puppet to be dragged up and down those damned stairs three times a day while jug-headed rogues stand by and ridicule me."

"You certainly are not, m'lo . . . Lyon. No puppet

I've ever seen could talk and curse with such fervor or frequency." She moved toward him. "But in spite of your many faults, I will promise you that—other than two of your own men who shall help me move you—no one will be standing about and watching."

"This shall *not* be." He spoke more forcefully.

"Indeed, it shall." She matched his tone.

"I am content to remain here."

"Before, you were content to remain unconscious and to starve. Right now, you are content to play the part of the angry bear and constantly flash those teeth at me."

"Come closer, my dear wife," Lyon threatened in a low voice, "and I'll show you how contented I am."

A soft blush spread evenly across her cheeks, but instead of backing away, she placed her hand on his shoulder and leaned toward him until they were face to face.

"Despite the tangled beard and uncombed hair that successfully give you a certain mad look, I don't believe you look very frightening from this distance. Maybe if I were to shave your face—"

His left arm darted out and took hold of her arm, toppling her onto his lap. She gasped in surprise and fell against him.

"No one touches my beard."

She seemed lost for words. This close he could tell her gray eyes had silver speckles in their depths. Her skin looked so soft. Lyon's gaze fell on her lips, and without another thought he found his mouth had captured hers in a rough kiss.

She did not pull away, but rather leaned into him and clutched his shoulders. Blood pounded in Lyon's body. Her lips were so soft and giving. He slanted his mouth over hers and was about to deepen the kiss when suddenly she dragged herself off him and away from the chair. She was blushing furiously, her hand over her mouth as she backed all the way to the far side of the room.

Lyon tried to calm his unsteady breathing as he watched her flushed face. She touched her brow, tucked loose tendrils of hair behind an ear. With trembling fingers she tried to straighten her dress. He followed the movement of her hands and told himself she was his wife. After three weeks of being in each other's company constantly, this was to be expected. Still, though, what had happened between them was totally inexplicable to him. What he felt was confusing as hell. She finally turned to him with a polite smile pasted onto her face. But he could see through the mask. She was visibly shaken.

"We cannot live the rest of our lives in this one room, m'lord."

His thoughts, however, were not in agreement with hers. He still wanted to be left alone here, with one small exception . . . Millicent. Surprising as it was, he wanted her here with him.

"I believe it would be good for both of us to get out of this chamber."

Us instead of *you.* Anger began to seep into Lyon's bones. Every time the door had opened this morning, he'd hoped to see her. And now she was playing games with him. He forced himself to look away from her lips, cursing himself for this additional layer of dependence on another.

"No one asked you to spend so much time in this room. I was content without you. *I* live here. You do *not.*"

"You are mistaken." Once again her fire returned. "I am your wife. Where you are, *Lyon*, I shall be. Where you eat, I shall eat. Where you—"

She cut the words short, but Lyon knew what she was about to say. *Where you sleep* . . .

"Do as you please, and the devil take you," he barked irritably. "I do not care to discuss this further. I don't need you. I am tired of seeing your face. And I'm bored with your incessant chatter. Out."

Lyon turned his head away without waiting for her response. Staring out the window into the courtyard and the fields beyond was his only escape. Silently, he tried to convince himself that she deserved his sharp tongue. So what that they were man and wife? Kissing her had been an impulse—a mistake. He only wanted her to let him be.

There was no sound for a long time. She had not moved, but she said nothing, either. Lyon wondered if she was finally going to give up.

"Actually, there is another reason why I wish to drag you out of this room." Millicent had the matter-of-fact tone back in her voice. She was not ready to let him alone.

"Is there, madam?" He did not look at her.

"From what Gibbs tell me, before your accident you took an active interest in many of the Aytoun family business matters. He said you never felt it was beneath you to oversee the management of your estate in the Borders and your lands in the Highlands. You served as a most valuable resource to many of your less capable peers. You are educated and obviously quite shrewd when it comes to getting what you want. And you are here."

"Your skills at flattery need work. Shrewdness is not a noble quality."

Lyon turned his head and saw her run a nervous hand down the front of her dress to smooth an invisible wrinkle. He knew what she was doing. This new strategy of hers was nothing if not transparent.

"I should like to introduce you around Melbury Hall."

"No."

"This is not a social request, but one regarding . . . well, business. There have been a few matters having to do with the estate where I have needed guidance. I would very much appreciate it if I could occasionally ask your advice on these concerns."

"You have the income now. Hire a better lawyer."

"I already have an excellent one, thank you," she replied, continuing tenaciously. "But you know that the law considers women feeble, at best. You also know that, as my husband, you are wholly responsible for the actions of your wife."

He snorted.

"Therefore," she went on, "I am giving you the opportunity of being involved. But again, considering your reputation in the household as a tyrant, perhaps I need to rethink my suggestion. After all, only a fool would want to have you meddle in things that you quite possibly know nothing about. It would not be the first time people's perceptions of a man's abilities have been mistaken. Or Gibbs may simply have been speaking out of blind loyalty. Then again, I may have inferred more about your abilities from what he said than he intended. Never mind. I don't know what I was thinking."

"Nor do I. Your vexatious nagging almost stops my breath, madam. Almost."

Lyon let the weight of his gaze travel down the length of her body. Despite the somber face that tried to mask the woman's feelings, despite the plain cut of her dark blue dress, despite the simplicity of the way she piled her hair upon her head, he knew at that instant that being confined in one room with Millicent was having a disquieting effect on him.

"If leaving this room means you will no longer plague me with your constant mindless chatter, then I will do it . . . and gladly."

Chapter 12

Preparing a dinner for the royal family would not have rattled Millicent as much as planning this meal for her husband. She wanted everything to be perfect—the food, the wine, the dining room. She had questioned Gibbs endlessly about Lyon's likes and dislikes with regard to the menu, and she had made certain every detail was conveyed to the cook and to Mrs. Page. Now, shortly before she was scheduled to go to her husband's chamber to supervise Will and John in bringing him down to dinner, Millicent was overcome with yet another reason for uncertainty. What could she wear that was appropriate? Of course, she wanted to dress presentably, but she also knew that what she chose for this occasion could relay a specific message to the earl.

She'd not had any time this afternoon to dwell on what had happened earlier, but she was still rattled by his kiss and by her own response to it. Avoiding intimate contact with any man had simply become Millicent's way after the physical abuse she'd endured under Wentworth's cruel fist. This had been one of the reasons why she had found marrying Aytoun so unobjectionable. Because of his physical inabilities, there would be no possible way that any such demands would be put upon her. Her insistence on a clause allowing for an annulment had been spurred by that very problem. Of course, she told herself as she stared into her looking glass, a kiss should not necessarily constitute any change in her thinking on the matter.

Millicent forced the thoughts to shift and settle in her

mind as her maid Violet rushed about the room laying
out petticoats and stockings and other pieces of clothing.
It was a kiss and nothing more. Millicent silently vowed
not to think about it again, and nodded at the blue embroidered dress Vi held up for her.

"If you're sure you'll not wear the wig, m'lady, I can
work some matching ribbons in your hair and—"

"We have no time for that, Vi." Millicent stepped out
of her dress and donned the petticoats. In a moment,
she was pulling on the blue dress with Vi's help. "I cannot chance having the earl change his mind about leaving his chambers. I told him seven o'clock, and I need
to be there on time."

"At least allow me to tie a ribbon at your neck,
m'lady. The square neckline of this dress looks far too
plain without jewelry."

A glance in the mirror at the low neckline and she
agreed. Violet had a good eye for colors, for what was
becoming and what wasn't. There were many times that
Millicent had thought the young woman's talents were
wasted staying here, but Vi seemed content.

"Too bad you no longer have that sapphire the squire
gave you when you married. The blue stone always
looked fetching with this dress."

"I like this simple ribbon much better."

Millicent felt no regret about having sold her jewelry
after Wentworth's death. Regardless of whether they
were his gifts or handed down from her own family, she
had no use for them. They all had been sold to take
care of her people.

"Thank you, Vi. I think I'm ready."

"Wait! You need to change your shoes." Violet
fetched a pair of matching slippers from the wardrobe.
"Perhaps this is not the time, m'lady, but I was wondering if you would mind if I were to spend two days away
at the end of this week."

"Visiting with your family in St. Albans?"

"Yes, m'lady."

Violet crouched before Millicent as she stepped into

the slippers. She thought the young woman looked thinner.

"I don't see any problem with that at all. But are you feeling unwell?"

"No, m'lady. I am quite well."

"I think you have been working too hard, Vi. In fact, if you speak to Mrs. Page about it, perhaps she can arrange to have one of the grooms drop you off while he is running errands for the household and pick you up again on another return trip."

"Don't fret about any of that, m'lady. I'll take care of the arrangements." She rose to her feet. " 'Tis almost seven, I think."

Millicent looked at the mantel clock as it began to chime.

"Indeed, it is," she said, and hurried to the door.

Try as he might, Lyon couldn't find anything to object to about the evening. The light from a dozen candles cast a soft glow over the room. A small fire crackled on the hearth. The food had been exquisitely prepared; the wine was excellent. He let his gaze run appreciatively over the woman seated near him. The company was enchanting.

Instead of taking the chair at the far end of the table, Millicent had chosen to sit beside him. After the food had been taken away, she had dismissed the servants, including Gibbs, and the two of them sat together. Lyon could tell she was in good spirits. Not only had he followed through on his promise, allowing his men to carry him downstairs, but he had also consumed small portions of fish and venison.

He watched her graceful movements as she poured more wine into his crystal glass. He was glad she had not retired to the drawing room and left him to drink alone.

"Frankly, I'm surprised that you trust me with this." Lyon nodded toward the glass.

"Are you referring to drinking the wine or breaking the glass?" Millicent asked lightly.

"The wine. I understand your late husband had some difficulties in that regard."

A small furrow formed on her brow. She reached up to smooth it with the tips of her fingers, and Lyon noticed the redness of her ears and the blush that had crept into her cheeks. "He had many difficulties."

"I am sorry to hear that your life was less than ideal."

"Thank you. But you are full of surprises. Here I had been afraid that you've been spending every moment perfecting your gibes."

"I enjoy a change of pace every now and then." He sensed her distaste of the topic, but he decided to press her on it, anyway. "And what were his other faults?"

He watched the delicate column of her neck as she took a sip of her own wine. The soft curves and the ivory skin above the neckline of the dress glowed in the candlelight, and for an insane moment he wondered if she tasted as sweet as she looked. He forced his thoughts away.

"Your husband's faults?"

"I am afraid I don't consider that a topic for dinner conversation," she answered as brightly as she could. "And I should tell you that it is senseless to listen to household gossip here at Melbury Hall. With the exception of a trusted few, the rest of these people are fairly new in their positions."

"And why is that?"

"I suppose it is just the natural progression of life in a household like this."

"Is it? And what is that progression?" Lyon stared at her flushed face, awaiting an answer. There was no point in retreating now. She had used the business of the estate as a lure. He had every right, therefore, to know what had brought Melbury Hall—and Millicent—to this point.

"I should hate to repeat what you already know. So why not—"

"Start from the beginning."

"Beginning of what?"

"You are being evasive." He caught her wrist when

she started to rise. "Sit, Millicent. You wanted me down
here. You asked for my help. I am here, but I need to
know your situation. *Our* situation."

"Very well." She sat down again. "As long as we can
keep my personal life and my first marriage out of the
discussion, I have no objection to telling you what is
happening at Melbury Hall."

His nod was a lie, and he knew it. Leave out her
personal life? Not likely. The person inside was what
interested him the most. The truth behind the lingering
sadness in those gray eyes was a mystery that was beginning to nag at him. He'd been told so little by his mother
and Maitland before agreeing to the marriage. The dowager had been looking for someone to provide some care
for him. Millicent, a widow, had been in financial need.
That had been all he cared to know at the time. But the
situation was changing now. He was improving every
day, and he wanted to know everything about her. To
achieve that, Lyon knew he would have to summon up
his patience—certainly the least exercised of his virtues.

She took another sip of wine. "Perhaps you have noticed that a large number of black men and women live
and work at Melbury Hall."

"Freed slaves."

She nodded. "Over the period of five years that I was
married to Squire Wentworth, these people were
brought in from his plantations in Jamaica to work the
land here. Most of them"—she shook her head—"no,
all of them were severely abused by a score of brutal
bailiffs who were also brought back from the islands to
oversee them."

Lyon watched her closely as she pushed her glass
away. The candlelight danced in her gray eyes, now glistening. He knew many men who had made or saved
their fortunes by investing in sugar plantations in the
West Indies. Even as stories about the barbarous conditions of the places trickled back, many excused the practice, saying that the slaves that were transported to the
islands were all criminals and captives of war. Lyon
knew the excuses were falsehoods, however, for he him-

self had seen young children on the ships tied up at Bristol's Long Quay.

"You freed them."

"After the squire's death, I tried to return a small portion of what had been taken from these people. While I let go those servants who were loyal to my last husband, I felt it only just to replace them with the freed slaves. As a result the household has continued to function, but the farms have suffered." She rubbed her temple absently. "I do not wish to bore you with details of what was then and what is now. What I am really in need of advice on regards how to balance the needs of both Melbury Hall and its farms."

"Did all the people you freed stay?"

"Most of them."

"And do you pay them all wages?"

"Of course! They do the same work as anyone else. They should earn the same wage."

"I am not being critical." He matched the tone of her voice. "You married me because you were approaching financial ruin. Was Melbury Hall the cause of it?"

Millicent paused to answer, and he could tell she was contemplating how much to reveal. "No. I was confronted by other debts passed on to me. Large sums beyond what my annual income could afford."

"Left by your husband."

"That is correct. But, having become the recipient of your gracious generosity, I can say that those debts are now paid, and I am even left with enough money make some desperately needed renovations."

"Renovations to this house?"

"No, to the cottages adjacent to it. But that is a project with a one-time expense and not the subject of my greatest concern. As I look over the books from previous years, I realize that Melbury Hall has never been able to sustain itself financially. During the years when Wentworth was alive, it seems that he used the profits from his plantations in Jamaica to support this place."

"Such things are not uncommon, depending on the

amount of land and the quality of the farms here. Are such funds still available to you?"

"No! I lost those lands to one of Wentworth's friends. A man to whom my husband was deeply indebted. But even if I still owned those plantations, I would never consider it," she responded passionately. "I could never have drawn any profit from them. Before I knew I had lost the Jamaican properties, my plans were to free the Africans there as well."

Lyon noted the rising color again in her face. He could see the passion of her beliefs in the flash of her eyes. She looked so incredibly alive. Almost beautiful.

"Also, I am not willing to place the burden of this place on you. I am determined, however, not to pursue any solution that would mean turning out anyone else or cutting wages to make things work here."

The high degree of intelligence and compassion in the woman was a rare mix that Lyon had not come across very often. He studied her with new interest. Another scrap of information he had learned since arriving here was that Millicent was almost thirty years old, and that she'd borne no children in her first marriage.

"You are fond of your large household," he said. "I respect you for wanting to keep it together. I also admire you for all that you are trying to do."

The trace of a smile on her lips washed over him like a warm breeze.

"Gibbs tells me that Melbury Hall has been cursed recently with a line of incompetent stewards. That alone could have been the reason for the poor management of its lands and crops. With capable stewards in charge, you might not have any problem at all."

"My mind would rest more easily if I could somehow be assured of that, but for too long I have felt myself buried beneath a mountain of debt. Now, thanks to you, I feel I finally have the opportunity to breathe fresh air. I cannot leave the future to chance, though. I will not allow things to continue on as they have been."

"I understand. I would be happy to go over the account ledgers and review the crop books. I would also like to see a map of your lands, if you have one."

"I do. It is in the library."

"Then, whatever they are worth, I shall share my thoughts with you."

"You will?" She placed her hand on his arm. "I am so impressed with this change in you. The truth is that in dealing with the financial areas of running an estate, I have often felt adrift in a rudderless boat. Would you mind greatly if I were to look over your shoulder and ask the hundreds of questions that I have?"

"Dozens I might be able to endure. But hundreds?"

Millicent's laughter danced around them and lifted his spirit. Lyon didn't know if it was the effect of the wine or her. This was the first time in months, he realized, that he had spent a couple of hours thinking about someone else, rather than drowning in his own misery. He glanced down at her hand still on his.

"I'll be content with whatever time you can give me, Lyon."

Her chair slid closer to his. The touch of her knee against his leg was warm. She leaned forward and picked up the napkin that had dropped off his lap to the floor. He admired the soft curves of her breast gently spilling over the neckline of the dress. She folded the cloth and put it back on his lap, beneath his right hand. The image of her pressed against his chest this afternoon rushed back to his mind. His gaze moved up to her lips.

"I hope this will not be too much asking for one night," she continued, obviously unaware of the direction of his thoughts. "Mr. Gibbs has been a great help to me, assisting me with so many of the daily business matters. Your valets tell me how involved he was with running the household at Baronsford and again at your town house in London. Would you object if I were to ask him to take over some of the steward's responsibilities here? I know he wouldn't even consider the job unless he had your blessing."

She continued to talk, but Lyon wasn't listening. With a shock, he realized that he was growing hard for the second time in one day. For over six months he had considered himself less than a man. No feelings, no desire, no thoughts of ever lying with a woman again. But after all this time, when he'd felt Millicent's body pressed against his this afternoon, as he'd ravished her mouth with his, he'd felt the stirring of desire. He had cast the feeling aside as his imagination. But to have it happen again now! He'd just been watching her talk, and the sensations had returned.

Instead of excitement, embarrassment drenched him in a cold sweat. The fact that his body responded physically to hers held out no relief to him. He was still not whole. He could not forget how little remained of him in body and soul. He was relieved that she was unaware of these changes.

"I am ready to be taken upstairs."

His sharp tone caused Millicent to look at him with alarm. "What's wrong?"

"I am tired. Ready to retire. I wish to be carried upstairs. Now."

"I shouldn't have brought up all that about Mr. Gibbs. I know how much you rely on him, and I have no intention of reducing the care—"

"I don't give a damn what you ask him to do. I'd be content not to see his ugly face ever again." Irritated, he shoved away the plate before him on the table. The glass next to it fell against the plate and the stem snapped. Before she could stop it, a piece tumbled off the table and onto Lyon's lap. She was at his side in a moment.

"Oh, my Lord! That cut you. I am so sorry. You're bleeding."

Lyon was already staring at the beads of blood forming on his right hand. It was nothing—only a nick caused by the falling shard—but he continued to stare.

His muscles had reacted of their own accord. Without consciously trying to move them, his hand and fingers had moved. But damn him if he could move them again now.

"Call John and Will and have me taken up," he

growled. "If you ever want me to leave that room again, you will have it done *now*."

Millicent hovered in the background while the two valets worked diligently by the light of a single candle, readying their master for bed. Everything about tonight had been special until something had happened. She couldn't understand what had caused the sudden change in Lyon's mood, and her uneasiness was undiminished as she considered the tense wall that had arisen between them. She knew it didn't have anything to do with her question about Gibbs becoming the next steward. Lyon hadn't even seemed to be listening to what she had been saying then.

John bowed his way out of the room first, and Will followed shortly after, closing the door behind him. This had become the nightly routine. The attendants would leave, and Millicent would spend the night dozing in a chair or pacing the room or staring out the window. She did not want Lyon left alone as yet. Then, as dawn was breaking, Gibbs generally came in to take her place.

"I do not want you to stay."

Millicent cringed at the roughness of his tone. Pushing her feelings aside, she reminded herself that despite the pleasant hours they had spent together tonight, he was still recovering from his illness. And she had already learned to expect the sharp alterations in his moods.

"Well, I am not going anywhere."

"Do as you bloody please." He closed his eyes, shutting her out.

Millicent realized she was more disturbed by his indifference than his rejection. Gathering her resolve, she moved close to him. The covers were tucked around him—the left arm lay on top, the right one beneath the blanket. She thought of the cut on his hand, but decided she would not disturb him to check it.

She stared at the dark beard and the long lashes that lay against his handsome cheeks. The memory of their kiss this afternoon came back into her mind and an unexpected warmth spread through her body. She stared at his hard lips and, without thinking, smoothed the bed-clothes. As she did, Millicent wondered if he would ever kiss her again.

Bothered by her thoughts, she drew back and looked about the shadowy room. During the last few nights he had often been sleepless, but other than carrying an argument when he started one or responding to his gibes, she really had not been needed.

She was tired and he didn't want her here, but Millicent couldn't think of anyplace at Melbury Hall that she preferred to be than here in this room. She sank into her chair by the foot of his bed and gazed at his pale face, wondering what he had been like before.

Everyone in the servants' hall was rushing about, obviously concerned about Moses, who was standing in the back door, wringing his hands. A black serving maid hurried up the steps to an upper floor after Mrs. Page whispered an order to her. Holding the large man's arm, the housekeeper led him to a bench by the fire. There, one of the cooks handed her a steaming cup of drink, which she pressed into his huge hands as she continued to talk to him in a low, reassuring voice.

Gibbs had entered in the midst of all this, but instead of meddling he stood back and watched the scene unfold before him. Moses was saying something in a broken voice, and it looked to Gibbs as if there were tears standing in the old man's eyes. Someone appeared with a blanket that Mrs. Page threw around his shoulders. All the time speaking soothingly to him, she ran a comforting hand over his back.

The household at Melbury Hall was roughly half black, half white, but what had struck Gibbs most impressively since arriving here was the familial feeling that held sway. Clearly Lady Aytoun's desire to treat all fairly, regardless of skin color, was a manner embraced by the people she employed.

The same servant who had been sent up the stairs returned, followed by the old woman Ohenewaa. Words passed between Moses and the woman. Almost immediately Moses stood up, shed the blanket, and the two of them went out through the back door.

Gibbs's gaze returned to the housekeeper. As she bustled about, he could not help but admire the efficiency with which she settled everything back to normal in just a few moments. He had to admit, though, that Mrs. Page's competence was not the only thing he had been finding fascinating lately. Inviting from a safe distance, but somewhat reserved whenever he came near, Mary Page had been drawing him in bit by bit. What was most interesting, though, was the fact that Gibbs wasn't even minding the feel of the hook she had in him.

"What was troubling Moses?" Gibbs managed to ask, once he was within arm's reach of her.

Mary's green gaze lifted, and she smiled tenderly. "One of the stable dogs that he has become fond of caught a leg in a poacher's snare tonight. Some of the grooms think the poor animal should be put down, but Moses wanted Ohenewaa to look at the injured dog first."

"So is this what Ohenewaa means to them? Is she a healer of some sort?"

Mary nodded. "Aye, but she is also seen as an elder and wise woman. Amina told me that Ohenewaa forms a sort of bridge for them to a part of their past."

"Ye mean Africa?"

"I believe so, Mr. Gibbs."

The Highlander followed Mrs. Page as she made her way out of the hall.

"Since the first day, I have not seen much of this Moses. But from all I can tell, the man appears to be well looked after."

"He deserves it." The same look of tenderness shone in her face. "Despite his scarred body and a weak mind, Moses is the gentlest person I have yet to meet in my life. I've heard stories of all that he regularly endured during the squire's time. The man cannot be blamed if he's a little slow when it comes to any complicated thinking. I think I would have lost my mind completely long ago if I were in his shoes. But Moses is devoted to the mistress and to those who were kind to him over the years."

Gibbs waited when the housekeeper paused at the bottom of the stairs to exchange a few words with Amina, who had just entered the hall. When they were finished and the young woman went off toward the kitchens, Gibbs gave Mary his most serious look.

"And if I were to confess my absolute devotion to ye, Mrs. Page, would ye treat me with the same affection as ye were treating Moses a few minutes ago?"

A blush crept into the woman's fair cheeks. "A cup of warm cider and a blanket around your cold shoulders, Mr. Gibbs?"

"A caressing hand on my back and soft words whispered in my ear."

Mary Page gave him a coy smile. "And why, sir, would someone with your looks and manners be wanting any such thing from an old widow like me?"

"Old, mum? I think not." He took her by the hand and pulled her into the shadow of the steps. "But ye know I'm going a wee bit daft trying to win yer affection, Mrs. Page."

"I don't know what you mean!"

"Don't ye now?" Gibbs dropped his head lower until he was looking into her eyes. "Ye wouldna ride back with me from Knebworth Village last Sunday. Ye have twice refused my offer of walking the grounds in the evening this week. Ye didna find the—"

"I should be honored to have tea with you tomorrow afternoon."

"Tea, did ye say?"

"Tea," she repeated with a smile.

He bowed, placing a kiss on the back of her hand.

"Tea! Well, I'll be dashed, mum, but I'm thinking ye'll be making me the gentleman yet."

"I would expect no less from the next steward of Melbury Hall." She withdrew her hand and fluttered past him. "You would be perfect for the position, Mr. Gibbs, and I do hope you are considering it."

*   *   *

Violet ran to keep up with Amina's longer strides. "How is Moses taking it?"

"He is very upset, Vi, and that is not helping anything," Amina replied. "Jonah wants to have Ohenewaa see to the dog's leg, but to do that, Moses has to keep the animal calm. We do not want the creature to bite anyone. But with Moses moaning and acting more wounded than the dog . . ." The young woman shook her head.

Inside the stables, a lantern was burning in one of the stalls, and at least a dozen people had gathered. Violet, followed by Amina, pushed through them to find Moses crouched on a pile of straw next to his dog. The animal's leg was a mess, and Violet could see what looked like bone sticking out of the bloody flesh.

"They should take off the leg," a groom said to her left.

"She won't make it," someone else commented. " 'Twould be better to cut her throat and put the poor beast out of her misery."

Violet shivered and looked at Ohenewaa, who was spreading out linen strips and some broken branches amid several bottles of salve a foot or two away from Moses and the dog. The old woman said something quietly to Jonah, and the bailiff bent over Moses and whispered to him.

Even from across the way, Violet could see that Moses's body was shaking and tears were running down his face when he stepped back and let Jonah take his place beside the dog as Ohenewaa approached.

When the healer touched the animal's head, Moses winced. When she reached for the paw, the man's whimper matched the dog's. The old man's suffering tore at Violet's heart, and she found herself pushing through the people and going to him.

"Moses." She tugged on his arm when she reached him. Eyes filled with anguish turned to her. "Will you please come and sit outside with me? I cannot watch this. It breaks my heart." When he hesitated, she held his arm. "Please, Moses. I need you."

The old man's feet slogged through the straw as they left the stables. Violet led him outside the open doors and sat down on a wall, pulling him down next to her.

"I took the basket you made me to the village this morning," she said, trying to tear his mind away from what was going on inside. "Will you show me sometime how you managed to weave all those pieces together? That was the best present."

"Do you think she can heal my dog, Vi?"

"Yes, Moses. I think she can heal her."

"M'lady gave her to me. My own."

"I know."

"Never had nothing of my own, Vi."

"I know, Moses." Violet looked into the face of the former slave. It didn't matter to her how hideous he looked. He was so kind and gentle. She held tight onto his arm and pressed her cheek against his shoulder.

"You shall always have at least one friend, Moses, as long as I live."

"I know that too, Vi. Friends."

Violet nodded, forcing down the knot in her throat. "Tell me about your dog, Moses."

It was past midnight when Millicent saw the shadowy figure of Ohenewaa trekking up from the stables. A couple of hours earlier, when she had gone to her own bedchamber to change out of her gown, Millicent had heard from Violet about Moses's injured dog.

Millicent's time had been so consumed with Lyon that she hadn't spent much time with the old woman. She had barely had the opportunity to thank Ohenewaa for the tea that she believed had helped Lyon through the first nights of going without the laudanum.

She thought back to the day that they'd spoken about the letter from Jasper Hyde. Millicent had listened to everything Ohenewaa said. She had already heard such horrors. And she had seen the same superstitious ignorance in others that might very well drive a man like Hyde to hold Ohenewaa responsible for his suffering.

Millicent's refusal to the plantation owner had been

clear and direct. Ohenewaa had no desire to meet with him, and neither did she.

The old woman was no witch, of that Millicent was certain. The fact that she obviously had a knowledge of herbs and medicines did not make her evil. No matter what others chose to think, Millicent felt deep inside that Ohenewaa could be trusted. She had felt it from the first day the old woman had entered Melbury Hall.

That was why Millicent had to see her again tonight. She needed her advice.

Turning away from the window, she watched Lyon breathing comfortably in his sleep for a moment. He had been correct in saying that he didn't need her. There were no more nightmares. No staying awake just to be difficult.

Millicent went to the door and quietly opened it. The hallway was immersed in darkness, and she stepped out of the bedchamber, pulling the door partially closed behind her. Almost immediately she saw Ohenewaa appear at the top of the stairs. The old woman's dark eyes shone like a cat as they fixed on her.

"How is Moses?" Millicent asked softly when the woman drew near.

"He was worried about the animal, but he is doing better."

"Did the dog live?"

"She has a broken leg, but Moses was taught how to tend it."

"We are fortunate to have you here. Thank you."

With a nod, Ohenewaa started past her.

"Would you consider, at some point in time, examining my husband?" Millicent paused when the older woman turned to look at her. "From what I can tell, none of the English doctors have seen any hope in him ever improving, in mind or in body. But we have already proven them half wrong. He is awake, aware, intelligent."

"And loud."

"That too." Millicent smiled. "This is why I cannot help but believe there might be something else—in his legs and arm—that they might be overlooking. So would you consider it? When the time is right, of course, and when I can convince him of it?"

The old woman studied her for a while and then nodded slowly. "When the time is right."

Chapter 13

Millicent was astounded.

No other word could describe her feelings at the flawless perfection of manner with which Lyon greeted and conversed with Reverend Trimble, despite the lengthiness of the visit.

Settling into a chair in the library as if he planned on spending the remainder of winter there, the minister touched upon one topic of discussion after another. Like a pair of old university friends, the two managed to engage themselves in occasionally heated discussions on everything from the political and social struggles in Ireland, to the changing face of industry under the visionary and exploitative influences (Reverend Trimble's phrase) of such people as Josiah Wedgwood, to Hugh Williamson's recent assertion that comets were positively inhabited. Having covered the rumors of land clearings in the Scottish Highlands, they moved easily into the latest news of the growing unrest in the American colonies. In someplace called the Carolinas, she heard Reverend Trimble say, British troops had recently been needed to suppress open rebellion there. And things did not look to be improving.

During the entire time, Millicent had remained attuned to Lyon's mood. She was ready to jump in at any time that her husband suddenly decided that it was time to be rid of the visitor. She did not want her old friend to be offended.

Despite the minister's customarily talkative nature,

Millicent maintained a great affection for him. Mr. Trimble had been a great ally to her and to the workers at Melbury Hall for a long time, even while Squire Wentworth held the whip over them all. It had been because of Reverend Trimble and Mr. Cunningham, the village schoolmaster, that a routine of tutoring the slaves had been established on the estate. Because of their perseverance and watchful intervention, more lives had not been lost to the brutality of the squire's bailiffs.

Mr. Cunningham.

Millicent's chin sank. A knot the size of a fist formed in her chest as she recalled for the thousandth time how the young teacher had lost his life while trying to protect her. She had asked him to come to Melbury Hall in the early hours of dawn to help free the frightened Violet of the lecherous advances of the squire. But Wentworth had thought the man was taking Millicent away with him. He had killed Mr. Cunningham that morning. And after all this time, she still could not free herself of the guilt.

She blinked back the sudden tears and tried not to think of the young man's affection—of how he had been her friend, her salvation during those horrible years. During his last days he had even thought that he was in love with her. But Millicent had discouraged his declarations. She had feared for her own life, but never guessed Cunningham would be the victim.

When Millicent looked across the room, she found Lyon's gaze focused on her face. The conversation between the two men appeared to have become one-sided. She realized they were talking about building construction—or rather, Reverend Trimble was. What had he just proposed? She had missed his point, and an awkward silence fell over the room.

"Would that be satisfactory to you, Lady Aytoun?" the clergyman asked.

Millicent had no idea *what* was satisfactory. She sent Lyon a silent plea.

"Has anyone checked this stonemason's references?" the earl asked, never taking his eyes off her.

"I believe so, m'lord," the minister replied. "He would not have been hired to work on the grange otherwise, and his work looks entirely satisfactory."

"And with the grange work nearing completion, you said he is willing to begin working here two days a week."

"That is correct."

"And after he is finished in the village, he can work a full schedule here?"

"That is what he says, m'lord."

"What do you think of hiring him then, Millicent? You have been anxious to start on your projects."

She gave a grateful nod to her husband and then turned to Reverend Trimble. "That would be wonderful. Thank you for seeing to this."

"My pleasure, m'lady. Well, I suppose I should be getting home, though I must say I have thoroughly enjoyed my visit."

The clergyman pushed himself reluctantly to his feet and said his farewells to the earl. Millicent escorted him out of the room.

"Once again, m'lady," he started as soon as they were heading down the hall toward the front foyer, "I must congratulate you on this union. Lord Aytoun hardly matches his reputation. I am so eager for Mrs. Trimble to meet him. What an intelligent man! So well-spoken and such wonderfully progressive views. Very edifying, indeed."

"He is a surprising man."

"And I understand that Lord and Lady Stanmore are returning to Solgrave in a fortnight. It will be such a happy occasion to have both your families here. Quite happy, indeed."

"Please send my regards to Mrs. Trimble," Millicent said before the clergyman could start in on another topic. A servant helped him into his coat and handed him his gloves and hat. "By the way, what is the name of this stonemason?"

"Ned Cranch. He is eager to start at this second job.

He told me confidentially that he could use the work and the extra wages."

"Could he?"

Reverend Trimble gave a nod. "I heard all about his two wee ones and his wife in Coventry. Says she's expecting their third child any day now. The man has mouths to feed."

"Tell him we shall have work ready for him as soon as next week, if he is free."

"I am certain he will be here."

Goldsmith's *The Vicar of Wakefield*, the book that Reverend Trimble had brought for Lyon, lay on the edge of the table before him. As he reached for it, though, the heavy volume slipped through Lyon's fingers and struck his leg. His left foot jerked along the carpet, and the volume landed on the floor. Lyon stared down in disbelief.

The sensations running up and down his leg were real. His leg had moved. He tried to move his foot again, but he could not repeat the movement. Then, as quickly as they had come, the feelings disappeared. No matter how hard he concentrated, he was not able to move his foot so much as an inch.

"Thank you for your courteous treatment of Reverend Trimble."

As Millicent came back into the room, the soft voice drew Lyon's attention away from his legs. Her smile dimmed a little, however, when she saw his face. He simply nodded curtly and looked down at the book at his feet.

"While I was watching you with him, I began to doubt that you were the same man I married. So I immediately became a student for the rest of his visit, trying my best to observe the techniques the good reverend employed to keep you in so agreeable a state." She crouched down beside Lyon's chair and fetched the book. "Did you wish to read this?"

"No."

At his sharp answer, Millicent put a hand on his arm. She continued to kneel beside his chair. "Is something wrong?"

"No."

After a moment of close scrutiny that he tried to ignore, she rose to her feet. "I am going to fetch Reverend Trimble before he leaves. I am going to ask him to stay and dine with us." She started for the door. "There must be something that I lack in—"

"Millicent!"

Lyon's call turned her around.

"Nothing is wrong. However, I want *you* to read this book to me."

Violet gasped as Ned shoved her hard, pinning her against the wall. His eyes were flashing with anger. She tried to get a hand between his forearm and her throat, but he pushed harder.

"I am sorry," she cried. "I am so sorry. But I heard you were going to St. Albans, and I thought you might want me to follow you here. Ned, we did plan to come together so you could meet with my—"

"*Ye* planned," he shouted into her face. "I did no plannin'. And by the de'il, woman, I should give ye a bloody lip for sneaking into this tavern and hiding in my room."

"I was just trying to make you happy, Ned," she whispered tearfully. "We're always sneaking off to your little room in the village. I thought here . . . well, I have two whole days off and—"

"Here I might just whistle and bring a few o' the lads up from the taproom and have ye play whore to all of us." He took his arm from her throat and grabbed her chin roughly in his hand. "Or maybe I'll just bind ye on that mattress there, with a gag for your mouth, and have my way with you a hundred different ways without never havin' to listen to your whinin' at all."

The young woman spoke through her sobs. "You are scaring me, Ned Cranch. You know you shouldn't say such things. You know I'm no whore. I only came be-

cause I thought you would be glad to have me here."
She gathered the front of her cloak tightly around her.
"I'll go. I am sorry to upset you like this. I was a fool
to think you meant all those sweet things you said. I
know now you only said them to find your way under
my skirts."

"Mind your bloody tongue or I'll . . ."

When Ned raised a threatening fist, Violet cringed
against the wall. She was relieved when he didn't hit her
and instead dropped his hand to his side.

"Get out o' here, ye brazen chit, before I change my
mind and decide to teach ye a hard lesson."

There was no doubting his words. The anger she saw
in those green eyes was sobering. It was as if he hated
her Violet moved away, circling around him and then
running for the door. Outside in the dark, foul-smelling
hallway of the inn, she let the tears fall.

What a wretched fool she had been, she thought, trying to get her bearings. She had believed every word he
had told her. She had believed him when he'd said he
loved her. Behind her, a woman laughed a drunken, sa-
lacious laugh, and Violet turned around in alarm. In the
murky light of a shuttered window at the far end of the
hall, she could see the woman bent over, while a trades-
man with his breeches around his knees held her hips
and slammed into her.

Violet felt her stomach rising into her throat. She was
no different, she thought. The tears came faster. She had
become a whore. She pulled the hood of the cloak over
her head and hurried down the hall.

At the stair landing, she ran into a small man coming
up. Kid gloves steadied her. She stared down at the
man's shiny boots.

"Pardon me, sir," she whispered.

One glove took hold of her chin and raised it. Violet
shivered as she glanced into the coldly amused eyes regarding her. There was no escaping him.

"Aren't you a pretty thing? And what a fortunate
wench," he exclaimed, glancing toward Ned's door.
"Come with me, girl. This will take just a minute."

On impulse Violet pulled her face away and backed up a step. He continued to hold her arm. "The stonemason just had me, sir. Perhaps you'd care to take me someplace else?"

His amusement changed to a look of mild distaste. "Very well. Wait here, then."

She was relieved when he let go of her and continued down the dark hall. As the man tapped on Ned's door, Vi turned and fled down the steps. Going down the stairs, she could hear Ned's greeting.

"Come in, Mr. Platt. Ye're early."

Chapter 14

Two maids were already scrubbing the wax and ash from the table. Another was washing the floor. The housekeeper had every window open and was waving the smoke out with her apron. Gibbs had the two hang-dog valets in the corner and was lashing into them like a prosecutor at a murder trial.

"Leave them be, Gibbs. The bloody candle dropped on the table; that's all. You are all making too much of a fuss over nothing." Lyon glared at the unsmiling woman who was scissoring through the sleeve of his jacket and shirt. "You realize you've just committed a capital offense in cutting my coat. And ruined a perfectly good one, at that."

"A perfectly charred one. And you can afford another," Millicent whispered absently, crouching beside him. She peeled back the sleeve of the coat and laid his arm on the armrest of the chair.

Lyon leaned his head back and stared in disbelief at the commotion around him. He had been going over the estate's books in the library when he had inadvertently bumped the candelabra on the table, tipping it over and setting the papers on the table on fire. Millicent had left the room only seconds before, but Will had been in here and had pulled Lyon's chair away from the table before dousing the small fire. What he had not realized immediately was that his master's sleeve was on fire, too.

Lyon flinched at the sharp pain in his arm. He looked down at the burned shirtsleeve. The cloth appeared to be stuck to his flesh. She immediately stopped trying to pull it.

"Mrs. Page, have someone get Ohenewaa for me. Mr. Gibbs, I want his lordship taken back to his room. It is getting far too cold in here." Millicent turned her gray eyes toward Lyon. "You moved your arm."

It was not a question but a statement.

"No, you're mistaken."

She gave him a look that he could not comprehend, and then the chair was lifted by the valets. Whatever concern Lyon had a week ago about being paraded through the household with everyone around had been cast to the wind. Every servant in the place was racing about, but no one seemed to have a moment to stand and stare. Millicent stayed beside him all the way upstairs.

Inside his bedchamber, Ohenewaa was already waiting by the window.

"I didn't do it intentionally," he barked at the black woman.

The wrinkled eyelids were open only a fraction. The dark stare told him she was not convinced.

"You two have met?" Millicent asked, motioning for John and Will to move him to the bed.

"We're old acquaintances."

Lyon became suspicious when Millicent and Ohenewaa started whispering together. When his wife started for the door and the old woman came over to check on his arm, he voiced his complaint immediately.

"Where are you going? Bloody hell. You really don't intend to leave me alone with her now, do you? Millicent!"

Millicent hid her smile before giving him an exasperated look over her shoulder. "I'm going nowhere." She stopped at the door and whispered some directions to a servant who was hovering outside.

Ohenewaa waved John and Will away from the bed. The old woman then approached him and began checking the burn on his arm. After looking at it for a few moments, she retrieved some sharp shears from the table and cut most of the fabric away from around it. In the meantime, the servant Millicent had sent away returned with a large bowl of white liquid.

"I am not drinking this," he groused when Millicent brought it to the bed. "Whatever it is."

"It is only milk."

"All the same, I'll not have it."

"As you wish."

Millicent sat on the edge of the bed and, following Ohenewaa's quiet direction, draped Lyon's arm over the bowl. Using a small towel, she poured the liquid over his arm again and again.

"Bloody hell!" he growled, gripping the bed with his good hand.

After a few minutes of the treatment, the aching pain started to subside. Ohenewaa directed her to lay the soaked towel on the wound. After the second or third soaking, he saw the fabric of his sleeve had loosened. Carefully, the two women peeled the cloth off, exposing fully the ugly blisters and raw flesh.

A few minutes later, Gibbs came into the room to check on him. Millicent assured him that everything would be fine and sent the Highlander and the valets away.

With the burn cleaned, Lyon thought the ordeal was over, but Ohenewaa had other ideas. Using featherlight touches, she started to examine his right arm and hand in the places that were not burned. She felt and moved each finger, following the line of each bone through the hand to his wrist. She gently felt the bones and muscles up to the elbow, being especially careful around the burn, and then worked her way up beyond the elbow until the material of the coat and shirt stopped her.

"Remove his jacket and shirt."

"The hell she will."

"I shall be back in a few minutes."

As Ohenewaa left the room, Millicent picked up the shears, and Lyon turned sharply to her. "What is this woman doing?"

"Ohenewaa is going to examine you, as any physician would."

"Why?" He caught Millicent's hand.

"Because she knows medicine as well as or better than the doctors you have been seeing. And because I asked her to do this," she said softly. "She won't hurt you, Lyon. I will not move from your side. Please allow her to tend to you."

He couldn't refuse her. "Very well, then. But no more cutting. Help me out of these." With her help he shrugged out of the coat. "You don't believe just because she healed a dog last week, she can heal me, too."

"She *liked* that dog, and you clearly don't believe she likes you."

"The old hag told me so herself."

"This is not the time to be so disagreeable," Millicent whispered. "Please, Lyon. I think she knows things that those highly educated physicians you have been dealing with have been blind to."

"And what do you think she knows?"

"Perhaps she can make use of the feelings and sensations that have been coming and going. The ones you ignore or try to hide." She met his gaze when he looked up startled at her. "I have seen it. Last week, when the glass cut you, your hand moved. Three days ago, when John was helping you out of bed, I think your foot was twisted, and I believe you straightened it yourself. And then, last night you were having a nightmare, and I saw the muscles in your leg move."

There was no rhyme or reason to what his body did, it seemed. Lyon had no control over what he was capable of moving and when. But he didn't want to say any of this to Millicent. He didn't want to raise any false hopes in her. Instead, he admired the loose ringlets that had escaped their tight confines and were now framing her face. She looked so soft. This was the way she had awakened him last night from his nightmare, and Lyon remembered how much he'd wanted to draw her mouth down and kiss her.

He wanted to do the same thing now.

"The movements were involuntary. They don't mean a thing."

Ohenewaa returned, carrying bottles of different liquids that she proceeded to line up on the table.

Millicent leaned closer, tantalizing him with her nearness. "I should like to grasp at every chance, no matter how small. Many people here believe in her, Lyon. I am not saying that she can heal you completely, but we would be fools not to give her a chance to help as much as she can."

"Do as you please." He let go of her hand. "But I think you are wasting your time."

Beneath his long, dark hair, his neck was strong and powerful. His shoulders were wide and his chest muscular. Lyon was thin, though, and his ribs showed through the skin, reflecting the weeks of refusing food and nourishment.

Millicent's throat was dry by the time she finished removing his shirt. They had been married nearly a month. She had spent her nights at his bedside. She had been present during the changing of his clothes and even during sponge baths by his servants. But none of those moments had felt as intimate as removing his shirt herself.

Ohenewaa came back to his bedside with a bottle of ointment and a few clean cloths. "Spread this gently over the burn on his arm and then wrap it loosely with this."

Millicent brought the jar to her nose. "It smells familiar."

" 'Tis a decoction of the bark of the elm tree. 'Twill dry the pus that will soon be forming, and help the healing process."

Millicent was grateful for having something to do, and she went to work while the healer started examining Lyon's body.

"You are too tense. Relax," Ohenewaa said softly to him. The woman's palm was pressed flat against the skin of his chest, moving in slow circles. "Let your body talk to me."

"You accused me of talking too much," Lyon retorted, moving his gaze momentarily from the ceiling.

"Close your eyes. Let your mind float away from here to a peaceful time in your life. Then your body will tell me where there is pain."

Millicent was surprised when he didn't protest or argue. She saw him close his eyes and give himself up to the touch of the old woman. She went back to her own task of dressing his wound. After she finished, Ohenewaa motioned to her to remain at the bedside.

It was soothing to watch her. Following the movements of the wrinkled hands over his chest and shoulders and arms, Millicent felt the calming effect of them on her as well. After a time Ohenewaa paused.

"Now I need to check his legs. You must remove his shoes, stockings, and breeches."

Heat rushed into Millicent's face. "I shall go and get one of the valets." She rose quickly to her feet.

"No." Lyon's eyes opened slightly. "I don't want any new rumors circulating in this house. You can manage it."

She took a deep breath. She had been sexually aroused simply taking the man's shirt off. Now his breeches!

Ohenewaa walked back to her table of medicines. Suddenly the room felt too hot. Lyon was lying on top of the bedclothes. Millicent took a folded blanket from the bottom of the bed and spread it across his middle. To make matters worse, he was watching her every movement.

"In case you're considering using those shears," he said in a low voice, "you can put that thought out of your mind. My stockings and breeches don't trust them . . . and the same thing goes for any parts of my body that you might encounter."

"Why don't you close your eyes and let your body talk to me?" she asked quietly, trying to inject some humor.

She moved to the foot of the bed and removed his shoes and peeled off the stockings. Without thinking, she ran her hands down one calf. Lack of exercise had shrunk the muscles somewhat. Her fingers moved up to the buckles below the knee on his breeches. Millicent's hands shook as she started undoing them. The skin beneath her touch was so warm.

"Keep this up, and you'll see very soon that my body

does indeed have something to tell you. That doesn't trouble you, does it?"

He was mocking her, teasing her. But his voice was beginning to sound a little strained. Steeling herself, Millicent held her breath and moved up to stand beside the blanket that covered his middle. The pulsing of her blood rang in her ears. She was thankful for the dimness of the chamber, for she could feel her face and ears burning. Her gaze remained focused on the weave of the blanket, and her hands brushed against his stomach as she reached under the covering.

"Get Gibbs."

At his curt direction, she leaped back from the bed and ran for the door.

"The news from the Borders is quite disturbing, m'lady. The Earl of Dumfries has begun to clear the farms to the west, raising the crofters' rents to exorbitant rates. As of the writing of this letter, it appears that some two hundred tenants have taken refuge at Baronsford since Michaelmas. My man says he's been told that perhaps five hundred more went to Glasgow with the hope of moving on to the American colonies." Sir Richard put down the letter that he had received from the Borders. "The earl should be told."

"No," the dowager asserted stubbornly. "He is not ready for this."

"As you wish, m'lady, but his lengthy absence is only adding more meat to the stew of rumor bubbling amongst the tenants. Many fear that with the earl's injury and the marriage to an Englishwoman—along with the fact that he signed the lands over to Pierce—Baronsford's farms will be next to go. They are already talking of him never coming back."

The dowager closed the book on her lap with a snap and glared at her old lawyer. "Under Millicent's care, Lyon is making great improvement. Relaying any such news to him now would only add strain and hinder further progress."

"You think she would not accompany him to Baronsford if he were to decide to make the journey?"

"I don't think it, Sir Richard. I am certain of it. And I do not believe anything of value will be accomplished if he were to go right now—for Lyon or for the people at Baronsford. Find some other way to put the tenants at ease. Pass on the news of the earl's progress. Write to Walter and have him lower the rents. Move every sheep off the farms, if that'll calm them. Whatever needs to be done, get their minds off such foolishness. Tell them I'm gasping for my last breaths, and they should begin mourning for me."

"That they shan't do, m'lady. The tenants at Baronsford are more wary of your tactics than your sons are. They all believe you'll outlive the entire family. But about the earl, you do realize that we can delay passing on this news for only so long. 'Tis his right to know if he is improving. And knowing your son, he'll be wanting to go back to Baronsford before the planting season anyway. How can we not tell him what he'll find there?"

"You are talking about the man he once was. You and I both know that Baronsford is no longer his responsibility. He might still simply tell us to notify his brother Pierce of all these problems. Have you forgotten his anger the last time he left Baronsford? He wanted never to return."

"I've not forgotten, m'lady. But that was the pain of the moment talking. Signing those papers was an act of frustration and nothing else. The tenants, Pierce, you, and I all know that he is the one who can save Baronsford. We all want to remember him as the man he once was, and *I* believe he will be that man again in time."

"I want to believe that, too," the dowager responded quietly. "But we have to give him time. We cannot push him into things that he is not ready for. He is coming along, it appears, but I do not want to set him back even a day."

Chapter 15

Lyon threw his napkin on the tray, hiding what he hadn't eaten of his breakfast. "What torture have you devised for me today, Madame de Sade?"

"Something very painful."

He noticed the dark circles beneath her eyes when Millicent leaned over him to pick up the tray. She was beginning to look paler and more drawn every day. "Excellent. When do we start?"

"Don't be impatient. Soon enough." She handed the tray to John to take out. "A few hours of uninterrupted sleep seem to have done you some good."

"You again spent the night here in this room, did you not?"

"I did."

"Why? I told you I have no need of a watcher, especially when I am knocked unconscious by the dark magic the witch is using to subdue me. I should ask her to use the same thing on you." He caught her wrist when she bent to pick up a cup and saucer that had been left on the table next to his chair. Her gaze flew to his in surprise. "You don't look very well."

"Thank you. But my health is fine."

"You look pale."

"I was born with this look, and there is not much I can do to change it."

"What I meant to say is that you look tired." She tried to pull herself free, but he tightened his hold. "We cannot allow you to become sick."

"Why?"

"Because then I would be left with no one to torment."

Gibbs cleared his throat at the door.

"Do not think it or say it," Lyon growled at his manservant. He let go of his wife's hand. As Gibbs went wordlessly to the hearth and began poking at the fire, Millicent went about quickly tidying up the room. Lyon watched her carefully. She had lost weight, too. Even her dress was hanging off her.

"The scheduled torture for today is to expose you to the ghastly out-of-doors. Sunshine, winter air." She took a woolen blanket from a chest in the corner. "We have selected a delightfully protected spot within the walls of the gardens and—"

"I am not going outside, nor I am going downstairs today."

She whirled on him, hands on her hips. "Why? I know you are too stubborn to admit it, but you have been enjoying—"

"Because you are getting ill."

"I am not."

"You will if you don't get a few good hours of sleep yourself—and in a real bed." He didn't give her a chance to voice a protest. "I'll tell you what I shall do. If you promise to retire to your bedroom this instant and settle into your bed for a few hours, I will pursue whatever bloody routine you have managed to plan out for me."

"It is only half past ten on a very beautiful morning. I promise to go to bed tonight."

"No." He shook his head. "You go now."

"There are other things that I need to see to today. The new stonemason will be—"

"Gibbs."

"Aye, m'lord?"

"Tell the man we shall pay him his day's wages and then send him away until tomorrow." Lyon turned back to her. "Anything else can wait or be handled by others."

She stood for a moment, looking at him. She must

have been genuinely tired, he thought, for no argument rose to her lips. At that instant, his physical shortcomings once again stabbed at him. What he wouldn't give to be able to walk Millicent to her bedroom right now, to be able to care for her a little as she had been caring for him.

Violet's heart climbed into her throat at the sight of Ned talking to Mr. Gibbs by the door to the servants' hall.

He was holding his hat in one hand. He had made an attempt to comb his blond hair and bind it at his neck. His woolen coat was open and his broad chest was visible beneath it. She saw two of the scullery maids giggle and cast flirtatious looks his way as they passed him heading to the kitchen. In spite of herself, Vi felt her claws emerge.

While the Scotsman continued to talk, Ned's eyes scanned the room and paused when he saw her. Vi held her breath, waiting for his reaction. She had cried her heart out last Saturday on her way back from St. Albans. She had promised herself that she would not go alone to Knebworth Village as long as he was still working there. She did not want to see him or be left alone with him for a minute. She had learned an ugly lesson, and she knew she was fortunate to have a respectable job and a bed to sleep in after such a huge mistake. But now, with that engaging smile appearing at the corners of his mouth, with those eyes seeing only her, Violet nearly forgot her name, never mind the promises she had made to herself.

Mr. Gibbs looked over his shoulder, following the direction of Ned's gaze, and Violet hurriedly moved on through the room. No one had made any announcement, but everyone at Melbury Hall knew that the Highlander was to be the next steward. And this suited just about everyone, including Vi. Mr. Gibbs was strict, but he had a sense of humor. He was also obviously sweet on Mrs. Page, a feeling that the housekeeper appeared to share. That in itself was a good sign that he was going to stay.

*   *   *

Millicent rolled over in the bed and stared at the half-light that surrounded her. For a few moments she was totally confused. The day, the hour, even how she had ended up in bed were a mystery to her. And then she remembered: She had come to her room before noon to rest for a couple of hours.

Whoever had lit the fire had obviously done it hours ago, for the embers on the hearth held only a faint reddish glow. She climbed out of bed, and the feel of the cold floor beneath her bare feet awakened her completely. Lighting a taper from the embers, she looked at the clock on the mantel. It was almost twelve. Midnight. But how could that be?

Millicent stood in the darkness, listening. The house was quiet. It appeared that everyone was asleep. A sudden thought made her reach for her wrap. Had anyone changed the dressing on the burn on Lyon's arm this afternoon?

As she washed her face and rinsed out her mouth, she glanced at her reflection in the looking glass. With her tousled hair hanging loose around her shoulders, she looked terrifying enough to frighten a ghost. She ran a hand impatiently through the mess and headed for the door.

The corridor was dark. She would just take a quick peek inside Lyon's room to make certain he was asleep. Passing Ohenewaa's door, she recalled promising the older woman the night before that she would stop to see her today for some ointments she was preparing for Lyon. Millicent could not believe she had wasted an entire day in bed.

She didn't knock. Quietly pushing the door open, she slipped inside Lyon's room. By the light of the dying fire, he looked to be asleep. She closed the door behind her and padded silently across the floor.

"Did you sleep well?"

She was startled to hear his voice and find his eyes open. He was watching her.

"Too well. I cannot believe how long I slept. I had

specifically asked Mrs. Page to send someone to awaken me by early afternoon."

"I ordered Mrs. Page not to allow a single person to disturb you."

"I see then that I was outranked." She smiled at him and looked down at his arm. "Thank you. I didn't realize how tired I was until I crawled between those sheets. Did anyone change the dressing on your arm this afternoon?"

"No, I wouldn't let them near me."

"I see." Millicent retrieved some clean dressings and the bottle of ointment Ohenewaa had placed on the bedside table last night. She sat carefully on the bed beside him. "So this means I have not worn out my usefulness."

"There is little chance of that."

Perhaps it was the words or maybe the way he said them, but Millicent felt a subtle warmth wash through her. She gently lifted his arm from under the blankets and laid it on her lap. His nightshirt had a wide sleeve. She started inspecting the wound.

"Does it still hurt?"

"Nothing to speak of."

Her feet were bare and cold, so she tucked them under her. The serenity of being here, of doing this for him, filled her with a feeling she had never experienced. Perhaps it was the privacy of the two of them as they were, while the quiet of the night surrounded them. Millicent couldn't explain it, but she felt happy and content. The blisters on his arm looked clean, despite a couple of them having burst. She gently applied some more of the ointment and started wrapping it again. "I expected you to be asleep."

"I tried, but I couldn't. The witch brought her potions in earlier tonight." He motioned with his good hand toward the window. Millicent saw the half-dozen bottles crowding the tabletop.

"Did she give you any instructions?"

"Of course. Don't eat them or inhale them. Only apply them. They are all the same thing. A new jar for each night, she said."

"Did you have someone apply them for you tonight?"

He gave her an incredulous look. "The . . . whatever it is . . . is to be rubbed onto my skin. Just the idea of Gibbs or Will or John spreading the stuff on me is revolting. Besides, I think Ohenewaa is a fake anyway."

"Why should you think that?"

"What kind of physician refuses to say what is wrong with you and whether she can heal you or not? The woman spent hours inspecting every mole on my body and still says nothing."

Millicent rose from the bed and walked over to the bottles of ointments. "She was not inspecting moles, and you know it. And even if it was only for one night, you had some uninterrupted rest."

She picked up one of the bottles and smelled it. There was something familiar and earthy about the scent. It was like something she might have smelled in the woods.

"Did she tell you anything else?"

"Are you actually going to use it?"

She carried one of the bottles back to him. "You don't have to look so horrified. I am going to try some on this same arm." Before he could object, she resumed her previous position on the bed and started rolling the nightshirt up as far as it could go.

She dipped her fingers in the bottle. It was oily but not unpleasant.

"It feels cold." She started rubbing it gently on his arm, above and below the burn. Beneath her touch, as she continued to spread the ointment, she could feel his skin begin to warm. "But it changes quickly. Do you feel it?"

He didn't respond. She carefully worked it into the skin, up to the shoulder.

Millicent looked into his face. "I'm using only my fingertips, but I feel the heat of it seeping into my hands, moving up my arms and through my body." To prove her point, she dipped her fingers into the jar again, but this time instead of his arm, she rubbed it on the narrow span of his chest showing through the open collar of the nightshirt. The muscles flexed and moved beneath her touch. "Do you feel it now?"

"I do."

Leaning against him, she dipped her hand into the jar again, but as she was going to return it to his arm, Lyon's left hand reached across and took hold of her wrist.

"I want to feel it here," he said, bringing her fingers back to his chest.

Between the dancing shadows of the room and the beard covering his features, she could see little of his expression. His hand remained on top of hers, though, guiding her as she rubbed his chest in wider circles. His skin continued to warm beneath her touch, but Millicent's body began to burn. This was more than the fleeting sensuality of touching his body. There was an intimacy and a silent awareness between them. Feeling him react to the gentle caress of her fingers thrilled her.

"Why not close your eyes and let this have its effect?"

"I prefer to watch you."

Their gazes locked. Millicent didn't know what was happening to her, but she found herself being drawn uncontrollably to him. She leaned on his chest, her fingers working a slow path up his neck. The memory of the kiss they had shared before filled her mind. Wordlessly, she brushed her lips against his—once, softly, gently, and then again. His lips were warm, inviting. Summoning her courage, she let her mouth linger a bit longer. Her tongue hesitantly teased the seam of his lips.

His good hand slipped around the back of her head. Millicent felt his mouth open up beneath hers, drawing her in. Enthralled with her position of control and by the curiosity of the heat that was spreading through her, limb by limb, she deepened the kiss. Their tongues danced and mated.

A hungry groan escaped Lyon's lips, and his fingers delved and fisted in her hair. She answered and matched his urgency with hers. She moved on top of him. Her hands held his face, she threaded her fingers through his hair, and she was lost in the play of their lips and tongues and the power of a kiss that continued on and on.

Though she had been married for five years, she had never been kissed or ever kissed anyone like this. Millicent realized that the joy of this one act exceeded by far the horrid sexual encounters she had experienced with Wentworth.

Her head angled to deepen the kiss, and Lyon's passion surged. She reveled in his taste and scent, and her body moved restlessly on him, unconsciously seeking a better fit. Suddenly his arm tightened around her, and he groaned in frustration. Breathless and mortified, she tore her mouth away.

"I am so sorry." She tried to scramble off him, but his grip only tightened more. "What have I done? Lyon, I am so sorry."

"Wait! Don't go." His breathing was as uneven as hers.

Millicent was too embarrassed to look into his face. She had practically attacked him. Tears of confusion rushed into her eyes. She remembered so vividly how helplessly she had lain beneath Wentworth's body, time and time again, while he had his way with her. And now she had become the monster, a predator.

"Get beneath these blankets."

With her heart in her throat, she looked at him in confusion. Lyon's hand moved from her back, and he gently wiped off the wetness on her face.

"You are shivering. Get beneath the blankets with me and stay."

It would have been so much easier to run away, to hide in her own bedchamber. But she could not run. This was different. The brutality and the sadness of her past forced her to open her eyes and face these unfamiliar sensations. She wanted better, and she was not running away. She was not going to be frightened.

Without another word, Millicent slipped beneath the covers and nestled against his warm body. Taking her hand, he pressed it against his heart.

*   *   *

The black child's heart was pounding hard. Jasper Hyde could see the vein at his temple pulsing relentlessly. On his face and neck and throat, there were more than a dozen dark pimples. The boy had passed a wretched night of fever and pain. Hyde had been told everything, but he could see for himself what was afflicting the slave. It was smallpox.

"Take him to the forecastle. Keep him away from the rest," Hyde said to the ship's master, who stood ready to pass on the order. "I want a general inspection of the slaves. The crew needs to be made aware, too. I want to know if there are any more cases."

He was pacing the quarterdeck when the answer came. It was a single case, but it could imperil the entire ship. He could lose his entire cargo of slaves. He called to the ship's master.

"Kill the boy. And the two who were nearest to him. Over the side with them all."

Jasper Hyde awoke with a gasp. His body was burning. Sweat dripped from his face, and he pulled off his periwig. Afternoon sunlight poured into the room from the large windows of his study. He must have fallen asleep in his chair after the late breakfast.

Suddenly panicking, he touched his chest, his neck, his face, checking for the rashes. None. He didn't have smallpox. There was nothing wrong with him.

As if to contradict his thought, a burning pain sliced through his heart. He grabbed his chest and leaned his head back. It was like the twist of a knife, the heat of a poker. He pressed his chest, trying to rid himself of the pain.

"Damn you, Ohenewaa," he cursed, trying to breathe.

The witch was everywhere, digging her withered hands into him and steadily tearing the life out of him, out of his fortune. The news had reached him this morning: A slave ship Hyde had invested over twenty thousand pounds in less than three months ago had been deliberately run aground on a beach near Accra on the coast of Africa. The slaves had mutinied and taken over the ship, murdering the captain and crew. Two hundred sev-

enteen slaves had disappeared back into the bush. The
ship was lost, all gone, and due entirely to the curses of
a filthy black witch.

Hyde barked at the door when he heard the knock.
The pain in his chest was easing, but he didn't dare move
when Harry's face appeared.

"Mr. Boarham is here to see you, sir."

"Who the hell is he?"

Harry's eyes motioned to someone standing behind
him. "The surgeon who bled Dr. Dombey before his
death. You sent for him."

Hyde realized his hand was shaking when he removed
it from his chest. "Send him in."

Boarham entered the chamber cautiously, and Hyde
watched the man's eyes darting from side to side, taking
in the whole room. Whether he was assessing the value
of every item in sight or making sure that a trap was
not waiting for him, Hyde had no way of telling. The
man had kept his hat, a greasy tricornered affair too
small for his head, and it was propped on top of an old
bagwig he was wearing. His face was badly pocked, and
for a small-shouldered man Boarham had a suspiciously
large belly. Hyde decided he probably carried his entire
fortune in a satchel beneath his coarse woolen coat and
matching waistcoat.

Boarham approached and doffed the hat with a nervous bow.

"Yer servant, sir. Ye're needin' to be bled, sir?"

"No."

"I've the finest leeches in London, sir. And I've served
the finest. Even the Lord Mayor's butler's cousin, sir."

"No." Hyde answered sharply. "You were with Dr.
Dombey when he died, weren't you?"

"Dr. Dombey? Oh, I know who ye mean. Nay, sir,
not when he died, but I visited him the night before. He
was good at taking his salts, he was. I had his slave
woman make some rice milk for him for supper. O'
course, I was astonished when she put an egg in it. But
he was right as rain when I went away, sir. As I recall
the next morning was market day. And 'twas sleeting.

Aye, the ground was ankle-deep with muck and mire when I went to the sheep pens. I didn't get back to Dombey until the old gent had passed on. You see I never like to miss market day, sir, and—"

"Dr. Dombey owed you money, didn't he?"

"Well . . ." The leech stuck his finger in one ear, took out a ball of wax, and examined it absently before flicking it across the room. "He had all kinds of creditors knockin' on his door, and I wasn't chargin' him much. But now that ye mention it—"

"I was hoping I might make good on his debt, Mr. Boarham. He left some money with his slave to give to you. I have it."

"That's mighty Christian of ye, sir." The drool practically hung from the man's lip.

Hyde leaned forward in his chair. "You are not the first one that she cheated—the slave woman—and that is why, being a good friend of Dombey, I have taken it on myself to set the wrongs to right." He opened a small wooden casket from the table beside his chair and took a bag of coins from it. "Now, how much did he owe you?"

Boarham's hands clutched the edges of his hat, and he held it to his chest. "I . . . I believe 'twas two guineas, sir."

Hyde drew a handful of coins from the bag and watched his visitor's eyes light up at the sight of gold. "And I thought he owed you so much more. I have fifty pounds here, Mr. Boarham."

"Maybe he owed me more, and I couldn't remember?" he blurted quickly.

"Perhaps he did. But I think your memory is very important, Mr. Boarham. Perhaps you might even remember that Dr. Dombey's death was caused by the greedy slave who is holding on to all his money."

"That old slave woman, sir?"

"The same one, Mr. Boarham." Hyde started stacking the gold coins next to him.

"I remember her well, sir." His gaze locked on the coins. "She looked to be a low-down poisoner, sir, if ever I seen one."

"Did you know she is a witch?"

The surgeon looked up startled and quickly crossed himself. "Is she, now?"

"Aye, my good fellow. And you are going to help me prove it."

Chapter 16

"The day is wasting away, man. Where the blazes is she?" Lyon bellowed as Gibbs entered the library with John in tow.

"Your wife is just finishing her interview with the stonemason. She said she will meet you in the gardens."

"When? Next bloody week?" he grumbled in annoyance.

Lyon's irritation had begun this morning when he had awakened to find Millicent gone. After that, while his valets were getting him ready for the day, she had poked her head in only fleetingly, mumbling excuses about the tasks she had to see to that morning. And she had not come back to see him even once, not even during breakfast. Now it was eleven o'clock in the morning, and Lyon was at the end of his damned patience.

" 'Tis a wee bit brisk out there, m'lord, though nothing we've not seen rounding the Cape of Good Hope on our way to India, I'd say. That aside, Lady Aytoun has insisted that ye should be wearing a hat."

Lyon took the hat Gibbs placed on his knee and fired it across the floor. "Tell her if she is so bloody worried, then she can come and see to it herself."

The valets lined themselves up on either side of his chair and carefully lifted him. As they tipped him ever so slightly, he blasted them all for their incompetence. With the air of a true martyr, Gibbs retrieved the hat and led the entourage out the door and through the house.

It was difficult for Lyon to understand, but last night had provided a fulfillment he'd not felt in months. The explosive reaction of his body to her kiss was stunning. And the warmth that had spread through him every time he'd stirred during the night and found Millicent still at his side had been remarkable. In the past, he had always felt the urge to leave a woman's bed when the evening's lovemaking was complete, but the feel of this woman against him last night had changed his mind.

Lyon knew he was starting to depend on Millicent. Perhaps he was just substituting her for the comfort that the opium drops had brought him. But hell, he thought, even if he was, the woman was flesh and bone, and he'd be dashed if it wasn't more interesting to lose himself in her kisses than to spend his time in a daze.

Outside, the winter air was indeed bracing, and Lyon took a few breaths, trying to adjust his lungs to the cold. They carried him down toward the old-fashioned formal gardens. Over the wall he could see trellises and arbors arranged amid symmetrically organized squares of herbs and flowers and paths of greensward. Beyond the lower wall of the garden, a landscape of fields and woods and evergreens stretched away from the house. Lyon glanced about him critically. The property needed some work, to be sure. But having glanced quickly at Melbury Hall's ledgers from recent years, Lyon already knew that renovation and upkeep of pleasure gardens and vistas were the last of Millicent's priorities.

He ducked slightly as they conveyed him through the gated and arched entry to the formal garden. Carefully they lowered the chair and positioned him next to a stone bench to the left of the gate. It was a place protected by trellises and stone walls that blocked most of the wind and yet captured the sun. A pair of cardinals flitted from branch to branch of a vine on the wall nearby. The male was more brightly colored than the female, and the birds went after the few bright orange berries still left on the vine.

"I am here. So where is she?"

"Here!" Millicent called breathlessly, walking briskly

down the path. She was holding his hat in one hand and some newspapers and a blanket tucked under an arm. Lyon stared at the well-worn woolen cloak. Its hood and lace edging framed her flushed face prettily. Wisps of steam escaped her lips.

"Leave us," he ordered his valets as soon as she arrived at his side.

"Thank you. I shall call you when his lordship is ready to come inside." She smiled at the men, and they bowed and took their leave. She dropped the papers and his hat on the bench and began unfolding the blanket. "We cannot have you catch a chill on your first day out, now, can we?"

"Don't *you* have something warmer to wear?" he asked irritably, watching her tuck the blanket around his legs. "Your servants dress better than you do."

"This cloak is quite sufficient, thank you, and you can put a stop to your peevishness. This is a beautiful day, and I plan for both of us to enjoy it." Picking up his hat, she placed it on his head and leaned down before him—cocking her head critically from one side to the other—checking the fit. "Your head must be growing, for that hat seems too small. Of course, the long hair and the shaggy growth on your face might have something to do with the fit."

"I do not wear the hat over my beard."

"If you gave any thought to hiding your brooding disposition, perhaps you would."

"And the logistics of that?"

"Quite simple, really." She trailed her fingers down one side of his face. "I can attach two long bits of ribbon to the hat to loop about each of your ears."

"Very stylish."

"Of course, we shall have to be clever about it and make them long enough to cross again over the front, thereby fastening the hat securely over your mouth before the ribbons are tied in a handsome bow above your head."

He couldn't stop a smile from forming on his lips. "So very clever."

"I thought so." She returned his smile. "And thank you, this is far more pleasant."

She reached up to settle the hat one more time, but he caught the ribbons at the neck of her cloak and pulled her toward him until their lips brushed, lingering for a moment before pulling apart.

"I think *this* is better," he said in a low voice.

Lyon was hungry for more. He had been fantasizing about her mouth all too often of late. She kissed with a fervor that was unmatched in any woman he had ever met. Her mouth was an instrument of desire, and she gave and took with more passion than most were able to summon even in the very act of lovemaking. But he sensed Millicent's hesitancy this morning as she drew back and sat down on the bench, just out of his reach.

"Why did you leave me in the middle of the night?"

"The dawn was already upon us when I left." A deep blush was coloring her cheeks. "And with your valets sure to come in to check on you, I just didn't know how appropriate—"

"We are husband and wife, Millicent. Though I do not recall the ceremony all that clearly, I have seen the documents." He hoped to see her smile a little, but her face retained its seriousness. "Therefore, not that I give a damn what my servants think, I do not believe they would think it odd finding you in my bed. Certainly it would be no stranger than finding you asleep in a chair, as they have seen you often enough this past month."

She was avoiding looking up at him. Something else was bothering her.

"Unless you find lying next to a cripple so demeaning that—"

"On the contrary . . . I find sharing your bed to be quite pleasing."

Her words fluttered shyly in the air between them, like butterflies testing their wings for the first time. Lyon was willing to wager she had never in her life spoken of such things openly.

"Then why did you slip away like some thief in the night?"

"I am not accustomed to it," she continued, blushing fiercely. "How am I to know what is appropriate behavior? I thought I was expected to leave at some point during the night."

"Is that how things were between your husband and you? You made love, and then each of you retired to your respective bedrooms?"

"Made love?" The color washed out of her face. "I don't care to talk of my first marriage."

Turning slightly to hide her face from him, Millicent spread the newspaper on her lap and turned her attention fully to it. "What can I read to you this morning, m'lord? News of the colonies or the continent?"

"Whatever suits you." That was a lie. He wanted to hear about her life. He wanted to know that she had been as eager this morning to see him as he was to see her.

As he listened to her clear voice, he realized what he would like to know was the story of the woman herself. Nothing would interest him more than to hear the reasons for her insistence on keeping the doors of her personal past so tightly shut. But Lyon knew he desired the same privacy regarding his own past life. There were limits as to just how far he would push her for answers.

They were two strange birds, he thought. Both of them were still drawn to the same brightly colored berry that they had each found so bitter in the past. And yet they were unable to pass it by completely.

"I do not wish to hear any news of the outside world," he barked, cutting her off when a news article she read referred to the regiment of his youngest brother, David. How many times during his months of being confined to a chair or a bed had he thought of him? Lyon supposed David thought him guilty of pushing Emma over the cliffs. He would naturally think the worst. Lyon had ruined David's dreams by marrying Emma. But it was another thing entirely to murder her.

Lyon pushed the disturbing thoughts away and tried to focus on the moment. He softened his tone. "Put that aside, if you will. Tell me instead about your interview with the stonemason. Or tell me about the village, or the mess that deuced Gibbs is creating while he decides if he can lower himself to take on the position of bloody steward."

She glanced worriedly from his face to the paper and back to his face again. Annoyed, Lyon wondered if she had guessed the connection. She folded the newspaper and put it with the others beside her on the bench.

"Very well." She thought a moment. "I received another letter from your mother, the dowager, with the packet of newspapers this morning. She is considering my invitation of coming to Melbury Hall for a visit."

"Since when have you been corresponding with that crafty old woman? And why would you do such a mean-spirited thing as to invite her here?"

"Twice a week from the first week of our marriage, and because I love tormenting you. Are these answers satisfactory?"

Lyon snorted.

"Very well, then we are ready to move on." Millicent clasped her hands in her lap. "Perhaps you would like to tell me what you have found in those ledger books regarding the Melbury Hall farms. Then I can interrupt you and tear you to pieces for no reason."

The ridiculousness of her challenge was comical, and her words caught him off guard.

Lyon Pennington had always been serious to the point of surliness from the day he was born. He had maintained the reputation throughout his school years, during his years of service in India, and later among his peers. And then, after marrying Emma, he had added the fine quality of being vile-tempered on top of it. As a result, most people avoided confrontation with him at any cost. And those who didn't soon felt—quite painfully—the error of their ways. Indeed, from early on in his marriage, his enemies' only means of attacking him had been by way of rumor and innuendo. There were some who had gone to great lengths to connect scandal with his name.

"Are you ready for the inquisition, m'lord?"

"I will tell you what I perceive, and then you may do your worst, Madame Torquemada."

Lyon looked at Millicent's straight back and couldn't help but smile. She had courage and spirit, and he wondered how his mother and the family lawyer could possibly have possessed such foresight.

Chapter 17

⌒

Ohenewaa's examination of Lyon had not been limited to the time she spent with him after his arm
had been burned. The next day, Millicent learned that
the old woman had spoken with Gibbs extensively about
his master. And when she was finished with him, she
had tracked down John and Will and the other servants
who had helped with the earl's care after his accident.

Finding Ohenewaa in the kitchen—in a quiet corner
that had become one of her usual haunts—Millicent sat
down beside her. She wanted to know what the old
woman had learned and what she still needed to know.

The couple of hours she and Lyon had spent outside
this morning had done a world of good for him. His
coloring had improved; his appetite had grown. Of
course, his temperament could still be as foul as ever,
but she now found it flecked with silvery touches of
humor. After they had come in—while Millicent had
been busy working with Mrs. Page—Ohenewaa and
Lyon had spent some time together. And now, with him
lost in the books again in the library—this time with
Gibbs—Millicent was impatient to learn what she could
of his condition.

"The only information I lack comes from not having
seen the surgeon set the bones." Ohenewaa paused
thoughtfully. "You know that any English doctor would
either laugh at you or commit you to Bedlam for putting
your husband's care into an old slave's hands."

"That matters very little to me." Millicent smiled gently. "Will you share with me what you have discovered thus far?"

Ohenewaa nodded. "Aye. And you should know that whatever I tell you your husband already knows. I even asked him if I might relay it all to you."

"Was his response, 'Do as you bloody please'?"

"Not quite so polite as that, but he said something similar."

"Why does that not surprise me?"

Ohenewaa's eyes opened more than usual, and one gray eyebrow arched expressively. "Despite his bad temperament, he does not suffer from madness."

"I never thought so."

"I believe he suffers from what old Dombey would have called partial palsy."

This confirmed what Gibbs had said of the first surgeon's opinion. Millicent kept her silence, though, waiting for Ohenewaa to offer more.

"The earl had a great injury inflicted upon his head when he fell from those cliffs last summer. I have talked to those in his service. At the time the greatest worries were the breaks in his legs and arms. No one wanted to amputate his limbs. While they worked on him, his lordship spent two full days lying unconscious. Of course, that was good, too, for it saved him much pain."

Pain of all types, Millicent thought. She already knew that these same cliffs, on the same day, had claimed the life of his wife. And how ruthless the gossips were to proclaim that Lyon had been the cause of that fall, when he had nearly died himself.

"His manservant tells me that once your husband regained consciousness, it took another fortnight before he was able to control his muscles or feel anything from his shoulders down. He even had difficulty breathing. His condition remained so severe that the family considered what arrangements needed to be made for a funeral."

His brothers were content to bury him rather than nurture him to health, Millicent thought cynically. When his siblings would do nothing, the dowager had taken responsibility for him, in spite of her own infirmity and advanced age.

"But the feeling and movement gradually began to return. A month after the accident, the earl could sit up. In another month, when the splints were off both arms, he had gained the full use of his left hand and arm. But then another fall—this time from a chair—and he broke the right arm again. I am told the splints from this second break were not removed until a few days before your marriage."

Millicent rose to her feet and walked to the window. From here she could see just the corner of the garden where she and Lyon had spent the morning. She had heard him laugh once this morning. The vibrant sound of it, like music, continued to play in her mind. No matter where she would go and what else might be on her mind, Lyon was now a part of her daily existence.

"You are saying they were gradual improvements for the first couple of months, but nothing after that?" She turned around to face Ohenewaa.

"So it appears. I think his impatience with the confinement, added to a constant melancholy that plagued him, inhibited the progress. He is a man whose spirit cannot be fettered or shut in. Instead of improving, Gibbs told me, he became worse, and the various medicines from the physicians did nothing to make him better." Ohenewaa could not hide her disgust. "There was no effort made to exercise and strengthen the limbs, but only to keep him confined in a bed or a chair. There was no one to clear and challenge his mind. Instead, he was kept subdued and out of the way. If you tie the legs of the great lion and keep him in a dark hole, he will soon refuse to eat. And then he will die. Kill the spirit, and the noblest of creatures will die."

Having lived with Lyon for over a month, Millicent understood more than ever how a situation like that would have killed him. The dowager's plea to her that first day to marry him made so much sense to her now. The old woman knew what was happening to her son.

"True, they managed to save his limbs, but in the process they were cutting off the sustenance he needed to live."

"What can be done for him now?" Millicent asked.

"He does not want to believe it, but there is no saying that he shan't be able to regain more movement in his limbs. Considering the extent of his injuries, the length of time he has been healing is short."

"One thing my husband lacks is patience. Is there anything that might help his body and not dull his mind?"

"I already have given him an ointment I call Matthiolus salve. 'Tis good for all pains in the joints. Something better than that would be an ointment of leopard's bane, but I do not have all that I need to mix that here. Jonah tells me, though, that the apothecary shop in St. Albans might have what is required."

"Leopard's bane. Even the name sounds fitting," Millicent said wryly. "I shall send someone for it today. And if you need anything else, that can be purchased as well."

"Another way of helping him is to force him to move those joints."

"Do you mean having someone else move them for him?"

She shrugged. "I already know no one could force him to sit through any exercise like that unless he himself is willing. But if he can be persuaded, he may heal more quickly."

"What do you mean?"

"All the ointments will do is help to warm and stimulate the joints. For him to walk again, though, he needs to ignore the voice in his head that says he cannot. Your husband's body is healing, but he does not believe it."

Millicent's head reeled with all this information. This was not at all what she had been expecting a month ago. Everything was changing so quickly, but this was not the time to confuse herself with the thoughts of that.

"Do you really believe that he has a chance to recover fully?"

Ohenewaa nodded her head. "You are the only one

who can persuade him to do things that he resists doing. 'Tis in your hands to nurture his spirit to health, too.''

The afternoon's sun was still bright and warm through the single window of the steward's office, and Lyon stretched with pleasure at the feel of it. The farms' books lay open in front of him. He looked up as Gibbs and the bailiff, Jonah, entered the room.

Lyon looked at the young bailiff. He was not a big man, but he looked strong and his eyes were clear and intelligent. From what Lyon had heard from Millicent, Jonah had been outspoken and somewhat rebellious during his servitude to Wentworth, and he had suffered greatly for it. Still, he had managed to establish himself as a leader among the workers at Melbury Hall, and Millicent had apparently trusted him. Since being made bailiff, though, he had not yet shown the confidence that the position required. It must be difficult, Lyon thought, to go from the depths of slavery to a position of authority. Who could blame the man if he took a while to feel comfortable in his new role?

Lyon noticed the amity that already existed between Gibbs and Jonah. *A good thing,* he thought.

"Gibbs and her ladyship both speak highly of you, Jonah," Lyon said after the initial introductions. "What do you say we put our heads together about these properties?"

Together, the three of them discussed Melbury Hall's farms and lack of income. Throughout, he encouraged the two men to be open in their thoughts on ways of improving things. Before long, the ex-slave was expressing himself without hesitation.

Jonah's detailed assessment of the present situation was clearly based on close scrutiny and thoughtful analysis. Lyon listened carefully as the bailiff spoke at length.

"There are tracts of land in the east farms, m'lord," he concluded, "that are surely capable of yielding many good crops. But they lie fallow, and the farm buildings are tumbling down from lack of use. The land is used only for sheep grazing. Even the dairy farm. Makes no sense to me, begging your pardon. Wool prices are down. The squire was partial to his horses, too, so we have too much grazing land here at the home farm. Solgrave, the estate to the west of us, plants barley, rye, some oats, and acres of wheat."

When Jonah paused, Gibbs asked what was stopping them from doing the same here. The bailiff told them of the lack of people in the outer farms. All the Africans had previously lived in the Grove, and it was not practical for workers to travel daily to work those farms. But now, with Lady Aytoun's project of building new cottages, the hope was to plant those fields in the spring.

Lyon told them what he had heard of new methods that were being used throughout the countryside. Agricultural methods were changing, with progress being made using crop rotation, forage crops, and new field design. For an hour and a half, they discussed better uses of the soil and the land.

Finally, talk turned to the idea of reorganizing the outer farms, leasing the land to families, and helping them restore or build whatever dwellings or outbuildings were needed. By the time Jonah left the room, Lyon was confident that the man would do well. He also found himself looking at Gibbs differently.

"I am quite impressed with how suited you appear to be for the position of steward. Who would have thought that such a dog could rise to such heights?"

The giant man scowled at the earl.

"I am serious, Gibbs. You have established a workable relationship with this bailiff, who will be a great help to you. You know the household. Already you have had enough time here to learn your way around and get to know everyone. And as far as doing the job of steward, you have helped Campbell enough times at Baronsford to handle anything here."

"Och, I wish I could say for sure, m'lord. Men are born into these sorts of positions, I'm thinking. Perhaps yer wife should be looking someplace else to fill the position. Do ye think she might just be asking too much of me?"

"You are a muscle-brained ox, to be certain, Gibbs," Lyon snapped at him. "You have no more faith in yourself than a stewed prune has. She is not asking you to sell your soul to the devil, man. She is only offering you a position in the household. A position in which you will excel. Speak up, you Highland ape. What is stopping you? Out with it."

Lyon knew what his man was thinking. For ten years they'd been inseparable. Where Lyon had gone, Gibbs had gone as well. When he had taken a commission, Gibbs had joined to serve with him. When his regiment had been dispatched to India to fight the Dutch, Gibbs had been at his side. When he'd fought duels against any number of scoundrels, Gibbs had faithfully served as his man. Now the Highlander was being offered a position that would give him a place of his own, in a sense.

Gibbs's dark brows were a straight line when he finally looked up. "It has to do with responsibilities, m'lord—responsibilities and loyalties. After all these years together, I just cannot have ye thinking that I have forgotten what ye did for me."

"I dragged your arse out of an oyster house. That's all." Lyon shook his head in disbelief, but he remembered the day very well. Wandering into an Edinburgh establishment on High Street on King George's birthday, Lyon had found a tall, slightly inebriated Highlander refusing to drink to the monarch's health unless the rest of the drunken mob would drink to Bonny Prince Charlie's. They'd been ready to stuff his rebellious carcass into Mons Meg and fire him from the ramparts of Edinburgh Castle. "And that was over a decade ago. Do you know how many times you have repaid me over the years for that day?"

"Nay, m'lord. 'Tis been a very fine thing, serving in your house over the years. But I've ne'er had the chance to repay ye. For as many years as I have been serving ye, I've been the envy of every manservant from Baronsford to Bath. Ye have always treated me no less than as an equal, and I have much to be grateful for on that score alone."

Lyon expelled his breath in frustration. "You are not leaving me, you deuced son of a horse thief. You shall be put in charge of things and making a bloody difference."

"Och, by the devil. If ye are thinking—"

"I'm thinking that I shall be a great deal harder on you if you don't take yourself out of here right now and tell my wife that you shall take the position she has offered you."

Gibbs glanced at the door and back at Lyon. "If ye are certain, m'lord."

"Get out."

Lyon watched him go to the door and open it. Before going, the Highlander threw a glance over his shoulder. "Thank ye, m'lord. I'll do ye and yer bride proud."

"I know you will."

With the door to the bedchamber left open and a dozen candles burning brightly on every table and shelf, Millicent tried to dispel all appearances of intimacy in the room as she prepared herself for the task ahead. Following her instructions, the valets had dressed Lyon in a nightshirt with wide sleeves and deposited him on the bed.

While John was still in the room, Millicent applied the ointments to her husband's right arm and changed the dressing on his burn, which was healing beautifully. But the short, stocky servant then asked to be dismissed, and Millicent was left alone to apply Ohenewaa's ointments to the rest of Lyon's partially dressed body.

By the time she was finished spreading the healer's ointment on one of Lyon's legs, her face was on fire, and she was drenched with sweat.

"Why not just call in the bloody household to chaperon us while you are doing this?"

She gave him a startled look. "I don't know what you mean."

"Really?" He lifted his chin challengingly. "You have

been nervous since dinner when you thanked me for Gibbs's deciding to accept your offer to make him steward.''

"You took me on your lap and kissed me."

"What is wrong with that?" he asked with a wry smile.

"There were at least half a dozen servants around, still serving the meal."

"And?"

Millicent had been excited and embarrassed and confused. He had simply ignored all of the shocked glances and unsuccessfully hidden grins of the servers. Of course, the fact that she had practically melted into him hadn't helped either.

"And nothing!" she whispered, dipping her fingers into the ointment and spreading it on his other leg.

Her long talk with Ohenewaa this afternoon had opened Millicent's eyes to the short-lived nature of her present situation. On the first day of meeting with the dowager, she had demanded that in the event of the earl's recovery, a divorce would be uncontested. Now it appeared that he would indeed recover, and perhaps speedily.

Millicent was no fool. She knew she would never be an accepted member of the *ton*. As a young woman of average looks with a fairly respectable lineage, she had been barely attractive enough to suitors to secure a marriage to an abusive sugar plantation owner with social aspirations. And in the years since, her looks and her luck had only deteriorated. She didn't want to imagine how objectionable Lyon would find her as a wife once he was completely healed.

"You don't need to do this if it makes you uncomfortable."

"I am not uncomfortable," she replied, meeting his amused gaze. She had made a bargain, and she was going to fulfill her part of it. "This is only the beginning of these treatments. The groom I sent to St. Albans was able to find several herbs Ohenewaa was looking for. She has already promised to prepare another ointment for you tomorrow. And I shall need to have John or Will help me every day to exercise—"

"This is all a waste of time. I have no bloody control of those limbs."

"Today you have no control. But tomorrow . . ." She paused, having finished rubbing the ointment on his leg; she pulled the blankets over him. "Tomorrow is a new day, with new surprises and greater promises."

He caught her wrist when she was about to tuck the blanket around his chest. "That is what I have been doing for all these months. Thinking of tomorrow. Knowing that nothing would change. Certain as a man can be that I shall continue to be a pathetic cripple, stuck in a chair for ten thousand tomorrows."

"Well, I am determined to change your mind on that, m'lord."

"How? By becoming distant? By running away?"

"No, I am here." She would help him, but she had to protect herself—and her heart. But how could she admit this to him? "I shall be here whenever you need me."

"Very well. Then spend the night here with me. In my bed, beside me."

"I don't see that—"

"Last night was the only restful night I have had in months. I want you here. I need you here."

He had tipped his hat to her and whispered good morning. He had smiled at her when he'd entered the servants' hall tonight. Violet didn't see anything wrong with serving Ned Cranch the late supper. Clearly he had found his manners once again, and Vi liked the way he was treating her.

Violet topped his cup of ale and sat across the table, watching his large, callused hands handle the food on his plate. As much as she hated to admit it, she missed the feel of those hands on her body. She looked up at his wide chest and thought of the crisp, curly hairs and the feel of them rubbing against her breasts. And that mouth biting and suckling her. She must have made a sound, for Ned's green eyes lifted from his food and met hers.

"Don't let yer thinking wander too far south, lassie,

or I'll be taking you down by the stables. If we make it that far."

Violet blushed with embarrassment and stared down at the deep grooves in the dining table. He was handsome and charming and the only lover she had ever had. But at the same time she needed to force herself to remember that he was mean and rough and had not thought twice about kicking her out of his room at that tavern in St. Albans. Violet knew she had to force herself to behave coyly, to remain cool and reserved, the way Mrs. Page did with Mr. Gibbs. It definitely would not do to drool after Ned whenever he came near her.

"Who's that one think she is, the bloody Queen of Sheba?"

Immediately annoyed with his tone, Violet followed the direction of Ned's gaze and saw Will, the lanky valet to the earl, holding a door open while Ohenewaa carried in a tray. The woman definitely had the look of a queen.

"She is a great healer."

"What the de'il does that mean? She's a witch?"

"No," she snapped at him. "That's Ohenewaa. She's quite knowledgeable about herbs and medicines. She was a slave to an English doctor for some forty years before Lady Aytoun brought her here. The women here at the Hall say she probably taught that doctor more about healing than she learned."

Violet watched with great admiration as the old woman glided through the room and disappeared into the kitchens with Long Will on her heels.

"The stories they tell about her ability to heal things are so impressive. Most of the black folk here knew her from the—"

"Ain't your mistress afraid of letting her near the food? I've heard stories about them witch doctors in the sugar islands. When they're not stirring up trouble with the slaves, they're poisoning the masters." He shoved his half-eaten meal away from him. "What if this one decides to poison us all with one of her brews?"

"That's a horrible thing to say." Violet frowned at

him. "Everyone trusts Ohenewaa. She wouldn't do anything like that. And that includes my mistress."

He snorted in disbelief and stabbed at a big chunk of meat on the plate.

Feeling compelled to defend Ohenewaa, Violet leaned toward him and lowered her voice. "Lady Aytoun bought her at an auction. That old woman was brought here in nothing more than rags."

"Aye? So what?"

"Well, her ladyship values Ohenewaa's opinion more than those of all those fancy doctors that have seen to his lordship since his accident. More than that doctor who came out from London. That's what I call trust."

"How's that? That woman is looking after the earl?"

Vi nodded exultantly. "None of those other physicians is even allowed to come here anymore. Her medicines are the only thing the earl takes. What she says goes. The mistress has put her husband's life in this woman's hands. That should tell you how much she values Ohenewaa."

Chapter 18

The mattress shifted slightly beneath their weight, and Millicent awoke with a start. Lying on her stomach at the very edge of the bed, she pushed up on her elbows and watched him. While still asleep, Lyon was trying to roll onto his side. She considered how she could help without waking him up. Before her sluggish mind could sort out a plan, though, he whispered something under his breath and rolled successfully onto his right side.

Millicent had given in to his request of spending the night in his bed. As odd as it felt, she was his wife, after all. And last night had been special for her, too. What harm could possibly come of it if she were to crawl beneath the sheets after he was asleep? She could keep a safe distance between them.

Looking at how close they were now, Millicent realized that her assumptions had been wrong. She intentionally had slept on the right side of the bed so that his good arm would not inadvertently brush against her body. But he had rolled toward her and, as she watched, his left arm reached out and came to rest across her back.

His regular breathing told her that Lyon was sound asleep, and Millicent laid her head back down on the pillow. She could not sleep, though. She had never spent the entire night in a man's bed. She lay there as the dawn's light slowly brightened the chamber, studying her husband's face.

He had a high, intelligent forehead and a straight

nose. The closed lids and long, dark lashes hid the eyes that turned a dozen different shades of blue, depending on his mood. Millicent wondered what the man looked like without his beard. There was no doubt in her mind, though, that Lyon Pennington would be the handsomest man she'd ever seen. Like some lowly mortal facing a god, Millicent knew she would probably just want to run away and hide.

And that would only be right. Then he would not need to face the humiliation of introducing her as his wife.

Millicent knew very well the ways of the social world Lyon inhabited. She had been an eager eighteen-year-old when she was introduced into the marital meat market of the London *ton*, but that eagerness had soon worn off. Suitors had barely looked at her. She had been too plain. She had been too thin. She had been too quiet. She had been too clever. She had been too everything but special. Gentlemen like Lyon Pennington—those whose fortunes and accomplishments and looks and manners placed them in airy realms far above the rest— did not even notice her. The ones who did were penniless boors who saw only the size of her dowry as an enticement.

The years of healthy living and a suitable education and a good family name were not enough. Millicent's self-confidence quickly drained away. Soon relegated to that wall of aging spinsters, she had suffered through five London Seasons of mortification. Then, at the advanced age of twenty-three, she had watched her uncle step in. He would have sold Millicent to the very devil just to get her off his hands. In fact, that was exactly what he did.

Millicent closed her eyes to halt the welling tears. She couldn't live with herself if Lyon should wake up now and see her like this. She was finished with self-pity. After Wentworth's death, she had found surprising strength by standing on her own two feet. This was how she wanted the Earl of Aytoun to remember her when they parted ways. Let him remember her strength, she thought.

She rolled slowly until her back was to him. Before she could slip out of the bed, however, his arm curled around her waist. Gently, he pulled her slowly back against his chest. Millicent didn't protest. She didn't make a sound but simply waited. Looking over her shoulder, she found him still asleep.

He whispered something again in his sleep and then—to her utter surprise—one of his legs moved, sliding over the top of hers. Her shift had ridden up in the night, and she could feel his warm skin touching her thigh. Millicent rolled toward him, not believing what had just happened. Perhaps this was all a dream. But he continued to move until she found herself lying flat on her back with half of her husband's sleeping body draped over her.

He had moved his leg. She did not dare to breathe. Stunned by the discovery, Millicent felt her mind reeling with thoughts of how she was going to awaken him—how she was going to tell him. The impact of his ability to move his leg—and what his reaction would be—had her spirits soaring. Ohenewaa had been correct. She'd said that the decision to heal lay with Lyon himself.

Her heart pounded with excitement, and she turned her head on the pillow to awaken him. His face was only inches away from hers. She could tell he was caught in the middle of a dream. His brow was furrowed and he was whispering again, words that she could make no sense of.

"Lyon," she whispered softly against his lips.

His body jerked once in his sleep, and the arm that was curled around her stomach moved. Millicent felt his hand drop to the edge of her shift. Lyon's leg moved again, rubbing against the sensitive skin of her bare thigh.

Millicent felt her throat go dry. Her voice was barely audible when she whispered his name again. He didn't awaken, but his hand slipped beneath her nightgown and moved upward with maddening slowness, along her thigh, her hip, the curves and hollows of her stomach, until he was cupping her breast.

A dozen times along that slow journey, she nearly grasped his hand, stopped him. A dozen times, though, she held back, unable to decide what she wanted more— to be touched by this man or to be free of any man's touch.

Her heart was hammering fiercely at the walls of her chest. A tight knot of fire had coiled itself somewhere in her middle, and Millicent found herself arching her back ever so slightly, pressing into his hand. The heat awakened by the simple touch, the sensitivity of her body to his caress, thrilled her. She edged closer to him, and Lyon's hand brushed lightly across the sensitive areola of her breast, making her nipple harden in response. Suddenly she knew she didn't want him to stop.

"Lyon." Millicent turned her face to him and brushed her lips against his. He stretched slightly, and his hand came to life on her body. He ran his fingers down over her belly and then up again to explore her breasts, feeling the fullness of one and then traveling to the other. His gentle touch was enough to make her breathe in sharply. Her body was quivering with excitement, and she felt herself growing moist. He seemed to be awakening, but Millicent found herself praying desperately that he wouldn't push her away once he opened his eyes.

She kissed him again, this time using her tongue to tease the seam of his lips. He emitted a groan in his sleep, and her shivers gave way to shudders as she felt him gently pinch an erect nipple.

When Lyon's hand left her breast and moved down her belly to the small triangle of hair at the junction of her thighs, her head rolled back on the pillow. She stared at the gray of the ceiling, and her lips parted slightly. Instinctively, her hips rose against his hand, and her legs opened for him. A soft whimper escaped her as his fingers slipped into the folds of her womanhood, lightly exploring, then finding and stroking the sensitive nub of desire.

Millicent's vision blurred and her breath shortened. Her body began to pulse to a rhythm that she had always associated with fear and pain. But that was before. What

she felt now was desire and anticipation so intense she
was afraid she might cry out.

Lyon was stroking her harder. She turned her head
on the pillow and found his mouth searching hers. She
kissed him, but the moment his fingers thrust deep inside
her, Millicent's body erupted with volcanic force. She
gasped for breath and somehow managed to roll beneath
the weight of his leg to face him. Millicent clung tightly
to him as waves of passion continued to roll through her
quaking body.

Lyon came fully awake at the sound of a woman's
quiet cry. Startled, he found himself inches from Millicent's face. Her eyes were shut, but even in the dawn's
light he saw the tears squeezing through the corners of
her eyelids and falling. He was shocked to find his hand
tucked intimately between her legs. He immediately
withdrew it.

"Bloody hell," he muttered. "Millicent . . . I don't . . .
I was . . . By the devil, did I hurt you? Dear God, I—"

He stopped as she shook her head and wiped the wetness from her face. She looked up at him.

"Do not blame yourself. You didn't hurt me. We
were . . . I was caught up in . . . in something."

He saw the glistening tears forming again in her gray
eyes. He had been dreaming. He was at Baronsford. No,
it was London. A woman had come to his bed. His body
was still painfully aroused. It was Millicent.

His body. Lyon's mind started to clear. He was lying
on his side. He pushed the covers back with one hand.

"You rolled." She hurriedly pulled the nightgown
down. "You rolled in your sleep."

Lyon saw his leg and knee trapping her lower body.
It was impossible.

"How?" He tried to move the leg but could not. Frustration quickly replaced his shock. "How did I do this?"

"You were asleep. You weren't thinking about it," she
replied gently, pulling herself to a sitting position and
trying awkwardly to move his legs off hers. "You just
did it."

"That is not possible," he persisted stubbornly, trying again to make it move by pushing his knee. Nothing. "I cannot move the damn leg."

"Don't fight it, Lyon." Millicent managed to free herself. Covering him with the blanket, she finally succeeded in rolling him onto his back. "Your strength is returning. You just need to give it some time. Ohenewaa said that it might happen like this. That one day you would just do it."

"No," Lyon snapped, though he knew that no one else could have moved him into that position. Perhaps . . .

He said nothing about the other times. It was true that he had recently moved his foot and his hand. But each occurrence had come without warning, and the frustration of not being able to do it again seconds later was almost too much to bear.

"It was a freak accident."

"It wasn't," she said patiently, straightening his right arm, pulling the covers over him and tucking them carefully around his chest. "Give it time. Your body is healing."

Millicent's hair hung in a cascade of curls around her face. Lyon's thoughts shifted, and he wondered why he had not told her how different she looked like this, and how much he liked it. She slipped off the bed and went around it, tucking in the blankets.

"Are you warm enough?" she asked.

"Yes." Lyon's attention was no longer on himself. In the dim light of the room, he tried to focus on her face. She had been crying, and the sadness still lingered around her eyes.

"Can I get you something to drink? Some water?"

"No," he said, unhappy with himself at having the audacity to become intimate with her . . . without being awake.

She touched his leg once, smoothing the blanket, and took a step back. "Good night then."

"Where are you going?"

She continued to back away. "To my own bedchamber."

"Why?"

"It is almost morning." She had reached the door and was already pulling at the latch.

"Millicent, wait," he called gruffly.

"What is it?"

"What happened just now?"

"You rolled in your sleep. You moved your leg. That is great progress."

He was not fooled by her hollow attempt at sounding happy. "What else happened? Tell me. What did I do to you?"

She shook her head, but no words came out.

"I acted . . . I behaved . . . dishonorably toward you, didn't I?"

She again gave a quick shake of her head, but her gaze was riveted to the floor. Lyon cursed himself. One thing he was sure of: He had touched her without her consent.

"I must apologize for the way I behaved—for whatever I did—for whatever you are forgiving me for so gracefully. I promise you, Millicent, whatever it was, it shall never happen again."

"Nothing happened. Please go back to sleep." She whispered the words before backing out of the room and softly closing the door.

She was relieved to find the hallway deserted. The household was still sleeping. Millicent's vision was blurred, but she managed to hold her tears in until she was safely inside her own bedchamber. There was no holding back her emotions after that.

He had apologized.

Wentworth had violated and battered her body sexually and physically at every opportunity during their five long years of marriage. He had called it his right as her husband to "educate" her as he saw fit. He had hurt her, killed her unborn baby, almost killed her. He had trampled on her body as if it were dry chaff in the barns.

But Lyon had apologized to her for making that same body feel alive. He had been sorry for touching her without asking her first. Even in his sleep, he had shown her the moon and stars as Millicent never knew they had existed. And Lyon Pennington was her husband, too.

Millicent buried her wet face in the pillow. She had no right to feel bad because in his unawareness he had made her climb to unknown heights of ecstasy. She should be grateful for the experience of learning that there could exist more than just pain and fear between a man and a woman.

He was growing stronger. His limbs were beginning to function. One day soon he would simply walk away. And when that happened, Millicent would need to go on with her own life. The thought terrified her.

The tears came faster. A numbing sadness was wrapping around her soul.

Who was she, Millicent thought, to care so much for him?

A carriage stood at the corner of a dark alley in St. Albans. A groom, with his hat drawn low on his face, waited beside the horses, talking to the driver. The drawn shade hid the identity of the two men meeting inside.

"Mr. Platt's high praise for your efforts convinced me that I should come and meet you in person." Jasper Hyde studied the young workman's cocky expression. "Now, after hearing all about the slave woman and her influence on Lady Aytoun, I am certainly glad that I made the trip."

"As I was saying, Mr. Hyde, her ladyship is relying on her more and more. I doubt any offer of money would convince Lady Aytoun to part with the slave." Ned Cranch lowered his voice and leaned confidentially toward the plantation owner. "But as I have been looking about the place, I've noticed that no one watches her. And she does have a routine."

"And what is that?"

"The woman leaves the house about dawn and roams the deer park in the direction of Solgrave, collecting things in this large basket she hangs from her neck. She gets back to Melbury Hall about the time the kitchen is ready to send up breakfast for the earl."

"How convenient." Hyde felt the twinges of the pain between his ribs but tried to ignore them.

"If ye want, Mr. Hyde, I could just snatch her some morning when she's in the woods." Ned glanced at the drawn shade and lowered his voice to a whisper. "In fact, knowing ye're willing to make it worth my while, I could more easily cut her throat and make it look like she was attacked by some passing gypsy or tinker, maybe. Ye just say the word, sir."

"I will keep that under advisement, Mr. Cranch. Meanwhile, I have other plans in the works that might settle the matter once and for all." Hyde rubbed his chest as the pain started to increase. "But that is good thinking on your part. Right now, you continue to keep watch." He had difficulty lifting his arm enough to toss the man a bag of coins. Cranch had no problem catching it, though.

"Will ye be coming yerself or sending Mr. Platt next time?"

"We'll let you know." Hyde weakly waved toward the carriage door, motioning to the man to get out. He did not like anyone seeing him when he was writhing in pain. He refused for others to see the hold Ohenewaa had on him.

"Thankee, sir."

Ned Cranch stepped out of the carriage into the dark. As soon as the door closed, Hyde tore at his collar and cravat. He couldn't breathe. The pain scorched his chest with the same blazing heat that his bailiffs had used to brand his slaves' flesh.

Hyde had no voice or strength left at that moment or he would have called Ned Cranch back and asked him to go ahead and cut the woman's throat. If he only knew that was a sure way to end the she-devil's curse.

Chapter 19

"You are no more than a bloody bramble weed, Gibbs," Lyon complained as the new steward entered the library.

"Thank you, m'lord."

"Do you not realize that in taking the position of steward, you are supposed to be freeing more of her time? Instead, you're tying her up in knots."

"She's not one to take what she sees as her duty lightly, sir." The Highlander sat down at the writing table with a grace that belied his size. Taking out his pens and ink, he prepared himself to write the correspondence Lyon had wished to dictate this morning. "I've been trying to ease her ladyship's burden."

For three days Millicent had been running in every direction. With the exception of brief glimpses of her when breakfast and dinner were served, or when she was overlooking some devilish new concoction Ohenewaa had devised for Lyon's legs and arm, or when one of the valets was bending him this way and that, she had been difficult to find.

Worse, though, was the matter of her failing to come to his bed again at night. She was extremely tired, or she had to stay up late answering letters, or some such thing. Any excuse she could think of had successfully kept her from being alone with him for any length of time.

It couldn't go on, Lyon thought. He missed her. He missed everything that they shared, from the verbal skirmishes to the kisses that set his blood boiling in his veins. More than once Lyon had cursed himself for whatever it was that had happened that night he'd touched her in his sleep. That was the cause of all of this, he was sure. But staying away from her was not giving him any answers, either, and he needed to change that.

The papers being shuffled on the desk drew Lyon's attention back to Gibbs. The man looked positively dejected.

"Bloody hell, Gibbs. She's not been blaming her busy schedule on you."

"I'm not surprised, m'lord."

"In fact, she's been singing your praises."

" 'Tis like her ladyship to do that, m'lord. She's very generous with her compliments."

"Where is she this morning?" Lyon asked impatiently.

"She is looking over what Cook planned to serve Reverend and Mrs. Trimble tomorrow."

"How long will she be in with him?"

"Not too—" Gibbs stopped himself. "It could take all morning, depending on how involved Lady Aytoun wishes to be with the preparations. I'm thinking that she wants this visit to go well, m'lord."

"Is impressing some country cleric and his wife so bloody important?"

"Mrs. Trimble's lame, sir, and doesn't leave the rectory too often. The woman is making the effort just to meet your lordship."

Lyon snorted. "I don't suppose you would know where your mistress is going after her discussions with Cook."

"Aye, m'lord. The schoolmaster who generally comes out to Melbury Hall on Thursday afternoons is unwell, apparently. Whenever that happens, her ladyship tries to take over the lessons of the older children and some of the workers." Gibbs paused, and then immediately added, "Just so you should know, on occasion she also works with some of the wee ones on Friday mornings."

"There are children here?" Lyon asked in astonishment.

"Aye, m'lord. Black and white and running about everywhere. They're mostly the children of those working on the farms, but a few belong to the Hall."

"Why don't they go to school in the village? What is it . . . Knebworth?"

"From what I hear, they started teaching the wee ones here back in the days of that cur Wentworth. Reverend Trimble and the schoolmaster, a Scot named Cunningham, rode out to hold classes. Her ladyship wanted to continue with reading and writing and the basics of arithmetic. Some of these folks are far past school age, but this is the first opportunity that they've had, m'lord. Most of the younger ones go into Knebworth village for their schooling, but they all still look forward to this gathering at the Hall."

"Take me there." At Gibbs's surprised expression, Lyon gestured impatiently at the steward. "After we are done with these letters, I want you to arrange it so that I am taken to wherever my wife happens to be. Starting today, I wish to keep Millicent company in her daily endeavors."

Millicent was leaning over the shoulder of one of the women and guiding her hand on the slate when she heard the scrape of benches and surprised murmurs. When she looked up, everyone was on their feet and staring at the door. Straightening, she was shocked to see the valets carefully setting Lord Aytoun down just inside the door of the servants' hall.

"M'lord," she greeted him, startled by his appearance. She started around the table toward him.

"Disregard my presence here," he said to the group, motioning with his good hand. "Sit and continue."

Stunned, no one moved. Millicent found both valets were avoiding her eyes and instead staring at the floor.

"What are you doing here, m'lord?" she whispered when she reached his side.

"I've come to see you."

"You might have sent someone for me. If you could give me a moment, I can dismiss these people and—"

"No." He took hold of her wrist before she could step

away. "I should prefer to watch you teach. I have missed your company, but at the same time I understand about your responsibilities. So go about your work, and I'll sit quietly here. I promise to make no more interruptions."

Millicent stared at him, openmouthed. There was no way she could object. "Very well, m'lord. As you wish."

She withdrew her wrist gently and tried to appear composed as she turned back to her students. At her encouraging nod, all but Moses sat down. The giant watchman continued to stare uneasily at Lyon.

"Where were we?" she asked of the group.

Several mumbled hushed comments about being finished with their writing exercises. It was time to move on to reading. Millicent grouped the students in twos and threes and, giving a Bible to each group, assigned a passage for each, telling them to alternate reading every three lines.

Moses was still standing when she reached him, and she found the older man was clearly apprehensive. He also had no partner.

The idea came to Millicent unexpectedly, and she voiced it before she had a chance even to consider how preposterous it was.

"Lord Aytoun, would you consider acting as Moses's reading partner?"

Her question silenced the room. Everyone, Millicent included, was holding their breath. Lyon's gaze moved from Millicent to Moses.

"I should be delighted."

Millicent felt a knot loosen in the back of her throat. She could almost taste the saltiness of the tears that were about to escape. Lyon Pennington continued to surprise her at every turn.

Lyon gave a quiet order to his men, and she hurried to Moses's side to make room for the earl's chair. The black man appeared as surprised as she was.

"All will be well, Moses," she whispered to him.

No sooner had the earl's chair been positioned at the table than Lyon looked up at the older man.

"I understand you have an injured dog. How is it faring?"

"Better, m'lord."

"Did they take off the leg?"

"Nay, m'lord."

"Good. They didn't take off mine, either."

Moses's dark gaze fixed on Lyon's legs.

"Before we start to read, I want you to tell me about it," the earl said, casting a glance at Millicent. "That is, if the mistress does not object."

"Not at all, m'lord," she replied with a smile as Moses sat down.

Chapter 20

⁓

"Anything else I can do for ye, m'lord?"

The curtains were drawn. All the candles but the one next to the bed had been snuffed out. The fire on the hearth had been tended. Lyon had changed into his nightshirt, and Ohenewaa—escorted by Millicent—had come and gone. This looked too much like the situation he had been left with for three nights in a row. John would retire and no one would disturb him until morning. *Bloody hell.*

"Where is her ladyship now?" Lyon asked the valet.

"I don't know, m'lord. Sleeping, I should guess."

"Go find her."

"M'lord?"

"Find her and tell her I need to see her."

With eyebrows raised, John started for the door.

"Wait."

The short, round man turned and looked at his master.

"Tell her there is an emergency. Tell her . . . tell her I've fallen from the bed. On my bad arm. Tell her I am back in bed but in severe pain."

John gaped at the earl, clearly uncomfortable about carrying such a message. "Perhaps I should get Mr. Gibbs for this, m'lord. If I—"

"I am telling you to do it. And don't fret so. I shall take full responsibility for the outcome. Wait! Whatever orders she gives—sending for doctors or anything else—it is your duty to make sure nothing is done."

The valet scratched his head and continued to stand

by the door. "Can I say ye cut yer hand or burned yerself again, m'lord? Falling on that arm—"

"Do as I say, you cowardly ape." He gave his man a reassuring nod. "I shan't make her suffer too long. I promise."

When the valet left the room, Lyon pushed himself closer to the edge of the bed. He wanted her within his reach when she came to check on him. He couldn't remember the last time he wanted something as much as he wanted Millicent here right now. Spending the day with her had been fine. Lyon realized he had been more content than he had felt in months observing the many aspects of her involvement at Melbury Hall. This household was indeed like a great family, and Millicent sailed about like some queen mother, tending to all that needed to be done.

Lyon adjusted a pillow behind his neck. This had also been the first day since the accident that he had felt nearly whole. He'd had no time to regret what was lost or who had wronged him. Instead, watching his wife, he had been filled with the simple desire to touch her. And that was what he intended to do now, even if it meant tricking her.

Lyon heard Millicent's urgent voice in the corridor, and he pulled the blanket over his right arm. A moment later the door of his bedroom banged open and she came quickly across the floor to him. Her hair was flying wildly about her.

"Light those candles," she ordered John, who had paused by the open doorway. "Send Ohenewaa here and tell Gibbs to send a rider to St. Albans for a surgeon." She leaned over him and carefully lifted the covers off him. "Are you in great pain?"

Lyon wrapped his good arm around her waist and held her against him. "You can leave now, John. Assure everyone that I need nothing else."

The valet immediately closed the door, and Millicent turned to him sharply.

"How can you say that when you might have broken something?" Without waiting for an answer, she gingerly

pushed the sleeve of the nightshirt up to his shoulder
and started feeling his bare arm with her fingers. "Where
does it hurt?"

"Nowhere," he said, admiring her as she continued to
lean over him. She was dressed in her nightdress and a
robe that she had obviously not had time to tie at the
waist. He stroked her back with his hand.

"I cannot tell what is wrong." She glanced toward the
door. "Where is Ohenewaa?"

"She is not coming."

"What do you mean?" Millicent tried to pull away,
but Lyon tightened his hold around her.

"I ordered John not to get her, or anyone else, for
that matter."

His earlier direction to the valet finally registered, and
she turned to him. Waves of auburn hair framed her
pale face, and Lyon found himself staring. Her gray eyes
looked huge and almost silvery; her lips were full and
inviting, and he couldn't wait to taste them.

"Why?" she asked in a small voice.

"Because what is wrong with me now, no one but you
can mend."

"Did you fall on your arm?"

"No."

She tried to pull away, but his arm curved around her
tighter. She braced herself, planting her hands on the
pillow on either side of his head. Her eyes narrowed.

"You tricked me."

"I confess. I wanted to see my wife."

"You have been with me all day."

"I needed you now," he said softly.

"You could have sent for me, and I would have
come."

"I'm sure. But that would have been tomorrow morning, with three dozen people around."

"Not three dozen. One person would have been
enough."

"Indeed. One too many." Lyon's hand moved up and
down her back caressingly. "I must say I don't care for
it much when you stay away from my bed."

"Really?" There was a quaver in her voice. She seemed unable to tear her gaze from his lips.

"I miss you," he said under his breath. Her body moved slightly, and her breasts brushed against his chest. "I miss your attentions. And I miss your laughter. I miss this."

As he spoke, he pulled her down to him until her warm breath mingled with his.

"This?"

His gaze lifted, locking with hers. "This."

Lyon drew her mouth to his. She shivered and closed her eyes, and Lyon's lips began to move on hers, possessively exploring each tender curve and trembling contour as if it were an uncharted new world that he had discovered and claimed for his own.

"And there are other things I miss about not having you here, too." Lyon felt the shaking arms give away. Her breasts pressed against his chest.

"What else?"

The wild pounding of her heart matched his.

"Your beautiful body."

His hand glided over her hip to her thigh, urging her onto the bed. She complied, her body stretching out fully on his. Lyon deepened the kiss, plunging his tongue in slowly and withdrawing, realizing it was only an imitation of the act he was beginning to crave. He wanted her. He wanted to make love to her.

With a silent moan of surrender, Millicent cupped his face in her hands, and her lips started moving on his with awakening ardor.

Lyon's mouth became more demanding as he felt his body straining painfully with his arousal. His hand moved restlessly between their bodies. She shifted slightly, giving him room to caress her breast. She breathed in deeply, her flesh swelling beneath his palm, her nipple rising against the nightgown. He groaned in frustration and tore his mouth away.

"Make love to me, Millicent."

Her face was flushed, almost intoxicated, when she looked into his eyes. "I . . . I don't—"

"I'll tell you what to do. Help me make love to you."
He brushed his fingers lightly back and forth over her
nipple through the fabric of her nightdress. "I know the
other night I had started something that I did not finish.
I am sorry if I hurt you. But with both of us awake,
perhaps we can do better."

She started to push herself off him.

"Wait," he said, bitterness creeping into his voice.
"Very well. Whatever you want. I'm certain that when
you married me, you did not bargain for this. What
woman would want to take a cripple and then be forced
to watch him fail as a man? What woman would settle
for a straw man of a husband who might only make the
act of love something weak and foolish?" He shook his
head. "No. It is wrong of me to ask you to accept this
useless body that cannot move even to love you. I only
ask you to stay. I shall be content if you do just that.
And there will be no more demands for—"

"But I like your demands."

Millicent pressed him back into the pillow, kissing him
deeply. Her tongue slipped tentatively into his mouth,
then grew bolder. When she finally pulled back, breaking
off the kiss, they were both breathless.

"What should I do first?"

Her innocent question had Lyon draw a few steadying
breaths. "Take off your robe and nightdress."

With her knees on either side of his legs, Millicent
knelt up slowly. Lyon saw her hands were trembling
when they pushed the robe down off her shoulders. He
held his breath as she began to untie the front of the
nightgown.

"I am nervous."

"So am I," he replied softly. Lyon could feel her gaze
upon him as he pulled the linen material down. She did
not stop him until it clung tenuously to her smooth hips.

She was so beautiful.

Lyon's gaze drifted downward from her face, admiring
her cream-colored skin glowing in the candlelight. His
eyes lingered at the sight of her round, full breasts. He

reached out and touched the curve beneath one nipple, his finger brushing each tight bud.

"You are a treasure. An exquisite and beautiful treasure." He looked into her eyes. "I want to feel your body against me."

Lyon's hand glided to her waist. He slipped the nightdress over her hips and her knees.

"What else should I do?"

"Take this shirt off me," he said, sitting up, his voice husky with desire. Millicent reached over him and pulled the nightshirt up from beneath him, but got no farther.

Lyon stretched out his hand and caressed the smooth skin along her thigh, sliding his hand between her legs. Immediately, she froze and clamped her legs together.

"Don't be afraid," he whispered roughly, sitting forward and taking her breast between his lips. She moaned and arched her back, and this time Lyon's fingers began to probe the dark triangle at the juncture of her thighs, seeking entrance. "Give yourself to me, Millicent."

With a soft moan she relaxed, and Lyon's fingers slipped deep into her wet warmth.

After a moment he felt her begin to pulse against his hand. He stroked her and relished the feel of her growing passion. Her breaths quickened, and then suddenly, with a sob of startled pleasure, she was calling his name. She clutched him to her, burying her face in his hair and curling her entire body around his hand.

As the waves began to subside in her, Lyon smiled. He had never really thought so much about the enjoyment of giving pleasure to a woman. True, he had always prided himself on the ability to please a woman, but this was different. Better.

Even as the thought flickered through his mind, though, she moved one knee over him, and he positioned himself between her legs.

"Take me inside of you."

Millicent's hand moved ever so slowly between their bodies, and Lyon's breath caught in his throat when her fingers wrapped around him. He closed his eyes and groaned out loud as her fingers tentatively moved down his length and she positioned herself at his peak. He heard the gasp as the head of his shaft entered her.

"Now, Millicent."

Their gazes locked as their bodies joined together in a perfect fit.

Though he could not move his legs, he did not want to move at all for fear of losing control. The sensations running through him were those that he had thought he would never experience again. The pleasure of her tight sheath closing around him was incomparable. He was alive again, and Millicent had made it happen.

"You are so beautiful, inside and out."

Her answer was a single tear that escaped one gray eye and slid down her flawless cheek before dropping onto his lips. Lyon tasted it and then kissed her as the urge to move became maddening. His fingers threaded into her hair, and he drove his tongue into her mouth again and again with the same sensual thrusts that he was incapable of doing with his body.

When Millicent tore her mouth away, he almost groaned with frustration. The thought ran through his mind that she was already disgusted with his inability to pleasure either of them. But when he looked into her face, what he saw was wonder and passion. The lump of tenderness swelling in his chest was overwhelming. Lying there, he watched Millicent as she took his face between her hands and brushed her lips over his lips, his bearded cheeks, his nose, his ear.

Then she started to move, ever so slightly, on top of him.

Lyon's fingers tightened on her hip, and he tried to guide her body. It was obvious that she was not very experienced in the art of love. She was following the instinct that nature provided, her body pulsing to the rhythms within her.

Their mouths met again, and Lyon lay back, letting Millicent set the pace. He felt the pressure building within him. The roaring in his head nearly blocked out all other sound, and his body strained, desperate for release. But he did not want to let go. There would be no joy in the race if she were not there beside him. Her body was sliding against his, her hips grinding into him. She was panting, and he could see the color rising in her face.

"Lyon," she whispered against his lips. "I have never . . . never . . . felt this."

He moved his hand between their bodies. The moment he touched her, she tipped over passion's edge and cried out, convulsing around him, and Lyon, too, reached that point of no return. As his body shuddered, he erupted within her as a blaze of fiery colors exploded before his eyes.

The sounds coming from the room were unmistakable. A woman's whimpering cries. The man's groans of exertion. Violet put an unsteady hand on the wall and approached the closed door with hesitant steps.

She was no longer aware of the numbness in her hands and feet, or the weight of the basket of food she had carried all the way from Melbury Hall. Against her principles, against her better judgment, she had come. Now Violet felt ill as she stood frozen by the door.

Silently, she prayed that Ned was not in there. Perhaps someone else was using his room for the night. When he had not stopped for dinner at the hall tonight, Violet had thought he might appreciate it if she brought him some supper at the inn. Now she prayed that he had not come because he was away. Perhaps he had been called to St. Albans.

The noises inside increased in volume as well as cadence.

"Neddy!" The voice of the young woman spilled clearly into the hallway. "Oh, my God!"

Violet's insides churned. The handle of the basket slipped out of her hands and fell to the floor. She stared down at the food that had spilled out around her frozen feet.

Suddenly, her blood coursed hotly through her veins. Vi pounded on the door. A muffled curse came from

the room, and in a moment the door jerked open. Ned
filled the doorway, a candle inside the room shadowing
his face.

"By the de'il! What do ye want here?"

Violet stared at his bare chest. His breeches had been
pulled up to his hips, but hid nothing. She looked up
into his fierce glower and saw the temper brewing there.
She didn't care that he was angry.

"I brought you dinner."

He looked down and then viciously kicked the basket
with his bare foot. "I've already eaten. Get out."

He started closing the door in her face, but Violet put
a hand out to stop him.

"Who is inside there?"

" 'Tis none of yer bloody business."

"Who do you have there?" she said more forcefully,
shoving the door open.

With a malicious smirk, Ned let the door swing open.
Vi saw one of the young girls from the village peering
wide-eyed at her from behind a blanket on the bed. The
woman's clothes were heaped in a pile on the floor.
Ned's shirt and boots had been thrown carelessly beside them.

Even as she stared, Violet couldn't push away the
memory of her and Ned making love on this same bed.
Her head was still filled with his whispered words of
love. Her only dream for weeks had been that of Ned
asking her to marry him. Their future together had dom-
inated her every conscious thought. Another look at the
bed and the woman and Violet felt her temper rise, the
hot blade of jealousy cutting deep.

"Get out!" she screamed, shoving past Ned and
marching toward the woman. "Get out of here now!"

The girl only cringed behind the blanket, and Violet
gave a sharp kick to the woman's feet. "You despicable
wench. You harlot!"

"Who the de'il d'ye think ye are?" Ned grabbed Violet by the shoulder and spun her around.

Vi didn't see his fist coming. Suddenly she was against

the wall, stunned by the blow, half of her face numb.
Her knees buckled and she sagged against rough plaster.
She put her hand to her mouth. She could taste the
blood.

"You . . . you hit me," she whispered in disbelief,
trying to straighten up. Tears started blurring her vision.
"How dare you?"

Ned loomed over her. "Ye asked for it, slut. What
right do ye think ye have to come in here and spout
off?"

"The right of a lover. The right of a woman whose
honor you have defiled. Of one deflowered with lies."
With the back of her hand she wiped her bloody lip. "I
was a virgin, and you took me. You made me believe
that you had honorable intentions."

"Honorable intentions? Deflowered?" He gave an insolent laugh and poked a blunt finger into her shoulder.
"This is what books does for ye. Well, I'm telling ye,
those are big words coming from a brazen wench. Ye
spread yer legs willingly for me, an' ye wanted it the
first time ye laid eyes on me. Ye followed me around,
even into St. Albans, so as to get it from me. An' now,
like a bloody bitch in heat, ye can't wait for a man while
he goes elsewheres. Well, slut, ye can just wait yer turn."

Tears burned Violet eyes. She pushed away from the
wall and faced him.

"You'll be whistling a different tune when I tell Lady
Aytoun how you seduced me and then mistreated me.
I'll tell her you forced me. You'll be thrown out of that
job and run out of this village when I tell people how
you raised your hand against me. You are a low, insolent
dog, and they'll see you for what you are. You'll never
get work anywhere around here ever again when—"

Ned drew back his fist to strike her again, and Violet
cringed, covering her face with her arms. Smirking, he
lowered his hand.

"And d'ye think all these folk, including yer precious
Lady Aytoun, are going to listen to yer bloody whinin'
and not ask why ye came here tonight? Why ye keep

spreading your legs for a married man?" He laughed in
her face. "I didn't force ye to come here, ye stupid chit.
You came willingly. Like a bitch in heat."

He continued to berate her, but Violet's mind had
snagged on the words "married man." A knot the size
of a fist rose into her throat.

"You're lying," she said brokenly. "You couldn't be
married and come courting me the way you did."

"Courtin'?" Ned snorted derisively and yanked her
roughly toward the door. "This is all the courtin' ye'll
be gettin' from now on. Just ye get out of here, for I've
a lass waitin' who knows what's what with a man. An'
ye best not be spoutin' off back at the Hall, neither, if
ye know what's good for ye."

He shoved her so hard through the door that Violet
went sprawling onto the filthy floor.

"An' don't ye come back to my door again, slut, or
ye'll have more than a bloodied lip to show for yer
trouble."

Before Violet could reply, he slammed the door in
her face.

Millicent nestled her face into the crook of Lyon's
neck and nuzzled and tasted the saltiness on the stretch
of taut skin below his beard. Her body still hummed
with the sweet after-effects of their lovemaking, and although they were still connected in the most intimate
way, she had no desire to move or go anywhere, but
simply to stay right here.

Lyon's hand roamed over her back, and she heard a
soft laugh rumble deep in his throat. She immediately
raised her head and looked into his face.

"What?"

His blue eyes were filled with tenderness when they
met hers. "I was thinking that in all my adult life nothing
has ever approached what I just experienced. It was like
the first time."

Millicent couldn't tell him how much his words meant
to her. "I know what you mean. What you gave me just
now . . . well, never in my life . . ." Her words trailed off.

"Will you tell me someday about it? About your life?"

Millicent didn't want to think about any of that. "Those years have ceased to exist," she replied softly. She moved carefully, disengaging their bodies, but Lyon's hand wrapped around her waist, keeping her from moving away.

"I am not demanding any answers, Millicent. I am only trying to get better acquainted with my wife."

"I know," she said, laying her hand flat on his chest, feeling his strong heartbeat. "We never removed this."

"I'm a very modest fellow."

Millicent laughed, her fingers trailing down to the hem of the nightshirt, which was still bunched up around his waist. "I see how modest you are."

"But I am quite warm. Perhaps we could remove it."

"It will be a challenge."

"I've seen you at work before," he said, grinning mischievously.

"Very well." She undid the two ties at the neck and then pushed up the linen fabric as far as it would go—which wasn't far. Stretching her body on top of him, she shifted his weight from one shoulder to the other, managing to pull up the shirt to around his broad chest.

"Almost there."

"Hardly," he responded.

Glaring at him with mock fierceness, she sat up, straddling his stomach and pulling his right arm out of the wide sleeve. That worked. Before she could reach for the other arm, though, she found it straying.

"You are a miracle."

He ran his fingers gently across her nipples and down over the curves of her belly, and Millicent felt the rush of liquid heat coursing through her middle again.

"Why do you say that?"

"A month ago, the only plan I had for the future was to find a way to put an end to my miserable life. But now I find myself deliberating on tactful ways of getting you to make love to me again."

"Is that so?" Millicent said, inching backward. The feel of his fully aroused manhood nestling against her body spread another wave of heat through her. Lyon's fingers trailed lower, and Millicent took hold of his hand. "First, I have to remove your shirt."

"Save that for later," he said, gently pulling his hand free and continuing to caress her belly. As he reached the soft mound, Millicent rose up slightly to meet his touch. "It may take any number of tries to get this shirt off."

Chapter 21

"These accusations are quite serious," the dowager said sharply to her physician.

"I am not making accusations, m'lady. I am simply passing on information that has been brought to my attention, information that I felt you should hear. Before conveying it to you, I considered the seriousness of the matter as well as the source—in this case, Dr. Parker—and I decided that Lord Aytoun's health necessitated my speaking to you. I did not believe 'twas in anyone's best interest to allow his lordship to fall victim to any evildoers."

"Evildoers, is it?"

As Dr. Tate waved his assistant out with his medical bag, the dowager motioned to one of her maidservants and whispered instructions to her. The woman hurried out of the room.

"When was the last time you spoke with this Parker?"

"Two days ago."

"And what exactly did he have to say about my son's condition?"

The thin shoulders of the physician straightened. "He was quite concerned. In fact, if I might be perfectly candid, m'lady, he feared that you could be receiving disheartening news any day about his lordship. Without proper medication and regular examinations by qualified physicians, Dr. Parker believes Lord Aytoun is at great risk and may be endangering his life."

"And he was able to tell you this with certainty after only one visit to Hertfordshire?"

"A qualified doctor sees beyond the condition of his patient on a specific day."

There was a knock at the door, and Sir Richard appeared.

"Come in, Maitland." She motioned to another servant to put some pillows behind her back. Propped up in the bed, the old woman turned to the physician. "Can you, sir, in just a few words, summarize all this for Sir Richard?"

Dr. Tate bowed stiffly. "The information I have concerns a slave woman who resides at present in Lord Aytoun's new residence, Melbury Hall."

"The information you have is outdated," the dowager interrupted. "The woman you refer to is no longer a slave but a free woman."

"I beg your pardon, m'lady." The doctor turned his attention again to the lawyer. "I have come upon some distressing information regarding this same woman. She is suspected of having murdered the physician whom she served as a servant for many years. What originally was assumed to be a death by natural causes is now suspected of possibly being caused by poison."

"Suspected by whom?" the dowager cut in.

"Well, I assume by the man's family." The thin man ran a hand nervously down the front of his jacket. "By the proper authorities."

"So you do not know," Lady Aytoun snapped. "Is that it?"

"M'lady, as I am certain Sir Richard will tell you, even with Sir John Fielding's Bow Street Runners looking into it—"

"Which they are not," she retorted scoffingly.

"Even if they were looking into it, these matters take time." The doctor turned to Maitland for help. "Sir, consider the severity of the charges. If Dr. Dombey did not die of natural causes, but rather because of the actions of this slave expediting his end with diabolical brews and potions, what difference does it make if she is officially charged with the crime?"

"The difference is a matter of making false accusations," the lawyer replied calmly. "At her age, having nothing as a former slave, she has enough trouble without respectable people slandering her. Terms such as 'diabolical brews and potions' imply witchcraft in addition to murder, sir. Is that what you mean?"

"I only mean that if one considers the strong likelihood of this African woman murdering her master—and we all know that this is common in the islands—then the dowager's first priority should be to remove her son from this woman's clutches before she murders again."

"My son is *not* in this woman's clutches."

"But he is, m'lady. 'Tis clear that your daughter-in-law put an end to Dr. Parker's visits to Melbury Hall as a means of giving free rein to this woman."

"Are you now accusing the younger Lady Aytoun of wrongdoing?" Maitland asked.

"I am relating what I have heard," Tate responded defensively. "There are witnesses from a nearby village called Knebworth, I was told, who claim the black woman is referred to, unbelievably, as a great 'healer.' Apparently, upon arriving at Melbury Hall, this slave woman was given the best room in the manor house. There are reports of agents of this same woman visiting an apothecary in St. Albans. If your ladyship's daughter-in-law has fallen under this woman's spell and has become blind to—"

"Enough," the dowager ordered angrily. "You are obviously operating under some deluded notion of loyalty to your brethren, Dr. Tate, rather than any loyalty to my family—"

"M'lady, I have been your physician for quite some time now."

"Indeed, sir. Too long, perhaps. But to make you understand where I stand on this matter, I do not believe the gossip of scoundrels. Nor do I suspect every old woman with a wrinkled face, a hairy lip, a squinty eye, or a scolding tongue to be a witch."

"M'lady—"

"Perhaps because I fit that description myself. Now, I

suggest that you take your leave, sir, before I lose my temper. See him out, Maitland."

Beatrice Pennington, Dowager Countess Aytoun, glared imperiously until the physician, mumbling apologies, backed out the door under the stern eye of Sir Richard. Dismissing her maidservants with an impatient wave, the old woman stared darkly at the window.

She didn't want to believe any of this nonsense. All the reports coming from Melbury Hall indicated Lyon was improving. For the first time in months, Beatrice had begun to hope that things might turn out well for her son, after all. She had allowed herself to let go of the past. It appeared that Millicent was good for him.

With a soft knock, Sir Richard reentered the room. From the droop of his old shoulders, the dowager guessed something was wrong.

"Don't tell me you believe this foolishness."

He shook his head.

"Then don't stand there tongue-tied like a block of wood, man. Tell me what is on your mind."

The man sat down in his customary seat by the window. "I received a letter from your son this morning."

"From Lyon?"

"Indeed, m'lady."

"This is good news." She shot an angry look in the direction of the door. "And more proof that this one and the rest of them, too, know little of what they dwell upon. This is the first time Lyon has corresponded with you since his marriage, is it not?"

"Indeed, m'lady."

"A great sign of improvement in itself." She leaned back against the pillows. "So what the devil is bothering you, Maitland?"

"Before I heard Dr. Tate's accusations, nothing. But now, the more I think of it . . ." His voice trailed off.

"Speak up."

"In his letter, his lordship has requested that I send up a few of the Aytoun heirlooms to Melbury Hall."

"What does he want?"

"He mentions specific pieces of jewelry that are here in London."

"And what of it? They are his. He can do as he wishes with them."

"He also directs me to hire and send a secretary up there to him, as his man, Gibbs, has been given the position of steward at the Hall."

"All well and good. Time enough that Highland beast started using a bit of his brain."

"Perhaps we should not take this matter too lightly, m'lady," Maitland commented. "The change—dare I say the improvement—in Lyon has been remarkable. I do not discount the fact that these doctors appear to be overly keen about bringing us damaging reports. But perhaps our wisest course is for me to go personally to Melbury Hall to check on your son's condition. I can go up under the pretext of delivering what the earl has requested in person. And while I am there, I can assess his lordship's improvement and snuff out another potential scandal before it spreads through this idle London *ton*."

The old woman's response was immediate. "There is no need for you to go, Sir Richard. I shall be making the journey myself."

"M'lady, I do not believe the urgency of the matter will allow us to wait until you are well enough—"

"I shall go this week."

"But m'lady!"

"No arguments." She waved a dismissive hand. "The only person who can put an end to all this foolishness is I."

"But you are not well enough."

"Who says I am not?" she challenged. "Millicent has already invited me, and I have told her I would go there to visit sometime. The only difference is that now we shall be arriving without prior warning."

"Then allow me to come with you, at least."

"As you wish, Sir Richard. Besides, getting out of this dreary city might be good for both of us. Make the arrangements."

*   *   *

"I ran into the doorjamb in the dark last night," Violet explained to her fellow serving maid. The younger woman was hanging over her shoulder, looking at the ugly bruise at the edge of Vi's mouth. "Really, Bess. 'Tis nothing."

"If that's so, then why did ye ask me to go and help Lady Aytoun dress this morning?"

"I feel silly enough, and you know how she is." Violet finished applying more of the white powder over the bruise. "She gets worried for nothing. I thought if I wait a day or two, then she won't be pestering me about being more careful and all that."

The truth was that Violet had seen many bruises much worse than this on her mistress's face when the squire was alive. The young woman had a sneaking suspicion that her ladyship would not be fooled by the story of running into a door.

She had already asked around this morning. What Ned had said about being married seemed to be true, or at least some of the servants she talked to had heard that rumor, too. Violet wondered where her mind had been this whole time. How was it possible that she had made such a mess out of her life in so short a time?

The two women descended the back steps together. Violet paused by the door to the servants' hall, looking for an excuse not to go in. She could hear the voices of people gathered there for their noon meal. "I have to take a walk over to the stables. I'll see you later on."

"Come on, Vi. Ye had no breakfast," Bess chided. "Why don't ye go in, and I'll run and fetch whatever ye want from the stables."

Violet shook her head and started backing out. "I want to check on Moses's dog, and I promised to do some mending for him. I'll be back."

"But Moses is probably here, too."

Violet was already moving to the door as the young black woman finished her words. With a wave, she went outside and pulled the wool shawl over her head.

The true horror of how Ned had treated her had not reached her until now. As she made her way toward the stables, she realized that although she had been abused, she felt like she was carrying a mark of shame. It wasn't so much who did this to her that mattered, but that she somehow deserved it. Well, perhaps she did, she thought.

No, Vi argued silently. Ned had no right to strike her, even if he was a man. She felt sick to her stomach at how unfair everything was.

With the exception of a couple of grooms working in the stalls, the stables were quiet. Moses's dog—her back leg bound tightly with splints and strips of linen—hopped toward Violet, nuzzling her hand before flopping back down on the straw by one of the stalls. Violet moved past the tack room to another small room that Moses had been given.

The small area was clean and tidy, and his clothes were hung neatly on pegs along one wall. Vi found his pile of mending folded in a corner on a barrel by his mattress. Picking up the worn clothing, she sat down on the barrel, took her thimble and a needle and thread from her apron pocket, and went to work.

Her heart ached, and she found herself batting away occasional tears. Violet knew she wanted to stay inside the gates of Melbury Hall, but she was afraid that the time was coming when she would be cast out. That was what happened to girls like her. Girls who foolishly gave themselves over to what they thought they wanted.

She had to take what time here she was given and then face up to whatever the future might bring. She held up Moses's shirt. This was what she needed now. Time to be alone. Time to work and be useful.

The voices of people entering the stables made Vi pull the shawl tighter around her face. She looked up as Amina and Jonah came into the room with Moses behind them. She should have known Bess would not hold her tongue.

Amina was carrying a plate of food. Jonah held a

wooden cup. Both were looking at her with concern, but Moses's dark eyes were angry enough to set the building ablaze.

"Violet is hurt." He moved around the other two and came to crouch down beside her. He pushed the shawl away from her face. "Who, Vi?"

Her chin sank to her chest, but he gently lifted it.

"No one hurts Vi. I'll kill him."

The young woman took one of Moses's large fists between her hands and shook her head. The tears trickled down and she realized that she couldn't be alone and separate. These people loved her like family.

"I don't want you to kill anyone for me, Moses. You are here, and that makes me feel better. I'm safe here. I know that now."

His life had changed. Everything had changed. Before, he had been at the center of a world that was vibrant and filled with action. Now it was as if he were on the outside, looking at the world through a tiny window.

No, Lyon Pennington had never before had to look through this . . . this keyhole at his own life. And the view was so different. Oddly, he found himself focusing on and fathoming the subtle things, the small changes, concentrating on moods and responses, recognizing that so long as an individual had the ability to take a breath, he or she had a life to live. Embracing life despite the hardships was a concept Lyon was coming to appreciate.

This morning, before their guests had arrived, he had joined Millicent downstairs when she had been tutoring some of the younger children in the servants' hall. The group had been lively and noisy. She had been patient and encouraging.

The joys at Melbury Hall were simple. Life was uncomplicated. To Millicent's credit, no one seemed to dwell on how they had suffered before or what was different about them. She had created a haven where people worked hard and lived happily.

So different from Emma's vision for Baronsford. If, indeed, she'd even had a vision.

He shook off the thought. He had no wish, either, to think about his own past.

Lyon focused his gaze on the profile of his wife near the window. She was seated beside Mrs. Trimble. The rector's wife was continuing to speak, but Lyon could tell Millicent's mind was elsewhere. He wondered if she was thinking of the same things that had been occupying his mind for most of the morning—their hours of love-making last night. As he watched her, she absently touched two fingers to the full lips he had so enjoyed kissing.

Lyon admired the soft glow in her cheeks. She had been changing before his eyes since their marriage. Lyon could not believe that he had considered her plain once. Every time he looked at her now, a different aspect of her beauty presented itself. It was as though a different woman had been living within each of the veils that protected her. As her confidence seemed to grow, another veil was peeled away and another woman revealed.

Millicent's gaze flicked away from their guest and locked with his. He saw the memory of their intimacy and the promise of passion reflected in those sparkling eyes. The excitement of what was to come made every limb in Lyon's body feel alive. He wanted her alone again. She had awakened an insatiable beast inside of him, and he couldn't wait to have her again to himself. Apparently reading his mind, Millicent looked away, a blush darkening her cheeks.

". . . will take care of the additions and the renovations of the schoolhouse."

Lyon gave a nod to Reverend Trimble in response to whatever it was the rector had just said.

"The Earl and Countess of Stanmore feel 'tis the right time, considering the continuing growth in Knebworth Village. And though naming the school after Mr. Cunningham is unprecedented, they feel strongly that—considering how devoted that young man was to teaching our children—this is a fine way to keep his memory alive."

"Of course. A fine idea." Lyon recalled hearing the

former schoolmaster's name from Gibbs. "How long ago did this Mr. Cunningham die?"

"A year and a half ago," Mr. Trimble answered.

"He was a young man, I believe you said?"

"I suppose he would have been about your age, m'lord. He was a Scotsman as well."

"And how did he die?"

There was a slight pause. "He was shot."

"Really? A hunting accident?"

"I don't believe so, m'lord."

An uncomfortable silence fell over the room. Reverend Trimble cleared his voice and—sending a quick look in Millicent's direction—began to explain.

"Due to an unfortunate misunderstanding, Mr. Cunningham met his end at Melbury Hall . . . down in the Grove."

A haunted expression marked Millicent's face, and she dropped her gaze to her lap. Lyon remembered seeing the same sadness taking over his wife when Trimble had visited them here earlier. He couldn't help but wonder if the cause might be the same.

Millicent rose abruptly to her feet and walked to the window.

"Then the death of this Cunningham was intentional?" he pressed.

"I was not present, m'lord, when everything happened," Reverend Trimble replied.

"Tell me what you know."

"Those who were there," the rector explained quietly, "say that Squire Wentworth shot Mr. Cunningham."

Lyon told himself it was not jealousy, but curiosity was beginning to stab at him. "Was it a duel?"

"Nay, m'lord. The unfortunate incident had to do with some long-standing disagreements between the squire and Mr. Cunningham over the treatment of the black workers at Melbury Hall. Mr. Cunningham and Lord Stanmore and I—being fiercely opposed to holding slaves—were considered by the squire to be his enemies." Mr. Trimble cleared his voice again and darted a nervous glance at Millicent's back. "The story behind all of this is too long and tragic for such a pleasant afternoon as this. Sometime when your lordship is willing to spend an afternoon at Knebworth Village, I should be delighted to give you the entire history of it."

Before, Lyon had been willing to let the ghosts of their pasts alone. But after last night he needed to understand all of it. Millicent did not care for her first husband. That was obvious. But Lyon needed to understand the role of Cunningham in her life.

"Early next week," Lyon announced, "I shall try to convince my wife to bring me along to the village. There is much that I would like to learn about my new home and neighbors."

"There was no reason to assault Reverend Trimble with all those questions," Millicent said somewhat tetchily as soon as she was back from escorting their guests to their carriage. She leaned her back against the door. "Lyon, if there is anything that you need to know about Knebworth Village's past, I will be happy to provide the answers. If there are some deep-rooted secrets that you believe people are keeping from you, I am the one you should ask."

"And you will answer?"

"I will."

"And I can ask anything?" he challenged, his blue eyes piercing across the room.

She refused to be baited or to fight with him. At the same time, she was not going to allow the past to thrust a wedge of mistrust between them. Mistrust had marred her marriage to Wentworth, and Millicent was not about to let it poison this one. Especially now that she recognized how much she cared for Lyon.

"You may ask anything," she answered, pushing away from the closed door.

"Even if it involves your own past?"

"Even so," she said, determined to follow this through to the end. "Of course, I expect the same courtesy from you."

"I doubt that there is much that you do not already

know about me. Gibbs told me you spent a great deal of time in the dowager's company on the day of our marriage, getting answers to all your questions."

"That 'great deal of time' consisted of less than two hours. And how could I have possibly received answers to all my questions when at the time I didn't even know what our . . . our involvement would be?"

"Are you having regrets about last night?"

Millicent turned to face him. The sudden look of vulnerability she saw etched in Lyon's face opened her eyes. This man was not Wentworth. There had been no accusations, no distrust. This man wanted to know more about her.

"How could I regret the most fulfilling night of my life?"

Lyon stared at her for the span of an eternity and then raised his hand. His voice quavered a little when he spoke. "Come here."

She went to him without a second's hesitation. He pulled her onto his lap, and Millicent wrapped her arms around his neck and held him.

"I am sorry if I sounded like a man adrift," he said softly. "But the truth is that nothing between us has followed any logical path. We were thrown into this marriage, knowing practically nothing beyond the other's name. Having taken matrimonial vows, I was moved into your care, while neither of us had any idea what demands or expectations such a marriage would bring. And yet so much has changed from that first day." Lyon's hand caressed her and drew her tighter against his chest. "We have both been down this road before. We have been married. And I believe I am speaking for both of us when I say that we want to do better than the first time."

Millicent's head moved beneath his chin as she nodded. She couldn't live through these days dwelling on the fact that their future together could be so brief.

"What the dowager would not have told you about my past was that my first marriage was not as peaceful as she wished it to be. And as I spend more time thinking back over what was wrong, I realize now that the root of my problems lay with my lack of trust. I was a master of *asking* nothing but *acting* on anything that raised my suspicions. I assumed wrongly. I fretted over shadows. I acted rashly on things that I think now might easily have been explained. I didn't ask; I just expected to be told." He let out a frustrated breath. "You didn't even ask, and here I am explaining. Rambling."

"You are not rambling." Millicent pushed her head off his shoulder and looked into her husband's face. "I have been hesitant about discussing my past because those years were nothing but a succession of difficult memories and tragic events. I am almost thirty years old with nothing to be proud of in my life. When I look back, all I see is nothing but total failure."

"You are wrong about that," he said, holding her gaze. "Each step that we take leads us down the road that we were intended to travel. And even the little I know of you is filled with great things. All anyone has to do today is look at Melbury Hall. What you have succeeded in doing here is reflected in everyone who surrounds you, Millicent. You are a wonder—a prize."

His fingers delved into her hair, and Lyon kissed her with enough passion to make her believe.

"Do you know how lucky I consider myself to be your husband?"

Millicent couldn't hold back her tears. She was overwhelmed with everything about this man. He kissed the tears off her face, and his mouth settled on hers again.

"You have a way of making me feel special," she whispered when they broke off the kiss. "Desired."

"And you have a way of making me feel whole." Lyon's fingers moved to the conservative neckline of her dress and started tugging at the small buttons. "From our first moment together you have managed to cast aside all my notions of what I could no longer do."

"Are you referring to taking my head off with that sharp tongue of yours?" she teased, brushing her lips against his bearded cheeks, his lips.

"Well, that too." He smiled. "But do you remember the first day that I arrived at Melbury Hall?"

"You had fallen off the seat in the carriage where Gibbs had propped you up."

"And you tried to help me back onto the seat."

She looked down as his fingers undid one button and moved to the next.

"I learned you had a ferocious temper that day."

"If Gibbs hadn't shown up when he did, you might have learned other things about me, too."

"What other things?"

His blue eyes were mischievous. He took her hand and brought it to his lap, where the evidence of his arousal was pronounced.

"That day, wrestling with me in that confined space as you were, pressing and fitting all your beautiful curves against me, you made me realize that perhaps my manhood was not too far beyond redemption after all."

Millicent tentatively stroked his shape through the breeches. She looked down as Lyon's hand parted the neckline of her dress, revealing the lace of the low-cut chemise she was wearing beneath.

"I always considered myself plain, tedious, lacking passion," she said. "I am struggling with this new me who wants to come out."

"Do not fight it." He placed soft kisses on her face. His hand gently touched her breast. "Do not fight the passion that I know is within you."

"You make me think of doing wicked things."

His breath was more a sigh of delight. "By any chance, do your thoughts run along the lines of latching the door and taking off your clothes and coming back to me?"

Millicent looked up shyly. "Taking off my clothes?"

"Every stitch. I want to see your beautiful body. I want to touch and taste every bit of you before burying myself deep inside."

"You want to make love here in this room?" she whispered, shocked.

"Is that wicked enough?" he asked.

Touching him through his clothing had been the extent of Millicent's thoughts, but she held back her comment when Lyon's mouth captured hers in another kiss.

Blatantly carnal, he thrust deep, sampling and tasting and playing out what another part of his body was eager to do.

Millicent was quivering with need when he broke the kiss. She rose and went to latch the door, but as soon as she turned to him, all her insecurities rushed back in. It was still daylight. Someone could pass by the window. Any minute there could be a knock at the door. And most important, it had been so much safer to make love to him in the half-darkness of the bedchamber, where her flaws were not so obvious. Her back pressed hard against the door.

"Will you be my hands?"

Uncontrollably drawn to the magic of his blue eyes, she swallowed her protests and nodded slowly.

"Undo the rest of the buttons on your dress for me."

She looked down at the partially parted neckline. Her fingers shook when she started unfastening the rest. The weight of Lyon's gaze was on her. The last button ended at the waistline of the dress.

"Now part the dress in the front."

The dark tips of her nipples showed through the thin chemise when she parted the front of her dress. Her skin tingled and burned, and she wasn't even being touched. Not yet.

"Now push it down your arms and step out of the dress and petticoats."

Millicent started doing what he'd asked of her. "I do not think I can go beyond this. I am too embarrassed to reveal—"

"Come here, love."

The softly whispered endearment made her heart soar. She stepped out of the dress and made her way to him slowly.

"You are so beautiful." His voice was husky. Lyon leaned forward, his hand molding the thin fabric to her sensitive skin at her waist, his mouth taking hers in another kiss.

Millicent's fingers delved into Lyon's hair as his fingers gently caressed the curves of her belly, and she shivered when his thumb crossed her ribs and came to rest at the base of her breast.

"You have the most glorious hair. Take the pins out of it."

She reached up with both hands, taking each pin out slowly. All the while she felt his gentle fingers caressing the curves of her breasts. Her skin heated to his touch, and his gaze scorched her.

Her hair came down like a heavy blanket around her shoulders. She leaned her head back when Lyon's fingers combed through the waves.

"I have been daydreaming about this all morning," he said.

Millicent held her breath when Lyon pushed the chemise off one shoulder, revealing only the top of one breast. The sound of a couple of servants passing outside the door broke through the haze that was enveloping her, and Millicent darted a nervous glance in that direction.

"Maybe we should wait until—"

"There will be no waiting." Lyon reached up and pulled the chemise off her other shoulder and drew her back onto his lap.

"But Mrs. Page could be looking for me. Or Gibbs might come to check on you. What happens if they come to the door?"

He placed a kiss on her exposed shoulders, tasting her soft flesh. "I'll tell them I am making love to my wife, and that they can all go to the devil."

"Now I do feel absolutely wicked," she whispered. She undid a couple of the buttons on his shirt and slipped her hand inside, caressing the sinewy contours of his chest. "I think everyone already knows what we did last night."

"And everyone probably knows what we are doing here this afternoon. You might as well stop worrying about what others will think, for there is a great deal that I plan to do to you in the gardens and in the carriage and in every other room of this house." He traced the edge of her chemise, where the tops of her breasts rose and fell with each breath she took. "Now let me see you."

Millicent was too aroused to remember any of her earlier inhibitions. She stood up again and found herself standing between Lyon's legs. His mouth tasted her parted lips. His tongue thrust deeply into her warmth. As he pulled back, Lyon's hand cradled Millicent's face, then moved down one slender shoulder. He gently pushed the chemise down her body, until it pooled at her feet.

"You are stunning."

Tears once again sprang to her eyes as Millicent basked in the way Lyon's gaze paid homage to her body. She, too, felt whole and beautiful, and it was because of him.

He touched her deeply, stroking her moist folds until she cried his name out breathlessly, and then he kissed her again.

"Now love me, Millicent," he whispered against her ear as she continued to float on the waves of her release.

She undid the front of his breeches and straddled him, drawing him deep inside her body.

It was then—at that very moment as they rose together into those ethereal realms—that she knew she loved him in more ways than just this.

Chapter 22

When the carriage rolled to a stop by the Fleet Bridge, the stench of the canal rose around them, infusing the air with the foul smell of sewage and other things that Harry did not even want to consider. London was not Jamaica; that was for sure. The clerk looked through the darkness at his employer, sitting across from him, his cane by his knee and a loaded pistol in his hand. Whether they were in London or Port Royal, Harry thought, Mr. Hyde was the same. And Lord save the fool who crossed him.

"Do you understand me?" Hyde was saying, growing angrier by the minute. "You're to blame for this. If you hadn't mucked up the auction, we wouldn't be here now."

"Aye, sir. I'll make good tonight. Ye'll see."

"That I shall. And if you mess this, you blasted cur, the dogs will find your carcass in this fetid ditch. Do you hear me?"

"Aye, Mr. Hyde." Harry grew queasy at the thought of the canal and the unnameable things floating on the dead water. "I'll not fail ye, sir."

"Remember what I told you. Go up this alley a ways until you see the sign of the sheep's head. Around the corner from it you'll find the tavern kept by a man called the Turk. That's the place you'll find the men we want."

"Aye, sir. Half a dozen men."

"At least a half-dozen. You are to pay them a guinea each, with the promise of more if they'll sign on with us. But they'll get nothing if they say a word to anyone.

Tell them your master requires tight lips, or he'll see they swing for it. They're to just wait until we say 'tis time. We shall come for them within a fortnight, and they must be ready to travel. Do you understand me?"

"Do I tell them they keep the money even if ye didn't need them at all?"

"You're a blasted fool, Harry. You think these blackguards would give it back? You'll be lucky to get out of there without having your throat cut. You tell them they keep what you give them tonight. But there will be a much bigger prize if we need to take them with us to get the slave."

Harry looked up the dark alley. He was not particularly happy about going alone into the rat's nest of ramshackle buildings huddled along the edge of the canal.

"Beg pardon for asking, sir, but Mr. Platt seems confident that he can get the woman by lining up witnesses to say she's a witch. Now, to my thinking shouldn't we be waiting to . . . to pay good money to some low-life scoundrels till we're sure that the lawyer's way don't work out?"

In an instant, the silver head of Hyde's cane was pressed up against Harry's chest, pinning him against the carriage seat.

"You listen to me. I am not paying you to think. And I am certainly not leaving the outcome of this to fools like you or Platt or that roaring braggart Cranch. He's a blasted laborer and he thinks he can conquer the world himself. No, I'll not trust any one of you. I'll have plans and alternate plans, and I'll keep my own counsel until I have my fingers around that witch's throat."

Harry nodded meekly. It was true about Ned Cranch. The stonemason might have a way with the skirts, but the man was a bloody blower, to be sure.

"Now get out there," Hyde barked. "Remember, the sign of the sheep's head. And look to your back."

"If I might be so bold as to ask," Will started hesitantly as he scraped the razor over Lyon's throat. "Have ye told her ladyship about this?"

Lyon studied the lanky valet. "You're frightened."

"Ye do look a wee bit different, m'lord, with yer hair cut and yer beard all shaved clean. I'm only thinkin' Lady Aytoun deserves some warnin' afore ye scare her to death wi' yer new face."

"Scare her to death?" Lyon's laughter rang through the room. "Damn you, Will, she has been after me to shave from the moment she set eyes on me. If anything, the woman will be pleased."

Pleased. Absolutely. And not only about his appearance, Lyon thought hopefully. He had a great deal more that he was ready to tell her.

Testing his latest discovery, Lyon slowly pushed his feet along the floor away from the chair as far as they would reach. He then pulled them back. Long Will, intent on not cutting him, was oblivious to the movement.

The past four or five days had been miraculous. Lyon couldn't explain it, but somehow his body had made great improvements in the slow journey of healing. Actually, the improvements were quite small, but unlike the dozen times before, these changes appeared to be permanent. The movement of his fingers in his right hand. The ability to flex his knees and bend his ankles. He had not dared to put any weight on them yet, but the prospect was exciting.

At times during these past few days, especially when he and Millicent were making love, it had been almost impossible to hold back this new discovery from his wife. But Lyon had decided to wait until he was certain, and until he could surprise her with the magnitude of it.

There was so much that he owed Millicent. And there was so much more that he intended to repay.

The valet wiped Lyon's face with the towel and stepped back. Beyond Will, he saw Ohenewaa enter the room. No doors stopped the old woman from going where she wanted to go. Like an apparition, she came and went at any time of the day, and Lyon was accustomed to her ways.

Of course, he owed a great deal of credit for his

healing to Ohenewaa, too. She continued to see to him and prepare ointments for Millicent to administer. Unlike the other physicians who had found their way to his bedside since the accident, this one had believed in his recovery and given him hope. She was another one whom Lyon had yet to tell about the progress he was making.

Lyon saw the old woman's gaze travel down his legs to his feet.

"Is this any improvement?" he asked, touching his smoothly shaven face.

"Some," she responded. "Have you told her?"

"That's what *I* was asking 'slordship," the valet chirped in as he gathered up the shaving equipment. "No disrespect, m'lord, but ye look like a different man than the one her ladyship hitched herself to. An' we dunna want her to boot ye out of Melbury Hall, thinkin' ye're somebody else now."

"Get out, you prattling scarecrow."

With a broad grin on his face, Will left the room. Ohenewaa did not repeat her earlier question, and Lyon made no pretense of misunderstanding her.

"No, I haven't told her yet. But I intend to, this afternoon." He flexed the fingers of his right hand. "I have been waiting, hoping for the moment when I could make some grand gesture like taking a step, or sweeping Millicent off her feet, but I guess that isn't to be."

"Those things will come. You have to exercise your patience as well as your muscles." Ohenewaa put the bottles she was carrying on the table beside the bed. "Your wife takes her pleasure out of the little things in life. Small joys are rewarding, but the monumental ones can be overwhelming. She is much different than what you are accustomed to."

"Has someone been talking to you about my first marriage?"

Ohenewaa snorted.

"Are you so attuned to Millicent's moods and feelings?"

Ohenewaa simply stared at him with her slitted eyes, but said nothing more. Then she turned to the table.

Lyon studied the old woman for a long moment in silence. He watched her capable hands moving purposefully among the bottles and jars.

"Are you able to look into people and heal their souls as well as their bodies, Ohenewaa?"

The dark gaze turned and met his.

"I have met many men with vast experience in science and medicine in my life," he continued. "I have even run across a few spiritual men over the years. But none of them have had your confidence. Or your knowledge of healing."

"There is no magic involved in what I do, or in what I see. But I have seen too much real suffering. And what I have learned from those experiences is that wounds heal or people die. But I have also learned something else. Sometimes the suffering that plagues the body when there is no physical reason is caused by some memory that holds that person captive."

"Do you think guilt stopped me from improving before?"

"You say guilt. I did not say it. Guilt, regret, sorrow. If you look deep enough into your heart, you shall have your answer. But all of these"—she waved her hand at the bottles before her—"have been little more than trifles to distract you. You were on a path to destroy yourself. For your wife, I could not allow that. You are healing now because you have started to push open the door and let the pain that is past seep out. You are allowing the present to move in."

Lyon didn't think he would ever totally recover from the blow of his past. But Ohenewaa was right: He had stopped letting it rule his existence. He was no longer consumed by it.

He looked up to see the old woman gliding across the floor to the door with amazing self-possession.

"Do not forget," she said, stopping at the door. "Little steps."

*   *   *

"I need to get out to greet them. We're not ready. They weren't expected. We need to think of where to put them."

Overwhelmed by the sight of the visitors' carriages driving into the courtyard, Millicent glanced out the upstairs window.

"The dinner—"

"Cook shall see to it," Mrs. Page said hastily. "There will be plenty."

"Mr. Gibbs, please tell his lordship that the dowager and Sir Richard have arrived. Arrange for him to be brought down to the drawing room at once."

"Aye, m'lady."

She turned desperately to the housekeeper. "As far as rooms for everyone to stay in, is there any way we could avoid displacing Ohenewaa?"

"Surely. We'll move Mr. Gibbs into the steward's apartment," Mrs. Page responded. "His bedchamber should suit the gentleman. And if you don't mind giving up your bedchamber and moving in with your husband, m'lady, then we can quickly fix that up for her ladyship."

"Yes. Yes. That will work just fine," Millicent whispered, hurrying away through the house to greet their guests. Although she had invited the dowager to Hertfordshire, she was flustered with the abruptness of the visit. Naturally, she had hoped for a little warning prior to their arrival so that she could plan a perfect stay for the older woman.

It wasn't so much the need to impress, Millicent told herself, but her desire to raise the dowager's confidence in her. She wanted Lyon's mother to be reassured about her initial choice of Millicent as her daughter-in-law.

She paused at the top of the wide, curved stairs and ran a hand down the front of her green velvet dress. Taking a deep breath, she tucked a stray curl behind an ear. *Why tonight?* Millicent thought. On impulse, she had sought Violet's expertise to help her dress differently. She'd wanted to look special for dinner with Lyon tonight. As a result, the gown was too revealing and the style of her hair completely impractical. Of course, this would be the night that they would have guests.

Lady Aytoun and her lawyer had already removed their cloaks in the entrance hall by the time Millicent reached the foot of the stairs.

With a pair of maidservants on either side of her and a silver-headed staff to support her frail frame, the dowager received Millicent's greetings with a wave of one hand. "I shall not be making any apologies for the unexpectedness of my visit here."

"Nor should you, m'lady. We have been expecting . . . hoping for a visit from you for some time now." Millicent offered her greeting to Sir Richard in turn. "And how was your journey from London?"

"Horrible and long."

"We don't need to serve dinner until you have had some rest. But would you care to have a glass of wine or a cup of tea in the drawing room while your luggage is brought up to your rooms?" she asked pleasantly, trying to ignore the way the dowager's keen stare was taking in everything—from Millicent's hair to her gown to the very tips of her slippers. "There should be a nice fire going in there to help you warm up."

"I should like to see my son first."

"Then we can accomplish two things at once. His lordship is to join us in the drawing room as well."

Millicent was not oblivious to the look that passed between the dowager and the lawyer, but she said nothing and took her time escorting the older woman past the bowing Gibbs toward the drawing room.

"And how . . ." Sir Richard asked casually as he surveyed the marble stairwell and painted ceilings high above, "how is Lord Aytoun faring with the lack of visits from any physicians from London?"

"Quite well. In fact, as I have been mentioning in my letters to her ladyship, I believe he has made a vast improvement . . . in his disposition particularly."

"Have you engaged some country doctor, then, to see to him?" the man asked.

"No, Sir Richard. There has been no need for that."
Millicent slowed down to allow Lady Aytoun to catch
her breath. "But he has not been without medicinal
care, either."

"And how is that?" the dowager asked sharply.

Millicent saw no reason to hide the truth. "If you recall the day of our first meeting, I had come upon an
assistant to a deceased physician in London."

"The old African woman."

"Yes. As it turned out, m'lady, Ohenewaa's experience and knowledge in traditional and herbal methods
of healing have proved invaluable in treating your son."
Millicent was aware of a second look that passed between her guests. "As you shall see for yourself in a few
moments, his lordship is now in full control of his
thoughts and actions. He no longer depends on any sedating medications to calm his moods. He is independent
and willful, and Ohenewaa believes that it is only a matter of time before he overcomes the inability to move
his arm and legs."

Neither of her guests appeared convinced by her
speech. Millicent nodded to one of the servants to open
the doors of the drawing room. She peered in, hoping
that her husband was already there.

Someone was indeed there. But the handsome, clean-
shaven, and impeccably dressed gentleman sitting beside
the fireplace could not be her husband. The man's confident gaze took in their visitors before coming to rest
on Millicent.

Her pulse raced. Millicent took an involuntary step
backward and looked away as her heart sank like a stone
into her stomach.

The future she feared had arrived.

Lyon had eyes only for his wife. She was stunning.

The gown fitted her beautiful body like a second skin.
The auburn hair piled on her head was perfect, and
the curled tendrils that framed her pale face accentu-
ated her high cheekbones and sensual mouth. But he
could also see the look of uncertainty in the depths of

her gray eyes. More than anything else, Lyon would have liked to be left alone with Millicent. He wanted to tell her how lovely she looked. Reluctantly, he turned to the visitors.

"I'm sorry I cannot get up, Mother." She was staring at him in open disbelief. "Come in. Please."

Both guests appeared to be rooted to the ground they stood upon, and now that he thought about it, so was Millicent.

"Maitland, you do not look any worse since I saw you last. And you must be well, too, Mother, gallivanting about the countryside in the middle of winter. Come sit by the fire, all of you." He brought a hand up to touch his face and addressed Millicent. "What do you think?"

"I . . . I . . ." Instead of answering him, she turned to the guests. "If you would be kind enough to join his lordship, I need to oversee some arrangements. I shall join you all shortly."

Lyon sensed her discomfort. But he didn't know if it was the suddenness of the unexpected company or if it was something that he had done. Long Will's teasing words came back to him; so did Ohenewaa's questions. He decided not to press her, and as Millicent disappeared from the doorway, he turned instead to his mother and the lawyer, who finally decided to approach the fire.

"You look a little tired, Mother, but much the same as I left you."

"I cannot say the same thing about you." She sat down heavily in one of the cushioned chairs and dismissed her maidservants. The door of the drawing room closed and the three of them were left alone. "You look rested and fit. I can see the Hertfordshire weather agrees with you."

"My improved health is due to far more than the weather," Lyon corrected, drawing surprised looks from the other two. He turned to Maitland. "I assume you received my letter."

"I did, m'lord. And I have in my possession the pieces you requested. We have also brought with us Peter How-

itt, a young man who was trained by Walter Truscott
and was a clerk at Baronsford for—"

"I remember him," Lyon said. "Any news of Pierce?"

Maitland shook his head, and Lyon was sorry that he
had asked. Signing responsibility for the family estate
over to his younger brother some six months ago had
been Lyon's attempt at salvaging their family. He
planned to withdraw and let all the hard feelings gradually fade, while Pierce could take charge and bring
David back and the people of Baronsford could continue
with their lives peacefully, as they once had. Giving away
Baronsford had been Lyon's way of settling the future
for everyone, but Pierce had thrown it all back in his
face by not returning from Boston in the American
colonies.

"And how are things at Baronsford?" Lyon asked,
trying not to allow old wounds to begin festering again.

"Perhaps we could discuss this later, m'lord, when we
have more time." The lawyer cast a cautionary glance
at the dowager, and Lyon respected his wish to wait. It
had been so long since Lyon had cared enough to ask
about the place that Maitland was obviously concerned
that once the discussion began, the dowager would become overtired well before the two men covered all
there was to talk over.

He was right. Lyon had so many questions. And he
was well aware that his brothers did not share his passion for it the way he did. It was not the place that he
missed so much as it was the people. And seeing the
care that Millicent bestowed on everyone at Melbury
Hall, he now realized how neglected the people there
must feel.

"Before you two do that, I have some things I should
like to know." The dowager studied him keenly. "These
changes that I see in you—these improvements—what is
the extent of them?"

"I cannot walk as yet, if that is what you mean." Lyon
took satisfaction in watching their stunned expressions
as he stretched his feet slowly before him. "But I think
it will only be a matter of time."

"This is wonderful, m'lord," Maitland exclaimed.

"Witch or no witch, the woman is a maker of miracles," the dowager whispered in awe, staring at his feet.

"So you have heard about Ohenewaa," Lyon said.

"We have, m'lord. But no report was favorable until your wife spoke of her upon our arrival. And now this!"

Lyon turned to his mother. "Who else has been talking about her?"

"Dr. Parker is still braying like a stung mule over your wife's treatment of him. The man has been filling the ears of everyone in London who will listen to him about the danger Millicent has subjected you to." The dowager smiled. "And from Dr. Tate's description of the situation, this black woman's care should put you six feet underground in a fortnight at the latest."

"So that is the reason for this unexpected visit?"

Maitland started. "You had requested—"

"Indeed," the dowager cut in with her usual abruptness. "I hated to think I had been wrong about Millicent."

"You were not wrong about her," Lyon replied tenderly. "And as much as I thought the idea of an arranged marriage preposterous when you first suggested it, this is as good a chance as any to commend you and to thank you for choosing her."

Their last meeting had been the day Lyon was leaving for Hertfordshire. He had been heavily sedated and, from what little he remembered of their last words to each other, Lyon didn't think he had been very appreciative.

"It is because of Millicent and her stubbornness that I have come this far and improved this much. She is a fighter, Mother. The woman would not let me be."

The sense of relief that passed between the visitors was palpable. Lyon saw his mother lean back heavily against the cushioned chair. A weight had obviously been lifted from her.

"So she is done with all that nonsense about a divorce or an annulment."

Lyon felt a dark cloud form over his own head. He leaned forward.

"What are you talking about?"

"The countess demanded a provision to be included in the marriage agreement, m'lord," Maitland stated quietly. "In the event of your recovery, a divorce would be uncontested."

"Why?"

"Because of her first marriage," the dowager put in, lowering her voice. "Because of the scandalous abuse she received under the brutal hands of her first husband. Because of the shame she still carries at the thought of facing society. Because of not being loved enough even by her own family. Despite the rumors that circulated at the time, they would do nothing to rescue her from that horrible situation."

"I knew nothing of this."

"Reason enough, I should think, for any woman not to want to be exposed to the bonds of marriage ever again."

The fingers of his hand fisted in anger. The fact that Wentworth was a worthless human being had been obvious all along. But Lyon had not guessed at his physical abuse of Millicent. Bits and pieces started to fit into place. He realized his mother was again speaking.

"I am certain you already realize that your wife has great pride. It took a great deal of hard work and courage to take charge of this estate. She has made it a home for herself and for the people she cares about. Though financially strapped, she was happy here. Absolutely content. It took a great deal of persuasion on my part to convince her to marry again at all. But you should consider that what she asked for over two months ago might not be what she wants now."

A seed of doubt had already taken hold in Lyon's mind.

"I almost did not recognize Millicent when I laid eyes on her a few moments ago," the dowager continued in a reassuring tone. "She has changed as much as you have. She looks happy. She glows with an inner beauty. In fact, she is much different than the woman I met in London."

Millicent was happy when people needed her. She had risen to the challenge of dealing with him because of the needs that had crippled him. Recently, they had shared tremendous passion. But they had not spoken one word of the future.

To become whole but to pay the price of losing her was an option that Lyon was not ready to accept. He cared for her too much.

There was a knock on the door, and two servants bringing trays of tea entered.

"I shall forgo the tea. I should like to go up to rest before dinner."

"We keep country hours here, Mother. We dine at seven."

"Very well." The dowager pushed herself to her feet. "This is your chance, Sir Richard, to bring Aytoun up to snuff on all the news of Baronsford. I believe he is ready for it."

Lyon watched his mother go and wondered what else he could be told today that could top the distressing news they had shared about Millicent's bargain.

Pushing herself off her knees, Violet wiped her mouth with the back of one sleeve and leaned against the stone wall of the house. The wind carried spatterings of cold rain, and the young woman raised her face, relishing the feel of it against her fevered skin.

Tonight the taste of cheese had not sat well in her stomach. Yesterday morning it had been the smell of turnips that had sent her running. The day before, she couldn't hold down even a cup of weak tea.

Violet's heart drummed hard in her chest. For the past fortnight she had been sick to her stomach every day. She had stopped denying it: She was pregnant.

The consequences of what this meant, though, had continued to pound at her. Bearing a child out of wedlock. She would lose her position. She would bring shame onto her family's name.

"Are you coming tonight?"

Amina's call as the woman stepped out the back door

forced Violet away from the wall. "I am. I was waiting for you," she lied.

They walked together toward one of the recently repaired cottages just beyond the stables. Amina and Jonah lived there, and nearly every night Amina and a number of the other former slave women gathered there. Violet had been welcome among these women ever since the days just before the squire died. A bond had been formed when, out of fear of Squire Wentworth, she had taken shelter with four of the black women in their hut in the Grove.

Since that time one of them, having being freed, had gone to London. The rest of them, though, despite new positions or living arrangements or marriage, continued to get together in the room of one or the cottage of another nearly every night. For a couple of hours they would gather to talk or sew, enjoying one another's company. Violet had an open invitation to join them whenever she wished, and she often did.

Tonight's gathering was a great relief to the young woman. She felt safe here. And after so many hours of anguishing over her pregnancy, she had been desperate to step outside herself—even for an hour or two. She had no one in whom she could confide this, and that included Ned. She already knew what his reaction would be.

". . . never had a husband, but she left a child behind when they sold her to that Dr. Dombey."

Violet focused on the conversation that was going on around her.

"I had never heard anything about that." Amina lowered the sewing onto her lap.

"That was before your time, child," the oldest of the women commented. She had spent most of her life in the islands, but her talent as a brewer had caused Wentworth to bring her to Melbury Hall. "I have heard our people say Ohenewaa was an Ashanti princess, stolen away from the land to the west of a sacred river in Africa. She had real beauty as a child, and so she was taken up as a domestic servant. She never worked in the field,

like I did before I went to the kitchens. By the grace of
the Almighty, she never took no beatings the way the
rest of us did. 'Twasn't till she came of age that the
troubles started."

"Troubles?" Violet asked quietly.

"Aye. When she started showing signs of being a
woman. I don't know how old she was. Maybe twelve
or thirteen. But the master was quick enough to notice
it. I remember she still had some growing left in her,
the first time that she started swelling up with child."
The old woman shook her head sadly. "But she lost it
at birth. The master's wife wouldn't allow any of us to
go to her the night of her birthing. The mistress would
have been happy to see her die, too. I still remember
her crying out in pain and fear that night."

"You said she left a child behind," Amina said.

"Aye, that I did. This was all before she learned how
to end a pregnancy before it showed. I think it was the
year after or maybe the year after that that she swelled
up again. And this time a boy was born."

"Could she keep him?"

"No chance of that. By then the master was tired of
her. He kept the child in the house, though, and passed
Ohenewaa on to his bailiff and the men. But that woman
was too strong for them. She ran away. They brought
her back and branded her. But she ran away again. They
brought her back and whipped her good that time. But
she kept running."

"She was lucky to survive it," Amina said sadly.

"That is what the rest of us were thinking, too. But
you know, what was so impressive about her was that
every time they brought her back, she became stronger.
With every beating she became more a part of the rest
of us. She was still a young thing, but her name started
getting out. And we stopped thinking of her as the master's girl."

"I am surprised Dombey bought her."

The old woman stabbed the needle into the sewing on
her lap. "He was brought from Port Royal to see to the

master's wife. She was sick in bed with a fever, and that was when he accidentally ran across Ohenewaa. She was sick too then, but she was ailing from the latest lashing she got."

"I remember Dombey when he was much older," Amina said. "He wasn't too bad."

"I don't know," the old woman continued. "Maybe he did have more conscience than most of them. Whatever 'twas, by the time the doctor left, the master's wife died and Dombey managed to buy Ohenewaa."

"But that was only the start of her making a name for herself," another woman, who had been keeping silent, put in. "Quite a few of us got sold off to other plantations right after that." She looked at the oldest woman in the group. "That's when you and me went to the kitchens in that other place. We only saw Ohenewaa from time to time after that. Everywhere Dombey went, he took her, so we only saw her when the doctor would be called up to the plantation."

"She went everywhere, she did," the older woman said. "And being as smart as she was, she learned whatever she could from old Dombey. But she didn't only learn from him. When they was traveling aboard a ship to or back from Africa, she'd spend the passage with our people. As Dombey did as little as he needed to do with slaves, Ohenewaa needed to be down there, below decks, seeing to the sick, comforting them that felt their hearts being ripped out of them, and all the while learning what she could of the land our people was stolen from."

" 'Twas amazing to be working at a plantation and having new men or women come in who already knew Ohenewaa," the second woman said, going back to her sewing. "She became a common thread that linked us all."

The oldest woman smiled. "Especially the women."

"Aye, she knew how to deal with our kinds of problems."

"What happened to her son?" Amina asked.

The older women shrugged. "I don't think she ever went back to find out. Maybe he lived to be a servant or groom or something. Who can say?"

"And what plantation was that?" Amina asked. "Who was Ohenewaa's first master?"

"That was out at the Hyde plantation, child. That was where everything started."

Chapter 23

*S*he must have been crazy to think this arrangement would work.

Millicent laid the book down and rubbed her eyes. She had delayed going up the stairs to their bedroom as long as she could. The dowager and Sir Richard, tired from their trip, had retired soon after dinner. And as it had become part of their habit these past nights, the valets had taken Lyon up to ready him for bed as well.

Millicent walked out of the library and passed through the house. Slowly she started up the wide curved stairs. If this had been any other day—if she had not been so affected by the change in Lyon—she would have been thrilled to rush up there. But for the first time since her marriage to him, she felt out of her element. She did not belong. He was moving too fast, and she was not sure she had the strength to follow.

The reason for these pangs of insecurity was not just his looks. True, he was far more handsome than she had even imagined. He looked like a god. But there was the matter of his confidence, too. And power.

She could feel his masculinity growing. Tonight he had exuded the raw animal potency of a man taking charge of his life.

And that frightened her.

The arrival of the dowager and her lawyer had awakened the man who must have been sleeping inside her husband. When Millicent looked at him during dinner, as he debated the growing unrest in the American colo-

nies with Sir Richard, she had seen a gentleman of intelligence and wit, a member of the fashionable elite, a
nobleman beyond her reach. Lyon Pennington, fourth
Earl of Aytoun, was a man she barely had the right to
dream about.

Violet had moved some of Millicent's clothes over to
this room earlier, but she hoped that he would be asleep
by the time she reached the bedchamber. Pushing open
the door and peering in, Millicent found her hope had
been in vain. At least a dozen candles were burning, and
Lyon appeared as awake as he had been at noon. He
was propped up with pillows on the bed. A book lay
open on his lap.

"I was wondering if you would come up, or if I needed
to come down and bring you up myself."

"I would like to have seen you try." She closed the
bedroom door and leaned her back against it.

"Is that a challenge?"

The touch of a smile on his lips played havoc with
Millicent's insides. She cast about for safe ground to step
on. "You and Sir Richard were locked in the library for
some time this afternoon. It must have felt good to be
brought up-to-date with your business affairs."

"Good and distressing. Are you getting ready for
bed?"

Millicent pushed away from the door. She glanced at
the screen divider and the nightdress that had been laid
out on a settee beside it. Tonight the room felt much
smaller; the bed looked far too narrow. Lyon closed the
book and fixed his gaze on her.

"I never had the opportunity to tell you how beautiful
you looked tonight."

"I . . . thank you," she whispered, becoming more
flustered. She needed a place to escape to. The screen
served the purpose. She had just slipped behind it as a
soft knock sounded on the door.

Hurrying to the door, she opened it slightly. Violet
stood in the corridor.

"Are you ready to undress, m'lady?"

"Yes, come in."

"No!" Lyon ordered from the bed. "I shall help your mistress. Out with you."

Millicent felt her face burn as Violet stood looking from one person to the other.

"I shall manage, Vi," Millicent said, dismissing her. "Off to bed with you."

Closing the door, she crossed the room as casually as she could and ducked behind the screen.

"I said I'd help you."

"Yes, I know." Her voice sounded odd, even to her own ears. "I can manage."

"The buttons to that dress are in the back."

She cursed silently. He was right. Violet had helped her get into the dress. She needed someone to help her out of it.

"Can I help you?"

Millicent closed her eyes.

"I shan't shave my face again, even if you beg me."

He sounded like a sulking child, and an uncontrollable giggle rose in her chest. He sounded like her. The ridiculousness of how she was acting dawned on her. This was, after all, the same man with whom she had made love repeatedly this week. He was her husband. Clutching the nightgown to her chest, she came around the screen.

"The damage is done," she said. "Now I know how frighteningly handsome you are, so you might as well keep this look."

"Very well, m'lady. Your wish is my command." He tossed the book on the bedside table. "Come here."

Millicent sat on the edge of the bed within the reach of his left hand with her back to him. "If you would do the first dozen buttons, I can handle the rest."

"You cannot be serious," he said with feigned shock. "The 'rest' is what I have been looking forward to all day. So I do it all or nothing."

She looked over her shoulder at the smile on his handsome face. He knew exactly how to melt her heart. "You drive a hard bargain."

Millicent felt the first button open and then the second.

"Now that you mention it, there is something that I need from you."

She heard the change in his tone. "What is it?"

"I need to go to Scotland. I want you to come with me."

Her body tensed immediately. Lyon's fingers moved down her back, undoing a few more buttons.

"During these past few months I had been so far removed physically and mentally from Baronsford that I was not aware of the situation there. I had no idea that the problems going on in the Highlands were spreading south to us in the Borders."

"You mean the land clearings?" she asked quietly.

She knew a little about it. For nearly thirty years, since the defeat of Bonny Prince Charlie at Culloden, the government had been leaning heavily on the Scottish Jacobites and the Highland clans that had sided with the Pretender.

In the newspapers the dowager had been sending up from London, Millicent had read some of the speeches being given in Parliament. From what she could gather, the present problems had really begun in earnest some ten years ago in the Highlands. The value of money was not what it used to be, and the lairds had all begun to raise the rents. Because there were just too many people in the Highlands, wages remained low. Tacksmen—the increasingly affluent men who for decades had leased large tracts of land from the lairds and then sublet the land in smaller plots to crofters—were no longer able to make a living, and had started moving out. The lairds had looked for ways to make the land more profitable, and that was when the trouble really started.

"Sir Richard told me hundreds of vagrants are passing through Baronsford every month. Most of them are hungry, desperate for work. They need ways to feed their families. Others just want to earn enough to pay for passage to the colonies."

She turned to him. "I read someone's speech in the House of Lords. He said that with the tacksmen gone, the tenants' lives would only improve. They would have only one master to satisfy. But these vagrants—"

"Are those same poor tenants." He finished her sentence. "In truth, what has happened is that the farms vacated by the old tacksmen have been let to any stranger who would make the highest offer. These newcomers care nothing for the lowly crofters who have been working the soil for years. The new tacksmen have paid their rent and now are determined to squeeze from those beneath them as large a return as possible for their outlay."

"People can only take that for so long."

"And raising the rents is not all of their troubles, either," he added coolly. "Some of the landowners are combining the smaller farms, doing away with the tillage, and introducing sheep on a large scale. Now, each of those farms would have been occupied by any number of tenant families who worked the soil. The landowners have simply pushed those people out and pulled down their homes."

"How terrible!" She touched his hand. "You said the troubles have reached Baronsford."

"Some of my neighbors have begun the same practice." He held her hand. "Because I have been away for so long, rumors have begun to spread amongst the tenants. After the accident, I transferred control of the land to my brother Pierce."

Millicent already knew this, but she decided to keep silent.

"I assume he has been too busy to come back from the colonies or do anything about it. Still, I feel the problems were really mine, and I have to address them now." He absently caressed her hand. "I have no tacksmen, nor did my father before me, but many of the tenants apparently fear that Baronsford's farms will be next to go."

Millicent had sensed the same kind of fear among the Africans at Melbury Hall after Wentworth's death. Although relieved that their brutal owner was gone, they had been very apprehensive about who was to take over. Many had expected Millicent to sell what she could—including them—and then walk away from it all. But she could not turn her back on her people.

"You must go back. You must make them understand that you are not deserting them."

"I agree. I want you to come with me."

"I cannot," she protested. "I cannot be away from Melbury Hall for so long."

"We could go for a fortnight—maybe a month at most. Then we shall come back."

"But I am needed here. Things cannot function—"

"You know they can." When she tried to stand up, Lyon's hand grasped her arm, forcing her to stay. "You have competent people here who are doing their jobs. There is no reason why you cannot take a few weeks away."

"There are others who can go with you. The dowager—"

"She told me tonight that this is as far from London as she plans to travel. In fact, she is so taken with my recovery that she told me she plans to stay awhile at Melbury Hall. She thinks the place might do her some good as well."

"You see?" She nodded matter-of-factly. "All the more reason for me to stay here. Someone needs to keep her company."

"She has Maitland. And Gibbs and Mrs. Page will look after her perfectly well." He lowered his voice. "I'll tell you the truth. It is not her affection for you and me that will keep my mother here. I think she wants to stay and see if Ohenewaa can do her any good."

Lyon was right, and Millicent knew it. As much as she didn't want to believe it, Melbury Hall was beginning to run smoothly on a day-to-day basis. But still, a mild panic had taken hold of Millicent. It really came down to one thing—she knew she lacked too much to successfully function as an earl's wife at a place like Baronsford. All her ancestors didn't amount to a hill of tea. She was just plain, simple Millicent Gregory. She might be able to fill the role of a squire's widow in a small country estate like Melbury Hall, but beyond that she had no illusions.

"Tell me what is bothering you."

She looked up and saw Lyon's hurt expression. "I am frightened."

He tugged on her arm and pulled her into a fierce embrace. His lips brushed against her hair. His hand moved possessively over her back.

"When we barricade the door," he whispered raggedly into her ear, "the world outside seems to be a frightening place. I have fears, too. I fear the past. I think of facing my own people and I fear they will find me lacking. I am not the man they knew."

Millicent held him tight. She pressed her head against his chest and listened to the stout heart drumming within. Lyon's problems were much more significant, and yet hers threatened to freeze her like a sculpture of snow. She looked down at her legs, frozen with fear and unable to carry her into the future.

"When are you planning to leave?"

"I was hoping to go early next week."

She looked up into his handsome face. "Will you let me think about it?"

He leaned down and brushed his lips against hers. "Yes. But don't ask me to refrain from pressuring you. Or from trying to convince you. Or bribe you. Or whatever else I must do. I need you with me, Millicent."

And she needed him.

Chapter 24

❧

"You there. What's your name?"

"James Wakefield, ma'am."

The dowager glanced at a second boy who stood by the garden wall, keeping a safe distance. The two of them had burst out of the woods and come racing up to the garden gate, laughing and shouting and chasing after each other like a pair of colts. But upon seeing her coming out of the garden, the two had come to an abrupt halt.

"And who is your friend?"

"Israel. He used to live here at Melbury Hall. But now he lives at Solgrave with us."

"I see." The old woman studied James Wakefield. The lad was tall and wiry, though he couldn't have been more than twelve or thirteen. She noticed his misshapen hand, but didn't linger on it. She turned her gaze on the other one. Israel had the most striking green eyes in his handsome dark face. She looked back at James. "And what mischief are you two about today?"

"Mischief?" James answered, shooting a devilish look at his friend. "None at all. But if you forgive us, ma'am, we have some very important business that we need to attend to."

With a deep bow, the young boy backed away from the garden gate and joined his friend. A minute later the two were again laughing and racing each other to the house.

"He is Lord Stanmore's oldest son," the dowager's attendant told her.

Although she had never met them in person, the dowager knew a great deal about the family. Lord Stanmore was from good Scottish stock. His mother was a Buchanan, hailing from the hills around Loch Lomond.

Lady Stanmore was even more interesting. In finding out what she could about Millicent, the dowager had learned about the solid friendship between her and Rebecca Stanmore that had started back in the years when the two were students at an academy for girls in Oxford. Despite the ten years that Rebecca had spent in the American colonies, the two young women had easily rekindled their friendship during the summer that Stanmore had married Rebecca. It was the same summer Millicent had become a widow.

"His young lordship attends Eton, and the black lad, Israel, goes to the school in Knebworth Village," the attendant continued. "The two boys are best of friends, I gather, and visit here often. Cook already had some sweets ready this morning, expecting a visit from them."

Such fascinating lives, the dowager thought, welcoming the feel of the sun on her face. Standing just inside the garden gate, she filled her lungs with the cool morning air and thought, as crowded as Melbury Hall was with all types of people, she couldn't remember the last time she had felt so well.

At the edge of the trees from which the boys had come, she spied a tall black woman bending down to pick up something from the ground. The woman straightened and put her find carefully in a basket that she carried. As she did, the dowager had her first opportunity to look into the wrinkled face. This was Ohenewaa, she was certain. The dowager had been keen on meeting her since their arrival two days ago, but the woman had proved elusive thus far.

She turned to her attendant. "Go ask her to come and join me here for few moments."

The young woman hurried to do as she was told. From within the walls of the garden, Beatrice watched her attendant approach and say a few words to the black woman. Ohenewaa answered without looking toward the garden. The young woman hesitated, then hurried back.

"She asks why you'd like her to come here, m'lady."

"Tell her I should like to thank her."

The servant ran off again. The dowager moved out of the gate and, using her silver-headed staff, poked the cold soil of a flower bed. From here she had a better view of the other woman. The attendant hurried back again and was breathless by the time she arrived at the gate.

"She'd like to know what reason you have for thanking her, m'lady."

"Good Lord! Tell her I need to thank her for what she has done for my son."

The attendant hurried down the hill again. Beatrice noticed that Ohenewaa had taken a few steps up toward the garden. A moment later, the young woman was coming back again. The dowager walked along the path a few feet.

"What now?"

Instead of coming all the way, the attendant called from halfway up the hill, "She says, m'lady, 'twas all his own doing. That she hasn't done a thing."

"Modest, too," the dowager called out, moving down a few more steps.

"Modest, too," the attendant called out in Ohenewaa's direction.

"I did not tell you to say that," Beatrice scolded. She stopped her complaining when she realized Ohenewaa had started approaching her. She continued down the hill.

"What else should I tell her?" the servant asked, looking a little frayed.

"You should go up to the house and rest your voice."

The young woman turned around. "You should go up to the house and rest your—"

"Not her," the dowager snapped, having reached the young woman. "You!"

"I?" The attendant turned around, confused.

"Yes, you," Ohenewaa answered, having reached the halfway point as well.

With a curtsy to each woman, the attendant hurried off toward the house.

Ohenewaa turned her gaze on the dowager. "You should know straightaway that I do not respond well to being summoned."

"That was no summons. 'Twas a request. But no matter," Beatrice said impatiently, waving her hand. "I just wanted to spend some time with you, to get to know you a little, but I am afraid I am not very good at expressing myself patiently when I want something."

"Abruptness is part of your nature," Ohenewaa commented.

"I know."

"And rudeness, I think."

"Sometimes that is true."

"And stubbornness."

"When 'tis called for." The dowager frowned suspiciously. "And how is it that you know me so well?"

She shrugged. "I know your son. Now, what was it that you wanted?"

"If you could put up with a cranky old woman, may I keep your company while you walk and gather your plants and herbs?"

"Since you ask this way, why not? I think the eyes of two cranky old women may be far better than one."

Millicent burst through the library doors, and Lyon smiled as the energy she exuded displaced all trace of quiet in the room. It was a welcome change, and he studied every aspect of her appreciatively. The dark blue dress had a fitted bodice and low neckline. She was wearing a thin ribbon of a matching color around her neck.

"Sir Richard just went upstairs to change for dinner," she said. "The dowager is on her way downstairs. I thought we should take two carriages to Solgrave, as—"

"For days now I have been desperate for a moment alone with you."

Millicent came to an abrupt halt in the middle of the room and stood motionless.

Since the dowager and Maitland's arrival, either she or Lyon had been constantly on the go. Even in their bedchamber, time had been fleeting, for Millicent seemed determined to come up late and escape early in the morning.

Lyon knew what she was doing: She was avoiding giving him the answer he was after.

"You look beautiful tonight."

A soft blush crept into her cheeks. She smiled. "You look rather handsome yourself."

"I have a small gift here for you."

She glanced curiously at the box sitting beside him on the table. "You have given me enough, Lyon. I don't expect any—"

"I know. I want you to have it anyway. Please."

She approached hesitantly. "But what is the occasion?"

"I need no occasion to give my wife a gift."

Millicent reached his side. "But I don't have anything for you."

"You have given me more than I deserve." He took her hand in his, and she sat down shyly on his lap. He handed her the box, and she opened it slowly.

She gasped in shock and closed the top quickly. "These are so beautiful. I cannot accept them."

Shaking his head, Lyon opened the box for her again. "Yes, you can." He took out one of the diamond necklaces and laid it across the palm of her hand. "Will you wear this for me tonight?"

"But Lyon, this is too beautiful. I could never do it justice."

"Love, this is only a string of cold stones. By themselves they are nothing. You will give them life by wearing them near your heart." He turned her face and brushed away a single tear that had escaped her silvery gray eyes. "You are so beautiful. Please let me do this."

She leaned into him and kissed his lips, and Lyon realized that he was like those stones in some ways. She was giving *him* life by holding him near her heart.

*   *   *

The round face of the baby sleeping so peacefully against Rebecca's chest fascinated Millicent. This past year had gone by so quickly.

"He is truly an angel," she said quietly.

"In his sleep," Rebecca quipped, caressing the soft mat of dark hair on her son's head. "You should have heard him half an hour ago. That was why Mrs. Trent came to fetch me."

They were still an hour from dinner, and Millicent had left Lyon and the dowager and Sir Richard chatting comfortably with Lord Stanmore while she came up to the nursery to visit with Rebecca. She didn't know how to broach the subject, but she really needed her friend's advice. She had been putting off answering Lyon's question for three days. She absently touched the elegant necklace at her throat. Although he was not pressuring her, she knew Lyon wanted to know if she was going to Baronsford with him. And despite everything between them, she was still terrified.

"I cannot believe how much he has grown since I saw him last." She looked up from the child's face to the proud mother's. "But there is something about you that has changed, too. I don't know. But you seem to have this look about you. Are you . . . ?"

Biting her lip, Millicent let the question hang in between them. The immediate reddening of Rebecca's face was impossible to miss.

"You *are* with child again!" Millicent blurted out excitedly. "Is it true?"

The young mother smiled, rising to her feet. "I must be so transparent."

"When? When are you having this baby?" Millicent whispered her question for fear of waking up the sleeping child.

"Sometime toward the end of autumn. We just found out." She laid the baby in his crib and nodded to the nursemaid, who sat sewing by the fire. "Stanmore is thrilled, of course. We brought James home from Eton on a short holiday to celebrate. He is quite

excited, but wants some kind of guarantee for another brother."

Tiptoeing out, the two of them left the nursery. In
the outer room, though, rather than going straight out,
Rebecca turned around and took Millicent's hands in
hers. "I want to hear about you and your marriage. You
look wonderful. You look happy."

"I am, surprisingly. Very happy."

Rebecca gave her a fierce hug. "I am so glad to hear
it. My Lord, to think that I was so wrong about Aytoun!" She pulled back and smiled. "When we were in
Scotland, I received a letter from Reverend and Mrs.
Trimble, praising your husband to the skies. Just spending the few short minutes with him downstairs, I can see
he is nothing like the man rumor had portrayed."

"If there was any truth to those rumors, or if they
were simply vicious gossip, I cannot say, Rebecca. I cannot defend the man my husband may have been before."

"Do not be discouraged, though, if you hear more
talk," Rebecca warned. "The idleness of the *ton* pro-
vides a breeding ground for malicious slander."

"I will not allow them to hurt him. I will fight anyone
with my bare hands if I hear them besmirch his name
now." She let out an unsteady breath. "He has come so
far in his recovery, but he still has a rocky road ahead
of him. But I shall tell you one thing, Lyon Pennington
has already proved to be a wonderful husband and a
great friend to me. I just cannot describe in words how
much I have come to value him."

Rebecca looped an arm through Millicent's. "Just
watching him downstairs, watching the way his gaze fol-
lows you around the room, the way he stops the very
word on his tongue to listen when you are speaking
across the way, I know that he values you, too. And I
know how difficult it is sometimes to put these things
into the right words. But from my own experience, I can
say that this is what love is all about."

"Love?" Millicent repeated under her breath.

"I would say that it is clear you love him, Millicent.
And I think he shares your affection."

Millicent couldn't stop the sudden tears from rushing into her eyes. She turned away from her friend.

"What is wrong?" Alarmed, Rebecca came around to face her.

"I am so confused and terrified and . . . and . . . I just don't know what to do." She stabbed at the tears. "I am so desperate to do the right thing for him and for myself, but my heart just doesn't let me carry it through."

"Sit with me." Rebecca tugged her hand, drawing her down on a settee beside her. "I want you to tell me what is wrong."

She let out a couple of shaky breaths, trying desperately to calm her nerves. "He . . . Lyon has to go back to Baronsford. He has asked me to go along with him."

"What is terrifying about that?"

Millicent shook her head. "The problem is that I entered into this marriage knowing that it might not last forever. I made them agree that if Lyon were to improve then I would be released from the marriage. I even had Sir Oliver Birch put those conditions in the marriage contract so there would be no objection afterward."

"You were trying to protect yourself, in case he turned out to be not the man that you expected. But that was then, and this is now."

"You don't understand. I was also trying to protect him, too. You see, he is an earl, and I am just . . ." She shook her head. "He needs beauty, style, charm to grace his arm in public, not someone—"

"Stop!" Rebecca snapped. "Stop and listen to what you are saying, to what you are doing to yourself. You are not lacking in beauty or style or charm."

"If I could only make myself believe that."

"Then you must." Rebecca spoke passionately. "Millicent, you cannot allow Wentworth to continue to ruin your life. It is not you talking this nonsense, but him. During your marriage to that degenerate pig, he tried to strip you of your confidence, of your sense of self-worth. He tried to crush you in person and in spirit. And now, after his death, you are allowing him to continue to hurt you . . . even from the grave."

The truth behind her words made Millicent shiver. She forced herself to push away the murky cloud that was enveloping her. She wanted to be able to look into the future without fear. But it was so difficult.

"Your husband needs you. You say he has asked you to go. He wants you to go." Rebecca took both of Millicent's hands and squeezed them as she looked into her face. "If for no other reason, go with him and think of it as a test. Think of it as a way of proving to yourself that you have done away with Wentworth's ghost for eternity."

The valets backed out of the carriage after seating Lyon comfortably for the ride home. Millicent climbed in immediately, and the door closed behind her.

"I like them very much," Lyon admitted. "Both of them. Rebecca is charming and completely unpretentious . . . like you. And Stanmore's progressive views and the way he presents them makes me happy that he sits in the House of Lords. If we only had more people there like him."

"I believe the feeling was mutual." She sat on the seat beside him. "They really enjoyed your company, too."

"Just the two of us?" Lyon asked when the carriage started off.

"I sent everyone else in the other one. I hope you don't mind, but I wanted you all to myself for the ride back."

Lyon wrapped his left arm around Millicent's shoulder and slid her across the seat closer to him. "This is far too promising for such a short ride. Tell the groom to go back to Melbury Hall by way of London."

Millicent's laughter rippled over him. Something had happened tonight. Somehow, during the time that Millicent and Rebecca had spent upstairs, his wife had shed the anxiety that had weighed her down of late. He took her hand and raised it to his lips.

"Thank you."

"For what?"

"For smiling, and for wanting to be with me, and for these obvious plans of seduction."

Her silvery eyes danced with merriment in the dim light of the carriage. She leaned toward him and brushed her lips against his. "And I thought I was being so devious."

He caught her chin and captured her mouth for a much deeper kiss. "This shall be a challenge."

She laughed softly and pressed her body closer as the carriage rolled down the dark country lane. "I do not think there is much that I can do with what little time it takes to go to Melbury Hall. But the dowager and Sir Richard have already told me how ready they are to retire. So when we get back, there is always the prospect of our bed."

Her hand moved beneath his overcoat, and Lyon felt every muscle in his body flex and come to life.

"I don't know if I can wait that long. There is something about the motion of a moving carriage," he said seductively.

The carriage turned onto the road leading to Melbury Hall.

"You make it sound quite tempting, but our bed will have to do for tonight, I think." She stretched up and kissed his neck. "But of course, we shall have plenty of time to try out your carriage idea on our ride to Baronsford."

He turned to her. "You are coming?"

"If you still want me to come."

"Is this answer enough?" he whispered huskily, crushing his mouth down on hers.

"I am so sorry to do this to you, m'lady, just before you go away. But with my grandmum sick and Baronsford being so far away in Scotland and all, there was no way I could get back if she—"

"You don't have to explain any more," Millicent said gently. "I understand perfectly, Violet. Don't give it another thought."

"But I feel so bad about it, m'lady." She turned her face and began straightening brushes on the dresser and then wiping specks of invisible dust.

"You shouldn't," Millicent assured her. "In fact, I have been meaning to talk to you. I've been worrying about you. You've not been looking yourself lately. Why don't you take a holiday while we're in Scotland and go give your mother a hand with your grandmother in St. Albans?"

"I am so much obliged to you, m'lady. I know she could use a little help. But don't you be worrying about me now. I've laid out all your clothes, and Bess will do well for you. She is young and eager to please and is looking for a chance to show that she's able."

As Violet continued to talk about maidservants and dresses, Millicent's gaze kept focusing on the young woman's pale face. She couldn't count the number of times Violet had been sick in the past fortnight. She also had a hard time forgetting the suspicious-looking bruise that she'd seen on the young girl's mouth lately. Something was not right. But as with everything else, there was not much time to probe and prod. She only hoped that Violet would be wise enough to take Millicent's advice and actually go to her family in St. Albans.

"Violet," Millicent interrupted softly. "You do understand that if you ever are in any kind of trouble, you can come to me."

The young woman's eyes avoided meeting Millicent's. Her gaze was fixed on a ribbon she was nervously twisting around one finger.

"Things happen in life," Millicent continued, hoping to make the young woman feel more at ease. "We all make mistakes, Vi. We sometimes find ourselves in situations that we have no control over. What gets us through these things is our connection with other people. Loneliness is a curse; I know that very well. Please remember that I am here to help if you need me."

"I know, m'lady," Violet whispered, curtsying quickly and escaping the room.

*　　*　　*

Despite everyone's assurance that life at Melbury Hall would continue on smoothly, Lyon still saw the worry etched on Millicent's face when she climbed inside the carriage and sat across from him.

"Everything will be just fine. Just fine," she muttered under her breath as she settled herself. She turned to him. "It was very kind of the dowager and Sir Richard to stay for another fortnight or so."

"I hope you still feel that way when we get back. I did notice a certain look in the dowager's face that told me she has become quite content here. We might not be able to move her anywhere in the near future."

Millicent smiled. "She is welcome to stay forever, if it pleases her. I am indebted to her in more ways than she could ever imagine." She reached out and took Lyon's right hand affectionately in hers before turning to look out the window again.

A long line of people had gathered in the courtyard to see them off and wish them a safe journey. Millicent waved through the small window of the carriage.

"I don't see Moses," she whispered worriedly over her shoulder at Lyon. "Do you see him?"

Lyon leaned forward and pointed. "There he is, behind Jonah and Gibbs."

Millicent looked again and let out a sigh of relief. "Gibbs and Jonah are developing a solid respect for each other. Since Moses is devoted to Jonah, that makes him like Gibbs. I don't know if our new steward knows that he has taken a protector for life."

"That is the kind of loyalty that Highland cur understands best."

With a shout from one of the grooms and a final wave from the waiting throng, the riders and carriages started out. Millicent continued to stare out the window until the bend in the road blocked her view of her people.

Lyon's attention, though, kept moving from his wife's anxious face to where her hand was clutching his right hand desperately on one knee.

"I used to leave Melbury Hall for months at the time with no guilt whatsoever when Wentworth was alive, but now, going away for a fortnight, I feel like a deserter."

He tentatively entwined his fingers with hers. She didn't notice the movement.

"Last night," he said, "I was listening to Stanmore and Rebecca talk about how guilty they feel whenever they leave James at Eton. Even though he has made a number of friends and has established himself very well as a student there, their worry does not go away entirely. It has to do with family, I suppose."

"You said that to me before." She smiled. "That Melbury Hall is like a family to me. You don't mind that, do you?"

"Hardly. I consider myself damned lucky to be a part of it." He squeezed her hand.

Suddenly Millicent's gaze dropped to their entwined hands. "Do that again."

" 'Tis like making love, my bonny lass. A man needs some time to recover first."

Without letting go of his hand, she moved across and nestled against him. "First of all, that is a lie if I ever heard one. You *never* need time to recover during our lovemaking, and you certainly should not need any now. Squeeze my hand again, Lyon. Please."

Being able to use his hand was not new for him. But now, seeing her excitement, he was relieved to be able to share this progress with her. Lyon gently squeezed her fingers.

Her joyous laughter filled the carriage. Millicent looked up at him in amazement. "Show me more."

"This is the extent of it, for now."

"No, it is not," she challenged him. "I have become too familiar with you and your scheming. I know there must be more. I can hear the rumbling in your brain from here."

He leaned toward her and growled. "What you hear, m'lady, is the rumblings of a starved man, and the sound is not coming from my head."

"We ate not an hour before we departed."

"Sexually starved." He kissed her lips. "Remember all those promises you have been giving me about rocking carriages and straining bodies?"

"But it is daylight," she replied, trying to look shocked.

"That is what curtains are for." He slowly slid his hand onto her knee. "Weren't you asking me to show you more?"

"You are the devil, Lord Aytoun." She leaned forward hurriedly and pulled the curtains closed. "A tempting, scandalous devil who knows all my weaknesses."

Chapter 25

That afternoon Gibbs found the Dowager Countess Aytoun in the drawing room with a book on her lap, nodding comfortably in the chair by the window. The blue eyes focused as soon as he entered, led in by one of her serving maids.

"Do not tell me, Gibbs, that you are here to moan that you already miss your master?"

"Nay, m'lady."

"That's good. Well, I hope you will promise not to make such a complaint while he is gone."

"That depends on how well ye treat me, m'lady," the Highlander said with a half smile.

"From what I've been observing around Melbury Hall, there is a certain young woman whose manner influences your moods." The shrewd eyes narrowed. "So tell me, is Mrs. Page as sweet on you as you are on her?"

"Well, mum, I believe she tolerates me well enough."

The dowager sat back and smiled. "I knew there was a reason why I liked the housekeeper. She is obviously exercising good judgment."

"Och, and here I was hoping ye might put a good word in for me with her."

"Good word . . . that is something we shall certainly need to negotiate." She closed the book that lay on her lap and put it aside. "But I doubt you are here so soon after your master's departure for that."

"Nay, m'lady." He cleared his throat, his back stiffening again. "A messenger has just come down from London, looking for Lady Aytoun."

"Does he bring news from her family?"

"Nay, mum."

"Well, who is he? Out with it, Gibbs."

"He's sent by a Mr. Platt, who happens to serve Mr. Jasper Hyde in legal matters."

"That ghastly man again!" Impatiently, the dowager took the spectacles off her face, her mood obviously souring. "The last thing Millicent needs right now is to worry about someone like him. You didn't tell him that Lady Aytoun has gone to Scotland, did you?"

"Nay, m'lady."

"Good man." The dowager waved off her servants, and the two women hurriedly left the room. "Did you ask what he wants?"

Gibbs walked over and handed a sealed envelope to the dowager.

"It simply says 'Lady Aytoun.' That could be me, don't you think, Gibbs?"

"Without doubt, m'lady."

"And even if it were intended for Millicent, in this situation it would be perfectly acceptable to read it."

"Ye know best, mum."

"It could be a matter of the gravest urgency."

"I'm thinking it must be, m'lady."

"And didn't my daughter-in-law leave Melbury Hall in my hands?"

"Even so, mum."

She quickly broke the seal and scanned the contents. "That low, disgusting, horrifying man." She looked up. "He does not know when to give up."

"What does he want?"

"Ohenewaa," the dowager whispered, reading the contents of the letter a second time.

Gibbs felt his temper beginning to burn. "Mrs. Page told me, m'lady, that this same messenger came down from London some time ago with a proposal to take Ohenewaa back to Mr. Hyde. Her ladyship put him out on his arse . . . begging your pardon."

"Well, he has added a great deal more weight to his request this time."

"Wouldn't matter at all to Lady Aytoun," Gibbs stated flatly. "Ohenewaa would go nowhere, to be sure."

"I agree, Gibbs." She placed the correspondence between the pages of her book. "But we shall need to act quickly to take the wind out of the man's sails. You said he does not know Millicent is not here."

"Aye, m'lady."

"Tell the messenger Lady Aytoun will meet with this lawyer. Not to accept the proposal, necessarily, but to talk. But the meeting must take place here at Melbury Hall."

"Very good, mum."

"But I want you to put it off as long as you can. Use whatever excuse, but tell him that the meeting cannot take place any earlier than a fortnight off—and even later if you can manage it."

"How about when pigs sprout wings, m'lady?"

"That would be just fine, Gibbs."

"What do ye plan to do?"

"I need to talk to Ohenewaa first. Then I must send Sir Richard to London to look into the accusations Platt alludes to in the letter." The dowager's eyes shone with the challenge of what lay ahead of her. "When we are done with Mr. Platt and Mr. Hyde, Gibbs, I think neither one shall dare to bother our Millicent ever again."

Gibbs did not know the specifics, but he had no doubt that the dowager would succeed.

"Now fetch Ohenewaa and Sir Richard for me, and then go and get rid of that insect of a messenger."

"As you wish, m'lady."

"And Gibbs," she called as he reached the door. "I will be honored to put a good word in for you with your Mrs. Page."

The rain had beaten against the inn walls and the small diamond-shaped panes of glass all night. And this morning, as they were crossing the river Wear out of Durham at dawn, the biting wind had buffeted the carriages all along the arched stone bridge. Millicent pulled her cloak tightly about her and tried to smile at Lyon, who was watching her intently. He'd told her that they should arrive at Baronsford sometime in the middle of the afternoon.

Unlike their first three days of traveling, Lyon's good nature had deserted him once they climbed into the carriage today. And as they rolled northward in silence, the rain and the wind continued to increase with the same maddening proportions as Millicent's apprehensiveness.

They had followed the east road up through England, stopping at Peterborough, Doncaster, and Durham. For this final leg of their journey, though, they had left the better traveled road leading to Berwick, turning inland at Newcastle-upon-Tyne. Passing villages along the way, the carriage had meandered along valley roads and eventually made the steady climb over the Cheviot Hills. Once into Scotland, the rugged terrain, the ancient abbey towns, and the ruins of countless tower houses and castles had fascinated her.

As the carriage bumped and rolled over a rough section of road, Millicent tore her gaze from the wild countryside and looked at the furrows in the brow of her husband. At some point during the day, she had realized that her worries of going to Baronsford were not solely the result of her own lack of confidence, but also a reaction to Lyon's suffering.

And he was suffering; that she could tell.

"Will you tell me about Baronsford?"

He took a long moment to pull himself free of his deep thoughts. "What would you like to know?"

"Did you and your brothers grow up there?"

He looked away from her. Since that first day, when she had met the dowager with Sir Oliver, she'd had little curiosity about the two other Pennington brothers. But now, going back to Baronsford, she couldn't help but think that part of what was tearing at Lyon had to do with the conflict with his family.

"Aye, all of us grew up there."

"Was it a home?"

He frowned at her. "What do you mean?"

"Gibbs told me his reaction to the place the first time he saw it," she explained. "He described Baronsford as a fairy-tale castle with miles of footpaths weaving in and out along cliffs overlooking the river Tweed. He said there is a great deer park, a lake, beautiful walled gardens and greenswards, icehouses and more. But this was only the description of the outside."

"The inside is attractive as well, I suppose. Robert Adam himself did the renovation."

"Yes, Gibbs told me. But is it a home where a family could live?"

Lyon paused before answering. "At one time, Baronsford *was* a home."

She waited for him to say more, but he chose silence. Millicent glanced out the window again, realizing that she could not press him if he did not want to talk. Not now. Not when he was so close to facing the past that had crippled him.

She had faith in him. Despite the words that were still left unsaid between them, Millicent believed that he cared for her. And she was here to offer her support, not to demand attention.

Their knees brushed. Sitting across from Lyon, Millicent looked in time to see that every muscle in her husband's face had gone taut. She looked out the other window to follow the direction of his gaze.

In the distance, perched dramatically on a rocky rise, a monstrous castle reared up imposingly through the fog and rain. She did not have to ask what place it was.

"They lied to the clerk. They didn't say a word about Lord Aytoun and his wife already having left for Scotland," Platt explained. "If your Harry hadn't happened upon Ned Cranch in the village on his way back, I would be going up to Hertfordshire thinking I am meeting with Lady Aytoun."

Jasper Hyde had been wracked with pain during a bout that had struck him earlier this morning. It was over, but he could not shake off the feeling of doom hanging over him.

"Where is Ohenewaa?"

"Still at Melbury Hall."

"A steward would not take it upon himself to do such a thing. Who is running the estate up there?"

"Ned told Harry that the earl's mother, the Dowager Countess Aytoun, was still there. She is the same meddling old woman who arranged for Millicent's debts to be paid off." Platt sat down on the chair across from the plantation owner's desk. "She was the start of all of our troubles. I am not wasting my time going up there to talk with the likes of her."

"You *shall* go!" Hyde snapped. "If you had gone up yourself sooner, we would not have missed her. But it does not matter. They sent a message back saying Lady Aytoun has agreed to meet you. They didn't lie. You will go and meet with the old woman yourself. She has no loyalty to Ohenewaa. It may be easier to pry her loose from this stranger. I will make every attempt to settle this in a peaceful manner."

"And if it doesn't work?"

"Then I have to proceed with my other plans."

"Do you intend to use force?"

"The less you know the better." Hyde pushed to his feet. "Just know this—I *will* take what is mine. They cannot stop me."

Millicent had chosen to stay inside the carriage and wait until the valets had lowered Lyon into his chair. Lyon understood her apprehensiveness. The grim faces of the servants forming the long receiving line were more appropriate for a funeral than a welcoming.

A hard, cold rain continued to fall steadily; nonetheless, Lyon ordered his valets to leave his chair on the wet ground beside the carriage as Millicent climbed out.

If she had been nervous before, she looked terrified as she surveyed the gathering of liveried servants. He reached for Millicent's hand. She was quick to take it.

"I'm sorry for this bloody formality," he said under his breath. "They are here to greet us; that's all. They are not here to judge you. They really just want to see how injured I am. Remember that. Once we get through this, I shall have Howitt show you to your rooms immediately so that you can change and rest."

Peter Howitt, the young secretary whom Sir Richard had brought with him from London, appeared at his elbow. "If ye are ready, m'lady."

Millicent was reluctant to let go of his hand. From the direction of her gaze, he could see she was worried about walking by all these people without any introduction.

"Where the hell are you, Truscott?" Lyon growled.

"Here, m'lord." His cousin's deep voice answered from behind. He looked up to find the man's rugged face, already dripping with rain, smiling down at him. "It is good to have you back, Aytoun."

"What are you trying to do, you blasted mongrel, terrify my wife?" He motioned at the reception line.

"M'lady." Walter Truscott bowed politely.

"Please call me Millicent," she responded in a quiet voice.

"It would be an honor, Millicent. My deepest apology, but our people have been very keen for Aytoun's return, and if not for the rain, I believe the courtyard would probably have looked more like fair day. The tenants and farmhands and the folk from the village are equally eager to see him."

"You are fortunate they didn't show up, or I would have had to bite your head off. Now take her in out of this weather."

"Good to see you're back to your old self, Aytoun. And my sympathies to you, Millicent, for having to put up with him in a confined carriage for such a long journey."

"Somehow she managed to handle me perfectly well." Lyon squeezed Millicent's hand knowingly. Her cloak was already soaked, and droplets of water were glimmering on her face. There was a spark of mischief, though, in her eyes, and he was glad to see it. "This dog Walter here will make the introductions to Mrs. MacAlister, the housekeeper, and the steward Campbell, and will accompany you and Howitt as you pass along the line inspecting the troops."

She was reluctant to go ahead without him, but at seeing Walter's proffered arm, she finally let go of Lyon's hand and headed toward the house.

He watched Millicent walk in the rain with the gray stone structure looming above her. He saw the introductions being made and the bows and curtsies as she moved along. When she disappeared inside, Lyon raised his face into the rain and breathed in a chestful of air. Everything from the scents in the breeze to the chill rising from the ground told him that he was home.

When the valets lifted his chair, Lyon saw all those lining the courtyard staring at him. The last time he left Baronsford, he had been sedated to such a degree that he didn't know his name, never mind where he was or where they were taking him. Now Lyon focused on every face. He answered the greetings with a nod. With the housekeeper and the steward flanking him, he was carried in through the front door.

He motioned for his chair to be lowered in the entrance hall, and the valets started removing his wet cloak and jacket.

"Mrs. MacAlister, where have you situated my wife?" he asked of the housekeeper.

"On the second floor, m'lord. In the west wing." The tall, wiry woman spoke in her usual clipped manner. "The apartments looking over the loch. Hope that suits ye."

"It does indeed. Be sure she gets into dry clothes." He turned to the steward next. "Campbell, I plan to spend the next two hours with you and Truscott. After that, I shall meet with anyone from the village or the farms who needs to see me immediately."

"Aye, m'lord. I'll arrange it and join ye right off."

Lyon's gaze was drawn to the wide curved stairwell. Truscott was descending from the upper floors. Hun-

dreds of paintings covered every inch of available space
on every wall. Going back for generations, the likenesses
of his ancestors were portrayed on canvases large and
small. Lyon's eye lit on the life-sized Reynolds portrait
of a woman on the first landing. The bright red of the
roses covering an arbor formed a perfect frame for the
beautiful woman dressed in white. He looked up into
the proud face of Emma.

"Take it down." Lyon snarled as he motioned to his
valets to take him away. "Take it down now."

The bedchamber of her master and mistress had been
completely swept and aired days ago. Her ladyship's
dresses had all been cleaned and replaced in the wardrobe that had been moved in. Violet had no good reason
to be up here now, and she knew it. But she had come
anyway in the late hours of the night. She sat hidden in
the shadows of the darkened window watching Ned
Cranch leaving Melbury Hall.

Tonight, waiting for his supper, he had been flirting
with one of the young serving girls. Violet had not
missed the whispers passing between them, the light
touches, the deep blush on the young victim's face as
Ned had directed all of his charm her way. Violet had
felt sick witnessing the man's treacherous manner. She
had heard all his lies already.

· But what had made her feel even more ill was the
realization of how much she still hurt just watching him.

Violet saw Moses, with a lantern in one hand, cross
the gravel of the courtyard. A dog limped from the direction of the stables, and Violet's heart warmed when
she saw the way the giant black man leaned down to
greet the animal. Violet remembered days not so long
ago, during Squire Wentworth's days, when it was more
common to find Moses in the stocks on the muddy banks
of the stream in the Grove.

The first time she had ever seen him there he had
been lying back on the wet ground, one arm draped
across his face. She'd watched him for the longest time.

No movements. She had not even been able to see if his chest was rising and falling with each breath. Despite her fears, Violet had approached. She had called out to him, asking if she could fetch him some water or food, and Moses had moved his arm. She had been shocked at the face, scarred and misshapen from countless beatings, she had heard later. But what was more frightening to her, looking on him for the first time, was that the old man had no ears. They must have been cut off long ago, for the scars were long healed.

He had looked so wretched and old and lost that Violet's impulse to run away had left her. She had given him water and had stayed beside him for a short while that day. She had just talked. She didn't remember what she had said, but whatever it was, Moses had never forgotten, and a friendship had been forged on that muddy ground.

Every nerve in Violet's body went taut when she looked down into the yard and saw Ned Cranch walk casually back into the courtyard to speak to Moses. Though the black man showed no concern, the dog seemed wary of the stonemason, her hackles rising and her back legs stiffening. Violet watched Ned try to touch the animal's head, only to have her scramble back a few steps.

"Don't give him even a moment of your time, Moses," she whispered, fighting a worry that was forming deep in the pit of her stomach. Why Ned would be spending time chatting with him had Violet's mind reeling with suspicion. They were so different. While Moses was kind and naïve, Ned was brutal and devious. The black man spoke only the truth; the other never did, it seemed. Unless it suited his fancy.

Violet let out a breath of relief when Moses finally picked up his lantern to continue on his rounds. She saw Ned light a pipe and slowly start walking down the road, too. She was about to close the curtain when she saw the same serving girl with whom he had been flirting before appear from the servant's wing. Violet found her-

self choking with sudden tears. As she stared, Ned
turned and waited for the woman. Together they disappeared into the dark.

The urge to scream, to tear at everything of hers that
he had ever touched, flooded Violet's mind. She wanted
to forget. She wanted to go to sleep and wake up to find
herself free of him. She didn't want to have memories
of their lovemaking. She didn't want to touch her stomach and think of the child that was growing there. A
child whose father was Ned Cranch.

Violet's face was covered with tears when she closed
the curtain and immersed herself in the darkness of the
room. If she could only take back the time, correct the
horrible mistakes she had made.

The sound of a door opening and then closing across
the corridor startled her. Ohenewaa. She was just going
to her room. Ohenewaa, who had borne a child out of
wedlock herself. Her friend's words came back to her:
*Those were the days before she learned how to end a
pregnancy before it showed . . . before it showed.*

Violet slipped through the door and started toward
the old woman's room.

"What is it exactly that you want from me?" Ohenewaa asked.

She had not missed the red and puffy eyes, the
trembling voice, the shaking hand of the young woman
when she had come to her door. She had also understood Violet's whispered words about how she had been
sick to her stomach for days. But now inside, with the
door closed, she wanted to hear the truth.

"I wanted you to . . ." Violet hesitated. "I was hoping
you would help me to rid myself of this illness."

"Do you have a name for this illness?" She drawled
out the last word.

The pretty chin of the young woman sank to her chest.
No words formed on her lips. Her nervous hands were
hidden in the folds of her apron.

Ohenewaa saw and heard much more than others
thought. It was no secret to her that Violet was with

child. And what disappointed her was Vi's choice of the man who had fathered it. From what little she had seen of Ned Cranch, he was a man without a soul when it came to his dealings with women.

"I know that you can help me." Violet spoke softly. "I have heard you know ways to end what I am suffering with."

"Illness? Suffering? Young woman, these are certainly not the right words to use to describe the gift of life."

"You know?" The blue eyes started tearing when Vi looked up. "But I don't want it, Ohenewaa. So please help me get rid of it. I beg you, free me of this curse."

"I cannot help you."

"Please don't say that," Violet pleaded. "I heard the other women talk. They spoke of the ways you helped women on plantations end their pregnancies. I cannot—"

"Was this child forced on you?"

Ohenewaa's sharp question silenced Violet for a second. She wiped the tears off her face, but they continued to come. "No, but I didn't know—"

"Did you go willingly to the man's bed?"

"I did, but that was before I found out how horrible he was."

"I cannot help you."

"But why?" She sobbed. "You have done it before. You have your ways. What difference does it make if I was willing at the time or not? I was stupid. I was tricked and made to believe that we would have a future together. Why can you not think of me as one of the women you helped in Jamaica? Or on board the slave ships? Please, Ohenewaa, give me a new life to live."

"How could I ever think of you as one of those women?" Ohenewaa said harshly. "I cannot, but do you know why?"

Confusion flickered in Violet's eyes.

"Can you even imagine what 'tis like to be an African woman? To be a young girl stolen from your home and your family and dragged on board a slave ship? Do you know the horrors these women endure?"

Violet's chin sank onto her chin. "I . . . I have heard the stories. I cannot imagine, even in my worst nightmares, such suffering."

Ohenewaa approached Violet.

"Then how could you believe I could ever, in my conscience, think of you in the same way as one of those I did help?"

A choked sob escaped the young woman's throat. She shook her head.

"Do you believe this child growing inside of you has the same fate awaiting him or her as those slave children?"

She shook her head.

"Is she a curse, girl? Is she a sickness?"

"Please—"

"Will you hate her because she is a reminder of a *mistake?*"

"No! I can never hate her . . . him." Violet covered her face. Sobs wracked her body. "I don't want to do this."

"Then what are you here for?"

"I . . . I should never have come here. I'm just so lost. So sorry . . ."

Without another word, Ohenewaa took the weeping young woman into her arms and held her.

Chapter 26

"Overwhelming" was a word that kept pushing into Millicent's brain as she followed Mrs. MacAlister, the housekeeper, on a tour of the house. At some point during the afternoon, Millicent had lost count of the number of bedrooms, and the location of the old Eating Room and the second-floor salon, and which wing contained the old armory, and what floor the new library was on, and which sitting room she was supposed to write her correspondence in.

It was beautiful. It was comfortable. It was a marvelous representation of Robert Adams's ideas of aesthetics. No question about any of that.

But Baronsford was too big.

After having a brief dinner with a rather preoccupied Lyon in the old dining room, Millicent found her way back to her apartments, while her husband continued his discussions with Truscott. Wandering into the sitting room off the bedchamber, Millicent collapsed into a lovely upholstered chair and looked into the fire.

Though she should have been warm, she was cold. Though the tiredness of the days of travel should have begun to seep out of her, she was becoming more tense. The grandeur of Baronsford was certainly impressive, she supposed, but it was not the main thing lying like a weight on her spirit.

It was the memory of Emma.

She was everywhere. With Millicent's first steps into the entrance hall, she had found herself faced with a life-sized portrait of the woman. She was clearly beautiful. Then, in the course of her tour, she had picked up bits and pieces of information that told her Emma had had a greater hand in shaping Baronsford as it was today than had any previous mistress of it.

This had come through most clearly when Mrs. MacAlister had taken her through the east wing. The six luxurious bedrooms there, looking out over the gardens and cliffs and the river, had been renovated and decorated by Emma for a specific purpose. She had forbidden having family, friends, or guests stay in any of them. No, the entire second floor of that wing was to be a private haven reserved for her and Aytoun.

And there was more. The drawing room in the old tower was also for Emma's private use.

Millicent had also been told about the parties in the ballroom and the dinners in the formal dining room and the choice of dishes imported from France. "None of Mr. Wedgwood's things for her," Mrs. MacAlister had informed her.

Even the arrangement of the portraits and the specially woven carpets ordered from Persia. All Emma's doing.

Hours later, Millicent's head still echoed with everything she had seen and heard.

Before long her maid appeared, and Millicent moved into the dressing room while Bess helped her get ready for bed. As she stood watching the young woman hang her dress, Millicent questioned her decision to come. She was of no use here, no use at all. In fact, with all the work that faced Lyon, Millicent had no idea when she would even see him again.

Millicent felt insignificant at Baronsford, and she hated that feeling.

At a knock at the outer door to the bedchamber, Bess went to answer it. Millicent was surprised to see both doors from the hallway swing open as Will and John carried Lyon in.

"I am glad you are not sleeping yet. I would have

hated for these two clumsy brutes to have awakened you while getting me ready for bed."

Millicent gaped, lost for words. And the way his gaze moved down her body, as if she were not wearing a thick dressing gown, but rather the most revealing of nightdresses, did not help her to recover. To share a bedchamber with him at Melbury Hall, when they had been short on available rooms, had been one thing. But here! With so much space!

"Are you done with your work for tonight?" she asked for lack of something better to say.

"Tomorrow is another day."

The valets were wasting no time in getting him ready, moving quickly in and out of another dressing room on the far side of the bedchamber. Millicent dismissed Bess, then went to wait in the sitting room, giving her husband privacy.

She took a book from a shelf and sat on the chair. She tried to focus on the first lines. It was so like him to confuse her. Just when she felt totally useless, here Lyon came. And then, to look at her the way he did. She reread the first paragraph again. And then again. No use. No comprehension. She rose to her feet and went to the small writing desk. Perhaps she should write a letter. Again the words were not there.

"Are *you* not done with your work for tonight?"

Hearing his question, Millicent laid her pen down and moved to the doorway of the bedroom. Lyon was already sitting in bed. The valets were gone.

"Tomorrow is another day," she said softly, leaning against the jamb. In a hundred years, she thought, she would never get her fill of him. He looked so handsome, so confident.

"Then come to bed."

She started slowly toward him. "I am surprised to find you here tonight. I was told today that his lordship's apartments are in the east wing."

"You were misinformed. My rooms are where yours are." He reached for the belt of her robe when Millicent arrived at the side of the bed. "I missed you today."

"We have been apart only since this afternoon." She looked down as his hand undid the belt and let it fall to the floor. "And we did have dinner together."

"Too many people there. Tell me what you did this afternoon."

"I was shown around Baronsford."

"It is too damn big."

"It is impressive."

He pushed the robe off her shoulders and let it drop down around her feet. "Do you approve of the place?"

"Baronsford doesn't need my approval."

"I say it does." His gaze met hers. "You are the mistress of Baronsford now."

"I have never had aspirations so high," she replied softly.

Lyon's fingers looped around a tendril of hair that was dangling by her chin. He tugged it gently, bringing her lips closer to his mouth. "There must be something you aspire to."

Millicent placed her hands on his shoulders. She brushed her lips against his. Lyon's arm wrapped around her waist, encouraging her onto the bed. She pulled herself up and nestled against his side.

"Tell me about it." His lips placed feather kisses on her face.

"I aspire to this."

"This bed?" He smiled, pulling her more tightly against him. "This demesne of the night is yours to rule, m'lady."

"And I should like to rule your heart."

The seriousness that took possession of his features made Millicent sorry to have voiced her thoughts aloud. She searched for something to say to bring the smile back into his eyes.

"This is what being so far away from Melbury Hall does to me. I've become foolish, rambling on and saying things that should not be said. I—"

"You already do rule my heart, Millicent."

She watched in bewilderment as Lyon lifted his right arm tentatively, and his fingers brushed away the tears that had fallen on her cheeks.

"You are the only woman whom I have ever known who would have me—as incomplete as I have become—over this place."

She hugged him fiercely. "There is nothing incomplete about you. I love you as you are."

His arms wrapped tightly around her in return. "And will you stay with me always?"

"I shall stay with you as long as you want me."

"Or need you?"

"Yes." Millicent pulled back to look into his face. "I need to belong, though. I need to feel that I can make a contribution. I want to give."

"And take. Is that not part of marriage as well?"

"With someone like you, in a place like this, I am afraid that the scale may tip too heavily to one side. You have title and wealth and every means to give more than you take."

"And you object to that."

"Of course. I want to carry my weight. I want to feel I am as much needed as I need."

"Then perhaps my injuries add that balance to our lives."

She pushed herself up to a sitting position. "I don't know what you mean."

"You do, Millicent."

Lyon's hand was wrapped around her wrist. She wondered if he could feel her pulse beating wildly in her veins.

"If you and I had not married under the conditions we did . . ." He shook his head. "Let's go back even beyond that. Let's say that I was never injured. If I were to approach you, if I wanted to court you—"

"You wouldn't have."

"Why?"

"Because I am plain. Because there is nothing special

about me, Lyon. Not to mention the fact that I would
not even travel in your circles in society. You would
have had no opportunity."

"And I am telling you, you are wrong about all of
that. But what would you have done if I had made a
proposal to you and asked you to become my wife?"

"I would have said no. I wouldn't have known you."

"What if we had a torrid love affair, and you could
not keep your hands off me? What would you have
said then?"

"Still no. We are just not from the same—"

"Same what, Millicent?" he asked sharply. "At what
point in our relationship would you feel comfortable
enough to trust me with your love?"

"I would have told you I love you, and that would
have been enough."

"But it is not enough. I would have wanted a future
for us together. I would have wanted to know that your
love for me was stronger than the unfounded fears that
you had been living with for years."

Raw emotions welled up in her. "I am here now,
Lyon. Is that not enough?"

"Will you be here tomorrow?" he asked.

"I will."

"And the day after, and the month after, and the
year after?"

"I will be here as long as you want me."

"And need you?"

"And need me."

Rain spattered steadily on the roof of the carriage
waiting to take the lord of Baronsford to the village. In
the old days, no carriage had been required. It was a
familiar sight, for both tenant and villager, to see their
laird sitting atop one of his fine horses and riding
through the hills. In fair weather and foul, they would
see him stopping to talk as they made their way out of
their cottages, ready for a day's work.

Aytoun had always been an early riser, and he knew
that many of his people cherished this daily connection

with their earl. Grievances and complaints did not need to be made in formal settings. Good news passed from one family to another without any difficulty. Someone's hardship was often alleviated before it became a crisis. They were valuable rides he took those mornings. Though he had also been their landlord, the Earl of Aytoun was first and foremost a friend to all of them. And no one missed these morning travels more than Aytoun himself.

Lyon intended to start again. Instead of riding his horse, though, a carriage would have to suffice. Rather than going alone, he would need to take his two valets and his secretary, Peter Howitt, with him.

It would be different, but life down in the village and on the farms was different too, he was told. The village was crowded with vagrant families huddled together, protected from the weather. In the eyes of everyone, Truscott had said, one could see the worry about what lay ahead.

This morning before he left, he had asked Truscott to bring the housekeeper and the steward to the library. What he needed to talk to them about was as important to him right now as anything happening in the village or on the farms.

"I want the two of you to get every available worker and make a sweep of the house immediately." His words were specifically directed to Mrs. MacAlister and Campbell. "You will search out and remove every item that might in any way be associated with my late wife. This includes paintings, clothing, personal items, whatever might remind the new mistress of her predecessor."

Neither one of them seemed surprised by the request.

The steward spoke first. "I can only guess, m'lord, but I'm thinking the collection could be very extensive. What shall we do with it once we've gathered it all together?"

"Put everything in one of the bedchambers in the east wing, if you like. Just lock the door." He turned to his secretary. "Send a letter to Emma's mother, and tell Lady Douglas she is welcome to anything she wishes of it . . . starting with that bloody portrait."

"As you wish, m'lord."

Lyon turned to Mrs. MacAlister. "I also want you to make a point of asking the countess's opinions on everything. From now on, she is to be consulted on all decisions that pertain to the household here at Baronsford—the menus, the seating arrangements for dinners, the purchase of linens, the choice of wine, everything."

"Aye, m'lord. Not unhappy with me, I pray."

"Hardly, Mrs. MacAlister. There is no better housekeeper in the entire British empire."

"Thank ye, m'lord."

"Conferring with her should be no hardship. You will find dealing with Lady Aytoun quite different than . . . than with your previous mistress. I am leaving everything to your good judgment to make her feel welcome here."

He turned to Campbell next. "You will make sure that there is no idle talk by the servants in front of her. No comparisons with Emma will be made regarding her ladyship's actions or dress or conduct. Millicent is her own woman, and everyone shall treat her as such. I know she is English, but there is no finer woman anywhere, and I want the household to recognize that."

Not a word was voiced by either, and Lyon looked from one face to the next.

"Emma Douglas Aytoun is dead," he said flatly. "It is time we laid her ghost to rest. There is a new mistress of Baronsford."

Millicent stayed up in their apartments as long as she could. Lyon had told her that he was planning to spend most of the morning at the village. She asked for a breakfast tray to be sent up, thinking to stay put for the time he was gone. But after writing a letter to Mrs. Page and Mr. Gibbs, she found her attention was continually wandering to the window and the gardens and the lake and the blue sky slowly breaking through the clouds.

Finally losing her battle against temptation, Millicent had Bess help her into some riding clothes and stepped out of their rooms. A young servant hurrying down the hall careened right into her.

"Och, m'lady, there ye be." The girl curtsied. "Mrs. MacAlister sent me to fetch ye. She was wondering if she could have a few minutes of yer time this afternoon to go over some menus for dinners and such for the next few days."

"Tell Mrs. MacAlister I shall put aside as much time as she likes." She started off down the hall with the servant beside her. "I was planning to go for a ride this morning, but I could go later if you think she prefers to speak to me now."

"Nay, m'lady. At your convenience, I'm sure. With the house all helter-skelter as 'tis this morning, I'm certain Mrs. MacAlister—"

"Is there a problem?"

"I should say there is, mum, though I wouldn't know what for. But they're tearing through the east wing and the drawing rooms and the rooms in the old tower and rearranging the portraits and the closets as if the king himself lost his crown and couldn't find it." The young woman shook her head in disbelief. "Anyway, I'm thinking Mrs. MacAlister shan't be having time to even scratch her head while the place is turned upside down."

"And you have no idea what the reason might be for all the activity?"

The servant hesitated, then looked about her and lowered her voice. "We hear his lordship laid down the law this morning."

"The law?"

"Aye, m'lady. We hear he was not pleased that the last Lady Aytoun's things were still about. He said to have everything of hers plucked out and thrown away. He says he has no wish to see anything around Baronsford that reminds him of his old wife."

They were at the top of the stairs, and Millicent's gaze was drawn to the place where Emma's portrait had been hanging the day before. It was gone now, and other paintings had been shuffled about to fill the space.

Uncertainty mixed with a touch of guilt washed through her. She needed to talk to him—to ask why he had given such directions. Last night Millicent had felt that they had successfully passed through an important threshold in their marriage. It had been so wonderful to speak one's mind, to say what the heart was feeling.

Millicent started down the steps. "Please tell Mrs. MacAlister I'd be delighted to speak to her this afternoon."

At the bottom, the servant disappeared into another section of the house, and Millicent asked one of the doormen if either Mr. Truscott or Howitt were around. She was told that the earl's secretary had gone with his lordship into the village this morning, but that Mr. Truscott was in the courtyard at this very instant, ready to ride out himself.

Millicent hurried out and found him there, giving instructions to one of the grooms.

"Good morning, Walter. May I ride to the village with you?"

The tall Scotsman brought the head of his horse around.

"Of course, Millicent. And good day to you. I shall have a carriage made ready at once."

"No, I should like to ride along, if it is all the same to you."

"As you wish, mum." He nodded to the groom, who ran off to have a horse brought up.

"I was wondering," Millicent started again, determined to speak her mind. "Would it be too much out of our way if we were to ride by the cliffs overlooking the river? I should very much like to see where the accident happened."

Platt was beginning to feel like a criminal being led to the dock. He was led by two footmen from the carriage in the courtyard to the door where three liveried servants took his coat and hat and gloves and escorted him to a giant Highlander who glowered down at him with open hostility. This Mr. Gibbs, as he was addressed, said nothing, but gestured with a jerk of the head for the lawyer to follow. With the three servants flanking him, Platt hurried to keep up with the man.

This was not Platt's first visit to Melbury Hall. Some four years ago, while Squire Wentworth had still been alive, the lawyer had come here on business on behalf of Jasper Hyde. The cordial reception he'd received that day was far different from the one he was getting now.

"Ye'll keep to the point," the Highlander growled over his shoulder as he marched Platt through the house. "Ye will speak only when ye are asked to speak, and ye will hold your tongue and listen otherwise. D'ye understand?"

"My word," Platt huffed. "I cannot say but I take grave exception to such rude—"

Gibbs whirled on the lawyer, bending and glaring into his face. "I care naught for your exception or your grave, but ye *will* hold your tongue. D'ye understand?"

"Indeed! Indeed, sir," Platt spluttered, feeling his face redden with fear.

The lawyer fought to calm his nerves. Perspiration was forming on his brow, and when the Highlander finally turned away, Platt quickly mopped his forehead with his sleeve. He knew he should stop right there and thoroughly upbraid the insolent servant for his rude and barbaric manner, but the man was a Scot, after all, and what could one expect?

"See here, sir. I do need to know one thing."

Gibbs said nothing.

"I know Lady Aytoun is in Scotland. With whom am I speaking today?"

"The Dowager Countess Aytoun. And she will receive ye in the drawing room." He opened the door and Platt hurried by him. "Mr. Platt, mum."

The lawyer's confidence immediately returned as he looked upon the frail old woman who was sitting with a blanket on her lap on one of the cushioned chairs. Two young serving maids fluttered about the room. *This* he could handle.

Lady Aytoun looked over the spectacles perched on the end of her nose and studied him. "Mr. Platt?"

"Your servant, m'lady," he said with a deep bow.

"How kind of you to accept my request that you delay this meeting."

Platt had not thought he had much choice.

"With my daughter-in-law already en route to Scotland," the old woman said in a meek voice, "and me somewhat under the weather, if you will excuse the expression, I was certainly not ready to receive any company before."

"I perfectly understand, m'lady."

"Now, please do not stand by the door, sir." She pointed to a chair facing her. "Come and sit here, where I can see you without getting a pain in my neck."

Platt crossed the floor and took the proffered seat.

"The rest of you may leave." She waved at her maids. "You too, Mr. Gibbs."

"I should prefer to stay, mum."

"Why, there is no reason, Mr. Gibbs. This gentleman appears to be quite trustworthy to me. You may leave us."

"If ye insist, m'lady."

Platt cast a haughty look at the ape as he turned to leave. While everyone departed, he made a quick survey of the room. Sunny and quite comfortable. A lovely room. Not very long ago, he had found himself taken with Melbury Hall. In fact, if not for the old woman's meddling, he might have made Millicent an offer for the place. He could have picked it up for a trifle in return for paying off everything she owed to Jasper Hyde.

Indeed, he thought, eyeing the beautiful woodwork and furnishings. This manor house, with its renowned neighbors and its excellent location in the country, would be the perfect country place for someone like him, who was ready to make his mark among the *ton*. In fact, now that he thought about it, perhaps he wasn't too late, after all. Perhaps the younger Lady Aytoun, so busy with her responsibilities as the new mistress of Baronsford, might be willing to part with this country estate. Of course, there was the little matter of his client, Jasper Hyde, but Platt believed once the plantation owner had the slave, he would not care much about anything else.

"What might I do for you, Mr. Platt?"

The lawyer's attention snapped back to his hostess. "My apologies, m'lady. Every time I come here, I find myself more and more smitten with Melbury Hall."

"So this is not your first time here?"

"No, indeed, m'lady. I was a guest of Squire Wentworth's."

"Of course." The dowager nodded pleasantly. "From what I hear, Mr. Hyde and Squire Wentworth were acquainted."

"They were indeed, m'lady. In fact, they were fast friends. Indeed, fast friends."

"Friendship is a valuable thing, Mr. Platt."

"Indeed it is. If I may say, it is a foundation of our English civilization. The bond of friendship constitutes the very core of our gentility. It forms the foundation of our nation's moral superiority in the world today."

"And it is so much like an Englishman to rip away at the fortune of his friend after his demise, is it not, Mr. Platt? So morally superior to tear into the belly of the corpse like some jackal, leaving nothing for his widow?"

Platt cleared his throat. Hyde and Wentworth were cut from the same cloth, he thought. It would not have been any different if Hyde had been the first to pass away. Wentworth would have gone after anything he could get from the holdings of his friend.

"But we digress, do we not?" she said sweetly, putting a smile back on her face. "You were telling me the reason for your visit."

"Indeed, m'lady." He eyed the old woman, knowing he'd best not mince any more words with her. "My client, Mr. Hyde, has made repeated attempts to settle a small business matter with your daughter-in-law. With no success, I might add."

"What is the nature of this business matter?"

"There was a mention of it in the letter I sent."

"I am an old woman, Mr. Platt, with a failing memory. Please humor me. Do tell me all about it again."

"The matter regards a black slave woman called by the heathen name Ohenewaa. My client wishes to buy this woman from Lady Aytoun."

"Surely there must be some mistake, sir. My daughter-in-law does not believe in owning human beings."

"Please allow me to restate my client's request," Platt said patiently. "Mr. Hyde wishes to pay Lady Aytoun all of the expenses that this Ohenewaa has accrued. He would very much like to make an offer of . . . employment to the woman."

The dowager nodded thoughtfully before answering. "Now, why should an important plantation owner such as Mr. Hyde—someone who has made his fortune trading on the very flesh of innocent human beings, a gentleman who must own hundreds of slaves—why should he be so desperate to get his hands on one old woman?"

"The reasons for my client's philanthropy with regard to this woman are private, m'lady," Platt said uncomfortably.

"Ah, philanthropy. And my daughter-in-law declined Mr. Hyde's request when it was made before, I take it."

"There are new circumstances now that might change her ladyship's answer."

"What new circumstances?"

"They were mentioned in the letter."

"Please, sir. My failing memory."

Platt felt the perspiration forming beneath his periwig and trickling down his neck. Actually, it was too warm here in this sunny room. He edged forward on his chair.

"M'lady, I see I must be completely honest with you. I did not wish to involve you personally, out of respect for your position, but you leave me no choice. My client acts in the name of justice. It grieves me to tell you this, but your daughter-in-law may be harboring a murderess. Since your daughter's purchase of this slave woman, certain evidence has surfaced that points to this Ohenewaa as the person responsible for Dr. Dombey's murder."

"I see. And who has been ferreting out this evidence?"

"Why, the proper authorities."

"Pray, give me names of those authorities, and I shall see to it that—"

"I misspoke, m'lady. The names of the witnesses and the evidence against the woman have been collected by clerks in the employ of Mr. Hyde himself."

"And what does he plan to do with this material?"

"Hand them over to . . . to the authorities if his demand is not met. He would like to see justice done without any further scandal attaching itself to your family's name."

"It is so good to have a 'friend' like Mr. Hyde." The dowager smiled. "Is your client a complete dunce, Mr. Platt?"

"I beg your pardon, m'lady?"

"Do you both suffer from imbecility, sir?"

He stared at her, momentarily speechless.

"Do you truly think that my daughter-in-law would believe Ohenewaa's fate could be worse in the hands of the English penal system than in Mr. Hyde's brutal clutches?"

"We have no intention, m'lady, of—"

"I personally would not trust your 'we' with the fate of a dung beetle, my dear man," she said sharply. "Now, back to your accusations. Maitland, are you taking all of this down?"

Platt turned quickly around in his chair and found a door into the adjoining room had been opened. Sitting down at a table was Sir Richard Maitland, and behind him stood an old black woman.

"Incidentally, I have asked our good neighbor, the Earl of Stanmore, a prominent member of the House of Lords, to join us later as well. The complications of what are legal actions and what might be construed as extortion constitute a gray area in my mind—though I believe Sir Richard here would say you have placed yourself clearly in the area of extortion."

"Aye, m'lady," Sir Richard asserted.

"Nonetheless, I am hoping Lord Stanmore will be able to reaffirm our view."

Platt jumped to his feet.

"But about your supposed evidence," the dowager continued. "Since we do not know what it is exactly that you have collected, or what sums you have paid to certain individuals for their testimony, we will tell you what *we* have collected. Ohenewaa, perhaps you could start."

The black woman gazed disdainfully at Platt. "Dr. Dombey died of old age, hastened by his excessive drinking. From our first day of returning to London, the following doctors attended him. There was Dr. Gisborne—"

"From whom I have a statement here." Sir Richard indicated a piece of paper on his desk. "Dr. Gisborne clearly identifies Dombey's condition and his opinion on the reason of death."

"And Dr. Billings," Ohenewaa added.

The dowager's lawyer held up another paper. "And here we have a statement from this good physician as well. He is quite emphatic on the matter."

"I have spoken with a surgeon named Boarham, who was called from time to time to bleed Dr. Dombey before his death."

"Produce him at your peril, Mr. Platt." The old lawyer looked sternly at him. "We have looked into his character. The courts will see him for the corrupt witness he is. I believe he would sell his own mother if there was good profit in it for him."

As Maitland continued to speak, Platt ran a finger along the inside of his cravat. Accusations and false testimony by the likes of Boarham would not stand against accredited witnesses. He thought of Jasper Hyde's comment about other plans if a peaceful approach was unsuccessful. Happy to be ignorant of them, he decided that it was time to lay the problem back in his client's lap. They had clearly been thwarted here.

"If you would please sit down, Mr. Platt," the dowager directed, "we expect Lord Stanmore momentarily. Perhaps you can give him a summary of your own findings regarding this matter of Ohenewaa."

Platt shook his head and cleared his throat. "That won't be necessary, m'lady. I was only acting on behalf of a client, whom I can see has been misinformed and led astray by some rather corrupt individuals."

He started backing toward the door, praying that the blasted Highlander was not lurking outside.

"I shall not trouble you anymore, m'lady. Good day to you all."

With a stiff bow, he yanked open the door and hurried along the corridor. As he turned beneath an archway into the entrance hall, he bumped into a young serving woman who was passing. The woman's eyes fixed on him in surprise before narrowing with recognition.

The lawyer, however, had no time to dally. Grabbing his things from the doorman, Platt left from the house with a shout to his groom and driver. Hyde could do as he wished, but he himself was done with this business.

Chapter 27

On the drive north to Scotland, Lyon had spoken a great deal about his cousin. Walter Truscott was the second son of the dowager's younger brother, William, who had passed away many years ago, leaving the responsibility of raising the boy to his older sister. Having spent most of his years at Baronsford, Walter was much like a brother to Lyon.

Realizing early on that Walter's passion lay in the management of Baronsford, Lyon—immediately after inheriting the title—had asked his cousin to do exactly that. And based on what her husband told her, Millicent thought the young man was doing an excellent job of it.

His polite behavior and interest in her came as a pleasant surprise, too, and she was pleased to know she might find a friend in Walter Truscott. He was kind and considerate, and she sensed from the moment of her arrival that he was trying to make her feel welcome at Baronsford. At the same time, she understood that Walter's temperament lay somewhere between that of Lyon and the dowager. He was not one of those who dispensed meaningless praise. He was candid in saying what he thought.

"This is as far as we can go on horseback," Truscott warned, coming to a low hedge of wild undergrowth near the cliffs.

"Would you mind if we walked to the edge?"

As the man shrugged, Millicent dismounted. Leaving their horses with the groom who rode with them, Walter led her toward an opening in the undergrowth. "There is a narrow path that runs along the cliff here for a way."

He held a branch back, and Millicent passed through it. Immediately she found herself on the very edge of the cliffs. As she looked straight down, her stomach churned at the sight of the rocks below, some protruding from the water, others forming the base of the cliff. Mist rose from the white water moving swiftly over the rocks.

"Does the river always run this fast?"

He took Millicent's arm and pulled her a step back from the ledge. "Yes and no. The river always runs fairly quickly right here, but we have been having a wet winter. So the water is running unusually fast and high."

Millicent glanced down at the rocks below, imagining Lyon the way they had brought him to Melbury Hall. She envisioned Emma's broken body next to his. "Is this where they found them?"

"No." He pointed downstream. "Less than half a mile that way. There is a rocky descent down to a small stone beach where the river bends. Emma's body was found on the rocks near the beach. Aytoun must have been trying to climb down when he slipped and fell."

Millicent was relieved to notice no accusing edge to the man's tone. A cold wind blew in from the east, and she ran her hands up and down her arms to ward off the chill. "Who found them?"

"Pierce did."

She looked up at Walter's solemn face.

"You have not met the rest of the family. Pierce is the middle brother. Younger than Aytoun by three years, he is. And then there is David, the youngest of the three."

"Of course."

"Aytoun doesn't talk about them, does he?"

"I have heard him mention only Pierce's name, and that was in connection with Baronsford."

"Those papers he signed giving this place away are meaningless, I think. There has been no acknowledgment from Pierce. He doesn't want Baronsford, and I believe he would refuse to accept it in any case."

Millicent did not care who owned what. What mat-

tered most was the family that had been torn apart.
"How long has it been since they have seen each
other?"

"Since Emma's death," he said. "But I know a wedge
had been driven between them long before that."

Millicent wanted to ask why, but she held back. What
right did she have to question Walter? Besides, she herself was not very good at keeping in touch with her own
two older sisters. And she had yet to explain to Lyon
the reason for the aloofness of her family. No, any answers to the questions about his brothers—questions that
were burning a hole in her tongue—had to come from
her husband.

They started walking slowly along the edge of the
cliffs. "What do you think happened to Emma? Did she
slip and fall?"

"No. I believe she was pushed."

Millicent turned sharply to Truscott. "By whom?"

He shrugged and shook his head.

"You don't believe that Lyon did it, do you?"

"No. He had already put up with her for two years.
He was resolved to endure the curse his marriage had
become."

Millicent said nothing, trying to absorb Truscott's
stunning revelation.

"Emma grew up climbing these hills and cliffs. We all
swam in that river in the summer. Her family—she was
a Douglas—are neighbors to the east of Baronsford.
From the time she was just a wee lass, she spent all her
time here. I think even then she was planning her siege
of the place. In any case, she knew every slippery edge
and every loose rock as well as she knew the Pennington
lads." He shrugged again in a matter-of-fact manner.
"Despite the foul weather that morning, I do not believe
she could have missed a step."

"But Lyon fell. Why not her?"

"He was going down to rescue her, or so he thought,"
Truscott argued. "You stare down there and see someone's eyes looking up at you from the bottom, and it

can throw you. I saw her down there, too. I believe Lyon's fall was an accident, but not Emma's."

"But they were both on these cliffs together. If someone had pushed Emma, wouldn't he have seen it happen?"

Walter gave her a sympathetic look. "He hasn't told you anything, has he?"

"He has had such a difficult time recovering from his injuries. It hasn't been very long since he has gotten back to being himself. But no matter how curious I might be, I would never bring up anything that might slow his recovery."

"You are a good woman. Selfless . . . I can see that. After everything he has been through, it is about time." He raised his face into the air, as if scenting the wind. "I will tell you this because I know you will not ask and because I also know how impossible it might seem right now filling Emma's shoes at Baronsford."

It *was* impossible, Millicent thought.

"I mentioned it before." Truscott's brooding face turned to her. "Emma had been planning to be the Countess Aytoun, to rule Baronsford, from the time she was a wee lass. She married Lyon not for love of him, but for love of his title. He was the one who would inherit everything. And it was this that brought on the quarreling between the brothers."

He waited a heartbeat before turning his gaze on the hills across the way.

"Wild, beautiful, untamed she was. In their own way, each of the Pennington lads was enthralled by her. Each of them wanted to change her or protect her. Of course, we always knew that Lyon would be the winner. Or loser."

Millicent put aside her questions. She focused hard on every word that Truscott spoke.

"After me, David was the closest in age to Emma. As children, they were inseparable. As they grew older, she became the very embodiment of what a woman should be in his mind. Of the three of them, I think he was the one who was always in love with her. But of course, he knew he couldn't have her."

He started walking again, ushering Millicent to the side, away from the edge.

"Then there was Pierce. He was always the protective kind. A born hero, that Pierce. He worried about her from the time she could walk. Watched over her through all the wildness. In a way, I think he regarded Emma as a sister. It was his responsibility to teach her and guide her. He had high hopes, but Emma was willful to say the least. She could never be tamed."

Walter kicked a pebble with the tip of his boot, and Millicent watched it roll down the rugged cliffs and bounce high off the rocks before disappearing into the waters of the rushing river.

"Of course, Aytoun was the one with the greatest expectations and the most to lose. He tried, though. He did his best to make her happy in her role as countess. And she did conform to what was expected, I suppose, but only on the surface." He cast a sidelong look at Millicent. "Do you know why Aytoun was called 'Lord of Scandal' among the members of the *ton?*"

"Because of his temper? His duels?"

Walter Truscott nodded. "Duels to protect his wife's reputation. To salvage what he could of his honor. All of those men with whom he fought, every one of them, had supposedly had a relationship with Emma."

"But was it true?" she challenged. "Rumors have a way of starting with no justification."

"Who can say?" he said vaguely. "Emma liked to toy with men. One never knew if she was speaking the truth or lying just to get a reaction. Whatever it was, she thrived on the attention." He paused, frowning. "But she was also as ambitious as she was wild. And becoming mistress of Baronsford—as grand as that might have seemed to her before her marriage—it was not enough once she had it."

Millicent looked back in the direction of Baronsford. Even at this distance, it was immense.

"Most of all, though, she wanted to control Aytoun. She didn't know how to go about it, though, so she started this dangerous game of playing on his jealousy. She soon found that she could not easily manipulate him. The more she flirted, the more reserved he became. In a very short time, Emma became a burden that he was responsible for, but that was the extent of it. No affection."

The conversation she and Lyon had in bed last night came back to Millicent. In a perverse way, that was what she wanted out of her marriage, as well. Not to control her husband—and never by using the methods that Emma had used—but Millicent, too, wanted to know for certain that she mattered to him. That she was the only woman he wanted.

"One of Emma's unforgivable flaws, though," he continued, "was her insistence on pitting the members of this family against each other. She knew how much David and Pierce cared for her, so from the start of her marriage, she used them as a means of riling Aytoun. Complaints she had were not brought to her husband but to his brothers. If anything at all displeased her, she would run to one of them. Of course, the fault for every problem lay with Aytoun."

"Were they so blind?" Millicent asked passionately. "Couldn't they see what she was doing?"

"She had been a part of this family for too many years for them to doubt her."

"What about the dowager? She must have seen through her?"

"By the time she realized what was happening, there were not many choices left to her. Emma was already Aytoun's wife. The dowager's answer to the problem was simply to stay away and let her son work out his own difficulties."

"What happened the day of the accident?"

"Everyone had been invited to Baronsford for the dowager's birthday. Now, Emma had planned it, which made it very suspicious to start with, for she didn't have the best of relationships with her mother-in-law. But still, they all came. Even Emma's side of the family had been invited."

Truscott stopped again and turned to look down at the rocks. Not far ahead Millicent could see the stretch of stony beach at the bend in the river.

"The morning of the party, while most had gone out hunting, Aytoun and Emma had a row. I don't know why or who started it. And, to be honest, at the time I didn't even think it strange, for they often fought when they were together. But then, before we knew it, Emma had run off on foot, and Pierce and Aytoun were growling at one another in the gardens." He turned to her. "I don't know what was said or why Aytoun left Pierce behind, but suddenly he was running after his wife, coming in this direction. Pierce lingered here for only a few moments, and then he, too, went off toward the river. He followed Aytoun and found the two of them down there."

Millicent looked where Walter was pointing and shivered.

"You are sure when you say that someone pushed her down."

"I am."

"But why?" She searched Truscott's dark gaze.

"Because many had come to hate her."

"Jonah told me the stonemason was finishing the first section of the river wall in the Grove," Amina said. "Is something wrong, Vi?"

"Nothing's wrong. Thanks." Wrapping her worn shawl tightly around her shoulders, Violet hurried out the back door of the kitchen and moved down the path toward the line of trees.

Vi had immediately recognized the face of the man who had visited the elder Lady Aytoun. He was the same one she had run into on the stairs that night at the inn in St. Albans. The same one who was going up to meet Ned in his room. Just to make sure she had the name right, Violet had asked Mrs. Page about the dowager's guest. The housekeeper had said he was Jasper Hyde's lawyer, a Mr. Platt from London. Vi knew that Jasper Hyde was the scoundrel who had been trying to ruin their mistress before she had married his lordship, but now the connection with Ned made her furious.

Mrs. Page had also told her that Platt had met his match in the meeting with the dowager, and there was nothing to worry about anymore.

Violet had been too ashamed to admit to the housekeeper that she had seen the lawyer meeting secretly with Ned in St. Albans. She couldn't think of any way of letting them know without having to explain what she herself was doing in that tavern.

The double-dealing, lying, cheating devil.

Jasper Hyde's threat was not completely eliminated. With Ned here, poking his nose and anything else he could manage into the business of Melbury Hall, there was no saying he wasn't sitting and waiting for a chance to cause real trouble.

When she reached the trees, Violet gathered up the hem of her skirt and started to run. Now that she had her head on right, she recalled with a clarity that made her queasy all the questions Ned used to ask her about Melbury Hall. Her only consolation was that she didn't remember ever saying anything that could have caused any difficulties for her mistress.

At a bend in the path, she ran square into the devil himself. Ned Cranch reached right out to steady her.

"What's the rush, lassie? Eager to see me?"

She shook off his hand and stood her ground, refusing to let him intimidate her. " 'Tis finished, Ned. Your true colors having been shown."

"That's a good one, coming from a whore." His smirk turned to a frown. "But what do ye mean by that, I'd like to know?"

"Everybody has figured it out," she lied. "Everyone knows you're being paid by Jasper Hyde. The reason for your being here is to spy on Lady Aytoun and Melbury Hall."

"I don't know no Jasper whatever-his-name-is."

"Is that so? Then why did I see his lawyer, Platt, going into your room in St. Albans? You remember the night."

Ned's gaze narrowed and he grabbed her arm. "So are you going to let them know about us then? About how you played the slut for a married man to—"

"I already told them," she replied, twisting her arm out of his grasp. "And as we speak, Mr. Gibbs has some of the grooms coming down here looking for you. I probably just need to call out for them to come running."

"Ye're a lying wench."

"Believe what you want." Putting on a look of satisfaction, Violet started backing away. "Stand around and wait until they come for you, Ned. I'd love to see them give you the beating you deserve."

That night, when Jonah came up to the house complaining about the stonemason disappearing and leaving a job half done, Violet breathed more easily. Ned Cranch had gone away in a hurry.

Now her only hope was for him to stay away.

Chapter 28

The travels they had made to the neighboring estates had added hours onto their day. It was far later than Lyon had ever intended to stay away, but it couldn't be helped.

As soon as his chair was placed in the entrance hall, Lyon asked about Millicent.

"Nay, m'lord," Mrs. MacAlister said. "She's not yet retired. In the library, she is. Waiting for ye."

"She is not unwell?" he asked, trying not to sound anxious as the servants helped him remove his hat and gloves and cloak.

"She'd not admit it, I'm thinking. But she looks tired." Mrs. MacAlister shot him a look that bordered on reproach. "Her ladyship pushed herself today. Far more than necessary. This morning, a wee morsel of breakfast. Then she leaves with Mr. Truscott. Hoping to find you in the village, she was. By the time she arrives, ye had already gone off to hither and yon."

"Yes, Walter told me that she'd decided to remain in the village when he rode on to join me at Lord Dumfries's." He looked carefully at the housekeeper, surprised by her unexpected concern for Millicent.

"Well, he would have done better to bring her home, if ye ask me." The housekeeper sounded downright disturbed. "The condition of the folk passing through upset her. Her ladyship stayed down there far longer than she should have. And then she rode down along the river. There are more vagrants gathered in the camps down there, where ye allow the gypsies to camp in the summer. She spent time there as well."

As the servants readied themselves to lift his chair, Mrs. MacAlister continued. "I tried to tell her, m'lord. As mistress of Baronsford, I told her, she is far above getting herself personally involved with the needs of vagrants passing through."

"I can just imagine her answer to that."

"I do not see how ye could, m'lord," Mrs. MacAlister said with a note of pride. "But my new mistress said even if she were the queen herself, she'd never turn her back on those in need."

Mr. Campbell cleared his throat nervously, drawing Lyon's attention. "Her ladyship asked me about the number of bedrooms at Baronsford."

"Is that so?"

"Aye, m'lord. And how your lordship might feel about filling them up with *guests*."

"Guests?" Lyon asked, pausing for a moment before beginning to laugh.

She put the closed book on the shelf. She took it down again. She clutched it under one arm and then held it against her chest. She put it back on the shelf again.

Millicent fought to keep herself composed while the servants tried to settle Lyon onto the settee. The hours that they had been apart felt like months, and from the first moment Lyon came into the room, she sensed that his pleasure at seeing her matched how she felt about him.

"This is far better. I have never been so tired of that deuced chair as I was today."

The serving men had not even left the room yet, but Millicent could hold herself back no longer. Sliding onto the settee beside him, she threw her arms around him. He held her tight against his chest before pulling slightly back and smiling into her face.

"I missed you, too." He kissed her lips with such tenderness that Millicent melted against him. The door to the library softly closed behind the servants. It was some time before he pulled away, and even longer before Millicent felt herself floating back to earth.

"I'm sorry I left before you arrived in the village this morning."

She shook her head. "I needed some time to establish myself and get my bearings."

"I understand you did that and more."

His right hand cupped her face. Millicent nestled her cheek into his touch, still amazed at how quickly he was recovering the movement in his hand and arm. "I might have disappointed Mrs. MacAlister with my lack of sophistication."

"Disappointed? You have won her over completely. Out there in the entry hall just now, the woman spoke more words to me than she would have normally used in a year."

"I'm glad. I believe we shall get along very well. She is very capable and quite efficient, and despite her sharp manner, she is a very warm woman."

"Well, I must tell you that you are the first mistress of Baronsford who has noticed that quality in her. She did not have much patience with Emma, who would have dismissed her a dozen times if I hadn't refused to allow it. And as far as my mother goes, their temperaments were too much alike for anyone to guess they could even stand each other."

"She stayed, though, so I suppose your mother must have appreciated her efforts."

"I suppose that is true." Lyon stroked her cheek. "Since you do get along so well with Mrs. MacAlister, then probably you will not mind what I am about to ask of you."

"Is it painful?"

"Very." He settled back with a tired sigh. "We need to throw a party, very soon. I want to invite every landlord and member of the gentility within an hour's ride of Baronsford."

"How large a group would that be?"

"About a hundred. Perhaps a few more."

Millicent settled back heavily, too. "That is very painful."

"And did I mention that we need to do it soon?"

She nodded tentatively, trying to blot out of her mind the image of herself in a roomful of distinguished people where no one noticed her presence.

"Campbell told me you were asking about the number of guestrooms at Baronsford."

Millicent looked up at Lyon and smiled. "Yes, I was."

"This is the reason for the party."

"To compare the size of castles and manor houses?" she quipped.

"Even better. We will stuff their bellies at the same time that we try to shame them into not pushing out their tenants. We shall also try to get a few of them to offer positions to a few of the vagrant families. I tried to do that today by visiting some of the neighboring estates. But it is too difficult to press them one by one. Sir Such-and-such is in London. Baron This-and-that was interested only in hearing about you." He waved a hand impatiently. "We need to bring them all here and try to convince them at once."

"With this kind of agenda, do you think anyone will show up at the party?"

"I think they will *all* come."

"Why?"

"They are all beside themselves with curiosity about the new Countess of Baronsford. And . . ." He pointed to a chair. "More than few of these curs will jump at the opportunity of looking down on me."

"They'll burn in hell first. I shall arrange for you to be carried about on a pedestal ten feet high."

"Such language!" he said, laughing and pulling her more tightly against his side. "Does this mean you will arrange the party?"

"Absolutely. We must do something for those unfortunate wretches."

Lyon kissed her again, and Millicent felt the desire and even the love in his embrace. She felt cherished.

"I know this has only been your second day at Barons-ford, but I thought you should know that you have made a great impression." His fingers gently pushed a loose tendril off her face. "And though you have said you have no aspirations with regard to this place, the people here already respect you. They already see your en-dearing concern for all."

Millicent remembered what Truscott had told her today about Emma loving Baronsford more than Lyon. She imagined the pain that Lyon must have endured.

"I asked Walter to take me to the cliffs overlooking the river today. I needed to see the place where you fell. The place where you lost Emma."

"You mean where she died."

Millicent didn't miss the hard edge in his tone. "A wise man once told me about this road that both of us had once walked before. He told me that we need to do better the second time."

"A wise man, you say?"

"Yes. My husband. The terribly wise Lord Aytoun. Have you heard of him?"

"Oh, yes. The Lord of Scandal."

She leaned against him and traced the hard lines around his mouth with the tip of one finger. "I don't want any secrets between us, Lyon. I don't want any-thing left unsaid. No assumptions or misunderstandings. Only the truth."

"Truscott told you about Emma."

"And your brothers' relationship with her," she said quietly. "There was so much that I didn't know, and there is still so much about me and my past that you don't know, either. And today, after I left the village and rode down along the riverbank, I ran into so many people who have been pushed out of their homes. Fami-lies that have nearly lost hope. And I thought of the two of us and how we have been given a second chance at happiness, and how much I wanted to succeed in that."

Millicent let her hopes rise when Lyon's arm tightened around her. She tucked her head under his chin.

"Being down there also made me realize that now

Emma was no longer the supernatural creature that I had imagined her to be. Now, knowing more about her, I realized that she was simply a woman made of flesh and blood—a human being with all the strengths and failings that all of us have. Knowing that, I realized I could survive this road and perhaps even make a difference as I travel along on it. But at the same time, I recognized how important it was for me to tell you everything I could about myself, too."

The feel of his arm around her gave Millicent the strength she needed to continue.

"I was practically given to Wentworth at the age of twenty-three for the lack of a better marriage offer. My uncle, who had been my guardian, was too terrified of the embarrassment and the expense of having a spinster on his hands forever. So I had to go. It mattered naught by then who it was to be, no matter how bad the man's reputation or character." She let out a shaky breath, resolved to keep nothing back. "I remained married to him for five years, though I still find it a miracle that I survived that long. To my husband, I was just a bit of property, like his land, his sugar holdings, his African workers, his horses and dogs and sheep and cattle. And he saw it as his right to abuse us and to cut us down as he wished."

Millicent felt the tension in Lyon's body as his anger grew, but she continued to talk. "During those years—when I was at Melbury Hall and not trying to hide from him in London—I formed a bond, of sorts, with many of the black workers that Wentworth held as slaves. During this time I also had the good fortune of becoming friends with Reverend and Mrs. Trimble and with Mr. Cunningham, the schoolteacher at Knebworth Village. These good people, with the support of our neighbor Lord Stanmore, were trying to improve the conditions at Melbury Hall that the slaves there were forced to endure."

She pushed away from Lyon's chest and tried to force down the lump that was growing in her throat. "Although Wentworth had nothing to fear, my friendship

with Mr. Cunningham became a very sore subject with
him. He refused to see that the man's compassion was
his reason for visiting Melbury Hall. He preferred to
believe that we were lovers. We were *not*, though I think
Mr. Cunningham at the end confused his compassion for
me with love."

"Millicent—"

"There is more I need to tell you about Cunningham,
but let me first tell you something else. Wentworth believed that it was his right as master to use me as he
saw fit. In short, I found myself with child. He used to
say that it was his right 'to touch as I like and to punish
as I see fit.' He preferred to punish, and he beat me
once so severely during that time that I was confined to
bed for weeks. I also lost the child."

She shook her head when he tried to pull her back
into his arms.

"Let me finish. I need to tell you all of it." She blinked
back her tears. "After losing that baby, I was lost in my
own grief for months. At the same time I knew that I
was wearing out my value to Wentworth. It was only a
matter of time before he would kill me. He had done
it before."

She looked up into Lyon's face. His fury was barely
restrained.

"Wentworth's first wife's family owned a number of
plantations in Jamaica. That is where he made a small
fortune, but just before he decided to move back to England, she died . . . mysteriously. Wentworth told me,
during a moment of drunken boasting, that *she* had worn
out her value."

Millicent moved her hand over Lyon's fisted fingers.
"Then came the summer before last. I accidentally met
an old school friend at Knebworth Village. It was Rebecca. She had been in the American colonies for ten
years."

Millicent recalled those days of meeting secretly with
Rebecca in the Grove or at the church in the village.

"She helped me realize I had to find a way out of that
marriage, before I ended up like Wentworth's first wife.

We even went as far as planning an escape to Philadelphia or somewhere in the colonies. But then one day, before we could put our plan into action, Wentworth flew into a rage when Lord Stanmore took away one of the slave children who had been severely abused by the bailiff. After that, everything broke loose at once.''

"You are shivering.'' Lyon's arm wrapped around her shoulders, and he drew her against his side. Millicent forced herself to go on.

"It was June. We had hidden Violet in the Grove to protect her from Wentworth and his lechery. I sent Jonah to the village one night to ask Mr. Cunningham to come at dawn to take Violet away. And he did. But Wentworth and his bailiff, a brute named Mickleby, appeared and claimed that it was I who was running away with the schoolteacher that morning. Wentworth shot and killed Mr. Cunningham that morning.''

Lyon's hand gently caressed her. "And Wentworth was killed by Stanmore?''

That was the public explanation, but Millicent wanted him to know the truth. "After killing Cunningham, Wentworth went berserk. He wanted to murder everyone who mattered to me . . . before killing me. He decided to start with Jonah.'' She held Lyon's hand and looked up into his face. "No one knows this, but Moses killed Wentworth that morning. Stanmore arrived just in time to save Moses's life. To save Moses from having to face the law for killing a white man, and to spare me the scandal that might follow, Stanmore took responsibility for all of it. How much he told the magistrate of what really happened I don't know, but there were never any questions asked later on.''

"I knew I liked Stanmore, but what about the bailiff?''

"As he prepared to kill Moses, he died by Stanmore's sword.''

"Who else knows this?'' Lyon asked, concerned.

"Only the few Africans who were in the Grove that morning. And Rebecca and Stanmore. And I believe Violet learned of it later from one of the women who had been hiding her in the Grove." She held his hand. "You are worried."

"For Moses's life," he said solemnly. "If the truth of that day ever reaches the wrong ears, his life will be worth nothing."

"But no one will know," she said, determined. "Wentworth would have slain many people that morning, including me, if it were not for Moses's bravery. He saved my life. You know him. How gentle he is. And no one who was there would ever betray him."

Shadows flickered on the walls of the servants' hall, and Gibbs sat before the fire, staring into the dying flames. The house was quiet, the doors secured, and Moses was on his watch rounds, but the Highlander could not shake the feeling that was haunting him.

A memory kept nagging at him. A memory of his childhood.

He was only about five, but even then he knew that something momentous was happening. Something that would change his world. He and his mother and sister were sitting before the fire in their cottage on the hillside. His father and older brothers had gone off a few weeks earlier to join Bonny Prince Charlie in his fight against the Hanovers. As they waited that night, they heard the keening cries of the women in the glen, and he knew his father and brothers were not coming back.

This same feeling was haunting him now, and Gibbs did not like it at all.

Mary Page glided into the hall like an angel, guarding her bit of paradise. She was growing fond of him; he could tell. And for the first time in his life, the feeling was mutual.

"Come sit with me, Mrs. Page. Ye have been on your feet this entire day."

She snuffed a guttering candle and adjusted a stack of plates on the table before coming and taking the seat beside him. Her eyes were warm when they swept over his face. "You look as troubled as I feel, Mr. Gibbs."

He reached for her hand and she let him entwine his fingers with hers. "Tell me what is bothering ye, Mary."

"I don't know what is happening, but something is wrong. And I am not imagining this. The entire household is feeling it." She looked about the empty hall. "Violet didn't take a single meal today, and I saw her looking out the windows at the road a dozen times, if I saw her do it once. Ohenewaa has been keeping to her room, and every time I passed by her door, I could hear her chanting her African songs. And then one of the serving maids said she thought she saw Ned Cranch in the shadow of the woods, peering up at the house with an ax in his hand."

"That sounds a wee bit far-fetched, Mary. The stonemason not only left his job here; he has also emptied his room at the inn."

"Now, what do you think happened to him?"

"Maybe he got word that his wife had a bairn. What I don't understand is why he didn't come around to get paid for the work he'd done. Perhaps he's planning on coming back, though I do not know why he went off without telling us."

"You see, Mr. Gibbs?" Mary looked him in the eye. "Everyone is behaving strangely, and there is just no explaining it."

He ran his finger gently over the palm of her hand. "Ye know all this imagining could be the result of having Lord and Lady Aytoun away. From what ye told me yourself, the mistress is not one to spend time away from Melbury Hall. And 'tis ten years since I've been separated from his lordship."

"Do you really think that is all 'tis, Mr. Gibbs? Do you think we are worrying about nothing?"

The way Mary's large eyes were watching the movement of his finger, the innocent way the blush had crept up her cheeks, Gibbs couldn't stop himself from leaning over and pressing a kiss onto her forehead.

"I don't know, Mary. But I can tell ye I feel better having ye beside me."

"The same goes for me, Angus," she said in a small voice, moving closer to his side.

As the two sat and stared into the fire, though, their feeling of foreboding was not easily shaken.

"I did not mean to worry you so with what I told you earlier about Wentworth's death," Millicent whispered against Lyon's ear, curling an arm around his chest. "I am sorry. Now you cannot sleep, can you?"

His head turned toward her on the pillow. "That is not what is keeping me awake. I have been thinking of what Truscott told you about Emma."

"It was wrong of me to ask him to take me there. I should have waited until you were ready to—"

"No. I am glad you went. And I am relieved that you know as much as you do about her." His hand gently caressed her hair and her face. "What has been keeping me awake is the fact that I should tell you the rest of it—of what happened that day."

Until this moment Millicent hadn't realized how mixed her feelings were. The possibility of Lyon's somehow being responsible for Emma's death was a plausible reason for his melancholy after the accident. But she had never wanted to believe it.

Millicent looked beyond her husband and the bed at the half-light of the bedchamber. The flames were burning low in the fireplace. Despite the shadows lurking all around them, she thought, she trusted this man. How fortunate they were to have each other.

"Will you tell me?"

Lyon took hold of her hand and stared up at the ceiling. "We fought. We always fought. Everything about Emma and me was a mistake from the very beginning. We were ten years apart, but it may as well have been a hundred. We did not understand each other. We did not speak the same language. Could not comprehend the other's needs. And this was no one's fault but mine. I always thought I knew what she wanted. I had watched her grow up. I had watched her liveliness and beauty bloom. I thought she wanted only me." He gave a bitter laugh. "Arrogance leads us to make many mistakes. She didn't want me. She wanted Baronsford. And I was completely blind to it."

Millicent wished she could somehow make this easier for him, but she could not think of a way.

"What Truscott told you about our problems was all true. When she became unreasonable, I only became worse. When she withdrew, I became suspicious. As a result, we spent most of our marriage apart. When she was in London or Bath or Bristol, I made sure I was at Baronsford. When she came here with her friends, I would spend the time in the Highlands. And as great a fool as I was, despite all of our difficulties, our mockery of marriage remained tolerable so long as Emma would not disgrace us publicly."

Lyon's gaze turned to Millicent. "Because of Emma, my brothers began to hate me. Pierce and David and I grew further and further apart. But that wasn't enough, so she began to hint at affairs. And then she would question my honor. My manhood. And she would expect me to act on it."

"And you did."

"I was a fool. I think she hoped I would die in one of those duels. Instead, even greater fools than I had to die."

Millicent thought that it was a miracle that Lyon had lived through those times. She pressed her lips against his heart.

"The day she died—the day of the accident—I should have known she was up to something."

"But Walter said everyone was visiting because of the dowager's birthday."

"All of our families were there at Baronsford. Over two hundred guests were arriving for the ball in my mother's honor, but that was just an excuse to have us all there," he said quietly. "She had an announcement that required a worthy audience."

"What was her announcement?"

Lyon's eyes were hard when they turned to her. "She wanted a divorce."

Millicent felt herself go cold.

"The greatest scandal she could create, and a public announcement to disseminate the news. Emma wanted to have the sympathetic ears of everyone who admired and loved her when she announced why she could no longer tolerate being married to me."

Millicent thought of her own divorce request to the dowager and Sir Richard before marrying Lyon. But that had been under very different circumstances.

"What did you do?" she asked.

"I told her no, though not in so calm a fashion. We fought, and she told me she would do as she wished. She was going to make the announcement, and I could live with the scandal of it. And then she ran away."

"And you went after her."

"Not at first. I told myself this was all just another ploy. That she was playing with me like a toy soldier. That she would never do such a thing, and I was not going to rise to her bait. And then I came downstairs and ran into Pierce."

"He talked you into going after her?"

"Not exactly. He was angry because he had seen Emma upset, running away in the direction of the cliffs. He started lecturing me again on how I did not treat her well, and how I was undeserving of her love. He asked me how I could upset her so, considering her condition."

"Her condition?"

"Pierce told me that Emma was pregnant. She told him that she and I were going to make an announcement about it that night."

Anger washed through her.

"I went after her. I ran out there after Emma. But before I could reach her, though, I heard the scream. By the time I got there, she was at the bottom."

His hand rubbed his forehead, back and forth. "When I started climbing down those rocks, I wasn't in search of answers. I remember thinking, She cannot be dead."

His voice caught in his throat, and he closed his eyes. Millicent kissed the tear that squeezed from the corner of his eye.

"Lyon, I am so sorry. So sorry for what you had to go through."

"I think what hurt me most about everything was to wake up so much later and find my brothers had gone. They believed—they still believe—that I pushed Emma off that cliff."

"You cannot know what they believe." She soothed her husband without knowing those other men, without understanding them. "They might have left because of their own guilt with regard to your marriage. They had served as a wedge between you and Emma. Perhaps by going away, they were just trying to cope with their grief."

Lyon's gaze fixed on her face, and then he pressed her head closely to his heart. "Thank you for your trust in me."

She listened to his strong heart beating beneath her ear. "Did you ever find out if Emma was truly pregnant?"

"I was told later that she was," he whispered. "But I know that the child was not mine."

Chapter 29

The kitchens at Baronsford were a combination of modern and ancient. The bakery, with its fine new ovens and solid wooden tables and protected shelves for the dough to rise, offered a sharp contrast to the three huge open hearths with their iron spits and swinging arms. Within those wide stone arches, pork and mutton and beef had been roasted over fires in exactly the same way for centuries. Even now the smell of oat porridge wafted from the cauldrons that were hanging over the fires.

"I am very happy with everything you have chosen, Mrs. MacAlister." Millicent took another loaf of bread from one of the cooks and wrapped it in a cloth before putting it in the basket.

"Cannot be all good. An important party, this is. There must be something that displeases ye."

"Nothing at all." She smiled pleasantly as a servant took away two of the filled baskets and replaced them with empty ones.

"The selection of the late-supper dishes," the house-keeper pressed.

"Love them."

"The dessert menu."

"Outstanding."

"The china."

"Beautiful."

"The cakes with the topping of fresh berries."

Millicent shot Mrs. MacAlister a look. "That was not

on the menu you were speaking of this morning. Where are you going to find fresh berries in March?"

"I was just testing, m'lady. Just to see if ye were listening."

Millicent's laughter made the housekeeper's tight lips twitch—slightly.

"I cannot understand why you find it so difficult to believe how delighted I am with the arrangements you have made for this large party. I trust your judgment. You amaze me with your thoroughness. You are very good. You are amazingly good, Mrs. MacAlister."

The housekeeper shook one of the cloths open and handed it to her, ready for the next loaf of bread. Millicent considered this a peace offering.

"And ye are too good, m'lady," Mrs. MacAlister finally said. "It has been a few years since we've seen our mistress in the kitchens."

Before Millicent could respond to the compliment, Mrs. MacAlister took the bread from the cook and started wrapping it herself.

"But this is one thing we can do, m'lady. Preparing food baskets for the vagrants. And our mistress can spend a wee hour with the dressmaker. The woman was fetched from Edinburgh yesterday, she was."

"I asked for no dressmaker."

"I know," the woman said, a wicked gleam in her eye. "His lordship gave me directions, he did. Said to see to your wardrobe. And so I am."

"But—"

" 'I trust your judgment,' " the housekeeper said, mimicking Millicent's English accent. " 'You amaze me.' 'You are amazingly good, Mrs. MacAlister.' Now, should I trust your words or not, m'lady?"

"Verrra well, Mrs. MacAlister," Millicent said, mimicking the housekeeper's burr. "Ye have me there, so ye do."

As she was being led away by her own maidservant, Millicent was pleased to hear surprised laughter behind her.

*   *   *

Jasper Hyde paced the length of the rooms he had taken in the coach inn on High Street in St. Albans. The large windows of the front room looked out at the ancient clock tower, and with each passing minute, the plantation owner was becoming more impatient. When Harry led Ned Cranch in an hour and a half later than was expected, he was ready to shoot the blasted stonemason, and leveled his pistol at the man's chest to make his point.

"To get all the answers ye wanted, Mr. Hyde, there was no way I could get back sooner," Ned explained defensively, ignoring the gun. "But ye'll be happy to know I've figured out the whole thing."

"Start talking," Hyde snapped, "before I blast a hole in you."

The stonemason did not look frightened. "We can't go down the road to Melbury Hall, snatch her, and go merrily on our way."

"Why not? You were ready to do that single-handedly. Now you're saying it cannot be done with a half-dozen men?"

"Aye, it can." Ned spoke calmly. "But we have to go about it different now. Things have changed since the earl and his wife left for Scotland. I've been keeping watch over the place, and what I see is that the black woman don't venture into the woods no more. And even when she does move about outside, there's always a handful of other blacks hanging about her. 'Tis like they know somebody's coming after her. I think they've got wind somehow, and they mean to protect her."

"A handful of slaves are no match for the paid cutthroats we've hired, Mr. Cranch."

"Maybe, sir. Or maybe not." Ned shook his head and moved into the room. "I'm thinking these freed slaves are not like the ones you're used to on your plantation, Mr. Hyde. These have tasted freedom, so they're bound to be fierce in protecting their own. There's also another thing to consider here, too. The road out of Melbury Hall passes close to Solgrave and goes through Knebworth Village. Any open attack on Melbury Hall and they'll send someone through the woods to the neighboring estate or the village. We'll find ourselves trapped, unless ye wish to climb the Chiltern Hills."

Hyde's temper flared. "Then what the hell do you propose?"

"We need to be making a distraction." The cocky stonemason had the nerve to sit down on a chair. "I think ye should go and fetch your men and bring them back to St. Albans. We can all of us meet at the tavern where I am staying by the brickyards. In the meantime, I'll talk to my lass over in Knebworth Village and arrange a way to get me inside Melbury Hall on the night when ye're ready."

"You told me you had your women in the house itself."

"I did . . . I do. I've a couple of them on the string, sir." He shook his head. "But the servants in that house are a strange bunch. They're just too loyal to their mistress for me to rely in them in a situation like this."

The man's reasoning was sound. "What do you plan to do once you're inside?"

The stonemason's gaze was confident. "This is the way I see it. We meet at the tavern, and I explain the lay of the land to your men. Then we separate and meet at the Grove. That's a bunch of empty huts in the woods to the back of the Hall. Meanwhile, I have my girl hide me in her cart and take me to Melbury Hall. Once there, I sneak out and start a fire in the stables. Now, with all the commotion of the fire, everyone is sure to empty out of the house. We'll probably have folk rushing up from Solgrave and the village to help. That's when your men come out. We snatch Ohenewaa and go on our way." Ned Cranch grinned proudly. "What do you think?"

Hyde moved to the window as he considered the plan. Another minute ticked by on the clock tower. Time was running out, and he rubbed his chest.

"Forget the stables, Mr. Cranch. Burn the house."

She was huddled beneath a cart to keep out of the falling rain, a small bundle of woolen plaid with the face of an angel.

Millicent noticed her as she handed out the contents of a second basket of food to a family of five gathered around a smoking fire. The young girl's gaze flitted nervously to the groom who was carrying the last basket.

Millicent took the food from the groom and walked toward the cart.

"She'll take it, but the lassie willna eat any of it herself." An old woman stood at the head of an ancient cow still harnessed to the cart. "She's already hoarding half a loaf o' bread from the basket ye gave us yesterday. She thinks her bairn'll be born with a full set o' teeth."

Millicent crouched in the deep mud beside the cartwheel and held the basket out to the girl. "It isn't much, but you might take some of this bread and cheese and dried meat."

A thin arm reached tentatively from the folds of wool. A cold hand brushed Millicent's. As the girl took some cheese, Millicent caught a brief glimpse of the young girl's swollen belly.

"You are close to the time for having your bairn, are you not?"

The girl pulled the food beneath her plaid wrap.

"Why not come to the house with me," Millicent encouraged gently. "This is a rough place to bring a child into this world."

A look of terror appeared in the girl's eyes, and she shrank back farther beneath the cart and turned away.

"She'll not be coming out," the old woman called from her fire.

Millicent reluctantly pushed herself to her feet and turned to the woman who had spoken. "Is she your kin?"

"Nay, she's no kin o' mine nor anyone else's hereabout. But I've been sharing my cart with her since I found her on the Glasgow road."

"Do you know if she has any family she is going to?"

"She's going nowheres, mum. She has no kin, I'm telling ye." The woman glanced back at the cart. "All the poor creature ever says is that her name is Jo. I dunno if she's a faerie child or just cast out on account o' the child swelling in her. I reckon there's no man she's going to, and no husband she left behind. Leastwise, she never mentioned any."

"I should like to take her back with me to Baronsford. She'll at least have her child in a dry room with a fire to warm her. Will you ask her if she'll come with me?"

"She understands everything ye are telling her, mum, but she'll not listen to me any better than she does to ye." The old woman pointed beneath the cart. "Look at her. The daft creature is terrified now, just by ye asking."

Millicent looked for Jo and found the young girl had indeed crawled back away from her. Her plaid was pulled over her like a shroud.

"If you would come along, perhaps she would feel safe."

The old woman shook her head. "I ain't moving from here, mum. When the river goes down and these folk move, I need to be right here. Nay, I need no dry room for a day." She pulled her wool shawl tighter around herself and went over to the smoky fire.

Millicent forced herself to be strong, but the knot in her throat would not allow her to breathe. She looked once more at the mother-to-be.

Millicent had been ignoring the signs, but she was certain she herself was with child. As she looked at the frightened woman, the difference between them was crushing. Jo, with little hope of a future for either herself or her bairn, steadfastly clutched at broken scraps of bread beneath a cart in the rain. And Millicent, with a husband and a home, was delaying the moment of telling Lyon only because she wished to find the perfect time.

The groom touched her arm. "His lordship is here, m'lady."

Millicent looked up from the bank of the river and saw Lyon's carriage stopped behind the one that had carried her down here. Lifting the edges of her muddy cloak, she trudged up the mud-slick ground toward her husband.

As she drew nearer, Peter Howitt immediately

stepped out of the carriage and hurried down to assist Millicent up the muddy slope.

"Is there anything I can do for you here, m'lady?" the young man asked eagerly.

"I would be grateful if you would arrange for these empty baskets to be taken back to the kitchens. They need to be filled and brought back—with more blankets as well."

"I shall see to it immediately."

Stepping up to the carriage door, Millicent took one look at Lyon's outstretched hand before her tears began to fall. He pulled her inside and into his arms. The door of the carriage closed behind them, and she sobbed against his cloak, lost to her heartache over the misery outside.

"Certainly not the beautiful Scotland that you hear about, is it, my love?"

"It is so sad, Lyon." She wept. "These people have been stripped of everything. What is waiting at the end of the road looks to be nothing either. They've been torn away from their kin, their land, their homes. And still, they are so proud."

Lyon gathered her tightly against his chest, placing kisses against her hair. "These are a strong people, my love. They come from folk who survived the rough wooing of King Henry and his English raiders. They've fought off reivers and marauding armies and treachery of all kinds. Now these folk have been pushed out by the very people who have grown fat on their labors. But they are strong and proud, as you say. And with a little help from compassionate ones like you, they'll survive this, too."

He drew her face up and brushed away the tears. "But you cannot let yourself fall apart like this anytime you come down here. These people need you to be strong, too. They need you as I need you."

Millicent kissed him, knowing at that moment that she had never loved anyone or anything as she loved this man.

The carriage rolled gently toward the house. When

he broke off the kiss, she still could not stop the tears from falling.

"There was something else."

She nodded and closed her eyes to block out the image of the young girl beneath the cart. But it wouldn't go away.

"There is a young woman out there with no husband, no kin. She is about to have a baby."

"You could have brought her back to Baronsford."

Millicent shook her head. "I tried. She'll not come. But it is so sad. Why must it be like this? These people—these landowners—pushing their people out. These are their own countrymen. Their own clan folk, they tell me. How can we inflict this kind of injustice on another human being?"

Lyon lifted her chin and touched her face. His eyes glistened.

"That party is only three days away. That is our best chance to reach these landowners. We cannot change the minds of every one of them, the same way that we cannot save every poor vagrant out there. But we shall try. You and I together will do our best to make a difference."

Chapter 30

"It was bad enough that every member of this household was walking upon eggshells for the past few days, but now you assign a personal protector to watch over me as if I do not know to behave appropriately, or to dress properly, or to be at the right place at the right time." Millicent shifted her glare from Lyon to his secretary, who was standing right outside the closed carriage door, waiting for her to come out.

"I have no such concern. You are misinterpreting this entirely." Lyon took hold of her chin and drew her gaze back to him. "And the only reason why I am sending Howitt along is to get him off my back. He is more nervous about me not behaving properly tonight than Truscott and Campbell and Mrs. MacAlister together."

"Well, if you were an agreeable, good-natured, polite, and soft-spoken gentleman, none of these people would be so concerned, now, would they?"

He smiled at her. "Let the bloody wretches take their chances. You love me as I am, and that is enough."

Millicent looped her arms around her husband's neck, drawing her face near his. "This is a very dangerous relationship we have," she whispered. "You only say a few words, and you can have your way with me."

"You come back sooner from your visit of the vagrants along the river, and you and I might be able to retire to the library, or to our bedroom for an afternoon rest. Then I can work on perfecting other methods of having my way with you."

His mouth followed up immediately with a kiss, and Millicent was lost in the taste and texture and heat of their mating lips and tongue. She pulled back slightly to catch her breath.

"I think you have mastered the technique very well, in any case."

His hand reached under her cloak. "But there are a few other skills I still need to work on."

She leaned into his touch. "I was told the guests might be arriving anytime from the early afternoon on."

"We'll just let that nervous flock of titmice at Baronsford entertain the bloody intruders until we are ready for them."

He drew her more tightly against him, and Millicent relished the feel of his lips grazing her neck. Then she looked over her shoulder and found Howitt standing at a respectful distance from the carriage, moving impatiently from one foot to the other.

"I think your secretary is anxious for us to get started."

"Remind me to dismiss the scoundrel tomorrow."

"I'll do that."

Millicent still had stars dancing in her eyes when she stepped out of the carriage and stood waiting for it to drive away toward the village. She still had not told him anything of her pregnancy, but the news would wait until after the party tonight. A second carriage, which had carried more food and Howitt and couple of the servants, was parked on the road a few steps away.

"I promised Mrs. MacAlister to get you back by noon, m'lady," the young man said, having already lined up the servants with baskets of food to distribute. "So perhaps if we start in different directions and—"

"That would be just fine. But before we begin, you will explain to me why you are so uneasy." She stood before him, refusing to move.

"Why . . . nothing, m'lady." He was avoiding her eyes. "This uneasiness you refer to is just one of my many flaws—"

"Stop right there, Mr. Howitt," she scolded quietly.

"The entire household is a wreck, and you know it. Has the king been invited without telling me?"

The young man's gaze met hers nervously.

"I am much easier to deal with when I am *told* what the problem is."

He let out an agitated breath. "The truth of it is, mum, the last time Baronsford was preparing a gathering of this magnitude was the day . . . well, the day of the accident."

Millicent should have guessed. With Lyon injured, and Emma dead, there was no reason to celebrate after that terrible day. And more than a few members of the household at Baronsford were probably feeling a little superstitious.

"In spite of the tragic events of that day," the secretary continued, "many of the guests who stayed on that night behaved in a fashion that was less than genteel."

"Whispering about what had happened?"

"Speaking openly of scandal," Howitt said flatly. "That is why we are all determined to make this night so perfect. Begging your pardon, we understand and support what you and his lordship are trying to do. At the same time, we would like to show these people that Baronsford has not suffered from the previous countess's death. We'd like to show them that since your arrival, we are faring even better than before. We should like these guests to see how fortunate we are to have you."

"I am honored, Mr. Howitt, by your words." Millicent fought back tears and tried to calm her emotions. "We shall all do our best. So let us, then, be off. We shall see to our mission here and be on our way back to Baronsford with plenty of time to ready ourselves. We shall be back before they expect us."

As she turned toward the muddy river, Millicent never imagined that so soon after speaking those words she would be forgetting the hour, the day, and the guests. Her lapse in memory came just as she came upon the cart belonging to the old woman, and asked about the girl Jo.

*   *   *

The burly, muddleheaded Earl of Dumfries had taken it on himself to show up far earlier than everyone else at Baronsford. After two hours of being closed up with him in the library, listening to the man's whining, Lyon was ready to pick up his favorite pistol and shoot him squarely between his squinty black eyes. He refrained, however, unwilling to ruin the library's handsome Persian carpet.

Though he was in large part responsible for much of the problem in the Borders, he sulkily argued that if Lyon were to speak tonight for the protection of the land and its tenants, then he would be unfairly represented as a villain before their peers.

Just as Lyon was about to tell the earl that he was a fat, jabbering mealworm, Walter Truscott appeared at the door. The rest of the guests were beginning to arrive, and Lord Aytoun still needed to get himself ready. He was surprised, though, when his cousin followed the servants who carried him up to his dressing room.

"What's wrong, Walter?" he asked.

"Millicent has not yet returned."

"Howitt is with her."

"I believe he is. We have seen no sign of the carriage or the servants or the two of them."

"Did you send someone to the riverbank?"

"An hour ago. No news yet," he said with a frown. "I am riding down there myself right now. I don't want you to worry about anything. I shall bring her back. She must have been distracted and lost track of the time."

"Go," Lyon snapped. "I need to know she is safe. I don't care a straw about the strutting popinjays coming here tonight. I care only about *her*, Walter. Bring my wife back."

The doctor that Millicent had sent Howitt to fetch from Melrose had come too late. Jo had died with her tiny, tartan-swaddled daughter in one arm while her other hand had clutched Millicent's.

The crowd of onlookers just stared. No one whispered

a word, and then most of them simply shook their heads and turned away. Millicent didn't attempt to mumble words of solace. It was a hard world, and they knew it well.

From the few whispered words the dying Jo had spoken before the end came, Millicent had pieced together an understanding of what had happened to the young woman. It was a story of suffering. It was a story of betrayal.

She was relieved when Truscott arrived. He knew what to do, and he took charge of the arrangements.

After what felt like a lifetime later, Millicent found herself standing on the muddy bank of the river, holding the sleeping bairn beneath her cloak while her people wrapped Jo's body and carried it up to the village kirk.

The old woman who had shared her cart with Jo stood next to Millicent. "Ye will take the bairn?"

"I believe that would be best."

"Aye. Part o' that lassie lives on through her bairn. I heard her. What she whispered to ye about her life. Mayhap someday the wee one'll find justice for her mither."

Perhaps someday. But not for a long time.

"Will you stay with us? Come back to Baronsford. You can be there and watch her as she grows."

The old woman shook her head. "Nay, but thank ye. I may just come back, though, to see how ye've done by her."

"You are always welcome," Millicent whispered.

She watched Truscott's solemn face as he came down the hill. She knew it was time to go.

In the carriage, Millicent pushed back the cloak and gazed at the baby's pale face. She admired the small tightly fisted hands. She would do right by the child. She and Lyon would both cherish her and raise her with their own.

Millicent nestled the bundle in her arm more snugly against her chest. There were so many things that she needed to tell her husband—about this new addition to their family, and about the other one that was growing inside her now. She could hardly wait until everyone was gone tonight.

"From the number of carriages and horses and grooms in the courtyard and down by the stables," Howitt said, peering out the carriage window through the fading afternoon light, "it looks as if most everyone has arrived."

Truscott frowned. "We can pull the carriage around to the side entrance if you wish. No one needs to know you have returned until you've had a chance to change."

"No," Millicent said. "We will go in the main entrance."

She expected an argument, but he surprised her by immediately relaying her wishes to the grooms.

"And everyone was hoping so desperately to avoid another scandal," she said to Howitt.

Walter Truscott leaned over and touched her hand. "I shouldn't worry too much about that, m'lady. You do as you wish and let them see what their greed is doing to innocent folk."

The carriage stopped before the impressive entrance of Baronsford. Truscott stepped out and assisted Millicent from the carriage. She could hear the whispers even before reaching the open doors. A few late arrivals stood just inside, shedding expensive cloaks and hats. Millicent looked down at her mud-stained cloak, at the boots caked with muck.

"I can find my way from here," she told Truscott before going up the steps.

As Millicent stepped inside to the bows of the surprised footmen, no introduction was made. Instead, an immediate hush fell over those who were gathered in the entrance hall. Then like a giant wave, the whispers rolled and spread into the other rooms, through the great hall and the saloons and the ballroom. Then, like the calm before a storm, silence once again fell. Even the musicians in the ballroom ceased their playing.

Millicent stopped at the base of the great curved stairway and glanced at the place where Emma's portrait had hung. Then she turned and moved through the separating throngs of guests, looking for her husband.

She heard his voice, and then, just inside the doors of the great hall, Millicent saw Lyon. He was handsomer than any man she had ever seen in her life. She stopped a dozen paces from where he sat.

"I was by the river at the vagrant camp. At least fifty more families, with all their meager belongings piled on small carts or on their backs, came into the village. There is hunger, sickness, but they somehow retain their pride. They have nothing else."

Millicent's voice quavered but she continued to speak as if there were no one else there. She was talking only to Lyon.

"I was delayed in returning. Today we lost a young woman." She shook her head. "No, she was really little more than a child. Without a home, with none of her kin at her side, without anyone who loved her or knew her to help, she died on a stretch of mud on the bank of the river giving birth to this beautiful girl."

She gently pushed back the cloak to show the tiny infant in her arms.

"That was why I was late. I hope you understand."

Millicent pulled the cloak over the sleeping baby and, without looking back, went out through the hall and up the stairs.

By the time Millicent reached the top of the steps, her entire body was shaking. She could hear the voices of the guests as they all began to speak at once. Hurrying servants pulled the doors to her bedchamber shut behind her as sobs began to wrack her body in waves.

She didn't know what she had been thinking. She had made a fool out of herself before everyone who mattered. Mrs. MacAlister hastened into the room right behind her.

"I shall take care of this angel, m'lady. Ye must change." The housekeeper gently took the baby. Her soft words and gentle manner made Millicent cry even harder.

The servants' hands tugged at her clothes, undressing her and dressing her again, brushing her hair. Millicent endured it all in a daze. She wondered how Lyon was managing with the embarrassment of his new wife's behavior. How was he going to explain her to these people?

I hope you understand. She shuddered.

The dress they had pulled onto her had silver threads woven into the fabric. Millicent sat and watched skilled hands frantically trying to arrange her hair.

"One of the women in the kitchen is nursing her own bairn of two months," Mrs. MacAlister explained. "I think this wee one is just waking up. She'll be looking for some food, too, she will."

Millicent nodded gratefully to the housekeeper and watched the woman disappear out the door. All the tugging and pulling and arranging suddenly come to a halt, and they all stood back. She stared into the looking glass at the strangely familiar woman staring back at her.

Millicent slowly rose to her feet. The idea of walking out of this room and down those steps was terrifying.

There was a knock at the door, and someone opened it.

A hush fell over the room, and Millicent turned to see who was at the door.

It was Lyon, standing in the open doorway.

Her breath caught in her chest. Tears welled up in her eyes, blurring her vision, and she reached a hand toward him just as she felt the room around her begin to whirl.

Two servants caught Millicent just as her knees buckled beneath her. By the time she regained her senses, she had been conveyed to a settee and Lyon was beside her, growling orders at everyone. She sipped the wine that was being held to her lips.

"I'm fine." She took his hand and, despite his objections, pulled herself to her feet. "You're standing. You—"

"I wanted to surprise you, but I never thought I would frighten you like this, my love." His arms wrapped around her, drawing her against him.

"How? When?" The tears would not stop. "This must be a dream."

" 'Tis no dream. I shall explain everything later."

Millicent remembered the guests. She recalled the importance of the gathering. At the same time, she could not stop thinking of his legs supporting him. She held him tight, fearing he might fall, but she was the unsteady one at the moment. She took a deep breath. "We should be downstairs."

"Are you certain you are feeling better?"

"I am. I am indeed." She wiped the tears and took his arm. She was ready.

Chapter 31

As recently as a fortnight ago, Millicent would have considered this night a borrowed dream. A lifetime of doubt had been cast to the wind, though, as she had stood proudly beside her husband in the ballroom of Baronsford, discussing everything from politics to the living conditions of the vagrants to what might be done to improve their situation.

At times, Millicent had surprised herself. Here she was, speaking with such passion. She cared naught if the scrutinizing looks directed at her were critical or approving. She was happy with who she was and how she looked. What meant the most to her, though, was the fact that the most important person in that room, Lyon, was openly proud of her. For the first time in her life, she felt complete.

It was only after the rest of the guests had either retired or gone home that the earl of Dumfries—the first guest to arrive, according to Lyon—decided to leave. As his carriage rolled away from the door, Millicent sank against her husband's chest.

"You were magnificent," he whispered in her ear, his arms wrapped tightly around her.

"And *you* are standing." She looked up with amazement at him. "I still cannot believe it. Standing."

Lyon had not been able to climb the stairs. When he had appeared in the ballroom, standing beside his wife shortly after going up after her, though, word had spread with amazing speed through the assembled guests. Millicent had seen many staring as if they were witnessing a miraculous event. Others stood looking on in silent awe. Many of Baronsford's household staff came up to admire their laird's recovery, as well.

"And do not forget the steps I took, too."

Millicent hugged him fiercely, fighting back her tears. "I shall never forget that. But how long have you been hiding this from me?"

"The feeling in my limbs has been coming back slowly, and I was looking for the right opportunity when I could share with you something significant." He brushed a tear off her cheek. "Seeing you tonight coming in here with that bairn in your arms and facing these wolves so bravely, I could wait no longer. You taught me, showed me, this had to be the moment."

"I love you, Lyon." She kissed him. "I shall never forget this night."

When she pulled away, she saw him lean heavily on the cane he held. She quickly motioned Lyon's valets to bring in his chair.

"You are not putting me back into that."

"We shall only use it to manage the stairs for a while." She lowered her voice. "This is the quickest way to get you upstairs and to our bedroom."

"In that case"—a wicked grin broke onto his face—"there are other things about my recovery that I am looking forward to showing you."

Millicent blushed at his suggestive words.

Will and John positioned the chair behind Lyon. He handed the cane to Millicent and sat down without the aid of the valets. "When will I get a chance to meet the new addition to our family?"

This time Millicent could not hold back her tears. He understood. Without her having to ask, Lyon knew that they would be raising the child as their own. She walked ahead of his chair as they ascended the steps. "I checked on her once tonight. She was fed and sleeping. I shall ask Mrs. MacAlister to bring her to us if she is awake."

He nodded. "Have you named her?"

"I thought perhaps she should be called Josephine. Her mother's name was Jo."

"That is a beautiful name."

When they reached their apartments, Millicent went to her own dressing room, where Bess was waiting to get her ready for bed. Mrs. MacAlister sent word that the infant was asleep and it would be best to wait for the morning for his lordship to see the bairn. Millicent returned to their bedchamber to find the valets gone and Lyon already in bed. He had been told the housekeeper's recommendation.

"I suppose we should enjoy this night of sleep, as I can only imagine we shall have some sleepless nights with a bairn in the house."

"Will you mind it?"

He laughed and stretched a hand toward her in invitation. "I've been waiting a lifetime for this."

"Have you really?" Millicent removed her robe and climbed into the bed. "Do you really mean it? Do you want a child of our own?"

"A houseful of them! And I do not care how we get them, either." He pulled her close to him. "What hurt me most during the years that I was married to Emma was being separated from my family. I felt isolated, alone. After the accident on the cliff, I realized that my brothers had severed the last ties that bound us. They had moved away from me, and that cut me deeply." His hand cupped her face. "I have made a vow to mend that rift, if they will allow it."

"That is a good thing."

"But that is only a small part of what I dream of for the future."

"What else do you dream of?" she asked.

"Of making you happy. I love you, and I promise to do my best to make up for all the sadness of your past."

"You have already done that, love."

His fingers delved into her hair, and he brought her mouth to his. She cherished his tender touch and felt her body come alive. He peeled away her nightgown, and Millicent looked into his face.

"When you mentioned the houseful of children . . ." Her voice trailed off.

"I meant it. It matters naught how we get them," he repeated. "I will not have you worrying about heirs and other such nonsense. There are hungry bairns and orphans amongst the poor. There are those who need a home wandering tonight on the London streets. There are the children of Africans who have been stolen away from their homes who need families. We'll have no trouble filling up our house, I should think."

She pressed a finger against his lips. "And there is the one who is growing inside me now. Do you think we might raise this one amongst all the rest?"

It took a moment for her words to sink in, but then he was the one overwhelmed with emotion. His fingers threaded into her hair.

"Do you mean it? Right now?" His voice shook. "You are carrying our child now?"

Millicent nodded and wiped away the tear that trickled down his cheek. "Yes, my love. A part of the two of us is growing inside me right now."

"Tonight, when you became light-headed, I should have guessed there was something more than excitement. Our child!" He lifted her chin. "But how are you feeling? You are not eating properly. You are certainly not getting enough rest. Doctors. We have to find a good one to look after you. But . . . Ohenewaa! She can—"

"Stop," Millicent scolded with a smile. "You shall not fuss over me like this."

"I shall do as I wish. I intend to provide perfect care for my wife and bairn." Lyon rolled her on the bed until she lay beneath him. "Wait, this might not be a good position for you, bearing all my weight."

Millicent looped her arms around his neck and pulled him back to her.

"I shall tell you what is good for me," she said, silencing him with a kiss.

Chapter 32

Violet asked the groom to wait with the cart by the shops facing Knebworth Village's market square and walked up the hill toward the rectory. Mrs. Page's basket of baked goods for Mrs. Trimble hung from one arm. In the other, she carried a bundle of London newspapers she had been told she should leave with the new schoolmaster.

The morning sky promised to be clear, and the smoke from the breakfast fires and the fragrant smell of bread baking somewhere smelled domestic and good to her. Passing the blacksmith shop and the livery stable, Vi was startled by a woman who jumped at her from behind a cart, grabbing her arm. Violet immediately pulled her arm away and took a step back when she recognized her.

"Don't you dare talk to me."

"Please, I've something important to tell ye."

Violet stepped toward the middle of the street, turning away from her. The last time she had seen the wretch had been in Ned Cranch's bed at the inn.

"Please, Violet," the girl pleaded. "I know yer name's Violet, and ye work up at the Hall."

She reached for her arm again, but Violet shook her off. "Get away from me, I'm telling you."

"He's coming back," she hissed, looking around nervously. "And he means to do something wicked out there at Melbury Hall."

The warning cut through Violet's anger. She took a few more steps toward the rectory before she stopped and glanced over her shoulder. The young woman was standing by a carriage in the yard of the livery stable. She was watching Violet.

Glancing up and down the street at the few people who were moving about, Violet backtracked to the miserable creature.

"If you're lying, I swear . . ." The words withered on Violet's tongue as the young woman pulled away the shawl around her neck, showing Vi the black and purple bruises there.

"He was better to me than he was to ye. At least folks won't see these unless I show them myself." She covered up the marks again. "He almost choked me to death, though. The bastard. He was just using me. Using us."

Vi did not want to feel any sympathy toward the woman, but she could not help herself. Ned was the one at fault. They were just two simpletons who managed to fall victim to his charm. How many others were there? she thought. "Why did he do this to you?"

"Because I wanted to know why he wanted me to take him to Melbury Hall." The young woman's voice quavered. "He said 'twas none of my business, and if I didn't do as he wanted and keep my trap shut, he'd kill me."

"When is he coming back?" Violet asked.

"Tonight." The girl's eyes scanned the street again. "He told me he's coming back before supper, and I should take my pa's cart. Says I'm to hide him under a tarp in the back with the iron bars and casks of tacks I take up from my pa's smithy to the Hall every fortnight or so. He wants to get to yer place around dinner, so's he can slip out when we get there, and no one will see him. He's up to no good, I just know it. But I don't know what to do about it."

"Do you know where he is now?"

"St. Albans. I think he's staying in the tavern where he always goes to—the one out by the brickyards."

Violet looked up the street and saw the wagon from Solgrave that carted milk to St. Albans every morning. She knew the driver. Shoving the basket and piles of

newspapers into the woman's hands, she quickly gave
her directions what to do with them. "After you're done,
tell the groom waiting by the shops that I had to go to
St. Albans. Tell him they should watch out for trouble
tonight."

"I can't tell them nothing about Ned. He'll kill me."

"You just tell the man what I told you and leave Ned's
name out of it. I'll take care of the stonemason. Be sure
to tell them to watch out for trouble coming their way."

Without another word, Violet hurried to catch up to
the wagon rolling down the village street.

At noon on the final day of traveling, Lyon reached
out to help his wife climb into the chaise. After stopping
to warm up at a wayside inn, she had reluctantly handed
the infant, Josephine, back to the nursemaid riding in
the carriage behind.

"I've uprooted everyone," she said again. "And so
soon after our arrival at Baronsford."

"You did not. We had planned on being away only a
fortnight." He pulled her next to him on the seat. "We
have done everything we could possibly do at
Baronsford . . . for now."

"Walter Truscott told me before we left that the mood
among the tenants is much improved. He says there even
appears to be progress on some of the other estates."

Lyon entwined their fingers. "Unfortunately, all of
these could come to an abrupt end when some other
landlord decides to clear his land. The people's confidence is fragile. With good reason."

Millicent's voice was hesitant. "Truscott also told me
that I should encourage you to get in touch with your
brother Pierce. Since you signed those documents some
months ago, the possibility exists that he might decide
to go against your wishes and sell the properties . . . or
even clear the land himself."

"Pierce would never do that to Baronsford," Lyon
replied confidently. "But I do need to reach him. I just
wish that this first attempt to communicate with him did

not have to involve the business of land and inheritance."

Lyon needed to think seriously about how to approach his brother. He didn't care a rush about getting back the properties. The last thing he wanted was to have Pierce merely send back a signed document, reversing everything. More important, Lyon wanted his brother back.

Millicent placed a kiss on his clenched jaw, and he smiled at her upturned face.

"You shall do what's right," she said. "I have faith in you."

Violet stood in a dark corner of the tavern and watched him.

The place was packed with men, and a traveling fiddler sat on a stool in the corner, sawing away feverishly at a jig, his battered hat in front of him with a couple of dull copper coins peeking imploringly from it. The men in the room were singing and roaring with laughter as two drunken brickmakers danced in a circle, jostling those nearby in their hilarity and drawing shoves in return.

Ned had one hand around a cup of ale and his other arm around a buxom wench. As Vi watched him, she realized he didn't look quite so handsome to her. His features were thick, his limbs heavy, and his movements jerky. His eyes glittered from the drinking.

He was supposedly going back to Knebworth Village in a couple of hours. The question of what no-good he was up to gnawed at her.

When Ned's attention was drawn to the door of the crowded tavern room, Violet looked at the half-dozen rough-looking men who all entered together. Behind them she saw Jasper Hyde's clerk, the same one who had been sent up to Melbury Hall a number of times. She drew back when she saw a swarthy gentleman enter behind the clerk. He had to be Jasper Hyde, she decided. Leaning on his cane, the man motioned the group to a corner, where Ned joined them.

Violet moved closer, keeping to the shadows along the wall. She could hear snatches of the conversation over the din of the room.

"Ye all stay in the Grove until you see the flames coming from the house," Ned barked. "Harry and the master here both know what we are after. As soon as they point her out to ye, make a grab for her and head out again toward the Grove. We shan't be using any roads getting out of there."

Fear gripped Violet's stomach as Ned continued to talk. They were going to steal Ohenewaa, and they were going to burn Melbury Hall to do it. Violet pushed away from the wall, not knowing how to stop them, and yet knowing somehow that she had to try.

The noise in the room was getting louder. More people were coming in. Violet could not even hear herself think. Ned looked to be through with his talking, and the men were ordering ale and talking amongst themselves. She saw him say something to Jasper Hyde and motion to the ceiling. As Ned got up to leave, however, an eager wench latched onto his arm.

Violet realized he was going up to his room. The stairs. She remembered vividly the dark corridor. Her gaze searched the room and came to rest on a man stretched out on a battered settle near her. In spite of the ruckus, he was snoring away with his mouth wide open. The blade of his knife glinted beside his hand.

She walked toward him with purpose. The man didn't stir at all when she took the knife and hid it under her cloak.

Violet looked over her shoulder and found Ned had succeeded in shedding the woman. He was heading toward the door leading to the stairs, and Hyde was giving orders to his clerk and the other men. Pushing her way through the crowded room, she hurried out ahead of the stonemason.

The narrow hall at the base of the stairs was dark, with the exception of a little light coming in from the tavern. Violet moved into the shadows and waited. Her fingers clutched the handle of the knife. Ned's large frame broke through the light. He walked toward the stairs, and Violet stepped out.

"Ned."

He turned, his surprised expression quickly giving way to anger. "What the devil are ye doing here? Following me again, are ye? Can't get enough, ye silly chit? Well, I'm through with ye."

"This is not about me, Ned." She came closer. "You cannot destroy Melbury Hall. Too many people's lives depend on that place."

"Ha!"

"I have a little money, Ned. If that's why you're doing this, I'll give it all to you."

Understanding made his eyes glint in the dark. "Bugger off, slut. What I'm going to make out of this job, ye shan't be dreaming of making in yer lifetime."

"He wants Ohenewaa. He is daft to think she's a witch. That's all a lie. Don't ruin so many lives because of some nonsense."

"What do I care? She's a filthy slave." He towered over her, and then his face changed as a thought occurred to him. "And ye're a greedy whore. Ye came here because ye want yer cut, don't ye? Ye heard I'm using my other woman to help me, and ye don't like it that I didn't ask ye."

"No. I'm here to stop you from doing the wrong thing. From hurting good people. You cannot—"

Violet winced in pain as Ned grabbed a fistful of her cloak and hair and jerked her about. "I think ye fancy those slaves, especially that stupid one, Moses. That's why ye want to save them. Ye filthy whore. Admit it. Ye fancy the thought of letting them—"

With all her strength, she drove the knife upward into his chest. His hand on her hair tightened. He took a step back, stumbling as he dragged her with him.

"The black bastards."

"You are the bastard," she hissed into his face. "And yes, I choose their lives over yours. And even over my own."

Vi jerked the knife upward, and he stumbled again,

falling backward against a wall but still taking Violet with him. When he struck the wall, she felt the knife sink deeper. His eyes went glassy, and his knees buckled under his weight. As Ned sank slowly to the floor, Violet went down with him. Small bubbles of blood appeared at the corner of his mouth, and his breathing stopped with a single shudder. His grip eased on her hair.

"Ride 'im good, lass." A drunkard laughed and slapped Vi on the side of the head as he stumbled by in the narrow hall and started up the stairs.

Violet's fingers uncoiled from the hilt of the knife. As she stood up from his lap, she saw the dark stain of the blood on the front of Ned's smock. She took a step back and stared at the man she had once thought she loved— at the father of the child growing inside of her. Violet pulled the cloak tightly around her and stepped into the merry commotion in the tavern.

There were people all around, but their faces were all blurred. She had killed a man. The wailing sound in her head blocked out the music, the shouts. She pushed her way out of the tavern and onto the street.

The air was fresh and clean, and as she started up the street, her mind suddenly grew clear. There was no way she could make it back to Melbury Hall in time. She had warned them. She had done what she could.

Her only path now led away from here. She had to go someplace far enough away that she wouldn't bring shame down on her mother and grandmother. Or on Melbury Hall. The thought of leaving them, of never seeing them again, sent a shaft of hot steel through her heart. But she had no choice. She could not shame them.

At another inn just up the alley on High Street, the daily mail coach was preparing to leave St. Albans. The driver was climbing up and the team of horses snorted and stamped impatiently in the cold air. Vi stopped and counted her money. Ten shillings and a few pence.

It was enough to take her away from St. Albans, at least. And when the coach would take her no farther, she would just walk from there as far as her legs would carry her.

Chapter 33

"I am always complaining about people arriving unexpectedly at Melbury Hall and here I have done the same thing to you," Millicent said as a way of apology to the housekeeper.

Mrs. Page and Gibbs had been racing around for the past two hours and had succeeded in settling everyone new who had come back from Baronsford. "We started a couple of days earlier than we had planned and never sent a rider ahead to warn you."

Mary looked adoringly at the baby in Millicent's arms. "You bring back this kind of joy to the house, m'lady, and you think we'd mind an army of guests? Not at all. May I hold the little darling?"

She handed the sleeping Jo to the housekeeper. This had been the same kind of reaction she had received from everyone. The dowager, Ohenewaa, Amina, even Gibbs. So far Sir Richard had been excluded from holding the infant, since he had been sequestered in the library, discussing some business affairs with her husband. "By the way, where is Violet?"

"She went to the village this morning on an errand, and then ran off to St. Albans."

"To see her mother and grandmother?"

"I don't believe so, m'lady." An anxious look crossed Mrs. Page's face. "The groom she went to the village with this morning said she'd sent a message about trouble coming our way. He said that Violet went on to St. Albans to see Ned Cranch."

"The stonemason?"

"Aye, the missing stonemason. He left in the middle of his job, right after you and his lordship went to Scotland. Mr. Gibbs can tell you everything else about it. But there have been some strange doings with that man . . . and I am afraid Violet is involved with him."

"How?" Millicent asked worriedly. "He is a married man, is he not?"

"He might be, m'lady, but I don't think our Violet knew anything about it when he started courting her."

"When was this?"

Millicent could hardly believe what she was hearing as Mary went on to tell her that as far back as Christmastide, Ned Cranch had been wooing Violet at every opportunity.

"Violet hasn't been feeling well, either," Mary whispered. "I am only guessing, but I'm starting to think she might have gotten herself into trouble."

Millicent remembered the bruise on the young woman's face and her inability to hold down food. "Will you look after the baby while I go and talk to Mr. Gibbs? I want someone to go to St. Albans after her."

"Of course, m'lady."

Everyone made mistakes in life. But after holding Jo's hand and watching the young mother die after childbirth, Millicent was not going to allow another young woman to be lost to the world. She knew Violet would not go to her mother's house. She wouldn't want to bring disgrace to their doorstep.

No, Millicent had to bring her back to Melbury Hall.

Jasper Hyde could tell the London men were becoming restless. They stood in a circle a distance from him, leaning on their cudgels and shooting quick glances his way as they muttered together. Night had already fallen. Through the break in the trees, they had seen that a number of carriages and riders had recently arrived at the Hall.

As the hours passed, the danger of a watchman or

dogs discovering their hiding place was becoming more likely. And still there was no sign of Ned Cranch.

"Blasted cowardly braggart!" Jasper Hyde cursed under his breath.

"I thought he left the tavern before us," Harry complained in his ear.

The last Hyde had seen of the stonemason, he was going up to his room. Burning sensations and a squeezing pain filled the cavity of his chest, and Jasper Hyde thought of a dozen different ways he would make the stonemason suffer if he did not appear soon.

Hyde had considered staying behind at St. Albans and letting those whom he had paid so handsomely finish the job. But the nagging feeling that something might go wrong—that like so many other recent instances his damnable luck might turn on him—had persuaded him to come along. Now at least he was satisfied with that decision. He would carry this through no matter what the danger. No matter what happened to Cranch.

One of the men he had sent to spy on the house came running back. "No sign of 'im. And no sign of any cart comin' from the village. But I couldn't get inside the stables, in case the rockhead might be hidin' there."

"Any place closer to the house to hide?" Hyde asked.

"There's the stable, but there are a couple of grooms still seeing to the horses. And the carriages are out front. They'll be bringin' them around soon. There's gardens in the back of the house and by the servants' door."

The pain was getting sharper, and Hyde knew time was running short. He called the men together. "You two go to the front and keep watch there. You four come with me to the back of the manor house. Harry, you set fire to these cottages."

The clerk looked around at the circle of decrepit buildings.

"Once you are through here, go to the back of the stables and set fire to them, too."

"Now ye're talkin'," one of the men said with a grin. "We come fer action."

Holding the pistol in one hand, Hyde had to put all his weight on the cane to keep up with the others moving through the woods. He was having trouble breathing. Fatigue was wrapping a tight fist around his chest. A pain in his head was clouding his vision as they got closer to the house. Suddenly he saw a shadow run ahead of them in the woods. But as he looked again, he saw nothing. His mind was playing tricks.

"The little bugger did it," one of his men said over his shoulder. The crackle and spark of flames could be heard rising from the Grove through the winter wood. Hyde tried to hurry to keep up with everyone else. Somewhere ahead the shouts of warning about the fire could be heard.

The pain stabbed him again in the chest. He saw the shadow pass closer to his left. He realized who it was. But it couldn't be.

"Tano," he whispered.

"D'ye say something?" The man closest to him turned around.

"No, go on. Look for an old black woman as they come out of the house." Hyde's mind was giving way to strange thoughts. Uncontrollably, he was crossing the great divide of many years. He remembered a night like this. He was a child, running barefoot with his friend through the meadow above the canefields. With Tano.

The edge of the woods lay ahead of them. More shouts came from the vicinity of the stables. Harry had reached there as well.

The pain in his chest and his head was unbearable, but he pushed on. There was a rustling sound in the trees to his right. He lifted his pistol and turned sharply. He was there, as clear as day. Tano was hanging in irons, left to die. His dark eyes were open and accusing.

Hyde backed away and tried to run, but his feet were too heavy, and he stumbled to his knees. One of the London men stood over him.

"Damn you, Ohenewaa!" he cursed into the night, shaking off the man's hand. He pushed himself to his feet, clutching his chest with one hand.

Through the remaining fringe of trees, he could see people pouring out of the house. Servants were running in every direction and shouting. Horses, freed from their stalls, were running about wildly.

Hyde stopped by the edge of the trees and stared at the chaos. Tano, named after a sacred river in the western lands of the Ashanti, was two years younger than Jasper in age. They gave him the Christian name Thomas, but his name was Tano. From the time they were young boys, he had surpassed Jasper in size and strength and courage. None of this mattered, though, for he was black and Jasper was white. Tano was a slave and Jasper would someday be his master. But for as many things that set them apart, there were others that made them the same. As children they thought the same, dreamed alike, tolerated each other . . . and though no one spoke of it, they shared the same father.

"I don't see no old woman," one of the men said into Hyde's ear.

"Find your way up to the house without being seen. Set it on fire, and she will have to . . ." His words trailed off.

Amidst the smoke and mayhem, Jasper saw Ohene-waa walking toward them. There was no doubting it; she had seen them, but she was still coming.

After their father, Rufus, had passed away, Tano had become more openly rebellious. With every problem in the slave quarters, Jasper had seen evidence of Tano's involvement. He could look away only so long. But even after Jasper began to have him punished for his transgressions, the slave had only become stronger.

The pain in his chest was spreading. His hands were shaking, but Hyde dropped the cane and wrapped his fingers tightly around the pistol.

Last year, during one of the slave uprisings, Hyde had reached the end of his patience. One of his bailiffs had been killed. Three other white men had been injured. Over two dozen slaves had escaped to the western forests of the island. It was all he could take. He had ordered Tano to be hung in irons.

Ohenewaa continued to walk toward him. This close, he could see the woman's eyes flashing angrily in the dark. He stepped out of the woods and raised the pistol until it was pointed directly at her heart. Tano had died, and she had cursed him.

"You must die, witch."

A woman screamed from somewhere to his right, and he turned his head. Out of the corner of his eye, he saw someone standing beside him. Tano. And at that moment he felt the pain explode in his chest even as he heard the crack of a pistol firing.

Millicent saw Jasper Hyde go down on his knees, and she turned to see Lyon lowering the gun. A half-dozen grooms raced past her toward a retreating group of men. To her left, Moses had Hyde's clerk by the scruff of his neck, and Gibbs was running down from the stables. She turned her attention back to Ohenewaa and saw her crouching over the bloody body of Jasper Hyde.

Millicent rushed toward them and knelt beside the old woman. Lyon approached and kicked Hyde's pistol to the side.

Hyde's breathing was labored. His eyes were open, but there was a hole in his chest near his heart. "He's here. He wants to take me with him."

Ohenewaa sat in silence.

"I cannot bear the pain. The heat of the branding iron . . . is scorching my breast. Do you hear them . . . the sound of chains?" A tear escaped the man's eyes. "You cursed me, woman."

"This is Tano's curse."

"Release me," he whispered, the words barely escaping his lips. "Please . . . let me live . . . help me."

She placed a hand above the open wound on his heart. " 'Tis too late."

"Then . . . forgive me." Hyde's eyes looked up into space. "Please, Tano . . . forgive me."

Millicent saw a tear drop from Ohenewaa's face onto his chest. The old woman's hand stretched out over the dying man's head. "He forgives. Go now."

Hyde's breathing stopped and his eyes glazed over. The old woman closed the lids and touched the man's forehead. Millicent sat beside her until Ohenewaa turned to her.

"Who was Tano?" Millicent asked.

"My son," she said, looking back at the dead man. "Tano was my son."

Epilogue

"You should write a letter to your sons."

The dowager peered over the tops of her spectacles. "I thought you said you were not getting involved with my problems."

"I am not." Ohenewaa put the basket of new greenery on the stone bench beside her and glared at her friend. "But you should know that I consider you a stubborn woman."

"And why is that?"

"You have the power to put an end to all the trouble between these three boys."

"They are not boys, but men. They started their disagreement, and they should finish it."

"You are helpless . . . and blind, too . . . and pigheaded. And if you don't do something to help your son with his brothers—"

"You shall cast a spell on me?"

"I do not know any spells."

"Then show me how to do some other magic."

Ohenewaa's dark eyes narrowed. "Not that I know anything about the dark arts, but even if I had that kind of knowledge, I would never entrust it to *you*."

"What if I promised to do some good with it?"

"Such as?"

The dowager shrugged. "Maybe I shall use it to find perfect wives for Pierce and David, as I did for Lyon. Never mind any letters. Marriage is the way to bring them back again to the family."

"You underestimate your shrewdness, old woman. And Sir Richard's hard work. You managed all of this before with no magic."

"But I am getting old, and my days are numbered. And I am weak."

"You might save that idle talk for your family. It does not work with me. I know there is nothing wrong with you."

"I still believe you know about those dark arts. You are just an ornery old witch and holding out on me just to be spiteful."

"And I believe you should take less snuff in the morning. Now, start with small steps. Write Pierce a letter and have it delivered at the same time as Lyon's. Then you need to start working on your youngest son. What is his name?"

"David. Perhaps. I shall think about it."

The dowager took a deep breath of fragrant spring air. She admired the flowers that were springing out of the ground in every corner of the garden. Mrs. Page and Gibbs were pretending that they were looking intently at a rose arbor at the lower end of the garden, but she knew better. Gibbs was still as gruff as ever, but there was a certain boyish spring that had recently begun to appear in his step. It was love; no doubt about it.

The dowager's gaze was drawn to two young servants shaking out linens by the house.

"Has there been any more news of Violet?" Ohenewaa asked.

"No, they didn't find her in St. Albans. Millicent is still upset over it."

"At least she did not run off with the stonemason."

"Indeed, but what an ignoble fate he met with, to be murdered by some drunk in a tavern."

"He deserved it," Ohenewaa stated.

Again both women fell silent, content to watch the activities of the people coming and going around the manor. Lyon and Millicent were walking along the garden path. He was still using the cane, but his legs were getting stronger every day. She was carrying the baby.

"Perhaps they'll bring her here, so we could hold her," Ohenewaa said, a note of hopefulness in her voice.

"That baby is a perfect lady. And I even like the name Josephine."

"Joseph was the prophet sold into slavery, was he not?"

"He was."

Ohenewaa nodded with satisfaction. "It shall be a challenge when their own baby arrives this fall. Two infants in the house."

"That's what they have us for. To help them."

"Do you plan to stay that long?"

"I am, if you are." The dowager laughed, watching Ohenewaa's face crease into a frown.

Millicent heard the laughter, and she glanced over her shoulder at the dowager and Ohenewaa. The two women were involved in one of their daily disputes.

"It might kill them to admit it, but they really like each other," Lyon said, following the direction of her gaze. He laid his cane aside and sat down on a nearby stone bench. "Can I hold her now?"

She smiled and handed the baby to him before sitting down beside them. The swallows had returned, and a number of them were flitting and swooping about the chimneys. She glanced toward the path that led from the Grove, where once the slaves had lived. They had pulled down what remained of the huts after the fire. Construction on new cottages had already begun on higher ground. The damage to the stables had been small, and the repair work had already been accomplished.

Life was changing, Millicent thought. Buds of flowers and leaves were appearing on the trees. The fields were growing greener, and daffodils were poking their heads up along the walls and paths. Laughter, happiness, and contentment surrounded them. Melbury Hall was alive again.

She glanced back at her husband.

Josephine's small head was nestled against his chest.

His large hand was gently caressing the baby's back. His blue eyes were loving when they met hers.

"Next year at this time, I'll have two of them nestled here."

"Who ever would have imagined such a thing?" she whispered, smiling at the vision of her own dream.

Author's Note

$\mathcal{A}$s you might have guessed by now, *Borrowed Dreams* is the first in a trilogy of books about the men of Baronsford. While Pierce and David search out their own lives, they are subsequently drawn back to their home, where the mystery of Emma's murder waits to be solved.

Millicent Gregory Wentworth was first introduced to our readers in *The Promise*, where Rebecca Neville and the Earl of Stanmore forged a future together. We hope the change wrought in Millicent since meeting her in *The Promise* has provided a satisfying journey for you all.

As with all of our novels, with this book we have tried to depict a place and a time in a way that mingles the real and the imagined in an entertaining way. The issue of slavery in England and in the sugar islands of the West Indies is one that we have introduced in our earlier work. We hoped to give our readers another glimpse, through the eyes of Ohenewaa, of the trauma that innocents suffered throughout centuries of injustice. Many authors contributed unknowingly to our account of the slave trade through their work. We'd like to thank James Pope-Hennessy for his work *Sins of the Fathers: The Atlantic Slave Traders*, and Marcus Wood for his *Blind Memory: Visual Representations of Slavery in England and America*.

The Highland clearances were only touched upon in this book. In the following stories about the men and women of Baronsford, we will enjoy together more of the history of Scotland as it unfolds.

Finally, we'd like to acknowledge, with gratitude, the hard work of the many people at NAL who contribute to our books—Hilary Ross, John Paine, the production staff, as well as those in marketing and sales. Thank you all.

As always, we love to hear from our readers.

May McGoldrick
P.O. Box 665
Watertown, CT 06795
mcgoldmay@aol.com
www.maymcgoldrick.com

Read on
for a preview of May McGoldrick's
Captured Dreams

June 1772

Her mother had been locked away for twenty-six years. Tonight, Portia was determined to free her.

Holding her feathered mask to her face, she glanced at the various doors around the room, going over in her mind the floor plan of Admiral Middleton's North End mansion. She had paid good money to get a detailed layout of the house. She touched the locket she wore about her neck and prayed now that the information was correct.

Portia knew the masquerade ball held at the admiral's mansion on Copp's Hill to honor the king's birthday was the only opportunity she would have to free her mother. The admiral almost never entertained, so when else would she be able to gain access to the grounds? As it was, the guest list consisted of only the most elite members of Boston's Tory society, including the governor. Of course, no invitation addressed to any Portia Edwards had arrived at the door of Parson Higgins and his wife, where Portia was living, but she had forgiven the admiral the oversight. She had simply lied to a dear friend and deceived people who considered her part of their family. It had to be tonight.

"You are uncharacteristically quiet this evening, my pet."

My pet. Portia tried to not lose her patience at Captain

Turner's condescending expression. She turned to the officer. As always, he was standing stiffly over her and leaning forward as he spoke. She had caught him peering down the front of her dress a half dozen times already, and she dipped her mask to cover the low neckline of the borrowed gown. He looked into her face, and she pasted on a smile.

Captain Turner, a distant cousin to her friend Bella, had been the means for Portia to get into the mansion. Now, however, she was having some difficulty ridding herself of him.

"I am simply *numb* with excitement." Portia raised the mask again to her face and looked around the paneled ballroom in search of a distraction for her companion. The notes of the minuet rose and fell as the other guests paraded about. There were far fewer women here than men, though it appeared that some of Boston's more desperate Tory families had sent their daughters. "I do wish you would not feel obligated to remain at my side, Captain. I should hate to make enemies of all these lovely ladies by keeping you to myself."

"Nonsense, my pet. I would not dare ruin your opinion of me by neglecting you. You know that I have been waiting upon you for months to no avail. To be honest, I was about ready to give up hope. I do not need to tell you, therefore, how thrilled I was when my lovely cousin sent me word that you had agreed to allow me to call upon you. And when you consented to accompany me here . . . ah, what delight! And now you suppose that I would step away from the glow of your loveliness?"

Captain Turner continued to speak, and Portia lowered the mask, glancing with disbelief at the officer, whose eyes were again fixed on her breasts. He was a man in his forties, she judged, and though he had apparently been powerfully built in his youth, his physique was now beginning to decline into the softness of middle age. Still, she had underestimated the captain's ardent interest in her.

"Warm, is it not?" she interrupted. "Would you be kind enough to get me something to drink, Captain?"

Her escort bowed, only to turn as a passing servant

unfortunately appeared carrying a tray filled with cups full of punch. Portia silently cursed her luck and, with a weak smile, accepted one. When the captain again started to lean over her, she glanced desperately about the room.

"I have never had such an opportunity to see so many distinguished people. The military men look so dashing in their finery."

"I should be happy to introduce you to any of them, along with their wives," Turner offered jovially. "We have some particularly fine men serving His Majesty here in Boston, and their wives would be delighted to meet you, I am sure. Whom specifically would you care to meet?"

She looked about for some guest far from where they were standing. She had no difficulty finding one. Leaning with a haughty air against a column near the door, the man wore a black scowl that matched his dark attire.

"That gentleman . . ." She motioned with her mask. "I don't believe I have ever seen him before."

"I should be surprised if you had met the man, my pet." Turner's nose climbed an inch in the air in obvious distaste. "That is Pierce Pennington, a brother to the Earl of Aytoun. He comes from an old family, but he's a scoundrel of a Scot, to be sure. This past year, since coming to Boston, he has been making a name for himself in finance and shipping."

"Is this not a difficult time to be establishing oneself in such pursuits?" Portia asked with interest.

"Perhaps not if one lacks a certain . . . well, a certain respect for His Majesty's laws of trade."

"You mean he deals with smugglers?"

"I mean no such thing, officially. But if I could prove that . . ." Turner's gaze remained fixed on Pennington. "There is a great deal about that gentleman that I do not understand. But my superiors consider him completely loyal to the king and safely above assisting these troublesome colonists. In fact, Pennington's younger brother is an officer in the army and has a fine reputation, by all accounts."

"You make Mr. Pennington sound all the more interesting, Captain."

"You cannot be serious, Miss Edwards."

"Indeed I am." The sound from the courtyard of carriages and riders signaled the promised arrival of the governor and his entourage. Portia knew he never traveled anywhere now without an armed military escort. She put on her sweetest smile. "I know I am safe with you, Captain. Would you kindly beg an introduction of the gentleman?"

"Given all the fine persons in the room, my pet, I do not understand why you should be so determined to meet this . . . Scot."

"If you please," she cooed. "You know that Parson Higgins' wife is of Scottish ancestry. I should so like to tell her that you took the pains to introduce me to a distinguished countryman of hers."

"Distinguished," he scoffed, casting a sour glance at the distance that he would need to walk. "If you must, then why not come with me and—?"

"No, I cannot," she said, hiding her face once again behind the mask. "I could never allow the rumor to spring up that I was discontent with spending time in your company, Captain. You are far better acquainted with the rules of society than I, but I should think that if you and Mr. Pennington were to approach me, there could be no reason for gossip."

Giving the captain a gentle push in the direction of the man, Portia waited with anticipation. As soon as Turner had moved away into the crowd, she sprang into action. Floor-length windows stood open behind her, and in an instant she was crossing the flagstones of a terrace and running down steps into the moonlit gardens below.

Portia was thankful to find the gardens still empty of guests. If her information was correct, her mother was being kept in a suite of rooms on the second floor facing the rose gardens. The only way to reach her, without being seen, was by way of a low balcony off her bedroom.

Raising the skirts of the gown, Portia ran along well-tended paths bordered by boxwood and flower beds and soon found her way into the rose gardens. She immediately spotted the balcony situated above a small pear tree and flanked by sturdy rose trellises. It was just as it had been described to her, and she quickly climbed a small embankment to the house.

Portia Edwards had spent twenty-six years of her life blithely ignorant of her origins. Raised in an orphanage school in Wrexham in Wales, she had joined the family of Parson Higgins and his wife at the age of eighteen. She had never doubted the stories of her parentage that Lady Primrose had told her since childhood. Her mother had died in childbirth and her father, a high-ranking Jacobite supporter, had died not long after Culloden. Though she had often imagined longingly what it would be like to have a family, she had none.

Portia touched the locket at her throat and started climbing the trellis. About a month ago, her eyes had been opened to her true background, and her childhood wishes for the impossible suddenly appeared within her reach. When Mary, the parson's wife, had come down with a cold, Dr. Deming had paid a visit to the house in the lane off Sudbury Street. The physician, admiring Portia's necklace, had recognized the miniature portrait of the woman inside the locket. From that moment on, Portia had not rested until she had found out everything she could about Helena Middleton.

The narrow balcony served more for the sake of looks than function, for there was not even room to stand inside the railing. The windows had been closed in spite of the warm evening. Realizing that she still had her mask in one hand, Portia laid it on the railing and tried to peer in. Unable to see, she held on to the trellis tightly with one hand and leaned closer, disappointed to find the curtains drawn as well.

It was rumored far and wide that Admiral Middleton's daughter Helena was mad. In searching out information about the family, Portia had heard the old man continually praised for his devoted care of his daughter. Portia guessed at the truth. If her father was a Jacobite, then

Helena's affair would have been a tremendous disgrace to a trusted Crown official. But was this reason enough to lock a daughter away for more than two decades?

Portia tapped softly on the window. She understood that she had mere seconds to try to explain all of this to her mother. Their resemblance was hardly perceptible. In fact, it was not beyond reason to imagine that Helena might be completely ignorant of her daughter's survival. She tapped again and felt worry form like a hot ember in the pit of her stomach. As challenging as explaining their relationship might be, the more difficult task would be to convince Helena Middleton to escape this house with Portia.

The curtains pulled back sharply and the burning ember rose from Portia's stomach into her throat. The woman looked older than she had imagined. The resemblance to the miniature portrait, however, was unmistakable.

Helena was holding a candle in one hand. She wore nothing over the thin rail that she must have been sleeping in. As she opened the latch on the window, Portia realized that her mother had not yet seen her.

The rose trellis creaked perilously under her weight, and the young woman took hold of the balcony. She had been dreaming about this moment all her life, and now she could hardly breathe.

The window opened. Helena placed the candle on the windowsill and leaned out.

"Mother?"

Silence enveloped them, and Portia saw Helena's look of bewilderment turn to terror as the color drained completely from her mother's face. And then, as Portia reached out a hand, Helena let out a scream loud enough to wake the dead.

Pierce Pennington watched as the governor and his entourage entered the ballroom. Following the man's gaze as he swept into the chamber, Pierce noticed how Governor Hutchinson quickly took note of everyone and everything in the room—very much like a herding dog sniffing the air around his flock for the scent of a wolf.

He returned the governor's nod when the older man looked his way. Hutchinson immediately turned his attention on their host as Admiral Middleton approached to greet him. A small string ensemble began to play a recent Handel piece, and Pierce pushed away from the large column he had been leaning against. He had made his requisite appearance. He started toward the large open doors leading to the gardens.

"Mr. Pennington, you are not leaving us so soon, are you?"

A naval officer had moved to block his path, and Pierce recognized him at once. A few years older than himself, Captain Turner was not distinguished by his physical presence, and at first glance the man did not leave much of an impression on either friend or foe. Pierce sensed there was more to the man, though, for he had evidently served Admiral Middleton well for many years.

"I was on my way to the gardens for some fresh air. Why do you ask, Captain?"

"A young lady of my acquaintance desires to be introduced, sir."

"To me, Captain? Don't tell me she has already tired of your company?"

"I think not, sir," Turner huffed. "She simply wishes to meet a Scot, and you, I believe, may be the only person here who fits the description."

"A lady of discriminating taste." Pierce glanced over the officer's shoulder at the sea of scarlet coats, fresh ruffles, hoop skirts, and feathered masks. High-ranking British military men and their women filled the room. "I see no one waiting on you, Captain."

"Is that so?" Turner looked over his shoulder. "She was right there a moment ago."

"Is she beautiful?"

"Quite so," the captain replied vaguely, his eyes scanning the ballroom.

"Young?"

"Yes."

"Does she have a sense of humor?"

"I did not ask you to woo or court her, sir," Turner said, turning to him in annoyance. "A brief introduction will suffice, if you please."

"Then take me to her, Captain, if you think 'tis safe."

With a stiff bow, the officer led him in the direction of a refreshment table. This distraction was costing him precious time. He cast a glance at the large stone terrace overlooking the gardens. He knew his groom Jack was waiting by the courtyard entrance with the carriage.

Turner's course began to meander as he searched in vain for his escort. He finally stopped and glanced helplessly about the large ballroom. "I cannot imagine where she went."

"You probably frightened her off, Captain," Pierce replied, keeping his tone light. "Perhaps I shall have the good fortune of meeting this mysterious lady another time."

"As you wish, sir," Turner said, still looking.

As soon as Pierce moved toward the terrace doors, though, Turner was beside him.

"Perhaps she stepped out for air. She was just remarking on how warm it is."

With the officer still at his side, Pierce stopped on the empty terrace. Trying to appear unhurried, he looked out at the spires and rooflines of Charlestown across the moonlit river to the north and at the masts of ships in the harbor to the east.

"Your elusive maiden is not out here," he commented, breathing in the smells of the sea and freshly cut hay that mingled with the scent of roses in bloom. "Perhaps you should take another look in the ballroom."

"Indeed . . . perhaps . . ."

Turner's indecisiveness irked Pierce. "Perhaps you should go inside and ask a few of the other guests. A young and beautiful woman unescorted in a ballroom draws attention, Captain."

"Indeed, sir. My apologies." Without another word, the officer bowed and disappeared inside.

With a practiced air of leisure, Pierce casually made his way down the stairs and along the brick pathways through a small orchard. Although the guests were eagerly showing off their wit and clothes to their peers and their betters, there was no saying that some of them would not venture out onto the terrace. He did not want anyone to see him leaving.

Beyond a cherry tree, the path led toward the stable yards. He paused to cast a final glance toward the house. No one was on the terrace. All was calm.

Then, as he turned to go, a scream cut through the night.

This was clearly not the time to explain anything. At the sound of her mother's response, Portia nearly lost her grip on the railing.

When Helena staggered back from the window, Portia tried to regain her footing on the trellis. As quickly as she dared, she began her descent. All around her, it sounded as if the household had come alive. The barking of dogs in the kennels followed Helena's scream, and shouts of running servants could be heard through the open window.

Halfway down, Portia's dress caught on some thorns. Trying to disengage it, she felt the trellis begin to come away from the house. Portia had no choice. Tearing the dress free, she jumped, grabbing at a branch of the pear tree as she fell.

As she dropped onto the soft ground, she was aware of her dress ripping. Leaves and branches showered down on her, but she couldn't stop to worry about it. Quickly, she struggled to her feet and started running from the window and the commotion taking place in the chamber above. Crossing the rose garden, she spied an arched opening leading out and turned her steps toward it. Then, as Portia looked back at the house one last time, she collided with a tall and muscular body suddenly blocking the archway. Stunned, she fell back, but a pair of strong hands grasped her shoulders.

Portia looked up in panic, expecting one of admiral's servants. Instead, she was relieved to find her captor was the Scotsman she had sent Captain Turner after. Shouts of "Thief!" and "Housebreaker!" rang out in the darkness.

" 'Tis not what you think!" she exclaimed, already knowing that she could not reveal the truth if she ever wanted to come back here to carry her plans through.

"And what do I think?"

"I am no thief." She tried to move away, but the man's hand wrapped tightly around her wrist. She could hear the loud voices of servants coming across the rose garden. "They are mistaken. I was only walking in the gardens. I . . . I must have frightened a lady looking out her window."

"It must have been an arduous walk."

Portia winced when his free hand touched her cheek. She had scratched herself in the fall. He pulled a twig with leaves still attached to it from her hair.

The pursuers were almost upon them. She tugged on his arm and tried to hide in the shadows of the garden wall. Being caught would prove disastrous, she was sure. Admiral Middleton was vicious enough to lock his own daughter away, and Portia didn't want to think of what he would do to her if he guessed the relationship between them.

"I came here as a guest. 'Twas too warm in the ballroom. I needed to come outside for a walk." Panic seized her. If he held her for another instant, she would be lost. "Please, you must help me. It will be impossible to try to explain this to them."

"I agree. You are having difficulty explaining it to me."

"Mr. Pennington," she pleaded. "I beg you to believe me. I am no thief. Where I was and what I was trying to do is perfectly justifiable and explainable to a rational person . . . but not to a pursuing mob. If you would help me get out of here . . ."

"There!" The shout was nearby. "There is someone there!"

Portia glanced over her shoulder and saw men approaching. Several had torches. She shrank against him.

"Please," she whispered against his chest.

He pulled her wrist sharply, forcing her to his side as he called out.

"I believe I have the one you are looking for."

ONYX

MAY McGOLDRICK

Three sisters each hold a clue to their family's treasure—and the key to the hearts of three Highland warriors....

THE DREAMER
0-451-19718-6

THE FIREBRAND
0-451-40942-6

THE ENCHANTRESS
0-451-19719-4

"May McGoldrick brings history to life."
—Patricia Gaffney

"Richly romantic." —Nora Roberts

To order call: 1-800-788-6262

May McGoldrick

The Promise
0-451-20449-2

In America for the last ten years, Rebecca
Neville has raised her young charge as if
he were her own son. But now, his father-
the Earl of Stanmore-has learned of his
fate and sends for him from England.
Rebecca must do everything in her power
to keep her promise to the boy's dead
mother—and keep her heart safe from his
mysterious father...

The Rebel
0-451-20654-1

Jane Purefoy is a woman with a double
life masquerading as the leader of a gang
of Irish revolutionaries. But it's passionate
and determined Sir Nicholas Spencer who
tears her heart in two...

**"No one captures the magic and romance of the
British Isles like May McGoldrick."
—Miranda Jarrett**